measure OF A MAN

MEASURE OF A MAN SPECIAL EDITION

Cover Designer: Sommer Stein, Perfect Pear Creative

Photographer: Wander Aguiar

Editor/Proofreader: Beth Lawton, VB Edits

Created with Vellum

To all the women who've lost themselves by putting everyone else first. May you find your way back to you again.

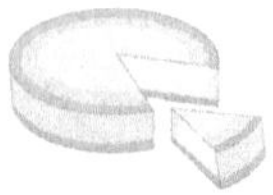

SERNIK - POLISH CHEESECAKE

Crust

- 2 c. flour
- 2 egg yolks
- 1 stick butter
- 2 T. powdered sugar
- 1 T. sour cream

Combine all the crust ingredients with room temperature eggs and butter until no lumps remain, and then form into a ball. Place in a bowl, cover with plastic wrap, and refrigerate for a half hour.

Preheat the oven to 350°F.

Line the bottom of a 10-inch springform pan with parchment paper and grease the sides of the pan. Roll out the crust dough until it's the about the same size as the bottom of the pan. Add the crust to the pan, using your fingers to press the crust toward the bottom/sides of the pan just enough to give it a small lip.

Pre-bake the crust for 15 minutes or until golden brown.

Cheese filling

- 2 lbs. farmer's cheese
- 6 eggs, with yolks and whites separated

- 1 c. powdered sugar
- 1 c. heavy whipping cream
- 2 tsp. potato flour
- 1 tsp. vanilla
- 1/4 tsp. salt
- 1 egg yolk
- 2 T. milk

Reduce the oven temperature to 325°F.

Cut farmer's cheese into a food processor and blend until most of the lumps are gone (about 5 minutes).

Separate the first six eggs and place the yolks into a bowl. Add sugar and whisk for 2-3 minutes.

In a separate bowl, combine potato flour, whipping cream, and vanilla. Then add to the egg and sugar mixture until combined well. Slowly add the blended farmer's cheese until all the mixture is smooth.

In a separate bowl, whisk the egg whites with the salt until they form a stiff foam. Fold this into the cheese mixture.

When mixed well, pour the cheese mixture onto the baked crust in the springform pan.

Whisk the egg yolk with the milk and pour this mixture on top of the cheesecake mix.

Bake cheesecake for an hour. The center should be set. Note that if the cheesecake starts to turn too brown before it's set, you can cover the pan with tin foil. When the cheesecake is set, shut off the oven, crack the oven door, and let the cheesecake rest for 20 minutes.

Sprinkle powdered sugar on top of the cheesecake if you wish, and cool cheesecake completely (about 4 hours in the fridge) before serving.

Enjoy!

PROLOGUE

ONE YEAR EARLIER...

The true measure of a man is seen in how he treats a woman, Justin. Remember that.

It's been nine years since my old man caught Gracie Janikowski and me steaming up my truck windows after our junior prom, and I still haven't forgotten his words.

But why they came to me this morning out of the blue, I have no idea. That is, until I pull into the Enders Excavating parking lot bright and early and find myself parked next to Rachel Perry.

"Morning, Jinx." The gorgeous auburn-haired woman flashes a cheery grin over the top of her car, then ducks down, disappearing to grab something from the passenger seat.

"Hey, Rach. Shouldn't you be at school already?" Last I heard, she was still teaching kindergarten at Cole Creek Elementary.

"Yep, I should," she says, reappearing and blowing

tendrils of long hair from her flushed face. "Could you grab this bakery box for me? I've got Craig's lunch and thermos, too."

"Donuts?" I waggle my eyebrows. "Say less."

She laughs softly as I jog around to the other side of her car. "It's been a while since I sent in treats, and since Craig forgot his lunch box and coffee, I figured today was a good day to remedy that."

"I sure as hell won't complain." I'll take free breakfast any day, even if guilt niggles at me. The last thing she should be thinking about is feeding us. The woman has enough on her plate already. She works full time, and she's raising two kids. Not to mention she's married to Craig Perry, the one guy on the Enders Excavating crew I don't like.

Pink and white box in hand, I close the passenger door and follow the click of her heels on the sidewalk to the front door. The whole way there, I crane my neck, trying my damnedest not to look at her ass in that snug navy skirt. I may not like her husband, but I'm not about to disrespect him by ogling his wife.

Laughter from the guys already waiting for our Monday morning meeting wafts into the vestibule as Rachel continues ahead of me. I'm only feet behind her, but when she catches the toe of her shoe on the rug and stumbles, there's no stopping the thermos and small cooler that go sailing through the air.

"*Shit.*" She grabs the doorframe to steady herself just as the thermos hits the ground with a *crack* and dark liquid seeps from the lid and onto the tile.

"Whoa, you okay?" Jesse rushes over and grasps Rachel's forearm. He checks on her quickly, then crouches and turns the thermos upright to stop the spillage.

"I'm fine." She pushes the hair from her face and rubs her fingers against her forehead, her gaze trained on the mess. "I'm so sorry. I just..."

"Hey, it's all right." Jesse squeezes her arm. "Connor, grab some paper towels from the bathroom, will ya?"

"On it." He jumps up from his seat and hurries off.

Craig, however, gives a deep sigh and slowly gets to his feet. "What are you even doing here?" he asks, his irritated tone instantly pissing me off. "Aren't you supposed to be at work?"

Rachel nods. "Yes, but you forgot your lunch, and I thought I'd bring donuts..." Her voice cracks as she balls her trembling hands into fists at her sides. "I'm just going to go. Jesse, I'm so sorry about the mess."

"Hey, no problem." My older brother's brow creases as he looks from her to Craig, probably wondering what his problem is, too.

"You sure you're okay?" I ask when she turns to where I still stand behind her with the bakery box.

"I'm fine," she rasps, as if the tears lining her honey-gold eyes aren't as obvious as the quiver in her voice. "Enjoy the donuts." With that, she hurries out the door and to her car without looking back.

My gut clenches. The urge to go after her is just as strong as the urge to punch Craig in his fucking face for not doing it himself.

"Sorry about that, man." Craig finally takes a paper towel from Connor and squats to help Jesse clean up the spilled coffee. "She's always been a klutz."

Jesse makes a throaty noncommittal sound, and I shake my head. Craig just won asshole of the week, and it's only just begun.

I glance back to the parking lot in time to see Rachel back out.

I may bite my tongue now, but one thing is for sure.

If I had a woman like Rachel Perry, the last damn thing I'd do is let her walk away.

ONE

EARLY JUNE...

RACHEL

"Don't forget to grab your cleats, Em. And Mase, Grandpa wanted you to help him with the garden this weekend. Take some old clothes so you don't get your good stuff dirty."

"Got 'em, Mom!" Emma calls from the pile of softball equipment she dumped at the front door last night after practice.

"Grandpa always makes me work," Mason grumbles as he slides off a kitchen chair like a limp noodle. "Why can't I just hang out with Dad?"

Because your dad's priorities are all kinds of messed up these days, kiddo.

"I'm sorry, baby. I know this is hard." I ruffle his dark hair as he slinks by.

He pulls away with a grimace. "Why won't he just come home?" My son's dark eyes are filled with a mix of sadness and frustration. At just shy of eleven years old, he understands far more than I wish he did, including the reason his father and I are in the middle of a divorce.

I've asked myself that same question a hundred times since Craig moved out. But four months into our separation, I've officially given up. More than that, I no longer *want* him to come home.

I just haven't figured out how to tell my kids that.

"That's a question only your dad can answer, Mase." I give him a sad smile. Smiles don't mend broken hearts, but it's all I've got.

"Can you pick us up early on Sunday?" he asks over his shoulder, a swoop of shaggy hair falling over hopeful eyes.

"That's up to your dad," I remind him. "But we can ask."

"Okay."

As he shuffles to his room, I let out the breath I've been holding and shakily pull in another. Eventually, this will get easier. It has to. One of these days, I'll be able to talk to my kids about their dad and not feel like I'm walking on eggshells. *Right*?

"Dad's here!" Emma announces, her nose pressed against the window beside the front door. "You're gonna be at my game tomorrow, right, Mom?"

"Wouldn't miss it for the world, Emmy Lou." I step up behind her and ruffle her hair—hair the same dark brown as her brother's *and* her father's—as my soon-to-be ex-husband hops out of his truck.

Fifteen years ago, the sight of his tall, bulky frame hurrying toward my front door gave seventeen-year-old me butterflies.

Now, it gives me anxiety.

"Hey, Dad!" Our eight-year-old daughter steps out onto the porch and launches herself at him, wrapping her arms tightly around his waist. Having come straight from work, his T-shirt is streaked with dirt and his jeans are even dirtier.

"You remember I have a game tomorrow, right?"

"Hey, ladybug." He tugs her ponytail as he props his sunglasses on top of his Enders Excavating ball cap. "Of course I remembered."

Mm-hmm. The crease in his brow says otherwise, but I won't call him out when Emma's within earshot.

Once she trots off, hauling her softball gear to the back of the truck, I tip my head toward the house. "Mason's grabbing his bag." Then I take a deep breath and spit it out. "He's really hoping to spend some time with you this weekend."

The line in Craig's brow deepens, and his lips turn down. "Isn't that why I'm here?"

It should be that simple, but it hasn't been. Either he doesn't realize it, or he does, and he's chosen to pretend otherwise.

"He wants one-on-one time, Craig. And he's old enough to know that you're not spending the night at your parents' house along with them like you say you are."

His scowl turns into a defensive laugh. He plants his hands on his hips and lifts one brow, hitting me with the condescending look he's so good at. "Oh, really?"

I rub my hands along my upper arms and swallow. I don't want to argue with him, especially not about *her*, but I'm sick of the way he's upsetting my kids. It was bad enough he hurt me.

"He wants to know he's your priority. And when you leave at night"—I wave an awkward hand—"to do what you do, you're telling him something else is more important than he is."

He narrows his eyes. "You sure this isn't you talking?"

Am I still hurt that he ended our marriage one month and started seeing someone else the next? Yes. Does it hurt even more that the woman in question is Cady Reynolds, his first love? Of course it does. But this isn't high school. One of us, at least, should remember that.

"I'm not going to have this conversation with you right now." I tilt my head, surveying Emma, who's come back to say goodbye.

"Right." Craig knuckles his nose and eyes the Pruitts' car, where it's backing out of the garage across the street.

I fake a smile and politely wave to them. It's bad enough the entire town knows my marriage failed and that my husband is back to fucking his old high school fling. I don't need them talking about how we're still fighting about it.

Mason skulks through the door with his duffel bag slung over his shoulder. "Hey, Dad."

"Hey, Mase. How was school?"

"Crappy. Five days until summer vacation." Without another word, he stalks to Craig's truck.

"Don't think you're leaving without a hug," I call after him.

His shoulders slump even more, but he turns around without argument.

"Love you, Mom." Emma gives me another quick squeeze before she returns to the truck and climbs into the back seat.

"The game is at noon at the field by the festival grounds," I mutter to Craig. If I don't tell him now, he'll text me for the details later.

"Thanks." He steps aside as Mason returns for that hug. "I'll have them back by four on Sunday."

Mason flicks a glance my way, silently pleading for me to ask about that earlier drop off, but I shake my head. He needs time with his dad, even if it comes in bits and pieces.

"I'll see you at the game tomorrow, okay?" I press a kiss to the top of his head and breathe him in, willing him to go without arguing.

"Fine." Once again, he shuffles away, and this time, Craig goes, too.

The moment the truck disappears down the street, I step back inside, close the door, and fall apart.

All in all, I've been okay since Craig moved out four months ago. My marriage wasn't perfect by a long shot, and this divorce is for the best. But watching him take my babies away? It's like there's a vise around my heart, squeezing a little tighter every time I'm reminded that this will be our reality for the next decade.

I hate it. And I hate even more that my babies are stuck in the middle of this mess. Craig and I were supposed to raise them together. Under this roof. But he called it quits on our family.

More specifically, he called it quits on *me*.

"I look at you, and all I see is their mother," he said when he told me he wanted a divorce. *"I respect you as the woman who's raising my kids, but I don't see you like a man should see his wife. The spark is gone, Ray, and I don't think there's anything more we can do to bring it back."*

A dagger to my heart would have been less painful. Hell, even a cleaver chopping it into hundreds of little pieces would have been preferable.

All I ever wanted was to be a good wife and a good mother, like my mom was for my dad and to me.

But I wasn't.

And I don't know what to do with that.

"DANG, GIRL! YOU'RE ON FIRE!" My best friend Crystal whoops. "You were imagining Cady's face up there, weren't you?"

I tip my head back and laugh. I sank two darts into the bullseye and hit twenty on the third, but the thought of her hasn't even crossed my mind. "No, but I bet I'd have nailed all three if I had."

Giggling, she takes her position at the line. "You can do that next time, and I won't even be mad when you beat me." With one eye closed, she takes her first shot. It bounces off the board and hits the hardwood floor. "Well, damn. Maybe *I* should imagine her face up there."

"Do what you gotta do, babe." Grinning, I return to our high-top table at the back of The Creek, Cole Creek's bar and grill.

Our PTA meeting ended an hour ago, but Crys and I stuck around for a drink and a couple of games. She needs a little time to herself to get through the rest of the school year, and I'm here hoping to forget my exchange with Craig. I'm not a big drinker, but desperate times call for desperate measures.

"Ugh, that was awful." Crystal collects her darts with a sigh and skulks back to the table, head bowed in shame. "I need practice. We should do this more often."

"True that." I tip my old-fashioned her way, then tip it back and finish it off with a little slurp. "But it's probably best if we don't. I like these too much."

She's grinning in response when the bells on the bar's

front door jingle and a group of young guys strolls in. They're dressed in T-shirts and swimming trunks, so they're probably cabin-goers looking for a little fun this weekend. Cole Creek comes alive this time of year. When the weather gets warm, we're inundated with city folk who love to leave behind the hustle and bustle in exchange for our quiet little town and its hospitality.

"Damn," Crystal mutters. "Look at all that fresh meat."

"Mm-hmm. They've got that look in their eyes, too." The kind that promises they're up to no good and not the least bit ashamed.

"Oh, the things I could do with a group like that."

I choke out a laugh, thankful I've finished my drink. Otherwise she'd be wearing it. "The *whole* group? What would Tony think about that?" I don't even bother to point out that they're probably twenty-one, twenty-two tops.

"He'd encourage me to fantasize all I want." She waggles her brows. "You know, like a good husband would."

I blink at her for a solid five seconds, equal parts shocked and jealous. Craig would have never been okay with me thinking about other men, let alone encourage me to do it.

"It keeps things interesting." She stirs her drink with her straw and lets out a dreamy sigh. "And my man never complains."

Ugh. My man—or rather, my *ex*-man—never complained, either. At least not until he told me he wanted a divorce because I was boring.

My stomach sours at the thought. Had *he* been fantasizing about someone else? Had he been fantasizing about *Cady*?

"I need a refill." I hop down from my seat and tug on the waistband of my jeans. I really don't need another drink, especially when I haven't eaten since lunch, but I'm desperate to wash away that last thought.

"You just want to get closer to all that man meat." Crystal smirks, a challenging glint in her eye that almost makes me think she's serious.

I hold up one hand and scoff. "Believe me, I don't." I have enough drama in my life. I don't need more from the kind of guy who's only interested in getting laid.

But on the other hand...

Maybe that's exactly what I need.

Not the sex, because I would probably break a hip. I'm only thirty-two, but it's been so long that I'm not sure my legs even move that way anymore.

But I could use a little fun. And the ego boost.

So if these boys are interested in making an almost-divorced mother of two feel desirable again...

Why not let them?

TWO

JINX

Ty: Dude, where the hell are you?

The text lights up my cell screen just as I pull it from my pocket to check the time.

Nine o'clock.

Shit.

So much for the early day I promised myself *and* my buddies.

Me: Unloading at the storage yard. Be there in ten.

I hit send and tuck the phone away. Then I get to work unhitching the lawn equipment trailer from my truck.

We're already operating at full bore, and with the summer just beginning, we're adding additional jobs every day. It's a good problem to have. I'm good at what I do, and I put in the extra time because I hate disappointing people.

Too bad the person I worry about disappointing the most hasn't noticed all the late nights I've been putting in.

Quit being a fucking baby, Enders. You're twenty-six, not twelve.

Giving myself a mental kick, I get the trailer situated in the landscaping garage and hop back into my truck, then head for the storage yard gate.

Though all us Enders kids were raised on big equipment and good ole Wisconsin dirt, Aiden, my oldest brother, bucked family tradition entirely by going into law enforcement, and our baby sister, Amelia, went her own way, too, with a career in graphic design. No one was the least bit surprised when Jesse and I stuck to our roots in Enders Excavating. That blue-collar blood runs deep, and I wouldn't have it any other way.

Jesse took over the family excavation company when he was just twenty-two. He oversees the bigger earth-moving projects, but I manage the landscaping part of the business. Lawn care, trees, gardens, you name it. If it's a residential project, then it's mine, and it's been that way since I was twenty years old. I may not have a financial stake in the company, but I take my work and my family's reputation seriously.

Hence the reason I'm late meeting up with Ty and Connor for the beers I promised.

I've just locked the gate and climbed back into my truck when my phone chimes with another text.

Ty: Saved you a seat, but if you don't hurry the fuck up, I'm giving it to Macy.

The hell he is.

Cranking the music, I hit the gas pedal. Five minutes later, The Creek comes into view. Between the weekend visitors and the locals here for the Friday night fish fry, the parking lot and the street in front of the pub are packed, but I get lucky and steal a spot near the front when another vehicle backs out.

When I finally step inside the bar, Ty hollers "about damn time" above the crowd and the country music playing on the jukebox.

As expected, the place has standing room only, but I'm a big guy, and I'm not afraid to shoulder my way through the patrons to reach my destination.

"Some people gotta work around here," I tell him when we clasp hands in a way that's more bro-shake than handshake.

Ty Crawford is a deputy with the Pine County Sheriff's Office and one of my oldest friends. We see each other more often in church than we do anywhere else because life is so damn busy. Of course, I'm rarely in church, much to my mother's dismay, so it's been months since I've seen him anywhere other than in his cruiser as he's headed through town.

"I thought you were clocking out a couple of hours ago." Connor hands me a bottle of beer. "Or were you making *house calls* again?" He uses air-quotes around the words and hits me with a smirk.

Connor DeLuca is my right-hand man at EE. Since I usually make him hang it up at five o'clock, he likes to give me shit about the hours I work and what I'm getting up to once he's gone home. I only wish it was as nefarious as he makes it sound.

Desperate for a little relaxation, I roll my shoulders and tip back a hefty swig of the ice-cold beer. It goes down way too easy, but I haven't eaten since I downed a slice of gas station pizza at lunch, so tonight, this will be my one and only drink. That, and we'd all be pushing the boundaries of the law if we had too much fun. None of us wants to put Ty in that position.

We spend the next forty-five minutes catching up on everything from work to the Brewers and the upcoming Packers season.

When a hoot of feminine laughter in the game area snags my attention, I lift my chin toward the back of the bar where a group of rowdy guys plays beer pong with a couple of local women. "What's that all about?"

Ty follows my gaze to Crystal, one of my cousin Bobbie Jean's friends, just as she slaps some dude's ass for nailing his round. "Sadie said the PTA met here earlier. Those two stuck around."

"You think I should cut them off?" Sadie, the bartender, saunters over, chewing her bottom lip.

"Tony would probably appreciate that." Crystal's husband is a chill guy, but his wife playing grab-ass with some frat boy might cross the line.

"She called him an hour ago to tell him she made some new friends. He told her to live it up, but keep her pants on, and that he'd be by at ten to pick her up."

I snort and glance at my watch. Only fifteen minutes to go. "On second thought, let her have fun."

"It's the other one I'm worried about, anyway." Sadie tips her head to the woman huddled close to a tall, lanky guy in the far corner of the game area. She has her back to the rest of the bar, but her wavy auburn hair and curvy body in those snug-as-hell jeans are familiar.

"Who is it?" I ask, leaning back and bringing my beer to my lips.

"Rachel Perry," Ty answers.

I lurch forward and damn near choke on my drink. "No shit."

"Yup." Sadie pops her lips.

Craig Perry, her soon-to-be ex-husband, is Jesse's lead man on the big earth-moving jobs. He does decent work, but I've never been a fan of the guy. Even before the rumors about him and Rachel—and the rumors about him and *Cady*—started going around.

"She comes in with the kids sometimes," Sadie adds. "But I've never seen her drink until tonight."

I haven't, either. Not that our paths cross often. Shit, I think the last time I saw her was when she spilled coffee all over the EE lobby.

"I obviously can't let her drive, and Bren isn't answering his phone."

"Saw his truck at Aiden's on my way through town. They're probably throwing back a few beers." Bren is the county sheriff and self-appointed Cole Creek cabbie. He's also my oldest brother's best friend.

"Ugh." Sadie sighs, her shoulders sinking. "Any chance either of you would do it?"

"Do what?" I ask at the same time Ty says, "No way in hell."

"Drive her home." She bats her lashes.

I hold up my empty beer bottle. "Probably not a good idea."

"You could drink a six-pack and not even catch a buzz, Jinx. Come on. Do me a favor. I don't want to call Craig and ruin her fun."

A burst of anger hits me at the sound of his name. Fuck that. He's the last person she needs showing up tonight.

I give a heavy sigh and take Rachel in again. The guy she's with is draped over her like a wet fucking noodle. His eyes are clear and his feet are steady, like he isn't drunk at all. In fact, he looks like he knows exactly what he's doing, and that doesn't sit well. I don't know Rachel well, but we look after our own in Cole Creek, and I can't in good conscience stand back and let this loser take advantage.

"She eat yet?" I ask Sadie.

She presses her lips together and shakes her head. "Not that I saw."

Great. "Can you throw on a couple of burgers?"

Sadie cocks a brow. "The kitchen closes in ten minutes, you asshole."

"You want me to drive her home or not?"

With that, she pastes on a fake-ass smile. "In that case, I'll throw in an order of fries. On the house."

I roll my eyes as she jots down the order.

Once she's headed back to the kitchen, I shift in my seat so I can keep an eye on the rowdy group in the back. Damn, I could use another beer.

Just a few minutes into the show, Rachel shakes herself loose and gets ready for her turn at the pong table. The wet noodle moves in behind her, grips her hips, and whispers something in her ear that makes her laugh... and it pisses me off.

No way in hell is he getting what he thinks he is tonight.

If she goes home with him, she'll hate herself. And something tells me she's already been hard enough on herself because of Craig.

With a sigh, I push off the barstool and make my way over just as she takes her first shot at the pong cups. She misses terribly, and her face twists with disappointment. But she quickly regains her focus, and with her expression pinched in concentration, she takes her second shot. This time, she easily makes it into one of the cups. "Yes!" She throws her arms in the air.

The guy behind her scoops her up and spins her around.

And I grind my molars.

"I should kiss you for that," the guy says.

Before he gets the chance to put his mouth on hers, I clear my throat. "Nice shot, Rach. Looks like you're showing these young bucks how it's done."

Every guy in the group turns his attention to me. Rachel narrows her eyes, probably assuming that since I work with Craig, I'm going to blabber to him. Then she blows a raspberry.

"Yeah, right. More like they're schooling me." She gives the guy who can't keep his hands off her a saucy grin. "Aren't you, handsome?"

The asshole grins right back, and this time, he dips in, going for that kiss.

"I wouldn't do that if I were you." I take two big steps forward and tug her from his grasp. I only meant to stop the kiss, but somehow, she ends up behind me, and I end up nose to nose with the young prick.

"What the hell, Jinx?" Rachel scoffs, trying to shove her way around me.

"She's drunk, and you know it," I grit out, keeping my grip on her firm but not too hard.

"What the fuck do you care?" The asshole puffs out his scrawny chest. "Are you her babysitter?"

"He's my friend's husband," Rachel interjects, slurring her words. "I mean, my husband's friend. *Ex*-husband."

"I'm her friend, too, and I promise that whatever you thought was gonna happen here tonight *ain't*. Not on my watch."

The punk's upper lip curls, and I brace myself for a fist.

One of his friends steps between us before that happens. "She ain't worth it, man. Let it go."

Behind me, Rachel slumps. I release her and glance over my shoulder to check on her, just in time to see her frustrated expression melt into defeat. With that small change, the energy around her shifts, and the temporary high she's been riding deflates like I just stomped on her balloon.

That's all right. I'd rather she hate me now than hate herself in the morning.

"Come on, Rach." I gently reach for her, and to my surprise, she doesn't balk.

In fact, she doesn't say a single word as she gathers her purse and walks with me toward the bar.

We're just approaching when Sadie exits the kitchen with a plastic bag in hand. "Perfect timing." Her gaze shifts from me to Rachel and back again. "Thank you," she mouths.

I nod and throw some cash onto the bar for the food. "Her car is okay here tonight?"

"Of course. Just lock it up."

"You didn't have to do that," Rachel slurs as soon as we step outside. Thank god she isn't wearing heels, or she'd probably break an ankle with the way she's swaying and sidestepping. "I wasn't going to do anything stupid."

"I'm not so sure about that." My guess is she's already going to have regrets, but what do I know?

When I hit the fob on my key ring and my headlights illuminate up ahead, she coos. "Ooh, did you get a new truck?"

"Sure did. Just a few months old."

She steps clumsily off the curb, and I snag her elbow just before she goes down.

"I like it," she husks, awkwardly pushing her hair from her face. With a hum, she reaches out and strokes her fingers along the paint. "Are you going to be my knight in shiny white armor tonight, Jinx?"

Not in the way you think, babe.

Still holding her arm, I stow the bag of takeout in the back seat, then I open the passenger door.

"Let me help you up." I gently grip her waist from behind, ready to bypass the chrome running boards and lift her onto the seat. But she turns before I get the chance.

"Is it true?" She lowers her lashes over her hazy copper eyes as she traces a fingertip down the center of my chest. "That men with big trucks are overcompensating?"

I laugh lowly. "Not in my case."

"That's what I thought." She bites the corner of her lip and smashes her tits against my chest.

Before I can stop her, she throws her arms around my neck and plants a fat kiss on my mouth.

"Whoa!" Still gripping her waist, I hold her at arm's length. "Whatcha doing, gorgeous?"

A satisfied smile flickers across her lips as she licks them. "Mmm, you taste good."

Jesus Christ.

"I think it's time to get you home." Before she can pull another stunt, I lift her onto the seat and buckle her in. "You good?"

She nods with that wistful look still in her eyes. "So good."

Sadie owes me a fuck of a lot more than fries for this.

THREE

RACHEL

I kissed Jinx Enders.

More accurately, I *threw* myself at him right there in The Creek's parking lot.

Okay, maybe that's an exaggeration. I didn't shove my tongue down his throat or try to hump him like a dog. But I did kiss him in a moment of drunken, mid-divorce insanity because I completely misread his chivalry.

Also, he smelled really, really good. Like spicy man, fresh cut grass, and fuel.

Oh my god, I'm going to hell.

Elbows planted on the kitchen counter, I pinch the bridge of my nose and pray for the ibuprofen to do its job. Every time my headache starts to ease up, I think about last night, and it starts throbbing all over again.

I'm not sure the kiss was even the worst part. Jinx laughed it off, and he wasn't weird about it when he sat with me on the front porch and made sure I ate the burger he'd bought for me.

No, the worst part about last night was that I'm pretty sure I cried to him about Craig. I don't remember everything, but I do recall Jinx telling me Craig was a selfish ass who didn't deserve me.

Which was really sweet of him.

Stoppp. I slide my arms forward and collapse against the countertop. The cool surface dulls the pounding in my head a little, at least.

Last night was full of weak moments, and I am not going to continue that craziness today. I will not swoon over a twentysomething boy who has a reputation around town for his laissez-faire attitude. A boy who also works with my soon-to-be ex-husband. *Ugh.*

When my phone pings, my first instinct is to cringe. I swear to god, if it's Craig asking me what the hell I was thinking last night...

Crystal: Hey, babes. Did you make it home okay?

Thank goodness.

Me: I did. How are you feeling?

Crystal: Like hell. Don't let me do that again.

I laugh and instantly regret it when my head revolts.

Me: Same. No more PTA meetings at The Creek.

Crystal: Bobbie Jean's from here on out. Coffee only. No more brandy.

Me: And no more whiskey

The clock in the living room chimes, reminding me that I need to get moving. The last thing I want to do today is nurse my hangover while the sun beats down on me, but I only have myself to blame for that.

Me: Heading to Emma's game. Talk later.

I grab my purse and keys and head for the door. I've got my hand on the knob when it hits me, and my stomach sinks. My Explorer is still at The Creek.

Great. Not only will I be pulling up to the game with a hangover, but I'll be late, too. Mom of the year, for sure.

I'm just pulling out my phone to text my dad—the only person I know who won't ask a million questions—when a familiar white truck pulls into the driveway.

My heart takes off at a gallop, and the nausea that, so far, has been mild, ratchets up. What in the heck is *he* doing here?

The driver's door opens, and a well-worn pair of boots hit the gravel. Then Jinx rounds the front of the truck looking far too bright-eyed and bushy-tailed. Which, of course, is a reminder that I have absolutely no business noticing how delicious he smells or how sweet he is or how good he looks in that snug white T-shirt. Also, he's twenty-five. Or is it twenty-four? *God.*

"Mornin'."

Dammit, that charming drawl is one more thing that shouldn't affect me.

"Thought you might need a ride into town to get your car." He arches one brow at the keys in my hand. "Looks like I'm right on time."

"Uh..." Embarrassment floods me. I want to die. I want

to go back into the house, curl up in bed, and die. "Yeah, I sorta forgot about that."

He lifts his sunglasses and rests them on the brim of his ball cap. The way his light eyes twinkle against the late morning sun is like a punch to the solar plexus. And don't get me started on the smile that stretches wide, revealing a dimple in his left cheek. Even with the light brown scruff on his jaw, the dimple is right there, looking as adorable as the man it belongs to.

He's trouble, Rachel. Jailbait. Maybe not legally, but morally. And you're not even divorced yet.

As subtly as I can, I blow out a breath, willing my body to chill.

"Happens to the best of us." He tucks his hands into the pockets of his jeans. Jeans that are well worn and—*stop looking!* "Anyway, I'm heading into town, so if you need a lift..."

"Uh, sure." I swallow down the butterflies threatening to take flight. "That would be great. Thank you." The last thing I need is to spend more time with him, given how much he's already derailed my sanity, but this saves me from having to call my dad for help.

A minute later, I'm buckled into his passenger seat just like I was last night, but this time, I've mostly got my wits about me.

Unlike Craig's truck, this one is immaculate. There are no fast-food bags on the floor, no half-empty bottles of Gatorade rolling around in the back, no tools that smell like grease and diesel fuel. It's all clean seats and that newer truck scent mixed with Jinx's spicy deodorant or body wash. And a couple of tubes of lip balm in a cupholder.

Huh. His? Or were they left by the many girls I'm sure he's had in here?

"What time is the softball game today?" he asks, one arm draped over the wheel while his other arm, thick and full of dark ink, rests on the console, his fingers drumming along to the rock song playing quietly on the radio.

"Noon." I swallow and assess him as discreetly as possible. "How do you know about the game?"

The corner of his mouth curls into another grin. "You told me last night."

"Oh." I clutch my purse to my abdomen a little tighter. I really wish I could remember all the things I told him. "About that... I probably owe you an apology."

He chuckles. "For what?"

The kiss, for one. And anything I said that may have made him uncomfortable. I'm sure the last thing he wanted to do on a Friday night was deal with an emotional thirty-two-year-old woman who's in the midst of a divorce.

"For all of..." I wave my hand, my stomach twisting itself into a knot. "All of *everything* last night."

He shakes his head, drawing my attention to the brown-sugar hair curling around the edge of his ball cap. "Not a problem."

"You were probably out with your friends and—"

"Hey..." He reaches over and gently squeezes my arm. Neither of us acknowledges the goose bumps that rise on my bare skin in response. "It's all good. I promise. I only stopped in to have a beer with Ty and Connor and grab something to eat. You were on my way home."

"And what about the cheeseburgers? You just happened to order two?"

The slightest blush creeps into his cheeks. "Sadie said you hadn't eaten, so..."

So he might've been driving past my house, but he still went out of his way for me.

"Thank you." I dip my chin and fiddle with my purse strap.

In my periphery, he nods humbly. "You're welcome."

We sit in silence as he drives into town, and I pray none of the people we pass recognize me.

I'm sure plenty of them saw us leave together last night, and I don't even want to think about who might've seen me kiss him. The last thing I need is for people to see us together again this morning and make assumptions about how we spent the night.

Then again, Cole Creek is a small town, and the rumors are going to fly one way or another.

"No offense, but I noticed that your lawn could use some TLC," he says as he turns onto the street in front of The Creek. "You need a hand with that?"

"My lawn? Oh. Mason takes care of that, but he mentioned something about needing more gas for the mower. We'll deal with it tomorrow afternoon when he gets home from his dad's. Er, his grandparents'. Thank you, though."

Jinx slows in front of the pub and pulls into the parking lot. "No problem. I'm happy to help out if you change your mind."

"I appreciate that." When the truck comes to a stop next to my car, I unbuckle and turn to him, suddenly feeling like an awkward teenager getting dropped off from a date. "Thank you for the ride. Both of them. And the burger."

He leans an arm on the driver's door and gives me another of those crooked grins. "You're too damn grateful."

I frown in confusion. "What?"

"You've thanked me no less than a dozen times in the last twelve hours for things anyone with a lick of conscience would do."

An ache forms in my chest. Craig wouldn't. He wouldn't have made sure I ate last night. He would have been too pissed off at the inconvenience of having to pick me up and deal with me. And he wouldn't have offered to give me a ride to my car today, either. I would have had to swallow my pride and ask. And then he would have spent the drive complaining about me acting a fool the night before.

"I'm not sure that's true, but th—" I pinch my eyes shut and let out a soft laugh. "I'm going to get out now."

He chuckles, too. "Bye, Rachel. Have fun at the game today."

"Bye, Jinx." *Have fun being too sweet and too swoony for your own good.*

And for my good, too.

"BIG CROWD TODAY." Bobbie Jean scans the people nearby as we hurry from our cars to the softball field with just a few minutes to spare before the first pitch.

Each of us has a lawn chair in one hand and a cooler full of water and Gatorade for the kids in the other. Even though it's Craig's weekend, loading myself down with every single thing kids might need is a hard habit to break.

"It's a nice day, so I'm not surprised." But there's no way I'm sitting in the sun with this headache. "How about we sit over there?" I jut my chin to a spot in the shade.

"Perfect." Bobbie Jean sets up her chair and makes a few hand gestures to her son, Casen, who's already taken off to play with his friends. "But I might sneak up to the fence later for pictures if Mariah gets to pitch."

"Oh." I nudge her with my elbow. "She's getting good, huh?"

Bobbie Jean smiles. "She really is. Too bad her dad is never here to witness the progress she's made."

Ugh. My heart hurts for Mariah and for Bobbie. Though after the horrible divorce Bobbie and her ex-husband went through, maybe distance isn't such a bad thing.

"I see Craig brought Miss Thing along today." My friend discreetly lifts her chin toward the bleachers on the other side of the field.

"Yeah, I noticed." I may not want Craig back, but seeing them still sends a shock of pain through my chest. We're not even divorced, and they're flaunting their relationship all over town just like they did when they were kids in high school. Good lord, grow up. Or at least wait until the ink is dry on the divorce papers.

"Mom!" Emma's voice snags my attention. "Drink, please!"

Ah-ha. Motherly intuition saves the day.

"Be right back." I stand and dig a Gatorade from the cooler, then walk it over to the field. "Hey, baby. Where's your brother?"

She backs up and holds out her hands, ready for me to toss the bottle over the fence. "With Grandpa," she says as she catches it. "He didn't want to come."

I figured that was the case once I saw Cady sitting beside Craig.

"Your hair looks cute." Her hair is done in two French braids that hang over her shoulders.

Her face goes red, and she ducks her chin.

"It's okay, baby."

My heart aches for her. I hate that she and Mason so

often find themselves in the middle of issues they shouldn't have to worry about. She can't braid, and my mother-in-law has never been the type to do hair, so it's not hard to figure out who's responsible.

"The braids look nice, and it's hot out today. They'll keep your neck cool."

Her shoulders drop in relief. "That's what Cady said, too."

"Good." I wish we were standing on the same side of the fence so I could give her a hug and reassure her. I don't love that another woman is playing a role in my children's lives, but I'm not going to force their loyalty when, thus far, Cady's influence seems to be a positive one.

"I'd better get back to the dugout." Emma tips her head.

"Okay, baby. Kick butt today."

With a thumbs-up, she trots off to join the rest of the team.

I watch her for a minute, unable to help but smile. When I turn to head back to the shade, I almost bump into Craig.

"Thanks for bringing her a drink," he says. Then, "What's this I hear about you going out last night?"

Without my permission, a breath huffs out of me. I should have known.

"There was a PTA meeting at the pub."

"I'm talking about after the meeting."

So the beer pong. "I'm allowed to have fun, Craig."

"With a bunch of college guys?" He regards me, brows lifted.

In the sun, it's so easy to see how much he's aged over the years. Of course, I have, too, and these past few months haven't been kind to either of us.

"Look, I really don't owe you an explanation." I don't

want to argue with him, but I will stand my ground purely on principle. If it's okay for him to already be in a new relationship, then I can go out and have fun. With whomever I want.

"At least tell me you didn't fuck around with Jinx."

If it were possible for my jaw to disconnect from my skull and hit the ground, it would have.

Hands fisted at my sides, I tilt my chin up, defiant. "Are you freaking kidding me right now?"

He lifts his hands in that innocent yet passive-aggressive way he's responded to most of our conflict over the past couple of years. Like he's just the messenger of whatever crap he's spewing without taking accountability for any of it.

"He gave me a ride home." I won't mention that Jinx kept me from doing something worse than playing games with those guys. He doesn't need more ammunition to use against me.

"He gave you a ride back this morning, too. Right before you came here." This time, he doesn't even try to soften the accusation.

"I'm not doing this with you." Here or anywhere else.

"You have kids, Rachel."

I rear back. "So do you."

But that doesn't matter. It's always been about me and what I am and am not. Never his shortcomings. Never how selfish he was for the entirety of our marriage. Never the things he got to do, the life he got to live, while I stayed home and raised our kids *and* maintained a job.

"Go back to your girlfriend, Craig." I will my tone to remain even. "And next time you want to come over and give me shit about what I'm doing with my life, maybe you should think about what you're doing with yours."

I shoulder around him, using all my willpower to keep the tears at bay, and march back to my seat by Bobbie Jean.

"What the hell was that?" she asks, frowning at Craig.

"Oh, you know." I drop into my lawn chair with a huff. "Just my soon-to-be ex-husband and his hypocritical bullshit."

"Does today's bullshit have anything to do with Jinx giving you a ride home last night?"

My spine stiffens and I spin to face her. "You already heard, too?"

"I saw your car was still at the bar this morning when I went into town to open the shop. I texted Sadie to check on you."

"Why didn't you text me?"

"What if you'd gone home with someone?" She smirks. "I wasn't about to interrupt your fun. Or your walk of shame."

"Oh my god." I press my fingers into my temples and close my eyes.

These people are out of their minds. I may be in the middle of a divorce, but I've never been that kind of woman. I'm not going to start now. "Sorry to disappoint you, but I slept in my own bed last night."

"So nothing happened with Jinx?" She frowns, her head tilted slightly.

Does she really look disappointed right now, or am I imagining things?

"He's a kid, Bobbie. And he's your cousin."

She holds up a finger. "For one, he's twenty-six and most definitely not a kid. And two, I'm related to half this town, so nothing is weird to me anymore."

I fight the urge to roll my eyes. "I'm not talking to you about this."

"This..." she repeats. "That implies that *this* is something."

"Ugh." I grip the armrests of my chair and push myself back against it. "No. Just... no."

"He's a nice guy."

I haven't had nearly enough coffee for this.

"It wasn't like that, Bobbie. He literally just gave me a ride." And he fed me. And talked to me. And didn't freak out when I kissed him.

"Hmm. That's too bad. I think you two would be really cute together."

Well, yeah. Because *he's* cute.

But he's young. And dating is the farthest thing from my mind right now.

Even if it weren't, I wouldn't even consider Jinx Enders.

As sweet as he was both last night and this morning, he has a reputation for exactly that... for being a total ladies' man. And me? I've been with exactly one man my entire life. I'd humiliate myself with someone like Jinx. Not that he'd even be interested in someone like me.

Craig wasn't even interested anymore, and he knew everything about me.

But did he really?

I shove a hand through my hair, close my eyes, and turn my face to the sliver of sun streaking through the trees.

No, that isn't true.

Craig didn't know everything, and to be fair, I didn't for a long time, either. I just became really good at convincing everyone, including myself, otherwise.

The truth is, I wasn't happy. With my marriage, with my life, or with myself.

And I can't blame Craig for leaving...

When I already blame myself for staying.

FOUR

MID-JUNE...

JINX

"Tell me you didn't do what I think you did." Amelia's tense, irritated voice grates through the Bluetooth in my truck Thursday afternoon.

It's eighty-six degrees in the shade, and beads of sweat practically run in rivulets down my back and make me stick to the leather seat, so I crank the air conditioning and turn all the vents to face me. The Pruitts are my pickiest goddamn customers, hence why I'm here doing their weekly lawn maintenance, as well as three hours' worth of tree trimming, instead of one of my guys. Between the heat and Cliff's request that I trim ten branches instead of the two on the service order, I'm in no mood for Amelia's guessing games.

"I have no idea what you're talking about, Lee, and frankly, I don't have time for this." As the youngest of us and the only girl, she's always pissed off. Having three older brothers makes it easy, I guess, so it could be any number of things.

"You called Theo my flavor of the week."

I have to bite back a smirk, because yeah, I did do that. The guy's weird mustache and gelled hair give off major creeper vibes. And by the way he went on and on about all the places he's "shot" as a photographer, it's clear he's more into himself than he'll ever be in Amelia. I did them both a favor by nudging him out the door.

Amelia scoffs. "You're not even going to deny it?"

"Nope." I tug at the front of my damp shirt to speed along the cooling process. "He cared more about his hair than you do yours."

"So? There's nothing wrong with valuing your appearance. At least he showers."

She's got a point there. One of the guys she dated last year was a hippie with a deodorant allergy. Water, too, apparently, because the dude was always ripe. He was creative as hell, I'd agree with Amelia there, but damn if he didn't stink.

"I know you're never going to stop doing the ornery big-brother thing, but did you have to make me sound like a skank? Theo was the first guy I dated in, like, five months."

"*Hmph.*" Five whole months. I'm going on eight or nine myself unless eating burgers on Rachel Perry's front porch counts.

The memory of that night has me peering over at her house across the street.

Her son, Mason, I realize, is messing around with a push mower in front of their garage.

It's a nice house. Ranch-style with brick veneer beneath dark gray siding. But the grass looks like it hasn't been cut in weeks, and it's been giving me anxiety almost as long.

"Look, Lee," I say, remembering she's still on Bluetooth. "I'm sorry. It was the first thing that came to my mind, okay? I'll do better next time."

"Next time. Right. Or maybe you could just mind your own business."

I half snort, half laugh. "We know that's never gonna happen."

"And here I thought there was hope for you." She sighs. "At least you're not as bad as Aiden."

Nope, not as long as he has a Glock to back up his scare tactics. Thank god she can't see my grin. If she could, she'd smack me.

"Anyway, I put some leftovers in your fridge before I found out about your comment to Theo. I was going to stop by and take them back, but I took a nap instead. So you're welcome, you asshole."

My chuckle is cut short when Mason slams a tool down onto the concrete, his face a mask of frustration. He's lucky the damn thing didn't smack him in the face when it bounced back up.

"Thanks. You're a good egg, even though your taste in men is shit."

She makes an annoyed sound but doesn't argue. Amelia is the more cultured and free-spirited sibling, but she's a small-town girl at heart. I don't see her settling down with a man who's all that different. She just hasn't figured that out yet.

"I hope you choke on those leftovers." With that, she disconnects the call.

I'm still chuckling when I turn back to watch Mason.

Now he's pacing back and forth across the garage apron with his head bowed and his fists clenched at his sides.

I should leave him be and mind my own business. But

just like I couldn't leave his mother to fend for herself at the bar, I can't let him struggle, either.

Turning my ball cap around, I snag my sunglasses and hop out of the air-conditioned truck.

"Hey, man. That thing giving you grief?" I call out as I jog over, already feeling the effects of the heat.

Mason turns to me, wearing a scowl, his forehead already beaded with sweat. "More like it's pissing me off," he grumbles as he swipes at his face, leaving a streak of dirt over his brows.

A laugh escapes me before I remember he just turned eleven. "Bro, don't let your mom catch you talking like that."

"I don't frickin' care." He shoves the mower away and then gives it a kick for good measure.

Damn kid could use some time with a boxing bag.

I lift my chin to the mower. "What's it doing?"

"Won't start."

"Hmm." Hands on my hips, I take a step closer to the offending machine.

"Started giving my dad problems last year, but now it won't even turn over."

Figures Craig would leave his kid to deal with this shit. "Mind if I take a look?"

Mason waves at the mower dramatically and then reaches for his bottle of Mountain Dew.

My stomach twists just thinking about all that sugar.

"Crap," he grumbles, peering into the mouth of the bottle. "There's a fly in it."

"There's a bunch of Gatorade in the cooler in the back of my truck." I tilt my head toward the street. "Go ahead and grab one."

He stares at the fly in the bottle for a beat before he wanders away and dumps the contents into the grass. As he's tossing the bottle into the trash, he looks back at me. "You sure?"

"Yep. Grab one for me, too, will ya?"

He gives a thumbs-up and jogs away.

Turning my attention to the mower, I give it a quick inspection. The issue jumps out at me immediately. There's oil all over the engine. The yard looks like it's been cut a few times already this year, so my guess is that Mason ran it with a leak and blew it up.

He comes strolling back with two bottles and sets one down beside me before cracking his own open. "You see anything?" he asks.

"Yeah, unfortunately." I run a finger through the oil on the carburetor. "This isn't supposed to be here. Hate to tell ya, but I think the engine is shot."

His shoulders drop and a flash of guilt crosses his face. "Mom is gonna kill me."

"Nah," I say, keeping my tone light. "It's just a lawn mower."

"Yeah, but we don't have money for a new one."

I kinda thought he might say that, but it's still just a mower.

"Your mom out running errands or something?" She should be on summer break by now.

"Emma had a dentist appointment. They'll be back soon."

I nod and, still kneeling on the concrete, survey the yard. "I'll come by tomorrow and cut the grass. Just do me a favor and don't tell your mom."

He smiles, as if he likes the idea of sharing a secret. "Why not?"

"Because she'll get stubborn and tell me not to do it. You know how those independent women are." I wink.

His response is a defeated sigh. "That's how I know she's gonna be mad about the mower."

"Your mom's got a lot on her plate right now."

He frowns and roughs a hand over the back of his neck. "She's been upset a lot since Dad left."

I dip my chin and pick up my Gatorade. "Yeah, I bet. Which is why I'm gonna come by and take care of your yard. Your mom doesn't need something else to worry about." And frankly, neither does he. "You playing football this year?"

"Nope." Man, if the kid's shoulders sink any lower, I worry it'll do permanent damage to his posture.

"Why not?" He's a damn good player. I know because back before work got so busy, I helped coach the team.

"Mom can't get me to all the practices. They're in Copper Crossing this year, since we combined teams."

"What about catching a ride with Sawyer?"

"He's playing baseball now."

Well, shit. "That's stinks, huh?"

"Yep." He sighs and takes a drink. "Hey, I almost forgot. Jesse said he'd have some work for me to do this summer."

I arch a brow. "He did?"

"Said I could cut grass at the shop. I think, anyway." He scans the yard, like he's trying to remember.

"Huh. I'll ask him next time I see him, but under two conditions."

The kid grins. "Okay."

"You keep your promise; don't tell your mom about me cutting the lawn. And you stop that cursing, too."

His cheeks are already flushed from the heat, but they flame now. "I was just mad at the mower."

"Maybe, but if your mom had heard that..." I leave the rest unsaid. I don't know how Rachel would react, but she doesn't need to deal with reprimanding her kid for spouting off.

"All right. I'll do my best."

I hold out a fist for him to bump. "Then we've got ourselves a deal."

RACHEL

"HOW MANY MORE DAYS?" Bobbie Jean arches a brow while she waits for me to slide my debit card into the reader. Between her, her sister Becca, and Crystal, there's no way I'll forget the day my divorce will be finalized.

"Exactly eighty." I sigh and slip the card back into my wallet. Once I've stuffed it back into my purse, I collect my go-to iced chai and a strawberry smoothie for Emma. "Seems like forever and yet so soon all at once."

She nods, her lips pressed into a line. "I remember that feeling. It's such a roller coaster."

"That's for sure."

These days, I'm not quite so bitter. It took time to see it, but I realized that my emotions were never about Craig moving on so quickly, though it definitely stings that Cady is the one he's moved on with. No, I was more upset that *he* was the one who had the nerve to call it quits. It should have been me, and I should have done it years ago.

Instead, I stuck it out. Because that's what good wives—good mothers—do.

"How are the kids?" Bobbie Jean leans a hip against the counter. "I heard Mason isn't playing youth football this year."

My heart sinks. "No, and it kills me. With Emma's softball schedule, there's no way I can get him to all those practices in Copper Crossing."

"What about Craig? Can't he help?"

I snort. "Craig take time away from work? Not a chance."

She crosses her arms over her chest. "Seriously?"

I shrug. He makes it to Emma's weekend games, so I haven't given him too much grief about the kids and their sports. Especially because he really does need to work. He has more debt than I do, with his truck and UTV payments and his credit cards, too. Plus, the judge ordered him to pay child support since the kids reside with me.

I'd rather he spend more time with the kids than give me his money, but that's not up to me. And maybe paying child support will encourage him to find a place of his own sooner rather than later. If the kids have dedicated space, they can stay with him more, and we can renegotiate.

"Mason's okay with it. Or so he says." I suspect he thinks he needs to be around more for me, which isn't true. I'm doing okay. But that doesn't change the fact that I can't commit to getting him to practice every day.

Bobbie Jean frowns. "Too bad he and Casen aren't closer in age. We could carpool."

"I appreciate that." The smile I give her is genuine. She's helped me so much these last few months. "Anyway, I have to get going. Emma's waiting in the car. This is her treat for no cavities at the dentist today." I lift the smoothie with a smile.

"Oh, good girl. Give her kudos for me."

"I'll do that. Thanks again."

She gives me a little finger wave in return.

Just as I'm closing in on the door, Janice Enders steps

inside the shop. Her bright blue eyes light up the second she sees me, and I almost trip over my own feet.

For one, Jinx clearly gets his eyes from his mother. I never noticed that before. And two, it's a lot harder to look at the woman now that I know how soft her son's lips are.

"Well, Rachel Kaczmarek. I haven't seen you in forever," the older woman says, fussing with her windblown gray-blond hair.

I smile awkwardly, and only partly because of her use of my maiden name. I suppose I should be used to it. She's called me that for years. I don't plan on going back to it after the divorce, but it's kind of ironic that she's used it all this time. Like maybe she knew something I didn't.

"Hey, Janice. How are you?"

"I'm better now that I've seen you." She swoops in for a quick hug, even though my hands are full. "How are you doing?" She looks me up and down, assessing me with a kind smile.

God, I hope the guilt isn't written across my face. "I'm hanging in there. That was quite the festival this year, huh?"

Her gaze brightens, if it's even possible. "It sure was. You and the kids looked absolutely adorable in your attire."

Adorable isn't the word I would use, but we had fun. Dad did, too, though the Polish festival hasn't been the same for him since Mom's been gone.

"You and the kids should come by sometime. Remember I was going to teach you how I make *sernik*?"

Ah, yes. Polish cheesecake. I vaguely remember a conversation about it several years ago.

"Oh, I'm sure you're too busy for that. I heard you're watching Jett during the day now that he and Hayden are living here."

Her eyes light up with pride. "I am. Come over one day. I'm sure he'd enjoy hanging out with Mason and Emma."

I'm sure he would. Mason and Emma would probably like it, too. But what would Jinx think?

More importantly, why does his opinion matter?

FIVE

JINX

"No way could I do that." Arms crossed over his chest, Jack stands back and watches as Connor scales a huge hemlock in the Bishops' backyard. The tree itself isn't the problem; the branches that hang over the Bishops' sunroom are. I removed the biggest of them a few weeks ago. It was by luck and luck alone that it didn't do any damage.

"Good thing tree-climbing isn't in your job description, then, huh?" I clap the kid on the back. Jack's been working with me for a couple of summers now, but he's only seventeen, so there won't be any tree spikes or harnesses in his immediate future.

"Any word on when the bucket truck will be fixed?" he asks.

Inwardly, I groan. Unfortunately, our unit has seen its final days. I thought I could milk it for one last season, but the lift is no longer stable, and I can't risk mechanical failure when one of us is in the air.

"The truck is officially out of commission. I've been gathering quotes for a new one. Just have to show them to Jesse and see what he thinks."

Jack nods, looking far more mature than his age. "Better safe than sorry."

My phone rings in my pocket, so I dig it out and give him a nod. "That's for sure."

Speak of the devil.

"Huh. Jesse's ears must've been ringing." I accept the call and put the cell to my ear. "Enders Exotic Adventures. This is Jinx, rendezvous master. How may I help you?"

Jesse snorts. "Master, my ass. Not unless you mean master-bater."

Tipping my head back, I grin. "I'm definitely good at that."

"I'm sure you are." He mutters something unintelligible under his breath. "Hey, I need you to do me a favor and take care of some trees at the Willis site."

"Take care of them how?" Any tree removal required for his projects is typically done with a chainsaw and a front-end loader, not my equipment.

"Lenny wants to keep some of them for landscaping, but we got some limbs stuck when we removed the trees around them. Figured it'd be easier to get the bucket truck over there and cut them out than it would be to wait for a good storm to do it for us."

Shit. "Hate to tell you, but no can do." I cringe and fuss with the brim of my hat. "The lift mechanism got stuck a couple of times on Thursday. Connor took a look and said the motor's shot. We're actually at the Bishops' now doing some tree work by hand."

Jesse's silence makes it clear he's not happy. And rightfully so. I should have told him about the truck right away.

In my defense, I wanted to get the quotes in order before I broke the news.

"Let's talk about this on Monday morning," he finally responds, his tone short. "I have to get out to the Willis place and come up with another plan."

Fuck.

I scrub a hand over my face. Despite trying to do the right thing, I still fucked this up.

Story of my goddamn life.

RACHEL

FIVE MORE MINUTES, *Rachel.*

Just one more song.

Gripping the bike's handlebars, I ignore the sweat dripping down my chest and pedal hard for the duration of the metal rock song pulsing through my earbuds. When the music fades and the next song begins, I sit back with my hands on my hips and heave in one deep breath after another.

Craig picked the kids up before dinner, and instead of crying, I focused my energy on working out. Unlike Mason and Emma, I've never been an athlete. Even so, pushing my body and getting my blood pumping effects more than just my physical health. It makes me feel mentally stronger, too.

Legs burning in the best way, I slide off the bike and head upstairs, already looking forward to a shower and the comfy pajamas I plan to put on early. I won't be sleeping or even relaxing, of course, because I have a continuing education class to work on, but there is a bottle of red wine in the kitchen, waiting to keep me company.

After a quick shower, I step out and towel off. My skin is still damp when the sound of a lawn mower passes by the bathroom window.

What the hell?

I stick my fingers in the blinds and move them just enough to see what's going on. My heart leaps into my throat a moment later when Jinx rides by on a mower.

In my backyard.

Dressed in what I'd planned to lounge in all night, I march outside, plant my hands on my hips, and wait for him to turn the mower around.

When he finally does, he grins brightly and lifts a hand in greeting.

I throw both of my arms in the air. "What are you doing?" I holler.

He points to his ear protection and mouths, "I can't hear you."

So, I wait again. The man takes his sweet time, making a couple more laps up and down the far end of the lawn before he finally drives over.

He cuts the engine and drops the ear protection to his neck. "What's up?" Slowly, he looks me up and down, one brow quirked. As if I don't already know that I'm barely dressed in a pair of skimpy sleep shorts and a tank top *without a bra.*

"Why are you cutting my lawn?"

"Needs to be cut."

"Obviously. But why are you the one doing it?"

He gestures toward the mower still sitting outside my garage. "Your mower is broken. Mine isn't."

Oh my god. "How do you... okay, you know what? Forget that." I didn't hire him to do this, so if he thinks he's getting paid...

Wait. A zap of anger courses through me, and I narrow my eyes on him.

"Did Craig send you over?" I demand. "Because I swear to god if—"

"Fuck no," he bites out.

Fuck no? What is that about?

"Are you sure?"

He removes his sunglasses, revealing those icy blue eyes of his.

I almost shiver.

The contrast between them and his tanned skin is startling. And sexy. Or it would be if I weren't so annoyed. And if he weren't so young.

"I don't talk to your husband," Jinx says, his tone still clipped. "Let's set that straight right now. He and I may both work for Enders Excavating, but he's on Jesse's team. And he's Aiden's friend. But he's not mine."

Tell me how you really feel. Jeez.

I cross my arms over my chest. "Okay. That still doesn't explain why you're here."

"Looked like you could use a hand."

Again.

He doesn't say it, but we're both thinking it.

"I'm not going to send you a bill, if that's what you're worried about."

I'm not. But I can't let him do this for free, either. "I don't expect you to work for nothing."

The smile he sends my way is far too bright. "But you didn't hire me, either."

"I'm going to pay you."

"Whatever floats your boat, Rach. Now, can I get back to work?"

Ugh. Why must he be so damn irritating and kind at the same time?

"Fine. Whatever." I wave a flippant hand.

With a single dip of his chin, he returns his ear protection to his head and his sunglasses to his face, and then he goes back to mowing.

I, on the other hand, close my eyes and turn my face up to the sky.

God, please give me the strength.

For what, I don't know just yet.

But I have a feeling I'm going to need it.

SIX

JINX

Rachel Perry is sexy as fuck.

This isn't a new revelation by any means. She caught my attention years ago, but she was married, so I was respectful and kept my eyes mostly to myself.

Now that she's in the process of remedying that problem, things have changed.

Of course, I still respect her. More so than just about anyone else. She's a good mom and a good teacher, and when we talked on her front porch a couple of weeks back, she proved she's got a good heart, too.

But it was damn near impossible to ignore her rockin' little body when she came out, hair still damp and skin glowing, to give me a hard time. Those tiny black shorts accentuated her long legs, making my hands itch to slide over that smooth skin. And the thin white tank top? Pretty sure she wasn't aware of all it revealed.

Thank god she went back into the house and stayed

there, because I was hard as a rock until well after I finished her lawn, loaded up the mower, and escaped before she could try and pay me.

I may have relieved myself of that inconvenience as soon as I got home and hit the shower... while I imagined her in her own shower before she put on that little outfit and came outside to give me hell.

She's a firecracker, that one. And damn if I don't enjoy lighting her fuse.

Just as I open the bathroom door to let out the steam, there's a knock at the front door.

It's almost eight o'clock, so it's probably Amelia coming to give me hell again.

But then again, my sister would've barged right on in and made herself at home rather than knock.

"Hold on a sec!" I holler down the hall. Then I pull on a pair of basketball shorts. I don't bother with a shirt, because if it's not Lee, it has to be Jesse or Aiden. Maybe even Connor or Ty.

My still damp feet leave footprints on the hardwood floor as I sprint to the front door and throw it open.

I almost stagger back at the sight of Rachel holding a plate of cookies.

"Oh." Her eyes widen, and the light from the entryway makes the golden flecks in her irises sparkle like glitter as she takes in my bare chest. "H-hi."

"Hi." I offer a smile. She's the last person I expected, but I'm not the least bit disappointed. Especially not when the blush on her face seems to indicate that she likes what she sees.

"I, um, I brought you cookies." She holds them out like an offering. "You left before I could pay you, and then I figured you probably wouldn't let me anyway, so I baked instead."

I give a crooked grin. "I love cookies. And if I'd have known this is how you do business, I would've cut your grass weeks ago."

The blush in her cheeks darkens. "They're just cookies."

Yeah. Cookies she made with me in mind.

I step aside and wave her in. "Come in. Have one with me."

"Oh, I can't. I have—"

"Another PTA meeting?" Damn, my grin is so wide it makes my cheeks hurt.

She pinches her eyes shut and lets out a light laugh. "No. No PTA tonight."

"Then come in. Please."

She hesitates, but ultimately gives in, her focus sweeping around the small kitchen on one side and the living room on the other.

Thankfully, I keep things fairly clean. I don't spend much time here, so there are no dishes piled up in the sink or dirty socks on the floor.

"Dang," she muses, wearing a small smile. "This is not what I expected."

"No?" I like that she's thought about it. "Were you expecting titty posters on the walls? Beer can towers?"

She gives another soft laugh. "Maybe."

"Wow." I rear back, feigning offense, even as a warmth spreads through me. I love that I've surprised her. "It'll probably blow your mind to know that the furniture is five years old, and there's not one beer or pizza stain."

"Oh my." She presses a hand to her chest, playing along

with my ribbing. "That's quite the accomplishment. Next, you'll try to tell me that all your plants are real."

I laugh and take a step closer. "They are."

"Shut up." She shoves at my arm.

"I'm serious. Look." I drag her into the living room like the dork I am when it comes to my plants. "Some guys have dogs; I have plants."

"I… don't know what to say." She reaches out and caresses a few of the leaves. "I'm definitely surprised."

I shrug. "I'd love to have a dog, too, but I'm not home enough."

"Understandable." She turns and regards me, her eyes soft.

"Anyway…" I tip my head toward the kitchen. "How about those cookies?"

"Ah, yes."

On the way, I snag a T-shirt from the laundry basket in the hall. The rest of the place may be tidy, but when it comes to laundry, I have no room to brag. It may look like I just took the clothes out of the dryer and set the basket there, but truthfully, it's been sitting there for weeks. And I'm not even sure the clothes are clean.

"Please, sit." I gesture to a chair at the table, then tug the shirt on. "Have a cookie with me."

"Oh no. Those are yours. I have some at home."

"C'mon." I pull out a chair for her and claim a spot across the table before grabbing a cookie. Not only are they chocolate chip, but they're still warm. "Damn, Rach. These are good."

"I'm glad you like them." She sits straight, keeping her hands folded in her lap. The playfulness she emanated a few moments ago has already vanished.

"Actually, I'm glad you stopped by. I wanted to talk to

you about Mason. He told me that Jesse planned on giving him some work this summer."

"Ugh." She closes her eyes. "They both know he's not old enough."

"I know, but I think we can work something out."

She cracks open an eye. "How so?"

"I do a lot of work off the clock. He can come along and be my helper. Jesse will pay him cash."

"I can't ask you to do that."

"Technically, it was Jesse's idea. And I could use the help." It's not really a lie, but the logistics will be a pain in the ass, for sure. Regardless, after my visit with the kid the other day, it's clear he could use someone to talk to. "The other thing is football."

This time, her face falls in a completely different way. Like this is something she's been struggling with already.

"How do you know about football?" she asks, her voice small and pained.

"He told me about it yesterday when I saw him messing with the lawn mower."

She scrapes her teeth along her bottom lip. "I feel awful, but Emma had already started softball when we found out that the football team would be combined with Copper Crossing's. All the practices are going to be over there, too. I can't be in two places at once."

"I'll take him."

"Excuse me?" Her chin drops, and her pretty mouth falls open.

"I'm helping Dalton coach this year. Figure if I'm gonna be at the practices and games anyway. Mason can come with me."

She snaps her mouth shut, and her nostrils flare ever so slightly as emotion brews in her eyes. "Jinx..."

"I don't mind. And like I said, I'm going to be there anyway."

She presses her fingers to the corners of her eyes and blinks back tears. "Are you sure? That's a lot to ask."

"Again, you're not asking. I'm offering." I'd offer a lot more if I knew what else she needed.

"I'll help with gas—"

"Rachel." I cut her off and zero in on her. "I got this, okay?"

She carefully wets her trembling lips and whispers a shaky "thank you."

"You're welcome." We'll need to hammer out the details before football starts, but I don't want to stir up more emotions. I'm sure that crying at my table wasn't on her agenda for tonight. "So, what do you have planned for the weekend? Anything fun?"

"Um, no. Not really." She gives a light sniff. "Not unless you think laundry and scrubbing floors are fun."

I chuckle and grab another cookie. "Hell no. I detest laundry."

She laughs softly, the tears finally disappearing.

"So, no hair appointment? No pedicure? You know, lady shit?"

She lifts a brow. "Lady shit?"

"You should take some time to yourself." I'm overstepping, but I get the feeling that someone needs to point this out to her.

"I take time to myself," she asserts, sitting a little straighter in her chair. "I never pass by Books & Beans without getting an iced chai. And I'm going to Madison in a few weeks with the girls."

"Good. You deserve that. What are you and the girls gonna do?"

"We have a teachers' recertification class."

I tap my fingers on the table and hum. "So you're working."

She frowns, and then it hits her. "Oh. I suppose I am."

I grin. "There will be drinks, though, right?"

"Oh, yes. There will absolutely be drinks."

"College guys, too?"

She tips her head back with a groan. "Will you ever let me live that down?"

"Not likely."

"Of course not."

She sighs, then, "Was it really that bad?"

"Bad in what way?"

"It's not like I took my bra off and tried to hang it from the rafters. I just had a few drinks and played some games. Sure, the guys were young, but..." Her worried expression morphs into one of annoyance, and her eyes narrow. "Why is it perfectly fine for guys to have fun like that, but the second a woman starts to let loose, everyone gets their undies in a bundle?"

"Hold up." I put one hand out in front of me. "Yes, I interjected that night, but not because I didn't think you were entitled to a little fun."

She cocks her head and surveys me quietly, waiting for me to continue.

"As far as I'm concerned, have all the fucking fun you want. Craig is a prick, and I already told you that he deserves to see you with someone else."

A crease forms in her brow. "You did?"

"Mm-hmm." I dip my chin. "That night on your porch."

"Oh. That's right." Color seeps into her cheeks. "My recollection of that conversation is a little spotty."

"I was thinking about *you* when I stepped in," I remind

her. "We may not know each other that well, but I'm pretty sure you're not a one-night-stand kind of woman."

She makes a throaty sound.

"Am I right?"

She purses her lips and narrows her eyes. "I don't like you very much right now."

I laugh. "Better me than you."

She shakes her head and crosses her arms over her chest. Thankfully, she's wearing a T-shirt and a bra now, but the stance still draws my attention where it shouldn't. "It's because I'm a mom, isn't it?"

"What?"

"The reason you saved me from myself."

I don't know how to answer that.

"That's what I thought. It's because I'm a mom, and moms are supposed to behave a certain way. We're supposed to set aside our own wants and needs and think about the kids." She sneers the last words, but a heartbeat later, she gasps, and her expression crumples. "*Fuck.*" She covers her face with her hands. "I shouldn't have said that."

"I didn't intervene because I disapproved of your behavior."

"Okay, then tell me why you did do it," she challenges.

I scratch at the collar of my shirt, which is definitely not clean, as an uncomfortable heat spreads through me. I want to be honest with her, but I'm not sure she's prepared to hear it.

"Just say it, Jinx."

"I didn't like that guy hanging all over you."

Her lips part, and her copper eyes dart back and forth between mine. "I don't think you mean that like it sounds."

"I do." I dip my chin. My movement is firm, even as my

stomach ties itself in a knot. "You're a beautiful woman, and you're also newly single."

Her lashes flutter quickly, but she says nothing.

Since there's no putting the lid back on this conversation, I keep going.

"I might've felt a little territorial." Hell, I wanted to break that asshole's hands every time he touched her.

She regards me for a moment and then nods, her expression neutral. "And this is a small town. I get it."

No, she doesn't.

But now isn't the time to clarify that. Her divorce isn't final, and she's still got quite a few things to work through.

But the day will come when she *is* ready.

And I'll make my move then.

SEVEN

RACHEL

With a fresh iced chai in one hand and a tall black coffee in the other, I clamber up the front steps of my childhood home.

I don't get to see my dad nearly as often as I'd like during the school year and with the kids' schedules, but I make a point to visit on Saturdays during the summer.

This year, I've come to look forward to our visits more than usual. Dad and I have always been close, but after my mom died, our bond grew even stronger. It remained that way for the six years when it was just the two of us at home. My brother Felix Jr.—FJ to the citizens of Cole Creek—had just started college when Mom had an aneurysm, and instead of coming back home like so many kids might've done, he stuck it out. I think putting his head down and working was his way of coping, just like mine was spending as much time as I could with our dad.

That is, until Craig and I started dating and my priorities shifted. In every aspect of my life, not just my relationship with my father.

"Hi-de-ho," I call out as I let myself in. Immediately, I'm assaulted by the smell of paint. "Uh, Dad? What are you doing?"

My father pops up from behind the kitchen table with a roller covered in lime-colored paint. His gray hair is doing some kind of Einstein tribute, and his denim overalls are more green than blue.

"Hiya, sweet pea. I'm painting. What does it look like I'm doing?"

As he goes back to work on the lower part of the wall, I consider whether this could be one of those weird dreams I have every now and again rather than reality. In those dreams, I'm back at home like this, but it's usually my mom who's up to something wild and crazy, not my dad.

"You do realize that's neon green, right?"

Dad glances over his shoulder at me with raised brows. "No need to break out the crayons, Ms. Perry. I'm well aware of my colors, thank you."

Someone's feisty today. Jeez.

"And for the record, Emma picked it out." Standing back, he inspects his work. "She said I needed some color in my life, and I happen to agree."

Oh, Emma. My heart pangs at the thought. The two of them have such a sweet relationship.

"Anyway, what brings you over?" He returns the paint roller to the tray and puts the lid on the paint can.

"I just wanted to visit." And maybe talk.

"I appreciate that." He leans in, careful not to get paint on my dress, and kisses my cheek. "No kids today?"

"No, they're with Craig this weekend. Which reminds

me... Emma's last game is next weekend. Do you want to come along? It's in Copper Crossing, so I was thinking we could do a little shopping and maybe grab something to eat afterward."

"Chinese food?" The eagerness in his voice is almost childlike.

I laugh softly. "Sure."

"I would have gone along anyway, but you know how I love those raccoons."

"Rangoon."

"That's what I said." He scowls as he wipes his hands on an old towel and sets it aside.

Right. "Anyway, I brought you a coffee." I hand it over and turn my attention back to the paint. "Do you want some help? I could get on the ladder and—"

"Nope. If you help, it'll get done faster, and we both know I like to keep busy."

That's true. He retired early from the iron mine, and if he isn't playing bunco with his buddies or working in his gardens, he gets restless and cranky.

"The fumes are getting to be a bit much in here," he says, holding his coffee aloft and motioning for the door. "Let's sit on the porch and get some fresh air."

So we do, and while Dad rocks in a rocking chair that once belonged to his mother, I claim the chair that was my mother's.

A warm summer breeze slips across the front porch, carrying the scent of fresh flowers with it, as if to remind me even more of her.

Dad's maintained her flower beds since she died almost twenty years ago. Most of them are significantly larger than when she kept them, because Dad can't let any of them go. It's one of the ways he pays homage to her still, after all this time. His way of letting her know that he still thinks about her. Still loves her.

"So, what's on your mind, sweet pea?"

"Who said there's anything on my mind?"

He rolls his head against the back of the chair, his all-knowing eyes seeing right through me. Damn him.

"I'm not sure where to begin," I admit. We've already talked at length about my split with Craig and what that means for the kids and our future. Early on, my focus was on making sure they were okay. Now that we've settled into a new normal, I've come to realize that I have a lot of work to do on myself. And that's perhaps the hardest part in all this.

"Start at the beginning," Dad says gently.

"We'd be here for hours."

"So? I like the company." He winks, and it takes me right back to when I was a little girl and he'd sneak me pieces of butter rum candy before dinner. He would always wink to make sure I knew it was a secret just between us.

I only wish the secrets I've been keeping these past few years were that simple.

"I think I've spent a lot of my life going through the motions," I tell him quietly, focusing on the chai I'm clutching. "Like a zombie."

"You look pretty alive to me," he teases. "And I noticed you got your hair cut. I like it."

I touch the locks, which I had trimmed this morning, thanks to Jinx pointing out how little I do for myself.

"Thank you. But what I mean is..." How do I explain this? How do I tell him that I spent most of my marriage living a lie? "It's like I was playing a role."

He nods, but he doesn't speak. He just keeps on rocking, waiting for me to continue.

"I feel so stupid for not realizing sooner. I'm thirty-two. Plenty old enough to know better. So, I have no excuse or reason—"

"You're human, Rachel. That's your reason."

Emotion builds in my chest, tightening around my lungs. I examine my mother's flowers, letting the comfort I always find there ease the ache. Their colors are vibrant in the sun. Shades of pink, purple, yellow, and green. And their leaves and petals flutter in the late morning breeze, standing so strong against it and inspiring me to garner a little strength, too.

"You've also spent the last decade raising a family, sweet pea. You've been busy. It's understandable that you'd find yourself distracted from time to time."

"It's more than that, Dad." I set my drink on the small table between us. "It's like... like I was one of those Stepford wives, running on autopilot. Like I was following the instructions in a manual rather than actually living my life."

More to the point, it's like I was doing everything I could to emulate my mother. The perfect mom, the perfect wife, the perfect teacher.

But somewhere along the way, I realized that wasn't what I wanted. At least not to the extent I'd taken things. I'd worked so hard to be the person I thought I should be that I almost lost who I was at the core.

Mason and Emma were young when I had that revelation, and I've battled with the worst kind of guilt since, trying to be what Craig needed me to be and what the kids *still* need me to be, all the while letting myself down over and over again.

And that doesn't even touch on the shame I feel for not wanting to be just like a woman who isn't even here anymore. A woman who was amazing and smart and... everything.

I'm grateful for what she taught me. Grateful that I had such a wonderful person to show me the way.

But I begrudge her, too, and that only compounds the shame. Especially because, according to Craig, I wasn't even that good at it. Or maybe I was too good. I don't know.

It just... it sucks. And for years, I've been stuck in this cycle of guilt and shame and confusion.

"Throw the manual away." Dad lifts his hands, as if the answer is that simple. "Burn it if you have to."

How the heck am I supposed to do that? That side of me is ingrained into every fiber of my being.

"Your mother wasn't perfect, sweet pea." He tilts his head and smiles sympathetically. "She's who you're thinking about, isn't she?"

I pinch my eyes shut and force myself to take another breath. "Yes."

"She wouldn't want you to be just like her. In fact, she'd want you to be as different as possible."

"I don't know about that." I laugh softly and wrap my arms around myself. "She was pretty amazing."

"And so are you." He says it so confidently, but I don't know if I agree.

I don't even know who I am anymore.

And I don't have the first clue how to be the woman I need to be for me while also being the mom my kids need.

"You gotta figure out what you want." He taps his chest with a weathered and paint-speckled hand. "In here."

In response, my own chest aches. If only my heart wasn't all over the place these days.

"If you listen close enough, you'll hear what it has to say."

I smile, even as I chase a tear away with my fingertips. "I might need to borrow your hearing aid for that."

He chuckles. "I'd let ya. I know there's been a lot of noise in your life lately. But things will settle down. You'll hear it and figure it out eventually."

"How long are you talking? Months? Years?"

His gaze drifts out across the big yard as he sighs. "That's the part we can't predict, sweet pea. Healing is complicated like that."

MUCH TO MY father's dismay, I spent the rest of the afternoon helping him paint. And when we were finished and everything was cleaned up and put away, even I could admit the lime green looked pretty good. I drew the line, though, when he suggested continuing the color into the living room. From there, we ended up at the hardware store, where he picked out a nice creamy coffee shade instead.

Now, at almost ten o'clock, I'm finally home with achy feet and sore muscles. The bed is calling to me, but my body has other ideas. Seemingly of its own accord, it heads straight into the master bath and the big tub I haven't used in far too long.

While it fills, I add a little of the coconut and brown sugar oil that Crystal bought me for my birthday a few months ago, then I undress and slip into the steamy water. Once I'm fully submerged, I nearly weep.

When Craig and I bought this house, I took baths all the time. Of course, I was pregnant with Mason, so life hadn't become crazy yet. Looking back, that summer after I graduated from college, before I started teaching, may have been the most peaceful period of my life.

Craig loved this house, but if I'm honest, the only reason I caved and agreed to put in an offer on it all those years ago was because I loved this tub and the huge bathroom so much. I would have preferred a piece of land outside of town and a home that we put our own blood, sweat, and tears into, but we were young with a baby on the way. So I set that dream aside.

Along with my plans to get my master's degree.

And my dream of becoming a school principal.

I also wanted to travel. Nothing too crazy, but at thirty-two, I've only visited a handful of states, and each one of them is within driving distance.

Eventually, I will travel. I still have plenty of time to make that particular dream happen. Even if I have to wait until the kids are in college or out on their own, I'll still be young enough to take that first flight. And if I'm alone, I can go anywhere I please.

With a sigh, I reach for my phone to turn on some music to occupy my mind before I fall back into the negative thoughts that have been plaguing me so much lately. Phone in hand, I tap the screen and am met with a new text message notification.

Unknown number: Hey Rachel. It's Jinx.
You got a second?

Jinx? What the heck?

Me: Depends on how you got my number.

Jinx: Stalked you online and paid for it on one of those info websites.

Oh my god, this man.

Me: Nice. I hope someone uses your credit card to buy a bunch of granny panties and has them delivered to you.

Jinx: *laughing emoji* As long as they're not used.

I snort-laugh and sink a little farther into the water.

Me: Ew. Anyway, what's up?

Jinx: Hold on. I'm going to call you.

No! Don't do that! I'm in the—

And then my phone rings.

Shit. I can't ignore him when he knows I'm by my phone. And after he's done so much for me lately.

Taking a deep breath, I hold still, desperately hoping I won't splash or slosh water against the side of the tub, and accept the call. "You realize it's after ten, right?"

"Is it? Shit, I'm sorry." There's noise on the other end of the line. The opening and closing of the fridge, if I'm not mistaken, and then the sound of buttons being pressed on a microwave. "I just got home. Wasn't paying attention to the time."

Obviously not. Also, why is he eating so late? "You weren't working, were you?"

Silence.

"Oh my god, were you not the one who *just yesterday* gave *me* a hard time about self-care?"

He chuckles, the sound low and warm. "It's sweet of you to be concerned, but I'm good. I promise. Anyway, I wanted to touch base about Mason and football. I talked with Dalton today."

Ugh. Avoidance at its finest.

"Okay..."

"Mason's going to need a physical and all of his paperwork done ASAP."

"He just had a physical in the spring, so we're good to go there. I'll get in touch with Dalton tomorrow for the other forms."

"Perfect. My other reason for calling is about him working with me. With football practice starting so soon, it's going to be hard to find time during the week. I was thinking we'd start with a few hours next Saturday and Sunday, if that works for you."

"Um, I think it does." I rest my head on the edge of the tub, careful to move slowly in the water, and study the ceiling. "I can't recall of any other plans right now."

"Great. Does he have a phone? I figured I'd touch base with him about this, too. Is that okay?"

"Of course." I smile at his thoughtfulness. "But I haven't had a chance to tell him he can play. Let me do that first?"

"Sure."

"I also need to make sure it's all right with Craig."

Another beat of silence. Then, "Okay."

Am I imagining the tension in his voice or...?

"Once you give me the go-ahead and his number, I'll start a group chat and include you so you can make sure our plans align with your schedules and whatnot."

"Thank you. I appreciate that." I tuck a lock of damp hair behind my ear. "How did you *really* get my number?"

"Bobbie Jean gave it to me. That's okay, isn't it?"

I bite back a groan. Freaking Bobbie Jean.

"Uh, yeah. I was just curious."

The microwave beeps on his end, followed by the sound of the door opening and closing again as he takes out whatever he's cooked. Probably one of those frozen meals. Poor guy.

"Hold on," he says, and there's a *thunk*, probably as he sets the phone on the counter. A second later, he puts the call on speaker. "Sorry about that. Had to take my shirt off. I got it full of pine pitch today."

Oh boy.

I bite my lip as the image of him opening the door last night dances across my memory. Not only did he look good, but he also smelled amazing, all fresh from the shower. I don't know what kind of body wash he uses, but if it comes in candle form, I want to stock up and burn one in every room.

And the sight of him bare-chested? Good lord. He fills out his T-shirts perfectly, but seeing those muscles without any barrier was almost my undoing, right there on his front step.

Jinx Enders is one heck of a gorgeous man. Blue-collar beautiful to the core.

Sighing, I slip down into the water, only to remember I'm on the phone.

"Shit!" I juggle the dang thing like a hot potato, barely saving it from the rice bowl.

"Wait, are you in the tub?" Jinx asks, his voice full of mirth.

"*No.*"

He gives a husky chuckle that sends a zing down my spine and straight to my nipples.

Goddamn.

Forget traveling. I'm going straight to hell.

"Don't lie to me," he admonishes. His low and growly tone reminds me of something else he said last night.

"I might've felt a little territorial."

Sweet lord, I know he didn't mean it like it sounded, but I went there for a second in my head. I imagined him standing up for me in a completely different kind of way. The kind that made me want to show my gratitude. On my knees.

"Rachel?"

Shit. Dammit. *God.*

"Uh, yeah. I'm sorry. I'm just... soaking my feet. I was painting with my dad today. They're, uh, sore."

"Oh." He chuckles, though I'm not convinced he believes me.

I scrunch my eyes closed and inhale deeply before slowly letting the breath out through my nose. I need to end this call ASAP.

"Anyway, it's getting late," I rush out. "I'll text you Mason's number after I talk to him and Craig, and we can coordinate for next weekend, okay?"

"Yeah. That sounds great."

"All right. You, uh, have a good rest of your night."

"You, too."

As I'm pulling the phone away, ready to tap the end button, he adds, "Enjoy your bath, gorgeous."

And I die.

EIGHT

JINX

I may not go to church every week—or even once a month—but I do make a point to join the family for Sunday lunch as often as possible. It keeps Ma off my back, keeps Dad from hiding all the shit he's not supposed to be doing at his age, and keeps my belly full, too.

Now that Hayden and Jesse are back together and she's living in Cole Creek and keeping him fed, the majority of Ma's leftovers come home with me. Amelia is too picky, and Aiden almost never shows up, so I've become the chosen one. And given my lack of culinary skills as well as my lack of time, I do not complain.

With lunch cleaned up and those precious leftovers all packed up and waiting for me in the fridge, Ma takes a seat at the dining room table across from Hayden and my nephew, Jett. He's working on a bulldozer puzzle and stuffing grapes into his mouth.

"So, Hayden," Ma says as she gets comfortable. "I ran

into Rachel Kaczmarek... er, Rachel *Perry*, the other day. I'm not sure if you've met her yet."

"Craig's wife. Uh, soon-to-be ex-wife," Jesse interjects, cringing just a little.

Hayden nods. "Ah, okay. No, we haven't officially met, but I saw her when we were at the ice cream shop a couple weeks ago. Mason's mom, right?"

"Yes, that's her. Such a sweet girl." Mom gives her a small smile. "Anyway, several years ago, she asked me to teach her to make *sernik*, because she's never been able to make it like her mother used to. Her mother died going on twenty years ago, I think, but regardless, I invited Rachel over for a baking lesson. I was thinking you might want to join us."

Whoa, whoa, whoa. My heart does a flip in my chest. Ma's been talking to Rachel?

"And if she has the kids, I thought Jett could come, too, and they could play."

"Her kids are kinda old for Jett, aren't they?" I point out.

And when *the hell* did my mother befriend Rachel?

Ma waves me off. "Not in the least. They're good kids. Jett will love them."

No doubt. But I don't know how I feel about Ma spending time with Rachel when I'm trying to do that same thing myself.

"I would love that." Hayden gives my mom a warm smile. "But I've never heard of *sernik* before. What is it?"

"It's cheesecake," Jesse grumbles, planting his hands on the island and shaking his head. "Just cheesecake."

"*Głupie gadanie*!" Ma raises her fist. "Polish cheesecake is *not* like other cheesecake, Jesse Alexander."

"Yeah, Jesse," I goad him, which I realize belatedly was a mistake.

"What was that?" he asks, sidestepping and hooking an arm around my neck for a headlock and noogie.

"Daddy!" Jett hollers. "Don't be mean to Uncle Jinx."

Everyone laughs, including me, even though the fucker messed up my hair and gave me a kink in my neck.

"Asshole," my brother mutters as he shoves me away. "Going and getting me in trouble with my own kid."

"Then get your fucking cheesecake right, man."

He narrows his eyes and watches me, like he's waiting for me to take off the way I used to when we were kids so he can chase me down and beat my ass.

I'm tempted for old time's sake, but Ma would kill us both.

"Anyway..." Jesse sighs and splays his hands on the island in front of us. "What's up with the bucket truck?"

Shit. I think I'd rather take a few punches.

"Uh, yeah. About that..." I scrub a hand around the back of my neck. "Let's go outside."

He cocks a suspicious brow but follows me out onto the back patio without a word.

I take a seat at the patio table, and he claims a chair by the railing.

"Like I said the other day, Connor thinks the motor is on its way out. It gave us grief last fall, but I figured it just needed a tune-up. We got that done over the winter, but then it started locking up last week. Had to get Connor down with a friggin' ladder."

Jesse scoffs and rubs a hand down his face. "Good thing OSHA wasn't around."

"No shit. We eventually got it down, but who knows when it'll lock up again. It's not worth the risk."

He nods. "I agree."

"I've been shopping around. I'll bring what I've found into the office tomorrow to show you."

"Yeah, do that." Thankfully, he leaves it at that rather than reminding me that he told me to do that weeks ago. "By the way, I might've told Craig's kid that he could cut grass with you this summer."

"Yeah, I already heard about that."

"From who?"

"Mason. I talked to him the other day. He's going to start next weekend."

Jesse blinks at me. "You did?"

"Yep."

"You talk to Rachel, too?"

I dip my chin. "It's all taken care of. All you have to do is pay the kid. Cash. And no less than fifteen bucks an hour."

He gives a laugh, one side of his mouth kicking up. "Yeah, right."

I lean forward and lock eyes with him. "I'm serious."

"He's *eleven*."

"Yet you told him you had work for him."

He blows out a breath. "That's a lot of money for a kid who's probably gonna stand around more than he does anything else."

"Nah, he won't be standing around on my watch."

"What kind of work are you gonna have him do? He can't do most of what our guys do."

"I thought the community service stuff would be best. The church and the cemetery. Probably my lawn. Rachel's, too."

He lowers his chin, and his eyes go wide. "I am not paying him to cut your grass."

"What else do you want me to do with him?"

He watches me for a long moment, then shakes his head. "That's highway robbery."

I lift my hands. "Again, you're the one who told him he could work. I'm doing you a favor by finding shit for him to do."

"You're raking me over the fucking coals is what you're doing," he mutters.

I laugh. "You're welcome."

"Fuck you."

RACHEL

"Hey, Mom!" Emma's voice carries through the screen door just after four o'clock.

I'm up to my wrists in flour and butter, trying to, once again, make a pie crust that isn't drier than my sex life, so I offer her a bright smile from the kitchen instead of a hug.

"Hey, Emmy Lou. How was your day?"

"It was good," she says, dropping her softball gear in the foyer. "Dad took us mini golfing."

"Oh, really? I bet that was fun."

Did Cady go, too? Mason's mood will tell me that, I'm sure.

"It was. Drake and his family were there, too. We had ice cream after." She grins. "I got blue moon."

"Yum!"

The door creaks open, and Mason strolls in with his backpack and, to my surprise, a small smile.

"Hey, Mom. Whatcha doing?"

"Trying to make the crust for a strawberry rhubarb pie. You want to help?"

He scrunches up his nose. "No, but I'll help eat it."

I give a soft laugh and brush at a wayward strand of hair with my forearm. "I figured. Is your dad coming in or—"

"I'm here." Craig steps through the door and lifts a hand. "Sorry we're a few minutes late. We just got back from Copper Crossing."

"I heard." I offer him a polite smile and step away from the dough to wash my hands. "Sounds like you had fun."

When I turn around, drying my hands on a towel, he's tucking his hands into his pockets. "Yeah. It was a good time."

"Hey, Emma," I say, setting the towel on the counter, "can you please take your gear to your room and get your uniform out so we can wash it?"

Her shoulders slump, but she does what I ask without a word.

Mason glances from me to his father and seems to read the room. "I'll go get my dirty clothes ready for the laundry, too." He heads toward the hall, but halfway there, he turns back. "Bye, Dad."

"Bye, bud. See you Wednesday night."

As soon as both kids are out of earshot, I turn to Craig. "I know we talked about Mason not playing football this year, but I think there's a way we can make it work. Assuming he still wants to play."

He lifts a brow. "How's that?"

"Jinx is helping Dalton coach. He'll be at all the practices and games, and he's offered to take Mason."

Craig assesses me for a long moment, his jaw tensing a little more with every passing second. "Jinx, huh?"

"Yeah. I saw him on Friday, and he mentioned it. He heard Mason wasn't going to play, and—"

"Who told him that?"

A flash of annoyance hits me at the interruption, but I keep my tone neutral. "Mason."

Craig tips his head. "When did he talk to Mason?"

Okay, the attitude is a bit much. "I guess he saw him messing with the lawn mower the other day. He stopped to see if he could help."

"Really." He gives a flippant scoff.

I ignore it, even as my blood heats with frustration. "I don't want to take advantage, but if he's willing to help, I think it would be good for Mason to continue playing. Especially with all the changes in our lives."

Craig rubs at his forehead. "I get that. I just don't know why Jinx talked to you about it and not me, unless..."

"Unless what?" I cross my arms and wait. I swear to god if he tries to make this about the night at the bar...

For a second, he watches me, his jaw working. Then he throws a hand in the air. "Fine. Whatever. If he's offering and Mason still wants to play."

"I'll talk to Mase tonight and let you know what he says."

"All right." He nods, but rather than heading out like he should, he holds my gaze, like he's waiting for me to cave and confess to a wild night in the back of Jinx's truck or something.

"I need to get back to my pie crust," I tell him, tipping my chin a fraction higher. "I believe you know the way out."

JINX

"What the hell are you doing, man?"

Aiden stands on my front step, cell phone in his hand and confusion in his eyes.

"What are you talking about?"

I should be the one asking him what's up since he blatantly lied to Ma and said he was out of town and couldn't make lunch today. His truck was parked outside his place both times I drove by.

"Craig just texted and said you're going back to coaching youth football. You don't have time for the shit you *have* to do, let alone the shit you don't."

Oh, that.

With a huff, I turn on my bare feet and pad back to the living room, where I've been watching the Brewers' game.

"You've got nothing to say or what?" He invites himself in and closes the door behind him.

"Other than it's my problem and not yours?" With a cocky smile, I drop back down to the couch. "Besides, I've been busier than this and I did just fine."

He makes a throaty sound. "One of these days, you won't be. One of these days, you're gonna have a heart attack from all those energy drinks you live on."

I snort and lean back against the cushions. "For one, I don't drink that shit anymore. And two, I think it's funny that you care about how much I work while our brother, *who's my boss*, doesn't have a fucking clue."

Aiden's brows lift. "You don't think Jesse's noticed?"

"Nope." If he has, he sure as hell doesn't seem to care.

"How the hell could he not?"

"Probably because he's had enough of his own shit going on?" I shrug.

He glares at me. "Here's a wild idea... why don't you just tell him you need help?"

I grit my teeth. "I can handle it."

"For fuck's sake." He scrubs his hands over his face and claims a recliner. "Why are you so goddamn bullheaded?"

"Learned from the best."

"Don't give me that shit. You know damn well you could ask for help."

Sure, I could. But it's easier to keep quiet and do what needs to be done.

As the third of four kids, it's always been this way. Aiden got the first-born honors, Jesse took over the family business, and Amelia is the only girl *and* the baby. I was—and still am—the sibling stuck in the middle.

I wasn't overlooked or neglected. Our parents did a damn good job raising us and loving us each the same.

But among the four of us kids? That's a different story. I'm not sure if it's because Jesse and I are sandwiched between Aiden and Amelia, or because we're the ones who stuck around Cole Creek to keep Enders Excavating going, but my relationship with him is the most strained.

The funny thing is, he's my best friggin' friend.

He's also the one person I can't help but compare myself to. And the one person whose opinion I respect more than any other.

"You gotta talk to him, Jinx. You gotta tell him about all this shit you've been doing for, what, three years now? Longer?"

I rough a hand through my hair. "We're meeting tomorrow." I hadn't planned on bringing up the overtime, but maybe the bucket truck discussion will open the door for that bigger conversation.

"That's good." Aiden nods, pressing his lips together. "I'm telling you," he says, sitting forward and resting his forearms on his knees, "he'll hear you out. Especially now that Hayden's here and she's taken over the admin side of things. He's in a better headspace these days."

I hope so. Because Aiden is right. These long hours are killing me.

"Now back to football..."

"I'm already committed. I'm not backing out." Not when there's an eleven-year-old kid across town who needs my help more than I need a break.

He gives a deep sigh and shakes his head. "I know. But Craig should be the one doing that shit, you know?"

Yep. But he won't, and I'm not going to let his son suffer because Craig is a selfish dick.

I arch a brow but leave it at that.

"Is there anything I can do to help?"

I laugh. "Dude, you literally work around the clock. Or you're out of town. Except for today, of course. I saw your fucking truck parked at home, you lying ass."

His face flames, and he lifts one shoulder. "To be fair, I *was* out of town until yesterday."

"Doing what?"

"I can't tell you that," he replies without missing a beat. As an investigator, he takes confidentiality very seriously. "Anyway, I wanted to come over and see if I could talk some sense into you, but I see that's not going to happen."

"Hey, I said I'm talking to Jesse tomorrow."

He nods. "And you're going to tell him about all the overtime he owes you?"

I give a guilty grin. "Now, I didn't say anything about *that*."

NINE

JINX

"Happy Monday!" Hayden grins from the coffeepot in the Enders Excavating lobby. "But you got my text that the staff meeting is canceled, right?"

I nod and scuff my boots on the entryway rug. "Yep. Thanks for that. But I'm meeting with Jesse."

Her brow creases. "Oh. I don't have that on the calendar. In fact, he asked me to cancel the staff meeting because they're running behind at the Willis site."

"It's all right, babe," my brother calls from the back. "I asked him to come in."

I offer an apologetic smile, but she shakes her head and rolls her eyes.

"Not your fault, Jinx. Jesse needs to learn to either communicate," she says loudly so he can hear, "or use the calendar app in his phone like I showed him."

"Yeah, yeah," he gripes as he appears in the doorway. "Gotta keep things interesting so you don't get bored."

She narrows her eyes and hums. The whole reason she's here is because the administrative side of the business is beyond his level of expertise and had been neglected for far too long. There's no chance of her getting bored. Homicidal maybe, but never bored.

"Anyway, come on back." Jesse waves me over and lifts his chin, focusing on Hayden. "Babe, we'll be in the office for a bit."

"All right. I'll hang out up here." She smiles sweetly as I pass.

Technically, the big office in the back is Jesse's, but since Hayden came on board, she's made it hers, and rightfully so. She's been in charge since the moment she arrived. She just lets my brother and his ego think otherwise.

"Have a seat." Jesse gestures to one of the leather chairs in front of the big mahogany desk that's been in this exact spot since the building was built some sixty or seventy years ago. This wood has seen just about every bit of EE business over the years, first when my grandfather ran the place, then when my dad did, and now that it's Jesse's. This is where the family business is run. And I might be a little envious that it'll never be mine.

"You said you had some things to show me?" Jesse takes a seat in his oversized leather chair and leans back.

"Uh, yeah." I slide the paperwork across the desk. "The quotes you told me to get for the new bucket truck. Some other info, too. Specs and whatnot."

He flips through the pages with a crease in his brow. "Holy shit, you actually got them?"

I frown and scoot to the edge of my seat. *Did he really expect me not to?*

"You said we needed them."

He looks up, head tilted, and surveys me. "You got all of these yourself?"

I dip my chin, reining in the frustration that hits me at his apparent shock. "Yeah. Went to two of the dealerships in person. The other one I got by email, but I called and talked to one of the guys at the dealer." I pull out my phone, bring up the notes app, and share the list of used options I put together, too.

Jesse's phone pings in response.

"That's the list of what I found online. They're all used and in-state. Two have delivery options, but we'd have to pick the other ones up if we went with any of them."

He continues to regard me for a long beat, then shakes his head with a laugh. "I honestly never thought you'd do it."

I see that. And it's irritating as fuck. Jaw clenched, I clear my throat. "I'm not incapable, you know."

"I know you're not." He cocks a brow. "I just wasn't sure if *you* knew that."

What the hell is that supposed to mean?

He holds up the paperwork. "Which one do you like best?"

"I like the brand new Dur-A-Lift in Janesville."

He tips his head. "But..."

"But it's more than we need and a lot of money. The first option in the used list I sent you is probably a better fit. It's only two years old and priced right. I know the guy selling it, too. Remember Mike down in Oconto?"

Jesse nods. "Yep. Decent guy."

"Exactly. He's only selling because he's not doing tree work anymore."

"Did you go and look at it?"

"Not yet. Wanted to see what you thought first."

Jesse taps the quotes against the desk. "Let me talk to Hayden about the financials. I'm sure it's all good, but I'll get back to you."

This is where it hurts. Rather than making decisions like this together, I give my input, and he makes the final call. But nonetheless, I appreciate that he isn't giving me shit about the current bucket truck being down.

"Thanks, man."

He shakes his head. "No need to thank me. This is your company, too."

Except it isn't. And maybe that's what really bugs me about all this.

Sure, I want his approval. And I want him to recognize how fucking hard I've worked. All the blood, sweat, and tears I've shed over the past six years. But I want more than that, too.

I want a stake in this business. And in our family legacy.

That's what's been holding me back. And seeing him sitting at this desk right now has finally made that clear.

Jesse's phone pings again, and he glances down and groans. "Motherfucker."

"What?"

"I gotta go. Craig and Lenny are having a disagreement at the Willis site." He gets to his feet with a sigh. "Craig has been such a fucking bear lately."

Yeah, well, Craig is also an idiot who's royally screwed up his life. I imagine he *is* out of sorts, and it serves him friggin' right.

Jesse tucks his phone into his back pocket. "By the way, I'm impressed."

"About what?"

"About you taking Mason under your wing. Something tells me he's gonna need someone like you to talk to."

"Yeah, I kinda figured that." I leave it at that. I have plenty of thoughts on the subject, particularly where Craig is involved—or rather, not involved—but putting them out into the world isn't going to do any good. What I can do, however, is be there for Mason.

And Rachel, too, if she needs me.

WITH THE BISHOPS' trees finally trimmed and Connor and Jack headed to the west side of town to start this week's lawn care rotation, I head east to do the same.

With the revelation I had during my meeting with Jesse running on repeat in my mind, I'm looking forward to a few hours of solitude. Thankfully, the first job on my list is the Kaminski place. Dave and Vera are in Europe for the month, so I won't have to stop to make small talk. I can get to work and—

Just as I pull into their driveway, a kid darts around the side of the house and into the backyard.

"What the hell?"

It's probably some little shit messing with the place while the owners are out of town. But that's gonna happen today.

Phone in hand, I hop out quickly and hurry around the back of the house. But whoever it is has already hidden.

"I saw you come back here," I announce. "And we both know you're not supposed to be here, so let's make this easy. How about you come out, and maybe I won't call the cops?"

A soft sniffle sounds from near the back patio.

Sorry, kid, but turning on the waterworks isn't going to work with me.

I'm headed for the patio when movement in one of the basement window wells catches my attention.

At first, all that's visible is a dark ponytail. As I get closer, a mint-green T-shirt comes into view, then the black shorts and the bedazzled flip-flops. But she keeps her face hidden in the knees she has pulled up to her chin.

"Do you have any idea how many bugs and spiders are down there?" I ask.

Her only response is a sniffle.

"Come on, kid. I'll pull you out." I drop to a squat and extend my hand, but she turns away.

"Go away, Jinx."

Ah, so she knows who I am. Okay, that should make this even more fun.

"If you won't come out on your own, I have some equipment that will do the trick. A backhoe maybe."

"A backhoe?" She finally turns to me, her expression set in a glower. "I saw your trailer. All you've got is a couple lawn mowers and a weed wacker."

Well, well. If it isn't Emma Perry and her mother's spunky attitude.

"Right now, sure. But all I have to do is make a call and—"

"Fine. Whatever." She gets to her feet and brushes the hair from her tearstained face. Then she holds her hand out.

I pull while she puts a hand on the side of the window well and pushes off.

"Now, can you leave me alone?"

"Afraid I can't do that. You see, these nice people pay me to take care of their lawn, and I'm here to work. Unless you've been invited to hang out here, you're technically trespassing. Maybe you don't know this, but my brother is a cop."

She crosses her arms over her chest and rolls her eyes. "So go ahead and call him. See if I care."

Hands on my hips, I bark out a laugh. "Who pissed in your Cheerios this morning, darlin'?"

Her face pinches in disgust. "First of all, gross. Cheerios are for old people. And you're not a cowboy, so don't call me darlin'."

Holy hell. They really do grow them different these days, don't they?

"How about Spitfire? Because you're spitting plenty of it right now."

Her gaze narrows for a moment, but her spite softens, and she shrugs. "That's better, I guess."

With a chuckle, I stroll over to the deck and lean against it. "All right then, Spitfire. You want to tell me why you're here?"

"Can't a girl just have a few minutes to herself?"

"Yes, but not on someone else's property."

"That's dumb." She kicks at the grass with the toe of her flip-flop, creating a small divot.

Crossing my arms over my chest, I raise one brow and pointedly look at her foot. "Now you're destroying property."

"Oh my god, you're so annoying." She stalks off toward the patio steps and drops down with a huff. "Can't I just stay here since you're here?"

"No. I have permission to be here, but you don't. And aren't you a little far from home, anyway?" She's, what, eight? And at least four blocks from her house.

"I'm not a baby, jeez."

"No, but your mom is probably worried sick about you."

She shrugs.

"I should call her and let her know that you're okay." I pull out my phone, bracing myself for her protest.

Rather than argue, though, she leans her head against the deck railing, suddenly looking teary-eyed again.

I drop my hands to my sides and take a cautious step closer. "Why don't you tell me what's going on before I do that?"

She picks at a string on her shorts. "You work with my dad, right?"

"We work for the same company, but we don't talk much." If that's what she's worried about...

"We don't either," she says, her little voice cracking. "Me and my dad, I mean."

Running a hand around the back of my neck, I take a seat beside her. "Yeah, I've heard things have been kinda rough in your family lately."

"He has a girlfriend now. Cady." She pulls in a hiccupping breath. "He really hurt my mom's feelings."

Well, shit.

"I'm so mad at him."

With my elbows planted on my knees, I duck my head. "I bet you are."

"I just want my mom to be happy again."

Damn, my chest aches for this girl. "Me, too, Spitfire."

She turns and looks at me with wide, hopeful eyes. "You do?"

"Sure, I do. Your mom is a great person. She has a big heart."

"Do you think she's pretty?"

Uh...

"Because I think she's prettier than Cady."

Ah. "Your mom is pretty. But I don't think that has anything to do with your dad moving out."

She bites her lip and studies her shoes for a minute, like she's considering that possibility. "I think she's beautiful," she finally says. "Maybe if she got a boyfriend..."

The back of my neck goes hot. From the sun, obviously, not the guilt that hits me for thinking her mom could use a good man in her life, too. "She probably will eventually."

"You think so?"

I nod. "I do."

She sniffs back her tears, seemingly satisfied with that response. "I just don't want her to be lonely."

Same, kid. Same.

"I like going to my grandma and grandpa's to visit Dad, but I feel bad leaving her. I don't want her to be sad when me and Mason are gone."

"I understand, but your mom wouldn't want you to worry about that, Emma. You're only eight, right?"

She tips her head and glares. "I'm almost nine."

I hold up my hands. "My apologies."

We sit in silence for a couple more minutes before I tap my phone.

"Do you want to call your mom?"

She swipes at her tears and nods. "I hope she isn't mad."

"She might be, but I think she'll be more relieved to know you're safe."

"O-okay."

I bring up Rachel's contact, hit the call button, and hand over the phone. "Here you go, Spitfire."

TEN

RACHEL

The best part about youth sports in small towns? The cozy, laid-back vibes that come with hauling out your favorite lawn chair and setting up a spot on the edge of the field in preparation for relaxing and sipping copious amounts of coffee from an oversized travel mug.

The worst part? Finding yourself stuck sitting just a few lawn chairs down from your soon-to-be ex-husband and his new girlfriend.

Or should I say old girlfriend?

New old girlfriend?

Ugh.

It's Mason's first game of the season, so of course they're here. I knew they would be. But being mentally prepared doesn't always spill over into being physically prepared. Case in point, the shaky restlessness that's plagued me since I arrived fifteen minutes ago.

I haven't touched my coffee yet, so I can't blame the jitters on caffeine.

Then again, maybe it isn't Craig's and Cady's presence that has me off-kilter...

Maybe the blame lies with the cute coach in cargo shorts, a black tank top, and a backward ball cap.

Jinx and I haven't talked much over the past couple of weeks other than a quick hello or goodbye when he picks up and drops off Mason for work and for practice.

The last real conversation we had was when he found Emma at the Kaminskis' and we shared a short heart-to-heart with her in the driveway before I took her home and snuggled with her on the couch while making her promise she'd never pull that kind of stunt again. I was seconds away from dialing 911 when she called from Jinx's phone and burst into tears.

And to think she's the kid I was least worried about. She's never complained about going back and forth for visits. She's never cried about missing me. She's certainly never said a word to me about feeling disconnected from Craig.

But she shared all of that with Jinx.

And he listened.

To *my* little girl.

When he could have just as easily called me or Craig and saved himself from the drama of it all.

My heart aches every time I think about it.

If I didn't already have a little crush on him, I would now. It takes a special kind of man to treat a child with care and respect like that.

"Hey, babes!" Crystal plops a chair down beside me, startling me out of my thoughts. "Did we miss anything?"

"Nope, not yet. The first quarter is almost over, but no scores."

Her husband Tony joins her a minute later, his chair in

one hand and a tray of coffees from Bobbie Jean's in the other. "I come bearing gifts," he says, offering me the tray.

"Oh, Tony." I accept the whole tray and put it on my lap so he can set up his chair. "You know the way to a girl's heart, don't you?" I already have a drink, but I will never pass up an iced chai.

"I gotchu, Rach." He winks.

Crystal backhands him across the stomach, forcing an *umph* from him. "Don't let him bullshit you. He almost got you an Americano. It's me who loves you, babes." She blows me a kiss.

Tony grunts and takes a seat. "You two are so weird."

"Don't be jealous." Crystal gets situated in her chair and bats her lashes at him. "There's nothing wrong with lady love."

He cocks a brow, the wheels turning in his head as he smirks.

"Good lord," Crystal scoffs. "Not *that* kind of love. Get yourself right."

I laugh and take my drink from the caddy before passing it to her. "I seriously love you both. Thank you."

"Anything for my bestie." She peers around me and wrinkles up her nose, clearly catching sight of Craig down the way. "Ugh. Really?"

"At least he's here."

"Yeah." She straightens the lid of her coffee and sits back. "But he could have come alone."

"It's not the first time, and it won't be the last." We've been avoiding each other at Emma's softball games for weeks now.

And that's what I continue to do. I successfully put them out of my mind, too, until the middle of the third quarter when a scuffle breaks out on the field.

My stomach drops when number 34 rolls another kid over on the grass. Mason pushes to his feet, using the kid as leverage a little too aggressively. To be fair, the other kid was the one who pulled Mason to the ground by his face mask in the first place. The frustration is warranted. However, the way he reacts when the other kid jumps up and shoves him isn't.

Mason shoves him back without hesitation and knocks the kid on his ass. His teammates laugh, and a whole group of boys from the other team steps out onto the field, as if they're going to rush Mason in defense of their friend. The refs, bless them, blow their whistles again and insert themselves between the kids before anyone can get hurt.

Dalton and Jinx rush onto the field, too, and herd our players toward the sideline for a much-needed timeout.

"Little punk deserved it," Craig hollers. "Where's the flag for that face mask, huh?"

My stomach sinks and my face flames at his outburst. *Oh my god, shut up.*

He heaves himself out of his chair, but he only makes it one step toward the bench before Cady jumps up and grabs him by the back of his shirt.

Kudos to her for that, at least.

"Sit down," she says sharply, pointing at Craig's chair. "Let the coaches deal with it."

"It's bullshit," he grumbles. "Mason should've laid that kid out."

I clench my jaw and bite my tongue. I don't mind that Mason defended himself, but taking things further than he did would have been uncalled for. Also, this is youth football, not the pros. The refs are high school kids, not seasoned vets. They're going to make mistakes.

Jinx pulls Mason aside while Dalton tries to calm the

rest of the team down. Dalton has to speak loudly to be heard over the chatter as he reminds the boys to play with good sportsmanship. Jinx's words to my son, on the other hand, are inaudible. From the look on Mason's face—his red, enraged face—he's still pumped up. But Jinx's expression is calm, mollifying.

As the seconds tick by and Jinx continues, Mason's shoulders begin to relax. The nod he gives Jinx and the thoughtful expression that crosses his face loosen the knots in my stomach.

Finally, Jinx smiles and grabs Mason's shoulder pad, giving it a little jostle. My son gives a small smile, too, and then Jinx wraps an arm around his shoulders for a side hug that has emotion immediately burning in my eyes.

It's when Mason gives him a quick side hug in return that I have to call upon every ounce of self-control I possess to keep myself from jumping and rushing over to hug him myself.

Mason jogs back to the team and stops directly in front of Dalton, likely apologizing, given Dalton's serious but accepting nod, and then sticks his helmet back on.

Jinx joins the rest of the team and quickly shifts back into game mode. But I'm still stuck on the interaction between him and Mason.

They've been working together for a couple of weeks now, on and off the football field, but until this moment, I hadn't realized how close they'd grown. Mason hasn't mentioned it, probably because he's usually so tired by the time he gets home in the evenings that it's all he can do to eat dinner and take a shower before he's zonked out. But there is no doubt in my mind that Jinx is someone my son needs right now. A friend and a mentor. And a darn good role model.

Because that's what he is. He may be a big goofball with a carefree reputation, but he is so much more than that.

He is amazing.

And I need to tell him that.

JINX

"First game of the season, and we're off to a shitty start with the refs. You gonna do anything about that?" Craig demands when the game is finished and he's approaching the bench.

Dalton looks up from his clipboard with a scowl. "What do you mean?"

"I counted at least a half dozen missed penalties, and that's just against our team," he adds, holding up six fingers to make his point. "That's bullshit."

"They're high school kids, Craig. They're learning just like these kids are." Dalton gestures to the team.

"They're not gonna learn if someone doesn't tell them they're missing shit left and right."

For fuck's sake, is this guy serious?

Dalton shakes his head but keeps his cool. "Let's not do this in front of the kids, okay?"

Craig's face turns red, and he fists his hands at his sides, like maybe he won't drop it. Cady joins him, her expression patient, and says something to him that only seems to piss him off more.

That's when I spot Rachel hanging back, watching but not getting involved. The way she's lowered her head and is wringing her hands makes her look more embarrassed than anything. Not for the first time, I'm glad she and this asshole are no longer together.

Also, she looks really pretty today with her hair in a braid and a ball cap on her head.

She catches me watching her and gives me a small but genuine smile.

I take that as my cue to stroll over. "Hey. You gonna give us shit about the reffing, too?"

She rolls her eyes. "Not even a little. He's so ridiculous."

Down the field, he and Dalton are still "discussing" the matter, but Dalton's at least got him pulled away from the kids.

"Mason handled that hit better than I would have," I say, returning my attention to her. "He kept his temper in check, though it was a little touch and go for a few seconds."

She laughs softly. "I noticed that. Thank you for calming him down."

I shrug. "Didn't take much."

She studies me for a second before she glances away almost nervously. "Mason has a lot of respect for you," she says.

Good. I've been intentional about fostering that. The kid makes it easy for the most part, but I still make a concerted effort to keep our time together positive. He's got enough shit to deal with, and more than anything, I want him to know he's got someone on his side.

"He's a good kid," I tell her.

He wouldn't be that way if it weren't for her. I'm sure there's plenty of Craig in him, too. Hell, his temper is obviously his father's. But he's got a big heart, and he puts his all into everything. That's Rachel, through and through.

"You taught him well." I nudge her arm playfully.

She smiles. "Well, I am a professional in that regard."

I laugh. "That's true."

"Anyway, I just wanted you to know that I saw you talking to him, and I really appreciate that."

I nod. I didn't do it for her, but I won't pretend that I don't like that she noticed. We may not have gotten off on the right foot with her kissing me and me having to reject her—and then me showing up and essentially trespassing to help her out—but she doesn't seem to hate me for any of it.

Now, if she'd only try to kiss me again...

This time, I'd do things a little differently.

This time, I wouldn't just kiss her back...

I'd take her fucking breath away.

ELEVEN

JINX

"Wow, you got it done in record time." Rachel grins from the front porch as Mason and I haul the weed wackers back to my truck. He's gotten pretty good with the equipment, and we've found our rhythm, so we can tackle a yard like theirs in less than a half hour.

Mason buffs his knuckles on his sweaty shoulder. "Yeah, well, when you're good, you're good."

I laugh. "Holy crap, kid. Rein that ego in."

He grins. "Only if you do."

"*Oh*!" Rachel's eyes go wide as she glances between us. "Do I sense a little ego war? I might have to withhold the cookies and lemonade."

"I'm just kidding." Mason climbs the steps and swipes a cookie from the tray she's holding. "His ego is way bigger than mine." Then, before she can steal the cookie back, he sprints into the house, claiming he needs to use the bathroom.

"You know, I'm second-guessing the two of you spending so much time together," she says, her eyes dancing. "You might not be as good for him as I thought."

Shoving my hands into my pockets, I take the porch steps slowly. "There's nothing wrong with self-confidence, Sunny."

"Sunny?" She pulls back with a frown, taking her tray of cookies and drinks with her.

I lean against the railing and survey her. She's got her hair twisted up in a messy bun, with stray strands falling down her neck and around her face. The summer sun has given her cheeks a soft glow that hides her freckles a little more than I like, but she's still the prettiest, sexiest woman I've ever seen.

"You do this thing," I tell her, tapping my fingers on the railing behind me. "When you're mad or thinking. You close your eyes and turn your face up to the sky."

The furrow in her brow deepens. "Okay..."

"It reminds me of a sunflower turning toward the sun."

All the confusion on her face turns to surprise. Pleasant surprise. Even as heat creeps up her cheeks.

"Oh. Uh, I didn't realize..."

I shrug. "I know. But I noticed." I've noticed a lot about her.

She brings the tray back within my reach. "You know a lot about flowers?"

I grab a glass of lemonade and nod. "I kind of have to. I can't plant flower gardens and shit and not know what I'm doing."

"Do you enjoy that?" She tilts her head in question. "Planting and gardening?"

I nod. "I do, actually. When I was a kid, I hated it. It seemed like I was always the one that Ma pulled outside with her to pick weeds, but I learned a lot from her. And I was able to apply that knowledge to the business."

She glances to the space on the other side of the railing, where one would expect to see flower beds. The stones and the edging are there, but it's nothing but dirt and weeds.

"Don't judge me," she says with a sigh. "I haven't planted these in years. There's never enough time. And when I have had time, it's the wrong season. Like now. It's too late to plant."

"Not really. We could put some blooming annuals in for the time being and get some perennials started for next year."

"We?" She tips her head with the sweetest smile on her face.

"Mason and I could do it." I wasn't thinking about Mason when I used the term—in fact, the image I conjured was one of the two of us on our hands and knees working up the flower beds. But if she's not interested in that, Mason will do just fine.

"Hmm." She carefully situates the tray on the porch railing and closes the distance between us. When her fingers ghost the stubble on my jaw, I grip the glass in my hand a little tighter to keep from touching her, too. "You collected a piece of grass," she says softly, pulling back with the speck of green between her fingers.

"Hazard of the job." I grin. "The rest of my face is probably full of dirt."

She scans my face, her expression soft. Her proximity and the intent with which she's looking at me has my blood pumping faster. I want to pull her against me and mess her all up. Kiss her until she's grasping at my sweaty T-shirt and trying to tear it off.

"It's a little dirty," she finally replies. Catching her

bottom lip between her teeth, she takes the tiniest step closer. "Did you want to go inside to clean up?"

What I want to do is go inside and show her just how dirty I really am. We can clean up after that.

"Nah, I'm good." Damn, it took everything I had in me to choke those words out. "Just heading home after this." To shower and enjoy every last bit of the fantasy that's already started in my head.

Mason comes jogging back outside, shaking his head. "Wow. Something sure has crawled up Emma's butt."

Rachel groans and steps back. "Again?"

"She's trying to wash her blanket, and she did something to the washing machine."

"Great." She sighs.

"Mom!" Emma calls from the house, her voice carrying through the screen door. "The washing machine is broken."

Rachel closes her eyes and tips her head up to the sky in that way I love so much. "I just did it, didn't I?" she asks, cracking one eye open.

I chuckle. "You did."

"Did what?" Mason asks, shoving another cookie into his mouth.

"Nothing." She shoots me a secretive smile, and maybe I'm making too much of it, but that smirk might almost be flirty. "I should go and help her with the laundry. She's just learning, so if I want her to keep it up, I can't leave her hanging."

"I get that. Did you want me to take a look before I go?"

"No, I'm sure it's nothing. Thank you, though." She gestures to the cookies. "Do you want to take some home?"

I grab a single cookie for the road and down the rest of the lemonade. "This is good. Thanks for the snack."

She presses her lips together in another smile that I can't quite interpret other than to say that it's different from the ones I'm used to from her.

Emma hollers from the house again, and Rachel and Mason groan in unison.

"I'll get out of your hair." I tip my head toward my truck. "Good luck with the washing machine."

"Thanks." Rachel sighs. "I'm gonna need it."

Do laundry or go to Ma's for Sunday lunch?

I look at the mountain of dirty clothes on my bedroom floor, then at my phone, which Amelia has been blowing up all damn morning, trying to convince me to be social today.

Even Aiden texted to tell me that he'd probably be there. As much as I'd like to give him a little brotherly support (yeah, right), I'm not in the mood today.

I'm freaking tired is what I am. I've been going balls to the wall for two straight months now, and today, I just want to crash on the couch, watch TV, and scratch my nuts when I feel like it.

My phone beeps again, the sound instantly causing a wave of guilt to wash over me.

> Rachel: Any chance your offer to look at my washing machine still stands?

The guilt turns to enthusiasm in a heartbeat. And suddenly, I'm not so tired.

> Me: Of course. It's still giving you grief?

I grab the only pair of clean jeans I have left and pull them on, followed by a questionable T-shirt and a hoodie. It's probably too hot, but it'll cover up any stains on the shirt.

Rachel: Grief is putting it mildly.

Me: You want me to come over right now or...?

Rachel: If you're not busy, that would be great. I know you're probably doing the family thing.

Me: Not feeling the family thing today, so you're doing ME a favor.

Rachel: No! I can't do that. Forget I asked. Seriously.

Me: Already on my way.

Rachel: Listen, I know how your mother is. That woman can hold a grudge, and I do not want to be on the wrong side of it.

Me: * laughing emoji * She'll be mad at me, not you, Sunny. See you in a few.

I brush my teeth and put on deodorant, then I'm headed toward the door. I stick my feet into my boots, not bothering to tie them, and grab a drill and my keys before heading out to the truck, where I text Amelia.

Me: Do me a favor and tell Ma I can't make it over today. Gotta help out a friend.

Amelia: Does this friend have a vagina?

Me: Not that kind of help, Lee.

Amelia: You didn't actually answer my question, so I'll assume that's a yes.

Me: Just tell her, okay?

When I pull into Rachel's driveway, she's already standing at the screen door, waiting.

"You really didn't have to give up your family time for this," she says with her arms crossed. "I feel bad enough asking you."

"Why?" I knock my boots off outside before entering the house and then toe them off. "I offered, remember?"

"Yes, but you do landscaping, not appliance repair." She wrings her hands together and hits me with a worried frown. "I left a message for my dad first, but today is bunco day. I would have asked Tony, but I'm pretty sure the list of things he still has to do around their house is a mile long, and I don't want to make it worse."

"Sunny..." I give her shoulder a gentle shake. "Relax. I don't mind. And I happen to be a jack-of-all-trades." I hit the button on my cordless drill, making it whirl to life noisily, and waggle my brows.

She huffs and drops her arms. "Okay. But if your mom takes back her offer to help me make cheesecake, I'm totally blaming you."

I give a small snort. "I heard about that. Ma loves to bake, especially when she can show off. She won't take her offer back, I promise."

With a sigh, she leads the way to the laundry room. It's situated just down the hall from the living room and before what I assume are the bedrooms.

"Where are the kids?" The house is quiet, with the exception of the low hum of jazz music playing in another room. The scent of lemon cleaner is heavy in the air, so I'm going to guess she's been cleaning.

"They're with Craig's parents today," she says over her shoulder. "Church first and then lunch, shopping, and a movie in Copper Crossing."

"Ah. So you have the day to yourself."

She makes a throaty sound. "To clean up after the heathens."

"C'mon. They can't be that bad."

She spins to face me in the doorway of the laundry room, eyes wide and a firm finger between us. "Oh no. There will be no siding with my children on the matter of their cleanliness. I found a half-eaten plate of spaghetti under Mason's bed this morning, and a bottle of orange Gatorade with something green and suspicious floating in it on Emma's nightstand."

I stick my tongue in my cheek. "Just one plate of food?"

She slugs my bicep. "Boys. Ugh! Anyway... the washing machine..." She waves a hand and gives it a glare. "It won't drain on its own. I took Emma's blanket out and used a bucket to get out as much water as I could from the washtub. I can't see anything stuck anywhere."

"It's probably a clogged drain pump." I tug my hoodie over my head and toss it onto the dryer. "Could I use a few towels? This is probably going to get messy."

"Yeah. Be right back."

As she hurries out of the room, I get to work removing the panel at the bottom of the machine.

"Whoa," she gasps when she returns with a stack of towels. "What are you doing down there?"

I chuckle as I remove the first screw. "The drain pump is behind this panel."

"It is? I thought it was in the back."

"You're thinking of the hose."

"Oh."

"If you can reach over me, see if you can use a couple of those towels to soak up some of the water in the machine. The more we can remove from the basin, the less that will come out onto the floor."

"Got it." She carefully steps one foot over me and toes up to push two towels into the basin.

She's wearing cropped leggings, but in my head, she's wearing a dress and giving me an accidental panty peep show.

Quit thinking about her pussy before you get hard, dumbass.

Three minutes later, with all the screws off the front panel, I carefully remove it and set it to the side. "This is the drain pump." I tap the white unit.

"Ah," she says from where she's deposited the wet towels in the laundry sink. "I had no idea."

"That's what I'm here for." I wink up at her from where I'm stretched out on the floor. "More towels?"

Once she's handed me a few, I position them where I want them. Then I remove the clamps from the hoses and carefully loosen them from the pump. As I do, water spills out, but the towels do their job and neither the floor nor I get too wet.

"I can already see the problem," I tell her, pointing to the dark shadow in the pump.

"What is it?" She squats down to get a better look, her foot accidentally bumping my leg.

"Guess we'll see." I pull the pump off, set it on a towel, then dig a finger into the end and hook the dark fabric.

The black *lacy* fabric, to be specific.

"Would you look at that." I crunch to a sitting position with the culprit in hand. Grinning, I unfold the lace and hold it up for her to see. I don't even care that it's dripping all over my T-shirt. Not when her face turns the sexiest, most embarrassed shade of red.

"Oh my god!" She takes a swipe at the thong, trying to snatch it from me, but I'm faster. With a chuckle, I hold it out of her reach.

"Hey now. Don't you know the finders keepers rule? He who fixes the washing machine or dryer gets to keep all the treasures left inside."

A gasp escapes her. "What?"

"You know... the loose change and shit?" Or in this case, her panties. "I've gotta say, I wasn't expecting this. But I'll take your wet panties any day."

Her eyes go wide, and that pretty color creeps down her neck and stains her chest. She opens her mouth a few times, trying for a comeback but coming up empty.

"Cat got your tongue, Sunny?"

"You're sitting there holding my underwear."

I take a better look at them. "They're pretty. Bet they look even better on you."

Her mouth drops open again, and she scoffs. "You did not just say that."

"Sure did." I push to my feet and stride to the wash-basin to wring them out. "And I'm not kidding about keeping them, either."

"Justin Enders." She marches over and tries to snatch them from me again.

This time I hold them up high. Her chest is flushed and her nostrils flare ever so slightly while her eyes shoot fiery daggers at me.

"Breaking out my real name, huh? Fuck, Sunny. Are you trying to turn me on?"

"Ugh!" She stomps away, and glutton for punishment that I am, I watch her ass as she goes. "Put my washing machine back together!" she hollers from another room.

I chuckle to myself. I hate being told what to do, but when she's the one doing it? It hits in an entirely different way. A way that makes me glad she's not in the room to see the bulge in my jeans.

I've never dated a mother or a kindergarten teacher before, but Rachel Perry just claimed her throne at the top of my MILF list.

RACHEL

What in the hell is going on?

More to the point, why is Jinx holding my thong hostage?

As if having him sprawled out on my laundry room floor like an appliance-fixing god didn't already have my heart racing, he had to go and confiscate my panties while shooting me that sexy smirk of his.

What on earth is he going to do with them?

Okay, maybe I don't want to know that.

Or maybe I do.

Who the heck am I right now?

I blink at the flushed woman staring back at me in the bathroom mirror, like I'm standing on the outside looking in. I don't recognize her. I don't recognize the fire in her eyes or the way her nostrils flare with every quickened breath she takes.

I definitely don't recognize the pulse of desire thrumming between her legs.

My legs.

My body.

Reacting to a man in a way it hasn't in years.

But not just any man. Jinx. Who is too young and too sweet and too *goddamn* sexy for his own good.

A light rap sounds on the bathroom door.

"You okay in there, Sunny?" His tone is still all tease. "You didn't die of embarrassment or anything, did you?"

"*No.*" I fling the door open and glare at him with narrowed eyes. "It'll take more than you manhandling my panties to do that. For Pete's sake, I spend half my time with five-year-olds who talk about farts all day."

He leans a shoulder against the doorframe, one corner of his mouth kicked up in a grin. "So I'll need to try harder next time."

Next time?

"Oh, and don't worry. When I tell Emma that the broken washing machine wasn't her fault, I won't tell her what the real problem was. I don't think she'll find that nearly as amusing as I do."

I cross my arms over my chest. "What's your angle here?"

"What do you mean?" he asks, even as his gaze drifts down my body like he knows *exactly* what I'm talking about.

"Are you playing with me just because you can? Because you know how attractive you are?" I tip my head to the side and give him a once-over to show him that two can play this game. "You should know that I'm not that distraught over my husband leaving me that I'll hop into bed with the first good-looking man who gives me a little attention."

His brows dart up. "No?"

"You're cute, okay? And I appreciate all you've done for Mason. Emma, too. And the yard work, but—"

"I wasn't referring to you not being distraught over your marriage, not your interest in sleeping with me."

I frown. "What? Oh." That. "It's complicated."

"Humor me."

A zap of annoyance runs through me at the sight of that damn smirk still on his face. "I am not talking to you about my broken marriage."

He shrugs. "Why not?"

Because five minutes ago, I imagined him lifting me onto my laundry table and making me come with that smart-ass mouth of his. The last thing I want to do is talk about the man who's never done something like that.

"Because I'm not." I shove past him and stalk to the kitchen, breathing through my embarrassment. "Is the washing machine put back together?"

"Yes, Mother. I did as I was told," he calls after me. The next words he utters are quiet, but they sound an awful like "damn, you're uptight."

I spin on him, true anger brewing in my stomach now. "You try being a single mom with a household to manage by yourself and kids who are a mess and—"

"Hey..." He holds up his hands and steps closer rather than backing away like I expect. "I wasn't trying to make you feel bad. In fact, if there's something more I can do to help..."

I open my mouth, but snap it shut again as guilt swamps me. He's been so good to me, and here I am, freaking out on him because of my *own* issues.

"Look..." I press trembling fingers to my forehead. "I'm sorry. I didn't mean to snap."

"You don't need to apologize."

"I do. You came over to help and probably to make me laugh a little and I..."

I like him *so much more* than I should.

But I'm not even divorced yet.

It doesn't matter that Craig has already moved on. I'm not that kind of woman, even if a part of me did think, for a few minutes at the bar weeks ago, that revenge was the answer.

But the way I'm starting to feel about Jinx... it isn't about revenge.

It's more. Something I'm not sure I'm ready for. And I don't know what to do with that.

"I don't want to unload my problems on you." I swallow hard and wet my lips. "I appreciate the offer, but—"

"Keeping it inside and ignoring it won't make it go away, Sunny." His voice is soft now. Soothing.

And damn if emotion doesn't swell in my throat.

"If you need a friend to unload it all on, I'll be that for you."

Except I already want to be more than friends. But I can't. Not yet.

He closes the distance between us and tips my chin up with rough fingertips. "If you don't want to talk now, that's fine. You have my number. You know how to get a hold of me when you're ready."

I close my eyes so he can't see the tears threatening to fall.

He slides his arms around my shoulders and pulls me against him, and the weight that's been bearing down on me for the past several months—the past several years—lightens. It's as if, in this simple embrace, he's already taking part of the load.

And I'm not strong enough to let go.

"Jinx?"

"Yeah?" he asks into my hair.

"Can you stay?"

TWELVE

RACHEL

"What hurt the most was that he was the one to go. It should have been me, and I should have done it years ago, when I realized we weren't working and never would. At least not the way either of us wanted. But I held on. I kept trying. And in the end, he decided it was over. I was mad at him, sure, but I was far more disappointed in myself."

"I get that." Jinx nods from the other end of the couch. He's leaning against one arm, and I'm kicked back against the other, each of us with one knee pulled up on the cushions.

"Now everyone thinks I was the problem. That he walked out on me, when the truth is that we were both done."

He fixes his gaze on me, his lips turning down. "No one thinks that, Sunny."

"But they do. I've seen the pitiful looks in town." Just thinking about it sends a pang through my chest. "They think I didn't measure up. I know better, but it still hurts.

And it makes me doubt myself, too. Because I did stay. I was too weak to leave. So they're not completely wrong."

He shakes his head. "No. They *are* wrong. And anyone who knows you—anyone whose opinion is worth a damn—knows the truth. Even me. Remember that day you brought him his lunch and donuts?"

"The day I almost face-planted in the EE lobby?" I chuckle softly and tip my head back against the couch, a hint of that day's embarrassment bubbling up inside me. "How could I forget? You obviously haven't, so don't try to tell me it wasn't a big deal."

He smiles. "I do remember. Not because you almost biffed it, but because of the way he treated you."

I swallow back a wave of shame. "You noticed that?"

"Fuck yes. Every one of us did. I thought Jesse was going to lose his shit. He wouldn't even look at Craig in the meeting afterward."

"Really?"

"I'm not going to sit here and bash him, because I'm not going to disrespect you like that." His expression is so serious, so sincere, and surprising coming from this man who's always teasing and always smiling. "You were married to him, and you have two incredible children together. But he showed everyone in the office that morning just how undeserving he was of you. And I bet there are people all over town who've seen the same on other occasions."

"I'd like to think that, but it's hard to pretend I haven't seen the way they look at me."

"It's the nature of the beast, Rach. People love drama, and in a small town like this, they're going to latch on to any tidbit of it they can get, even if they know better."

He's right, and what he's telling me isn't anything I haven't told myself a dozen times already.

"Fuck them," he adds, lifting his chin. "I know it's easier said than done, but fuck them."

His enthusiasm and vigor make me smile, which in turn makes him smile.

"I like that grin a hell of a lot more than your tears." He reaches out and nudges my shoulder. "But I meant what I said before. If crying is what you need to do, I'll be the friend who sits with you while you do it."

"You're so sweet."

"Listen..." He leans forward and lowers his voice surreptitiously. "If you could keep that between us, that'd be great."

I tip my head back and laugh. "Can't ruin your bad boy reputation, huh?"

"Exactly."

"I hate to tell you, but I think most people are onto you. I mean, you single-handedly keep this town looking like a *Better Homes and Garden* magazine spread."

He snorts. "I don't know about that. Besides, it's not just me. I have Connor, and Jack helps during the summer, too. Mason is starting to shape up pretty nicely, as well."

"Yes, but don't forget about all the work you do off the clock."

He lifts a brow.

"You didn't think anyone noticed?" For Pete's sake, he's always working. I've seen him cutting grass at seven in the morning and pulling weeds in the flower beds by the highway at seven at night. Never mind all the time he's putting in with Mason around town. "Your hard work does not go unseen, believe me."

He rubs the back of his neck and peers up at me. "Yeah, well, not everyone notices. I promise you that."

Is that a little passive aggressiveness I detect? "Who do you want to notice?"

With a grunt, he gets to his feet, then paces to the window. "We were talking about you, Sunny. Not me."

"Uh-uh. That's not how friendship works. It's a two-way street, mister."

He glances back, wearing a crooked grin. "Mister? First you break out my legal name and now mister?"

"You don't like the formality?"

He doesn't answer, just looks back to the window for a long, silent moment. "Jesse doesn't seem to notice." His words are so quiet that I'm not sure if he meant to say them out loud.

"I don't know how he couldn't."

He lifts a shoulder, still turned away from me. "I don't either, but he's never mentioned it. Maybe it's because he's been so busy with Jett and the business. Who knows."

All I know about his role in Enders Excavating is what Craig shared years ago. That Jesse offered Jinx a partnership, and he declined. But the defeat in Jinx's posture and tone makes me wonder if there's more to the story.

"I don't know what Jesse has going on, but I *can* say that raising kids can pretty easily distract a person from a lot of things. Especially if he's confident in the work you're doing."

"He might be too confident," he mutters.

"Is that a bad thing?"

He drops his head, then finally turns to face me. "You have an older brother, right?"

"I do. He lives in Virginia now."

"Are you two close?"

"Not really. I talk to his wife more than I do him these days."

He hums, mulling that over. "I'm close with all of my siblings. All of us living here in Cole Creek has definitely helped with that. But sometimes..." He breaks off as a shadow passes over his face. "Sometimes it makes it harder, too."

His situation is so much different from mine, but I recognize that look anyway. "Your brothers have left big shoes to fill."

He glances at me, brows lifted in surprise.

"My mother left some pretty big ones behind herself."

He comes back to the couch, shoulders slumped, and drops onto the cushion. "That's exactly it. Don't get me wrong—they're great guys—Aiden and Jesse are the fucking golden boys of this town."

"You're pretty shiny yourself," I tease.

He doesn't bite. With a sigh, he says, "They don't think so."

"Your parents?" I can't imagine that's true. Janice and Al have nothing but love and adoration for their children.

"My brothers." He lowers his head and stretches his neck. "Mostly Jesse."

"Oh." I don't know if I buy that, either. "Why do you think that?"

For a moment, he's silent, tracing lines on the arm of the couch. "Do you know how I got the nickname?"

"Uh-uh." Long ago, I heard a rumor about him, a girl, and another guy, but I'm pretty sure people were calling him Jinx long before he would have been old enough to partake in that kind of activity.

"I was eight. Jesse was playing youth football like Mason is now. It was Aiden's first year not playing, because he'd aged out, and I was a few months shy of being old enough. Anyway, they were playing one of the teams from down south. An easy team. Jesse was the quarterback, and he was working on his sixth win of the season. If they won, he would have beaten Aiden's record."

"Okay..."

"Dalton and Marcus Kaminski came down with a case of summer strep throat. That meant the team didn't have enough kids to play. Jesse was pissed."

Knowing all about brotherly competition from my students, I nod. "I bet."

"Dad decided to suit me up."

"But you said you weren't old enough."

"I wasn't, but no one really checks the records in youth football. At least, they didn't back then. Anyway, I'd been practicing with the team for a couple of years, so I knew the plays. But I had nothing on those bigger kids." He shakes his head in shame.

It's clearly something he takes very seriously. I have to bite back a smile at how cute he looks, revisiting this childhood memory.

"We not only lost, but Jesse got sacked three times."

I winced. "Ouch."

"He blamed the loss and the sacks on me. Said I was bad luck and called me a jinx."

"You weren't even old enough to play."

"Didn't matter." He lifts one shoulder and lets it fall again. "He had to blame someone, and I was the easiest target. For the rest of the summer, he found at least a dozen more things that were my fault, too, and he called me a jinx every single time. Pretty soon, it's all he called me. And then my family picked up on it, because they thought it was cute."

"Oh no." Poor little Jinx. Or Justin, rather. "Even your mom?"

He nods. "It took her longer to adopt it, but eventually her, too." He sighs. "It sounds so stupid now."

"It's not stupid." I shift in my seat, sitting a little straighter. "You don't like the nickname because the memories associated with it are painful. That's valid."

"I've never been able to live that shit down, and I hate it."

"But you don't have anything to live down. It wasn't your fault."

"Tell that to the pissed off eleven-year-old who thought he was King Shit."

I'm not sure what to say to make it better. God knows I'm still hung up on things from my childhood, too.

"Well, I'm not going to call you Jinx anymore," I declare, lifting my chin.

He quirks a brow. "No?"

"Not if you don't like it."

"It's not that I don't like it. It's the origin that sucks."

"Isn't it all connected?"

"The flip side is that at least he cared enough to give me a nickname, you know?" He lifts both hands, looking so adorable in his vulnerability.

"No offense, but you're kind of a mess."

One side of his mouth tips up a fraction. "Don't I know it."

"At least we're in good company."

"You're not a mess, Sunny."

"Oh, but I am. You just wait and see."

THIRTEEN

JINX

"And what's on the landscaping agenda this week?" Jesse swivels his office chair my way bright and early on Monday morning. The full EE crew, including Hayden, sits around us in the main part of the Enders Excavating office, most of them mainlining coffee in preparation for the day.

"We've got our usual residential upkeep, including the hedges by the school, and later today, I'm meeting with Wes and Lexi Carlisle to go over the design for their backyard water feature." I tap my notebook on the desk beside me. "Jack is gonna play football this year. Since varsity practice starts the second week in August, we've only got him for two more weeks."

Jesse looks at Jack with a grin. "No kidding."

He presses his lips together and nods. "Yep. Probably gonna get my ass kicked, but I want to play for Noah."

The chatter and the restless movement in the office come to a halt, and I give the kid an encouraging thumbs-up. This past spring, his best friend was in a car accident that left him paralyzed and cut his promising football career short. Jack, being the awesome kid he is, is stepping out of his comfort zone. Not only is he playing, but he'll be wearing Noah's number.

"That's friggin' amazing," Jesse says. "Is there anything we can do to help? You got all your equipment set?"

Jack dips his chin. "Most of it is provided by the school. Just gotta get my cleats and girdle."

"We'll cover that for you. Just let Hayden know what you need."

Jack's face turns red, but he nods. "Thanks, Jesse."

I grin with pride. I'll miss having him around for the rest of the summer. He's a good worker, and we've gotten close these past couple of years. He's like a little brother to me.

"All right..." Jesse sits forward in the chair. "Sounds like we're set for the week, hopefully finishing up the Willis project and getting ready for the municipal building site next week. Jinx, can you hang back for a minute? Wanna talk to you about the bucket truck."

I nod, and everyone else starts to clear out.

"We're gonna get started on our route," Connor says, tipping his head toward Jack.

"Sounds good. I won't be far behind you."

They head out as well, and Hayden gets up to refill her coffee mug.

"First things first," Jesse says, "I'm sorry it took me so long to get back to you."

"He was supposed to do it two weeks ago," Hayden chimes in from across the room.

"Is that so?" I lift a brow. I was starting to wonder what the hang-up was.

"I can't get away with anything anymore," my brother grumbles. "But yes, she's right. I got busy and put it off."

Another reason why me having a little more decision-making power would make things easier.

"Anyway, I called and talked to Mike this morning. He still has the truck for sale, and I told him we'd take it off his hands."

That's great news. But why the hell did he have to jump into the middle of a conversation I was already handling?

I rub a hand around the back of my neck and take a deep breath. "Thanks, but you know I could have done that."

He shrugs. "I felt bad about making you wait."

"It was my deal, man." Sure, he signs the checks and has final say in financial decisions, but I've been working deals on my own for years now.

Jesse furrows his brow. "I thought I'd help you out."

I shake my head. "I don't need your help."

The retort comes out stronger than necessary, and Hayden winces as she joins us again.

"What the hell is your problem?" Jesse snaps. "I'm fucking sorry it took so long, but you know how things get around here."

"Yep, I do." I look at Hayden and lift a tempering hand. "And no offense to you, Hay, because you coming on board has been a godsend." I turn back to my brother. "But maybe if you'd let me out from under your thumb, things would run smoother around here."

"What?" Jesse roars, pushing to his feet. "From under my thumb? What the fuck are you talking about? You have free rein over everything related to landscaping."

"Do I?" I challenge him. "Because you're the one who called Mike."

He laughs bitterly. "It was a phone call, dude."

I run my tongue around my teeth in a meager attempt to

keep my cool. Admittedly, I'm in a pissy mood this morning. All the late hours and coaching are kicking my ass, and I know I only have myself to blame for that.

Maybe it's time to come clean.

"Do you have any idea how many hours I work a week?" I ask, jaw tight.

He stares at me for a beat. "Is that what this is about?"

"Answer the fucking question, Jesse."

Hayden takes a careful and strategic seat between us.

"This is ridiculous." He turns away, scrubbing his hands over his face. "I know you work a lot, okay?"

"I put in fifty-four hours last week. Sixty, if you count the freebie work I do for the church and the cemetery."

Beside me, Hayden gasps.

Jesse spins around, eyes wide. "What?"

"Same the week before. And sixty-two without the volunteer hours the week before that." I shrug. "You want me to keep going?"

Jesse continues to stare in shock. "You don't get paid for that."

"No shit!" I laugh. "I told you last summer I needed more help, and you told me you'd have Ma put out an ad. Never happened. I told you in the fall when things slowed down that we should get someone else lined up for the summer, even another high school kid, and you told me we'd worry about it closer to summer."

Recollection dawns in his gaze, and his stance softens.

"I know you've had a lot going on. And it's only eased up since Hayden's taken some of the load off your plate. But if you expect me to uphold my part of this deal, then I'm going to need you to either do the same or give me more control."

"We can hire someone else, Jinx," Hayden interjects calmly. "In fact, I'll get something posted today."

"I'd appreciate that."

She dips her chin and jots herself a note.

"What kind of control do you want?" Jesse asks with an edge to his voice.

"I don't know." I lift both of my hands and let them drop. "But what we're doing now isn't working for me anymore."

We stand there like that, the truth finally out between us, for what feels like forever.

"Come up with a plan and then we'll talk," he grits.

I nod once. "I'm already on it."

FOURTEEN

RACHEL

After taking the kids for breakfast at Tulah's Diner and then dropping them off at the library for the Tuesday summer reading activity, I spent almost an hour of my morning chatting with Bailey Janikowski at Busy B's Boutique.

Okay, so maybe I did a little more than catch up with an old friend.

I might've also done some damage to my credit card. Not as much as I could have, thanks to two years' worth of Christmas gift cards from my dad, but enough to make me feel just the teensiest bit guilty when I put the bags in my car.

The truth is, I haven't shopped for myself beyond the requisite new socks and shoes in I don't even know how long. Long enough to be embarrassed that I'm still wearing the same cardigans and dresses for school as I was when my own children were in kindergarten, but I'd like to think that no one but me has paid attention.

"Mom, I'm going outside to toss the ball around with

Cody!" Mason calls from the front of the house shortly after we arrive home.

"Okay, baby, have fun!"

"I'm going to paint my nails and then read my new book!" Emma hollers as soon as the screen door slams.

"Make sure your nails are dry before you touch that book, kiddo. Miss Kimberly won't be happy if you bring it back full of polish."

"Ugh, *I know*!"

Of course she did. Because little Miss Emmy Lou knows everything.

I laugh softly to myself as I begin pulling my new clothes from the bags. I didn't go too crazy, but I did splurge on a couple of items that I normally would have passed over because of the price.

To be fair, I've never been a big shopper. But having kids and bills to pay more or less turned me into a non-shopper. At least, for myself. The kids never seem to stop growing and if we're not buying new jeans because their current ones are too short, then we're buying new shoes because their toes are poking through.

And there was Craig and his dirty, greasy clothes that never lasted more than a couple of months. And the fact that he blamed me for never getting them clean enough instead of acknowledging that maybe *he* could have tried harder to keep them clean in the first place.

I pull in a deep breath and let it out slowly.

"I'm not doing that today," I say to myself as I've begun to do more and more lately when negative thoughts like that pop up. In fact, it's what I told myself earlier, too, when I got to the door of the boutique and almost turned and walked away because the mom guilt started to chatter in my head.

But then I heard Jinx's voice telling me that I needed to take more time for me, and I shoved that guilt aside. Just thinking of him again makes my stomach flutter, and I pick up my phone on instinct.

Me: Can I get your opinion on something?

Justin: Depends.

Me: On?

Justin: Whether you want me to lie to you or be honest.

Me: What?

Justin: I'm kidding. What's up?

Ugh. Men.

Me: Okay, first of all, don't lie to me. Even if you think it's what I want to hear.

Justin: Noted.

Me: Which dress looks better on me?

I send him the pictures I snapped in the boutique changing room earlier. The red dress first and then the navy one. The *message read* notice appears beneath them, but it takes two solid minutes before the three little dots dance on my screen.

Then disappear.

And start again.

Only to go away a second time.

My stomach clenches in dread. Does he hate them? Is he trying to figure out how to tell me they're awful without hurting my feelings?

Me: Jeez, are they both that bad?

Justin: No.

Okay, so…

Me: That's it?

Justin: I'm trying to find the right words.

Ugh. See?

Me: They're just dresses.

Justin: Dresses on YOU.

Oh. *Oh*.

Justin: The red one is nice. But the blue one… holy fuck.

My cheeks are burning as I hold my thumbs over the keyboard. Now it's my turn to struggle with finding the right words. I wasn't fishing for compliments. At least not entirely.

Justin: Permission to be totally honest?

Me: I already told you not to lie.

Justin: Your tits look fucking amazing in the blue one. And the color is nice with your complexion. Draws out your freckles.

My face positively flames now.

Me: I hate my freckles.

Justin: Why? They're sexy as fuck.

My stomach flips, and I silently admonish my body for reacting to that comment. Now he's just flattering me.

Me: They're freckles.

I'm covered in freckles from head to toe, and I've hated them since I was old enough to notice that not everyone had them.

My phone vibrates in my hand, and his name appears on the screen.

Ugh. This was a bad idea. I never should have asked him.

"Yes?" I answer reluctantly, putting the call on speaker so I can hang my purchases in the closet.

"Buy the blue dress." His tone is low and husky, and it sends goose bumps washing over my bare skin. "You look beautiful in both, but that blue one? The way it hugs every one of your curves..." He breaks off with what sounds like a bitten off curse. Or maybe it was a groan. "Don't get me started on those freckles."

"I have so many."

"I've noticed. And I like them. A lot." He clears his throat. "I don't want to cross any lines here, but I'm going to say this anyway... Those are the kind of freckles that make a man wanna strip a woman bare and trace every single one with his tongue."

Oh my god. Did he really just say that? *To me*?

With my heart in my throat, I force myself to ask, "Any man?"

His responding laugh is low and almost feral. "Me, Sunny. I'm talking about me."

Not only is my face on fire, but my body has been engulfed in flames. I'm going to die. Right here in my closet. My children are going to find me with my phone and a bunch of flirty text messages from a man who is far too young for me.

Tamping down the mix of emotions coursing through me, I swallow and hope my tone is even, then say, "You're crazy."

"I'm a man who knows a beautiful woman when he sees one. And you told me to be honest."

I did. I just didn't expect *that* level of honesty.

"Then you'll be happy to know that I already bought the blue one."

He laughs. "Tease."

"What? Why am I a tease?"

"You asked me for my opinion of a dress you already bought."

"I wanted to make sure it was the right decision." And maybe push the boundaries a bit, which I realize now was a mistake. I think.

"Mm-hmm. What's this dress for, anyway?"

The answer to that is the other reason I texted him.

"It's for me."

"Obviously. But why?"

"Because I wanted it isn't reason enough?"

I can practically hear him grin through the phone. "Hell yes. I'm proud of you, babe."

Babe? "You're too much."

"I'm not enough," he counters. "That dress is perfect for a date."

"Whoa, there, cowboy. Who said anything about a date?"

"The day is going to come when someone in this town is

gonna have the balls to ask you out. And it's going to happen sooner rather than later. I promise you that."

Will that be him? Because I'd probably say yes. My heart takes off at just the thought.

"Can I ask you something?" he asks.

Oh god. I didn't mean, like, right now. "Uh, sure."

"Why did you want my opinion?"

Phew. Also, I'm not sure that's any easier to answer.

"Permission to be honest?" I repeat his words.

He chuckles softly. "Always."

"Because I don't have many male friends. And I trust you."

He's quiet for a moment, then, "So we're friends now?"

"Of course we are."

"Another question?"

"Justin..."

"Why would a man's opinion matter when you already love the dress?"

Well, crap. I put my foot in my mouth there, didn't I? Because he's truly the only man whose opinion I was interested in. For the dress and for other things, too.

"Sunny," he prompts when I don't respond.

"I *don't* care what men think. Not really." I pinch my eyes closed and come out with it. "But your opinion matters to me."

"*My* opinion?"

"Yes."

"I see." His voice takes on that husky quality again. The one that always makes me think he's in bed and nearly naked. The one that sends tingles down my spine. "We can call it mutual respect if that makes you more comfortable."

Mutual respect?

"I like you, too."

Oh.

"And if you need an opinion about anything—especially if it involves you looking like a million fucking bucks in a sexy-ass dress—I'm your guy. You got me?"

At the moment, I don't have anything, because I'm on the verge of combusting into a pile of ashes on my closet floor.

"O-okay," I finally squeak.

"Good." His voice drops another octave. "I'm glad we cleared that up."

Except I'm more confused than ever.

What does he mean he likes me?

And why is this conversation making me blush like a middle schooler?

I'm older than him!

But he is *clearly* more experienced.

"All right, Sunny. Breaktime is over. I have to get back to work."

"Oh, I'm sorry. I forget that not everyone is on summer break like me."

He chuckles. "Not a problem. You've given me lots to think about this afternoon."

"I have?"

"Mm-hmm. I'm gonna be thinking about all the other places you might have those sexy freckles."

Oh boy.

"See ya later, Sunny."

"Bye, Justin."

FIFTEEN

JINX

Me: Uno reverse. Can I get your opinion on something this time?

Rachel: Did you buy a new dress, too?

I laugh and lean an elbow on the console in my truck. The things I could do with that smart mouth of hers...

Me: As a matter of fact, I did. Can I stop by and show you?

Rachel: Oh, a fashion show. Bring it on.

Ten minutes later, she greets me at her front door, wearing a bright smile. "I don't see any dresses."

I lift my laptop bag. "It's in here."

Her mouth forms a cute little O as she steps aside and lets me in. "Online shopping, huh?"

"Don't tell anyone, but I have an addiction to those cheap foreign websites."

She giggles while I kick off my boots in the foyer. The house is quiet, save for the muted jazz she seems to like.

"No kids tonight?"

"It's Casen's birthday, so they're having a sleepover at Bobbie Jean's."

"Nice." At least I'm not interrupting family time, though the discarded laptop and blanket on the couch signal I've disrupted something. "Are you working on one of your classes?"

"Yes, but I'm just reading. It's not serious." She goes to the living room to close the laptop.

"Actually, keep it open. If you don't mind."

Tilting her head and eyeing me, she takes a seat on the couch. "Okay. I'm intrigued."

I claim a spot on the other end of the couch, a safe distance from her, and pull out my laptop. Fuck, I hope she doesn't notice the tremor in my hands. The only other person I've shown this to so far is Amelia, and her feedback contained more sarcasm than viable input.

"What's your email address?"

Rachel recites it as I type, and a few seconds later, an email notification appears on her screen.

"So mysterious," she muses. She gets cozy with the laptop and her blanket, then she clicks around and scans the document I sent her. "A business plan?"

I swallow hard. "It's rough, but I don't think it's too far off from what I want."

"And what is that?" she asks, keeping her focus on her screen. "To go out on your own?"

"I want to expand the landscaping part of EE. And"—this is the most nerve-racking part of all—"to tell Jesse I want to be a partner."

Her eyes light up, and the smile on her face is pure and genuine.

Relief cools some of my anxiety. I wasn't worried that she'd judge me. She's Rachel, after all. But I like her, and I want her to see me as smart and capable. And if I'm lucky, a man she might be willing to give a chance to in the future.

"You're finally going to do it," she says, shaking her head and grinning.

"What do you mean *finally*?"

"I've never understood why you weren't already a partner."

"Ah." I rub at my stubble. "That's complicated."

"Craig said you weren't interested."

"I wouldn't say I wasn't interested," I hedge. "I was young when Jesse took over. He was, too, but he'd finished college, at least. I was still taking classes. The timing was bad."

"Oh. I thought maybe there was another reason."

I blow out a long breath. "I didn't want to let Jesse down, either."

She tips her head with either pity or empathy in her eyes. I can't tell which. "Justin..."

"I know. It sounds weak, and I'm not proud of that."

"It doesn't sound weak at all." She sets the laptop aside and scoots closer, resting her hand on my thigh. "I think it's sweet how much you look up to your brothers and how much you want to please them."

A dry laugh escapes me. "Yeah, well..."

"But you're not a kid anymore."

The pointedness of her statement sends my gaze darting back to hers.

"You're ready now."

My heart stutters at the sincerity in her expression. "I've been ready for a while."

"Good." She squeezes my leg gently. "So you're going to talk to Jesse, then?"

"I might've started the conversation the other day. We were both pretty heated, though."

"Oh." She exhales slowly. "So you're worried he won't be open to the idea?"

"Honestly, I don't know. A few years ago, I think he would have jumped at the opportunity to unload some of the responsibility onto me. But now Hayden's helping him, and she and Jett are living in Cole Creek, too. It's only a matter of time before they have more kids, and I can see Jesse wanting to keep things as they are so he can pass the company down to them without having to worry about me."

She gives me a sweet smile. "You won't know unless you ask him."

With my lips pressed together, I dip my chin. "I know."

"Your plan looks good. But make sure he understands that this is more than just a business move for you."

She figured that out, did she?

I offer a small smile. "How do you know that?"

"You wear your heart and your passion on your sleeve." She tugs at my T-shirt to make her point. "It's not about the money or the notoriety. If it were about the money, you wouldn't work as hard as you do without getting paid for it."

Eyes narrowed, I frown at her. "I never told you about that."

She laughs softly. "It's in the business plan. You want to move from hourly to salaried. Your breakdown of what you're currently working and being paid compared to what you'd be making on salary gave it away."

"Oh." I cringe. That's embarrassing.

"Don't do that." She presses her palm to my cheek and turns my face to hers. "My point is, you love what you do, and you've been doing it for far less than what your time and energy are worth. My guess is that you just want the business that's been the lifeblood of your family to be as successful as possible. It's not about you."

"Some of it is," I admit. "I think I've worked hard enough to earn my place in the company."

"To earn your place beside Jesse, you mean. As an equal."

My chest is so damn tight it's hard to breathe. How the hell is she so good at this?

"Do you have a special key to my mind or something, Sunny?"

"So I'm right?"

"Maybe."

"Just maybe?" She shoves at my leg playfully. "Men."

"What is that supposed to mean?" I grasp her wrist and hold her hand away from me.

"Men never want to admit when a woman is right."

"Oh, really?" I hook an arm around her waist and playfully dig my fingers into her side. "What about me coming over to ask *a woman* for her opinion? Don't I get credit for that?"

She giggles and squirms *into* me instead of away from me. "Okay, fine. A little credit."

"Just a little?" I pull her onto my lap and stop tickling.

In return, she stops squirming and heaves one breath after another, recovering from the torture.

We stay like that, wrapped up in each other and the moment. And it's perfect.

I've spent the past few weeks wanting to touch her so

badly... to feel her lips against mine for longer than the split second they touched that night at The Creek.

But this is just as nice. This level of comfort. The intimacy.

"Have you had dinner yet?" she asks.

"Uh..." Did I eat? Hell, did I even have a break this afternoon? "I don't think so."

She jumps up and throws her hands in the air with an exasperated huff. "Well, then I better feed you."

Before I can respond, she marches to the kitchen, leaving me staring after her.

"Good thing I have leftovers," she calls over her shoulder.

I chuckle and toss my ball cap onto my laptop bag, then I haul myself off the couch and follow her. "You don't need to feed me."

She tips her head and gives me one of those motherly looks of disapproval. "No, but I'm going to."

Twenty minutes and two massive chicken salad croissants later, I sit back in one of her dining room chairs, wishing I'd stopped at home to change and put on joggers.

"Holy shit, I'm stuffed. Thank you."

Chin resting in one of her hands, she smiles from across the table. "And to think you turned your nose up at those grapes."

"Grapes and chicken aren't supposed to go together." I hold up a finger before she can protest. "But they worked here. This was amazing."

"See." With a pleased smirk, she gets up and takes my plate to the sink. "Any room for dessert? I have frozen cheesecake bites I might be convinced to share. It's not your mother's cheesecake, but..."

I stand and stretch, my belly fuller than it's been in days. "Did the two of you ever set a baking date?"

"No, not yet. It's been a busy summer."

"You should take her up on the offer when things settle down. She'd love that." I join her in the kitchen and spot several clean dishes on a rack next to the sink. "Can I put these away?"

"We'll see about the cheesecake, and not a chance on the dishes." She waves me off. "Confession?"

"Hit me."

"I don't bother putting them away anymore," she says almost conspiratorially. "It's easier to just grab them from the rack when we need them again."

Hmm. I can't help but smirk. I suppose I'm thankful for that. I've never put them away, and now I know she won't be horrified if she discovers that tidbit about me.

Embarrassed, she presses her hands to her cheeks. "That sounded ridiculous, didn't it?"

"No." I huff a laugh. "I leave my clean dishes in the drying rack all the time."

Sighing, she carefully folds a hand towel and hangs it over the oven handle. "My mother wouldn't go to sleep until the house was as perfect as it was when we woke up in the morning. Laundry done and put away. Dishes done and cupboards organized. My dad's shirts ironed and perfect..." She lowers her head and trails off.

"Sunny?"

She scratches at something on the counter, unwilling to meet my eye. "Yeah?"

I step forward, wrap my arms around her shoulders, and pull her against me. "You're a good mom," I say into her hair. "And I don't doubt for a second that you were a damn good wife, too."

She tenses for a beat, then a tremor rocks her body and she fists my T-shirt at my lower back. "How do you know that?" she rasps, melting into me.

"Because you're a good woman." I kiss her temple and then pull back so I can see her face.

In response, she burrows into my shirt and shakes her head.

"Don't hide from me." I lift her chin gently and search her watery eyes. "Don't hide who you are or how you feel. Not from me."

"You don't know me well enough to say that," she whispers.

"I know plenty." I hold an arm out and gesture to the dining room. "I know you're a great host. And an amazing cook." Then I wave toward the living room, where our laptops still sit. "You're smart, too. And kind."

She looks up at me, lashes fluttering, with so much hope in her expression that it almost breaks my heart.

This woman has been through so much, and something tells me that Craig and her divorce aren't even the worst of it. She's been hard on herself. Trying to live up to the legacy of a woman who isn't here to tell her to knock it off.

"It wasn't easy for me to come here tonight and share that plan with you, but you told me you trusted me, and I thought maybe I'd take a chance and trust you, too."

Her bottom lip trembles, so I swipe my thumb across it.

"You're enough, Sunny. More than enough." I lower my forehead to hers. "I want to kiss that quiver from your lips so badly right now."

Those pretty eyes widen, and she grips my T-shirt tighter. "Justin..."

"I know." I shouldn't say it. I shouldn't want it. I

shouldn't even be here right now. But there's something about this woman that I can't shake.

"I don't think you do," she whispers again, shifting closer so that her chest is pressed against my ribcage and my hardening dick presses against her stomach. "Because if you did, you'd know I want the same."

That's all I need to hear.

Hands to her face, I tip her head up and crash my lips against hers.

She tastes like something sweet, probably those damn grapes, and a woman who's denied herself for far too long. The way she grasps at me, trying to get closer, deeper, promises I'm right.

She's starved.

And I'm just the guy to feed that hunger.

Bending, I curl an arm around her ass and lift her to the counter. She spreads her knees wide for me, and I go eagerly, wedging my hips between her thighs so she can feel as much of me as I can her.

I can't begin to guess at all she needs, all she's been hungering for, but if I have it, it's hers.

I break the kiss and trail my lips to her jaw, then the curve of her neck, all the while doing my best not to lose my shit.

"Justin," she murmurs. My name on her lips is music to my ears. Fuck, I hope she never calls me anything else.

"What do you want, baby?" I nip at the skin below her ear, then soothe the sting with my tongue.

"I-I don't know." As the words stutter out of her, she slides her fingers to the hem of my shirt.

My heart is pounding in my ears, and every inch of me is a live wire, but I can't help but smile. She knows. She fucking knows, and I'm all hers if she wants me.

"I got you." I kiss her mouth again, then pull back and strip the shirt over my head. "Better?"

She gulps hard and nods, splaying her hands across my chest. The wonderment in her eyes is not lost on me. "You're so warm. And beautiful."

"I think that's my line," I tease, watching her fingers dance over my skin as she explores my pecs and biceps.

"Are you even real?"

I grind my cock between her legs until her eyes flutter shut and she moans.

"Does that feel fake to you?"

I don't wait for an answer. I kiss her again, this time to leave no doubt in her mind just how real this is. Tongue against tongue, teeth scraping lips, and hands everywhere until she's breathless and pulsing against me.

"Touch me," she begs. "Please."

"My fucking pleasure."

In one quick motion, I lift her tank top over her head and toss it to the floor. She's wearing a pink sports bra that easily gives way when I tug down with both hands.

"Jesus Christ," I murmur, my mouth watering at the sight of her pretty pink nipples, big and full and so fucking perfect.

I dip my head and suck one between my lips while I toy with the other. Only when she's writhing against me, her hands wound tight in my hair, do I switch and start the game all over again. Lick, suck, nip, tweak over and over again until she vibrates with need and is grasping desperately for my fly.

She flicks the button open and tugs at the zipper.

Halfway down, she pushes me away, chest heaving. "We can't do this." Her eyes are swimming with panic as she tugs her bra back into place. "Oh my god. Oh shit..."

"Hey..." I grasp her wrists to slow her down. "Breathe for me, baby. Just breathe."

She swallows hard and closes her eyes, pulling in one deep breath after another until the panic fades. Her lips still tremble, and I suspect she's holding back a wave of tears, but she keeps it together.

"Good girl." I cup her cheek and remain close. We might've let things get out of hand, but I'm not going anywhere, and I need her to know that. "Better?"

She nods, and then her eyes flutter open, revealing tears. "I'm sorry," she rasps.

"What are you sorry for, Sunny?" I stroke the pad of my thumb along her jaw.

"We shouldn't have done that. I-I'm still married." She whispers the words like they're a dirty secret.

"I know." I should have guessed her moral compass would be a strong one. "But we didn't do anything wrong. You know that, right?"

Her face flushes red, but she gives a subtle nod.

"Thank you for looking over the business plan." I stroke my knuckles along her jaw. "I appreciate that."

"I'll take a closer look and give you some feedback. If that's what you're looking for."

I nod. "If you want, sure."

"I'm happy to." She presses her hands to my bare chest, but with a sharp intake of breath, she pulls them away again. "I..." She worries her lip, eyes downcast for a moment, but then she takes a deep breath and meets my eye. "I enjoyed what happened here tonight, but it can't happen again."

I nod, but we both know this isn't over.

Sunny and me? We've only just begun.

SIXTEEN

JINX

What the hell did I just do?

I went to Rachel tonight because I respect her opinion, and then, like an idiot, I jumped the fucking gun and disrespected her as a woman.

"Fuck!" I climb into my truck, guilty blood rushing through my veins, slam the door, and throw my head back against the seat.

I offered to be her friend, and then I crossed the damn line.

"So fucking stupid." I scrub my hands over my face, then pound a frustrated fist against the steering wheel.

And how the hell am I supposed to go back now? Now that I've tasted her and touched her and smelled her?

"You are fucked, man. So fucking fucked." I turn over the engine and pull out of her driveway.

The worst part is that the regret I'm feeling probably isn't even half of what she's feeling.

She's still married. She has kids to think about, one of

which I friggin' mentor. And I know damn well she's battling some pretty heavy internal shit related to her mom.

My entire intent with her has been to help her out, not make shit harder, because I really like this woman.

And god dammit, I *do not* want to be her fucking rebound.

When I should go right to head home, I turn left instead, and three miles later, I find myself in the driveway of my childhood home. It's almost ten o'clock, but there's a dim light on in the kitchen, and inside, I find Ma sitting at the table with a puzzle book and a cup of tea.

"What are you still doing up?" I ask quietly, hoping not to wake Dad, who's probably been in bed for an hour.

"Eh, it's summer, and there's a storm coming in." She glances at the patio, where the warm night air is filtering in through the screen door. In the distance, the sky lights up in shades of silver and blue.

I was so distracted on the drive over that I didn't even notice.

"Sit." She nods at the chair across from her. "Can I get you some tea?"

"Nah, I'm good." I'm pretty sure I've never had a cup of tea in my life.

"Suit yourself." She picks her cup up off the table. "What brings you over at this time of night?"

I blow out a breath and lock my hands behind my head, unsure of what to tell her or if I should say anything at all.

"Oh boy," she says. "I know that look."

Dropping my arms, I frown. "What look?"

"The lady-trouble look."

Great. Not only do I wear my heart on my sleeve, but I wear my stress on my face.

"You obviously came over to talk about it, so tell me

what's bugging you." She tips her head, and her eyes twinkle in that sweet, motherly way they always do.

"I really don't know how I ended up here," I admit.

She presses her lips into a smile. "Something inside you knows you need to get it out. So you came to your momma. That's what momma's boys do."

"I am not a momma's boy." I totally am, but denying it comes with the title.

"Yes, you are. You and Jesse both."

Awesome. Yet another comparison between us.

"I've gotten myself into a bit of a situation," I finally tell her. "I tried not to, but... it sorta got the best of me."

She hums. "With a woman."

I nod. "Yeah."

"What kind of situation are we talking about, Jinx?" The sudden seriousness in her voice catches me off guard.

"Not that kind of situation." I laugh, a little uneasy. "This isn't a Jett 2.0 kind of thing."

"Phew." She sits back in her chair and blows out a breath. "Not that I don't want more grandchildren, but I'd rather see you fall in love first."

"Me, too, Ma." I laugh lightly and rub a hand over my head, only now realizing I left my ball cap in Rachel's living room. "It's just... I really like this woman. And I might be rushing things a bit."

"Is she on the same page?"

I lift a shoulder. "It's possible, but things are complicated. She's not really in a place in her life where she should be thinking about seeing anyone."

"What makes you think that?"

I press my lips together and lower my focus to the table in front of me. "That's not my story to tell."

"Ah. I see." She regards me for a moment while sipping

her tea. Then she says, "But she seems interested in you, too."

"If the way she blushes every time I'm around is any indication, then yeah." And like the sap I am, just thinking about it makes my face heat up.

Ma sighs again. "Listen, baby, we can keep being cryptic if you're not ready to say more, but if it's advice you're looking for, you're going to need to give me a little more than that."

"I can't." I wish I could, but I can't say anything now when I don't even know what's going on myself. "Let's just say that she's different. Getting involved with her isn't something I take lightly. Which, to be clear, I'm not. Getting involved, that is." Or am I? We did cross into new territory tonight.

"She must be special if you're this conflicted and you're not even seeing her yet."

"She's definitely special." One of the strongest women I've ever met. But she's fragile, too. "But, like I said, things are complicated."

Ma frowns. "Maybe I'm reading this all wrong, but, Justin, is she with someone else?"

A knot forms in my stomach, and I swallow hard. "Yes and no."

"Baby," she sighs, her expression pained. "I can't tell you that's okay."

"I know." Getting involved with me, or anyone, for that matter, right now isn't the kind of thing a woman like Rachel would take lightly. No matter that Craig has already moved on.

Ma reaches across the table and covers my hand with hers. "I'm sure there's more to this story, so I'm not saying it isn't okay, either. You're smart, and it's clear you've already been thinking about this. So I'm certain you will make the best decision possible for yourself and for her."

I hope so. It's what I've been trying to do all along, but the more we talk and text and the more time I spend with her, the harder it becomes to deny the pull between us.

Part of me wants to say fuck it all and jump straight into the fire.

But another part knows that's just asking for trouble.

I need to give Rachel the space she needs, first and foremost. And when the time is right, if the connection between us is real, then it'll happen.

If it doesn't... well, then it doesn't. I'll still have helped her through this the best way I know how. And at the end of the day, that's all that really matters.

SEVENTEEN

EARLY AUGUST…

RACHEL

"Mom! You cannot be afraid of the ball." Mason throws his head back in disgust when the football goes flying and I jump out of the way instead of catching it. "It's not going to hurt you."

"But I already jammed a finger!" I hold the digit up as proof, but he just shakes his head from a few yards away as Emma collects the ball and tosses it back to him.

"Just try and throw it back to me, at least."

"Okay." I line my fingers up on the threads like he showed me, pull my arm back, and launch the ball as hard as I can.

It hits the ground halfway between us, and Emma makes a pitiful "*wa-wa-waaa*" sound.

"I think you need a break," Mason snarks as he shuffles to retrieve my paltry pass.

"My form was good, though, right?"

He glares at me. "If I answer honestly, you'll ground me, and if I lie to make you happy, you'll also ground me. So, I plead the fifth."

Crystal bursts out laughing from the picnic table where she's been watching it all unfold. "He's got you there, Mom!"

I chuckle, too. "I'm not that bad, jeez."

"Jinx would say otherwise," Mason mutters before he tosses the ball for Emma to catch.

I roll my eyes and grab a bottle of water, then join Crystal at the table. "I thought I did pretty good."

Crystal gives a small snort. "For a mom, sure."

Ugh.

"Speak of the devil." My friend glances toward the park entrance, and I follow her gaze as I tip back a drink.

The familiar white truck with a trailer full of lawn equipment pulls in and parks by the tree line. A second later, Jinx hops out and drops the trailer ramps.

"Does that man have any help?" Crystal asks. "I swear, he's everywhere."

"Connor DeLuca works with him, and Jack Stroud helps during the summer. And of course, Mason."

She hums. "Don't get me wrong—I don't mind seeing him everywhere."

I almost choke on my water. "Crystal Denise!"

"What? He's nice to look at." She shrugs innocently and then shakes her head in appreciation. "I mean, those arms are like tree trunks. And that cake. Goddamn."

"Oh my god." I recap my water before I spill it. "You're crazy."

She swivels her head toward me, one eyebrow arched. "Don't you act like you haven't noticed. He did give you a ride home from the bar that one night *and* come back the next day to take you back to your car."

"So? Just because he's chivalrous doesn't mean I want him to bend me over."

She considers me for a moment, and then one corner of her mouth lifts into a smirk. "I didn't say anything about bending over, sweet cheeks. That was all you."

Well, crap.

"It's okay." She pats my knee. "Your secret is safe with me. Fantasize about the lawn boy all you want. Hell, do more than fantasize. After these past six months, you deserve it."

The lawn boy? Dear god.

"Hey, Mom!" Emma hollers. "Can we go and say hi to Jinx?"

"Go." I wave them on. "But don't keep him from his work."

Crystal sighs and glances out toward the lake in the distance. "Anyway, can you believe it's August already? School starts in thirty days."

"Yep. And thirty-one days until I'm divorced."

"And not soon enough. Too bad it's the first week of school. You deserve to get laid and take a vacation."

Don't I know it.

"It's okay." I stretch my legs out in front of me and sigh. "It'll be nice to get back into a routine again."

"You should come to the Dells with us next week."

A few days away from Cole Creek sounds amazing, but... "I can't swing it right now. I'm sorry."

Crystal tips her head. "I already told you, babes. The rooms are paid for and there's plenty of room for you and the kids. Tony got a nice bonus from the mine a couple of weeks ago, too, so we got you covered all around."

I seriously have the very best friends, but the offer is too much. "I can't let you do that. And it isn't that I can't afford the trip. It's my mental bandwidth that's stretched too far."

"Anything I can do to help?"

"I appreciate the offer, but I just need to slow down for a bit." Get myself ready for the school year we're both about to start *and* the one I haven't told her—or anyone—about yet.

I'm probably crazy, but the week after our drunken escapade at The Creek, I made a spur-of-the-moment decision and applied for an online graduate program. I was accepted, and classes start a week before I return to my kindergarten classroom. I'm excited, but I'm also nervous as heck. It's been a long time since I've been a student, and I want to make sure I can handle it before I tell anyone what I'm up to.

"Well, the offer stands. For the trip or the help."

"I love you." I lean over and rest my head on her shoulder.

"I know." She pats my head, all motherlike. "I'm a pretty awesome best friend."

Snorting, I shove away from her.

"Aw, look at that." She lifts her chin toward the kids and Jinx just as he pulls back and launches the ball. Emma and Mason scramble to catch it, and to my surprise, Mason lets his sister take the honors. "He just gets cuter and cuter, doesn't he?"

"Mason?" I smile. "He's a good kid."

She nudges me with an elbow. "I meant Jinx."

Oh, yes. Him, too.

"So..." she begins in a tone I know all too well. "When do you think you'll start dating again?"

Yep. Saw that coming.

"How about I get divorced first?"

"Why? Craig sure as hell didn't."

I give a light laugh. Funny how that fact doesn't bother me as much as it used to. "I'm not in a hurry. It'll happen when it happens."

"Hmm." She takes a drink from her water bottle, still watching Jinx and the kids play with the ball. "You'll need someone who's good with kids."

"Obviously."

"And he better know how to lay it down *and* go down."

I snort. "I should have never told you that."

"Darlin', a man who doesn't *eat* ain't got no place at your dinner table, either."

And this is why she's my best friend.

"I only wish you'd told me what a selfish prick he was sooner. I would've gotten you out a long time ago."

"I really do love you."

She curls her lip. "Cady deserves his no-pussy-eatin' ass."

Hell, yes, she does.

Of course, I'm still sex-deprived, but at least I don't have to pretend anymore. And after last week's kitchen counter escapade, I'm pretty sure I wouldn't have to fake a single thing with Jinx. He almost made me come from boob play alone.

I shiver at the memory and discreetly glance his way just as he lifts a hand in greeting.

"Hey, Rach!" he calls across the park. "I hear you need some lessons!"

Crystal chortles. "Go on, Rachel. Let the hunky lawn boy show you how to handle his balls."

I gasp and jab her with an elbow. "You're going to hell,

you know that?" Then to him, I call back, "Some of us are just better on the sidelines!"

He laughs and tosses the ball back to Mason before ruffling Emma's hair. The kids start to make their way back, and he returns to his work.

He really is an incredibly sweet, incredibly sexy man. But no matter what my body may want, my head and my heart know better. I can't let myself get caught up in the first man that pays me a little attention just because it's been so long.

But it's more than that.

My stomach tightens at the thought, and even my cautious heart agrees.

It's more than flirtation and attention with Jinx.

It's *him.*

It's his generosity. And his honesty. His compassion, too. And it certainly doesn't hurt that he's made me smile and laugh every time I see him.

Yes, he's younger, but he's already proven that he's all man.

And I'd be a foolish woman to deny that, in just a couple of short months, he's made me feel more like myself than I have in years.

EIGHTEEN

JINX

"Great game, buddy!"

Mason jogs off the football field, already unfastening his helmet. Even with it on, the smile plastered on his face is blinding. "Did you see that last play? I pancaked that guy!"

"Of course I saw it! Even heard him whimper like a little baby." I throw my hand into the air for a high five.

Mason laughs and gives it a good slap. "Yep. I heard him, too." He peers around me, craning his neck. "Have you seen Mom?"

"She's here somewhere." I turn and scan the crowd, but I don't see her or Craig. Interesting. "She probably ran to the car for something."

"Yeah, probably." He grabs a bottle of water and squirts a hefty amount into his mouth.

"Hey, Mason!" Dalton comes over wearing a huge smile. "What the heck got into you today? You were on fire out there!"

The kid continues to beam. "Ate my Wheaties this morning."

That has Dalton and me throwing our heads back and roaring.

Mason's back to looking past us. "There's Mom. Dad, too."

I turn and follow his line of sight. Sure enough, Rachel's there, standing with her arms crossed over her chest, looking down at the ground while Craig throws his hands in the air.

"They're fighting again." Mason sighs.

I ruffle the kid's sweaty hair. "Don't you worry about it. That's between them."

"Yeah, but it's probably about me or Emma. Or Cady." He says her name with a sneer.

Dalton cringes behind him. "Time to regroup," he says, clapping Mason on the back and pulling his attention away from his parents and their argument. "Come on."

With that, they're off, heading for the rest of the team for a postgame chat.

While I should follow, I don't want to put that much space between Rachel and me. Not while Craig's red faced and fuming. So I busy myself with cleaning up gear and water bottles for a few moments. Finally, Craig storms off toward the parking lot, and Rachel turns her face up to the sky like she always does, probably praying for patience or a goddamn miracle.

So I head over with Mason's things. His gear is the only excuse I can come up with to talk to her, and I desperately want to talk to her. It's been a week and a half since the night things got out of hand, and we haven't talked much since. She hasn't been avoiding me, but she's been quiet. I've backed off a bit, eager to give her some time to process and figure out where we go from here. *If* we go anywhere from here.

But it's killing me.

"Hey, Sunny. Did you catch that last play?" I hold out the water bottle and Mason's helmet.

She forces a smile to her face, clearly still irritated over whatever Craig was raving about. "I did. That other kid okay?"

I shrug. "Haven't heard otherwise, so I guess so."

She laughs softly. "That's good."

"You okay?" I tip my chin in the direction Craig just huffed off to. "He looked pissed."

"Isn't he always?" She tries to smile again, but it falls quickly. She ducks her head and sighs. "He was asking if there's something going on between us."

"What?"

"He heard about the ride you gave me a couple of months ago, of course. And then the lawn mowing..." She swallows hard, and I know what she's thinking. *Good thing he didn't hear about that night in my kitchen.*

"What'd you tell him?"

"That it's none of his business."

Damn right, it's not. And her response? Sticking up for herself rather than denying it to keep the peace? It's got my heart clenching.

A slow, genuine smile spreads across her lips, which, I've noticed, are free of any gloss or lipstick today. In fact, I don't think she's wearing any makeup. She's prettier than she's ever been with those freckles on full display.

"You look pleased to hear that."

"I am." I'm generally not into pissing matches, but... "If he thinks he's got something to worry about with me, then let him."

She playfully bumps her arm into mine. "Oh, really?"

"Yeah. I'm a big boy. I can handle his shit." Especially if it means taking some of the pressure off her.

"I knew I liked you." The confession seems to surprise her as much as it does me, because her eyes widen for a second before she laughs, clearly embarrassed. "God..."

"You can call me Justin. And I happen to like you, too."

She shoots me a *you did not just say that* look as the breeze teases strands of her hair across her cheek.

I fist my hands at my sides and resist the urge to tuck the wayward hairs behind her ear. I truly don't care what Craig thinks, but the last thing I want is for him to witness the move and start shit in front of the kids.

"I should get going," she says with a sigh. "Emma has a haircut this afternoon."

"You should text me again."

Her gaze flicks to mine, and we stand there for a beat, watching each other, so much felt but left unsaid between us.

"I'm a mess, Justin. You know that."

"I like messy, Sunny."

Those pretty lips purse and, if I'm not mistaken, the color that seeps into her cheeks isn't from the midday sun.

"Be careful what you wish for, Coach Enders."

Oh, it's going to be like that now, is it?

Bring it on, babe.

MOST OF THE kids and their parents cleared out pretty quickly after the game, but as I'm loading the water jug into the gear wagon, Emma jogs over.

"Hey, Em. Did Mason forget something?" I scan the

parking lot, stopping when I find Rachel by her SUV, helping Mason undress and remove his pads.

Instead of answering, Emma grabs my wrist, turns my hand over, and drops something into it. "I made this for you."

She what?

She pulls her hand away, revealing one of those friendship bracelets all the kids are wearing these days. The kind with colorful beads and some lettered ones, too. This one has round black and brown beads, with smaller white ones in the middle.

"Holy crap, Em. This is great. What does it say?"

She shrugs and toes the gravel, suddenly shy. "I don't know."

"Okay." I chuckle and spin the beads so I can read the word. "Spitfire."

Her cheeks flush a bit. "Do you remember?"

"Of course I do. But I thought you were Spitfire?"

She rolls her eyes. "I am."

I frown, and she huffs at my stupidity.

"Look." She holds out her wrist, where a half dozen bracelets just like the one she gave me, but in different colors, sit. "I have one for my friend Tessa." She points to a pink and green one with the initials TJM on it. "And this one is for Drake—"

"Who's Drake?"

"Ugh." She groans, dropping her head back. "A boy, okay? Anyway, we wear bracelets for the people we're friends with."

Hot damn. "Are you saying we're friends, Spitfire?"

She fidgets with her bracelets, arranging them nervously, then holds her arm out again and points to a white and red one with my name on it. "I have this one."

The strangest pressure knots itself in the center of my chest. A heart attack? Acid reflux? Shit, is this what it feels like to be considered cool by an eight-year-old?

"I don't know what to say. This is awesome." And easily the sweetest gift anyone has ever given me.

"It's okay if you think it's stupid."

"I don't think it's stupid at all." I slip the bracelet over my hand. It's a little snug, but it's stretchy. "Looks good, too."

"I didn't want to put my real name, because I didn't want it to be weird." She shifts from foot to foot. "I mean, you're old and stuff."

With a hand pressed to my chest, I feign offense. "I'm not that old."

She cocks her head to the side. "You can't go around wearing a bracelet with an eight-year-old's name on it, Jinx. People will think you're a pedophile."

I have to bite back a gasp at that comment. I'm not sure if I even want to know how she knows what a pedophile is.

"People will think that mine means 'Jinx, you owe me a Coke' or something."

"Fair enough." I hold out my arm and admire the new jewelry. "You give your mom one of these?"

She scowls. "Um, *no*. She's my mom, not my friend."

Ouch.

"Besides, if I made one for her, then my dad might find out."

"And you don't want to make him one?"

"I don't want to make Cady one."

Oh. There goes my heart, aching for her again. "Ah, I see."

She fusses with the bracelets on her wrist, gaze averted again. "She's not so bad. But Mom would be mad."

Rachel wouldn't be mad. Hurt maybe, but never mad if Emma really wanted to give Cady a friendship bracelet.

"How are things going with you and your dad?"

"Fine. Cady's teaching me how to diamond paint."

I have no idea what that is, but okay. "That's great. I mean, if you think it is..."

She nods. "Yeah. It's fun. And my mom seems a little better, too."

A smile splits my face at that. "That's great. I'm glad to hear it."

I don't know what I expected to happen today beyond the football game that just ended, but this conversation wasn't it.

Emma continues to reorganize her bracelets, putting them in a different order. "Grandpa Felix says that divorce isn't always a bad thing."

"I think he's right about that, Spitfire."

A wide grin slashes across her face. "See? It's a good name for me, right?"

I chuckle. "Yeah, it's a good name." Propped up against my tailgate, I cross my arms. "So, who's this Drake kid?"

Her eyes go wide, but she's saved when Rachel hollers for her.

"I have to go." She takes one step back, then another. "Don't tell anyone, okay?"

"Your secret is safe with me." I zip my lips and throw an imaginary key over my shoulder.

"*Ew.*" She cringes. "Don't be weird."

A laugh bursts out of me as she turns and runs back to her mom and her brother.

I may be weird, but I just got myself a pretty awesome friendship bracelet from a pretty awesome girl.

I'll take that any day.

NINETEEN

RACHEL

"Hey. I'm so sorry." I climb out of the car and pull open the back door so I can collect the groceries.

When I pulled into the driveway, Craig was already waiting to pick up the kids for a visit.

"My dad called as we were leaving town and asked if I could pick up some butter. He got chatty with the kids when we dropped it off. You know how he is."

Craig gives a half-hearted smile. "No problem."

"Hey, Dad." Mason hops out of the front seat. "Just gotta grab a charger from my room." He jogs toward the front porch, but at the base of the stairs, he comes to a screeching halt. "Whoa. When did this happen?"

"When did what happen?" Grocery bags in hand, I lean to one side, peeking around Craig.

Mason turns back to us. "The flowers."

Flowers?

"Damn. You've been busy," Craig mutters.

I frown, clueless as to what they're talking about.

That is, until I round the rear of my car and see for myself.

The old flower beds on either side of the front steps have not only been dug up, but they've been planted with a mix of perennials and annuals. The colors are bright and vibrant and breathtaking. They're also exactly what I would have picked for myself.

But I didn't pick them out. And I didn't plant them, either.

I can guess who did, though.

A comforting warmth spreads through me as I take it all in. "Wow. This is beautiful."

"I bet it was Jinx," Mason says with a grin. "He said he was going to."

Oh god. With Craig standing nearby, that warmth turns into unease instantly.

Emma skips over to us. "He did good. I'm gonna get my book, Dad. Be right back."

Both kids head into the house, leaving me alone with a confused Craig.

"Jinx did this?" He frowns at the flowers, then at me.

"Probably. If he told Mason he was going to."

"But why?" He scowls, his confusion turning to irritation. "Did you ask him to?"

Oh, he's getting ballsy with his accusations. "I'd really like to tell you yes right now."

He scowls. "What?"

I shake my head and sigh. "No, Craig, I didn't ask him to. But I did tell him that I wanted to fix up the flower beds someday."

"You're still talking to him?" He puffs up, his face an angry mask. "What the fuck, Rachel?"

Okay, now he's pissing me off. "Mason still works with him, *Craig*."

"I know that, but—"

"But what? What are you really upset about? That someone did something nice for me? A man, at that? Or is it because he did something you never bothered to do?"

He snaps his jaw shut, and fire blazes in his eyes.

"You might as well know that he's also the one cutting the grass. With your son. Every week." Guilt swirls in my stomach, even if I don't regret the comments. I know I'm just stirring the pot, but I'm sick and tired of being the one to bite my tongue and hold back. God knows he didn't give a single thought to my feelings when he started another relationship a month after he left.

"I'll turn him in for working a minor," Craig seethes.

A dry laugh escapes me. "Oh really? You'll have to turn Jesse in then, too, because he's the one who pays him."

He lifts his chin, his jaw hard, and looks down his nose at me.

I shake my head. "I have to get these groceries inside. The kids will be out shortly." I turn and head inside, forcing myself to count and breathe.

"Got my book." Emma races down the hall and throws her arms around me. "Bye, Mom. I love you."

"I love you, too, baby. Have fun tonight."

She's gone without another word, the screen door slamming behind her.

Mason appears just as I set the bags on the counter.

"I texted Jinx to ask if it was him," he says, grinning at his phone. "I already know it was, though."

I laugh softly. "You text with Jinx?"

"Uh, yeah. Work stuff." The *duh* goes unsaid.

"Oh. Right."

Mason rolls his eyes. "Anyway, I'll see you later."

"Yes, you will." I pull him in for a quick hug and press a kiss to his forehead. Pretty soon, I won't be able to do that. "I love you."

"Love you, too." He wriggles away and rushes to the front door, and a minute later, Craig's truck backs out of the driveway.

I don't wait to put the cold food away before I dig out my phone.

Me: What have you done?

Justin: You like it?

Me: I love it. The kids, too. Craig, not so much.

Justin: He saw, huh?

Me: He just left with the kids. Wednesday night visitation.

Justin: Ah. So you're alone?

Me: I am.

Justin: What are you doing for dinner?

I twist my lips and consider the food in front of me. I have lots of options, but making something just for myself is never as appealing once it's time to actually do it.

Me: Not sure yet.

Justin: Wanna come over and share this rotisserie chicken with me?

Me: You're done with work already? Dang.

Justin: For now. Was thinking about going back out after I eat.

Me: I'll come over.

No way am I letting him go back to work. Poor guy needs a break.

Justin: Don't play with me, Sunny.

Me: Not playing. I'll bring a salad, and I have a bottle of wine, too.

Justin: Hell yeah.

Me: See you in ten.

"SHE CAME out in her robe, Sunny." Elbows on the kitchen island, Jinx forks another bite of salad and shakes his head. Much like the last time I was here, he's fresh from the shower and smelling delicious while his light brown hair rises in damp spikes on the top of his head. My heart stumbled over itself when he answered the door wearing a white T-shirt that complements his tan and a pair of gray jogging pants that complements *everything* else.

"Mrs. Janikowski *is* old," I reason, though I already have a pretty good idea where this story is going.

"Oh no," he counters. "I'm not talking about a normal robe. I'm talking about one of those silky things that barely covered her ass."

Yep. I saw that coming. "You should see your face right now." I laugh.

"It's not funny. I really thought she was gonna bend over and show me the whole southern border."

"Were you on the riding lawn mower?"

He nods as he stuffs a bite into his mouth. "Mm-hmm."

"She was probably hoping to make you crash so she could come to your aid. You know, a little TLC. Or CPR."

He swallows and glowers. "I would rather die."

And I laugh all over again.

"Anyway, that was my day. How about you?"

Trying to regain my composure, I reach for my glass of wine. "It was good. The kids and I went to the lake for a while, and my dad called when we were on our way back home. He asked if I could pick up some things from the store, so we visited with him for a few minutes. By the time we got home, Craig was already there to pick the kids up."

He gives a crooked grin. "That's when he saw the flower beds?"

"Yep." I pop my lips. "Fabulous timing with that, by the way."

He chuckles and gathers another bite. "Not my intention, but hey..."

"How did you get all of that done while we were out today?"

"Connor and Jack helped me. Might've had some assistance from your dad, too."

"My dad?"

He nods confidently. "Yep."

"When did you talk to my dad?"

He lifts a shoulder. "Earlier in the week, and again today when we dug up some of the flowers from his place."

His place? As in... "My mom's flowers?"

The slightest color tinges his cheeks. "Yes. But don't give me all the credit. Technically, Mason gave me the idea."

There goes my damn heart again. "You're kidding."

"Nope. I asked him what kind of flowers we should get, and he said you liked the ones at your dad's. I drove out there to take a look, and when I asked if it would be okay if I dug up a few, he insisted I take as many as I wanted."

"Justin..." My voice cracks, and I swallow hard to fight back the tears prickling at the backs of my eyes, but it's no use. "I don't know what to say."

"You don't have to say anything." His voice is as gentle as the hand he places on my thigh. "I didn't mean to make you cry."

"Oh, please." I laugh softly while I knuckle away my tears. "You had to know I would love this."

He tips his head from side to side, smiling adorably. "You're right. But it was the surprise I was really after."

"Well, you succeeded in the best way." I slide my hand beneath his on my thigh and tangle our fingers. "Thank you."

His eyes go a little hazy as they drop to my lips, and I don't think twice. I lean in and kiss him.

For a moment, he's still. And after the way I freaked out last week, I don't blame him. But I'm sure this time.

"Sunny." He growls my name and cups my face, his mouth finally moving against mine.

The feel of his calloused palm and the soft, sensual caress of his lips is the perfect paradox. I melt into him and slip my hands around his neck, absorbing his warmth, while the heavy thrum of his pulse beats beneath my fingertips.

I could so easily get lost in this man. And yet, when I'm with him, I feel stronger and more empowered than I ever have.

"Hey..." He pulls back suddenly and rests his forehead against mine. "What time will the kids be home?"

"Oh, um..." I glance at my phone for the time. "Probably not until ten."

"Do you want to go for a ride with me?" He smiles, a plan of some kind clearly in mind.

"If we'll be back in time."

"Don't worry, Cinderella. I'll have you home before your carriage turns into a pumpkin."

I give a soft laugh. "Okay, because I'd prefer not to have to walk home."

He gets to his feet and takes our plates around to the sink. "Don't judge me, but I am not washing these now."

"Hey..." I hold up my hands. "I've already shared my deepest, darkest secrets when it comes to dishes, so you have nothing to worry about with me."

He grins as he rinses the plates and sets them aside for later. "Did you wear decent shoes?"

"Oh, this sounds like an adventure. Good thing I wore sneakers."

Five minutes later, with his ball cap on backward and "Feels Like Tonight" by Daughtry blaring through the truck speakers, he drives toward Copper Crossing.

"Too loud?" he asks above the music.

"Not at all. I love this song!" It takes me back to high school. "It reminds me of my first boyfriend."

He tips his head to the side and gives me a *come on* glare.

I laugh. "Sorry!"

"That's all right." He flashes a crooked grin. "I know what I have to offer."

Holy swoon. "Can we roll down the windows? It's warm in here."

He dramatically hits the power buttons, and both of the front windows lower. "Better?"

"Yes!" I throw one arm out the window and let the wind whip through my hair. "I love this."

He chuckles as he watches me from the driver's seat. "You need to get out more."

"I do." I've always loved driving with the music cranked and the windows open, especially on summer nights like this. It's so reminiscent of my younger, carefree days, when my biggest worry was if I had enough money to buy fast food with my friends.

A few minutes later, he hits the blinker and turns onto a dirt road that I've passed hundreds of times over the years but have never been down. In no time, the trees on the sides of the road give way to massive fields, some with tall, swaying cornstalks and others that will probably be cut for hay.

"Are we still in Cole Creek?" I ask, holding my hair back from my face.

He shakes his head. "Nope. This is technically McAllister."

"Ah. I've never been back here before."

"Really? And you've lived here all your life?"

I huff a laugh and lift one hand. "I really do need to get out more."

With a smile, he shakes his head. He's quiet for the rest of the drive, only speaking again when he slows the truck and turns into a long driveway leading to a farm set back in the middle of several fields.

"You know Ty Crawford?" he asks as we pass a herd of grazing cattle.

"The cop? Yes."

"This is his parents' place."

"Oh."

Then what are we doing here?

"Just trust me." He winks like he can read my mind.

An older man in overalls and muck boots exits one of the barns and waves as we pull up.

"That's Ty's dad, Lawrence," Jinx says, turning the radio down. "Hang tight here while I talk to him."

He hops out before I can question him about what he has up his sleeve. He hurries over to the man and shakes his hand. With his hands on his hips, he listens to Lawrence intently while they chat for a few minutes. Then the older man lifts his chin toward a two-rut road that hooks around the rear of a different barn.

Jinx claps him on the shoulder and jogs back to the truck.

"What on earth are you up to?"

"You'll see soon enough." He flashes a mischievous smile, and in seconds, we're bumping along that little road, well behind the barns and headed toward a small thicket of trees in the middle of one of the fields.

And then I see the sunflowers.

"Oh my goodness, look at them!" Hand held to my chest, I lean forward to get a better view. "Is this what you wanted to show me?"

He nods humbly. "Yep. They just hit their peak growth."

"Can we get out? I want to take pictures."

"Of course. Let's go."

We meet in the front of the truck, and he takes my hand and guides me across the uneven ground toward the rows upon rows of tall, stalky flowers with crowns of golden petals and bold bronze centers.

"Why would they plant these way out here?"

"To keep people like us from stopping to ask if they can see them."

"Oh." I laugh softly. "Okay, then."

"I have special privileges." He winks.

"How is that?"

"I helped plant them."

I face him fully and study him in the fading light. "Did you really?"

He dips his chin. "Yep. For the last few years, I've been helping them plant. In return, they give me seeds for the gardens I plant around town."

"Is that an even trade?" It sure doesn't seem like it.

He chuckles. "Not really, but I don't mind. I've been friends with Ty since elementary school, so the Crawfords are like a second family."

"That's really sweet." Every time we're together, I learn a little more about this man, and each time, I'm a little more impressed with him. "Can I be really cheesy and ask you to take a picture of me with the flowers?"

"Babe, I got you covered." He pulls out his phone and ushers me closer to the beauties.

It isn't until I'm right next to them that I realize they're taller than I am.

"I had no idea they actually got this big!" I prop my hands on my hips and flash a smile.

After he's taken a couple of photos, I throw my hands in the air and twirl. He snaps away while I live out my runway model dream in front of a field of sunflowers.

"Damn, babe, you're a natural," he teases.

I laugh, and then remember. "Wait. One more!" Closing my eyes, I turn my face up to the setting sun and pull in a deep breath.

"Ah, fuck, that's perfect."

It really is. This night and this trip. These little

moments that probably seem silly to him but feel like so much to me.

"Hey..." He's beside me when I open my eyes, his big hands sliding around my waist and pulling me into him. "Do you have any idea how beautiful you are?" he asks, peering down at me with those crystal blue eyes.

"You've told me a time or two." I toe up and press my lips to his. "Do you have any idea how handsome and amazing you are?"

He gives a crooked grin. "Amazing, huh?"

"So amazing." I kiss him again, wishing I could somehow get closer. Right now, kissing isn't enough. I want to wrap myself around him, and I want him to do the same to me. I want him to feel my heartbeat and know that it beats a little stronger these days because of him and all the selfless things he's done for me and my babies. I want to feel his heart and hope that, in some way, we've made an impact on him, too.

He breaks the kiss and pulls back, holding up his phone again. "I want a picture of us. If that's okay."

It's more than okay. "Only if you send me a copy, too."

He grins, and we tip our heads together for the picture.

"One more." I press up and kiss his cheek, and he snaps one last shot.

"Look at that." He shows me the image.

God, we look so perfect together that my heart aches in the best kind of way.

With a kiss to my temple, he murmurs, "We're a good-looking couple."

I swallow against the pressure in my chest. "We are, aren't we?"

He tucks his phone away, gathers me against him, and nuzzles his nose into my hair. "I don't want to rush you,

Sunny," he says softly. "In fact, I think it's best if we take our time. I don't want you getting sucked into something you're not sure you really want all over again."

Fisting his T-shirt against his back, I nod against his shoulder. What I really want to do is tell him that I already know he's what I want. But that's fear talking. That's fear of losing what already feels so good and so right between us, because it's been such a long time since I've felt anything remotely close to this.

But he's right. The last time I fell for a man, I was seventeen. I thought he was everything I ever wanted. And I was wrong. So, how can I trust that I know what I want now?

"I have one more small surprise." Jinx places a quick kiss on my temple and then produces a small pair of garden shears from his back pocket. "Pick out the ones you want to take home."

I barely contain a delighted shriek. "Really?"

"Gotta give you something to make you think of me when I'm not around."

Oh, Justin Enders, I don't need a reminder. You're already unforgettable.

TWENTY

JINX

I may work weekends, but Friday is still my favorite day of the week. Maybe it's knowing that there won't be anyone around to bother me. Kinda like that feeling of freedom that comes when the boss is away. When the atmosphere is more relaxed, yet more gets done. Or maybe it's because I still believe that one of these Fridays, I'll actually shut down at five o'clock and take a full two days to myself.

Fucking idiot. I laugh and shake my head. I cut back during the week when football started, and now that the season is winding down, I've been slow to get back to the late nights. I don't see myself reducing my hours any more than that.

"Hey, Jinx!"

I quickly finish tightening the strap on the last mower, then turn to Hayden, who's standing at the back door of Enders Excavating. She shields her eyes from the morning sun as her long blond hair and skirt ripple in the breeze.

"Morning, gorgeous!" I call back to her from the mower trailer. "What's up?"

"Can you come in for a few minutes before you head out for the day?"

"Anything for you!" I blow her a kiss, knowing full well Jesse is glaring at me from across the storage yard lot.

We still haven't said more than a few words to each other since the blowup in the office a couple of weeks back, and that's fine by me. I've been tweaking the business plan with Rachel's help, and it's only a matter of time before I lay my cards—and my heart—on the table. I have no idea how he'll react, but maybe Hayden can help soften the blow.

"You called for me, Your Highness?" I flash a cheeky grin as I prop one shoulder against the doorframe of her office.

She laughs and spins the big chair my way. "I did, kind sir. Please enter."

Chuckling, I take a seat in the guest chair. With her behind the desk, I don't expect the envy that hits when I typically sit across from Jesse, but it's still there. Still sitting heavy between us, just like that damn desk.

I clear my throat. "What's up?"

"I wanted to show you the applications that have come in so you can tell me who you'd like to interview for the landscaping position." She slides several sheets of paper across the desk.

Lips pressed together, I eye them, then her. "Did Jesse already look these over?"

"No." She shakes her head. "I didn't give him the option."

I lift a brow. "Why not?"

"Because this is your area. You should decide who you work with, don't you think?"

Yes, absolutely. But Jesse's always vetted my preferences.

"You should consider hiring two people," she adds, folding her hands on the desk in front of her. "Given all of the extra hours you've been working, it's apparent we need to add more than one new person to the crew."

"Can we afford that?"

She tips her head and shoots me an annoyed look. "Do you think I'd suggest it if we couldn't? Of course, we can, Jinx. You guys are killing it out there."

Hell yeah, we are.

"For what it's worth, I think I know why you did it. All the overtime, I mean."

My gaze lifts to hers in surprise. I expect to find sympathy or pity, but all I see is understanding and maybe a little challenge. I shouldn't be surprised. Hayden has become like a big sister since she and Jesse got their shit straightened out and got back together. She won't coddle me, but she will push when she thinks I need it.

"I just want him to stop seeing me as a kid, you know?" I haul myself to my feet and pace to a picture on the wall of my grandfather and the governor back in the early days of EE. "And maybe I regret my decision to not partner with him when he gave me the chance."

"I didn't know he'd considered that. When was that?" she asks, remaining seated.

Head bowed, I turn to face her. "Back when he first took over."

"Wow." She surveys the room, her expression thoughtful. "You were, what, nineteen?"

I dip my chin and stuff my hands into my pockets. "Yeah."

"So, you said no because...?"

"Because I was a kid." I make my way back to the desk, my boots heavy against the hardwood floor. "I had no idea what I was doing."

"In turning down partner?"

"In life." I laugh, dropping into the chair again. "I knew I wanted to be part of this company, but I didn't have the business skills like Jesse. I only had a year of college under my belt. The only thing I was good at was drinking beer and raising hell."

She smiles. "If I recall correctly, your brother was pretty good at that as well."

I sit back, knees spread wide. "Yeah, but he had a head start on all the shit that matters, and I didn't want to hold him back or disappoint him."

"But you've worked for EE all this time."

"Yep."

"And you've grown the company alongside Jesse."

An uncomfortable heat creeps up my neck, making me shift in my seat and run a hand over the burning skin. "My part of things hasn't made even a fraction of the money his side of things has. But yes, I've grown my part, too."

She sets another sheet of paper on top of the applications. "You certainly have."

I lean forward and take a closer look. It's an expense and revenue report that details the income our landscaping work has brought in over the last five years. The numbers align with those in my business plan, though her records are probably more accurate since I've been loosely keeping track for my own peace of mind.

"You've grown the landscaping business by nearly four hundred percent in the past five years, Jinx." She points to one of the lines on the spreadsheet. "And since you've done all this with only one full-time employee beneath you, you've turned one heck of a profit."

The number she points to next is one I'd already calculated, at least roughly, but it's still staggering.

"We can afford help, Jinx. You don't need to work yourself to death to prove you can handle the responsibility." She smiles and laces her fingers on the desktop. "Because that's what you've been doing, isn't it?"

Deflating, I shrug. No point in denying it when she's got the proof in front of her. "Maybe."

She sits back in the big leather chair and gives a short laugh. "Good lord, you Enders men are stubborn."

"Hate to tell ya," I say, unable to stop the smile that takes over, "but you're raising one, too."

"Ugh." She tips her head back dramatically. "Don't I know it. But seriously. Hire two people. And for the love of god, take a damn vacation."

"Yeah, I don't know about that."

"I do," she argues. She arches her brows in challenge, making it clear there's no point in arguing. "And sit down and have a heart-to-heart with your brother." She raises her hand, readying herself for my rebuttal, but I've got nothing.

"I know, Hay. I've been planning on it for a while now." I gesture to her numbers. "This reinforces that decision."

"Good." She sits up straighter. "Do you want me to schedule something so it's official?"

My instinct is to tell her no, to pull Jesse aside when the moment feels right, but that would leave room for me to second-guess myself. So with a nod, I agree.

"Let's do it."

"Next week?"

"The sooner the better."

She turns to her laptop, her fingers flying over the keys, and a moment later, my phone pings with a notification.

"Monday after staffing. I've given you two hours."

At the sight of the message, my stomach turns to knots. *Jesse & Jinx - Landscaping Expansion Meeting.*

Holy shit. This is really happening.

"Now," she says, turning back to the applications still spread out before me. "Let's pick some candidates, shall we?"

TWENTY-ONE

RACHEL

"So, it's settled, then? We'll order the bounce house and a couple of carnival games for the back-to-school event?" Crystal asks Friday evening during our August PTA meeting.

"Yep," I chime in. "I'll call both vendors tomorrow and make reservations."

"Perfect." She jots it down in her notebook. "Anything else we need to discuss tonight?"

Bobbie Jean raises her hand from a stool by the barista station. "What about the book fair? Given the trouble we had getting the order in last year, I think we should start planning early this year."

"Good call." Reese holds up his pen. "Anything I can do to help with that, Bobbie?"

"At the moment, no," she says with a smile. "But I'll let you know."

With a wink, he shoots a finger gun in her direction.

I bite back a laugh and busy myself looking over my own notes.

Reese could be best described as awkward single dad meets dorky fifth grade teacher—wild, mismatched wardrobe and all. Tonight, he's wearing camouflage cargo shorts and a navy button-down… with yellow flip flops.

"All right, then." Crystal picks up her phone. "We'll work on back-to-school event prep in two weeks. Suggestions for that meeting location?"

I raise my hand. "Let's stick with Books & Beans."

A round of suppressed laughter goes around the room, and I can't help but join in. That night feels like a lifetime ago, and the embarrassment has long since faded.

"Okie dokie. I'll send out a reminder text a few days beforehand." Crys closes her notebook and adjourns the meeting.

"Hey, Rachel…" Reese strolls over with his notebook in one hand and a coffee cup in the other. "Funny thing happened the other day."

"Oh yeah?" I ask, stuffing my laptop into my bag. "What's that?"

"I'm enrolled in a couple of graduate classes this fall. There's a Rachel Perry in both of them. For a second, I thought maybe it was you."

A wave of dread washes over me, and instantly, the temperature in the coffee shop rises uncomfortably.

"Oh." I laugh, quickly scanning the room to make sure no one is listening. "You're taking classes, huh?"

He nods. "Educational administration through UW-Superior."

Small world. And inconvenient, too, because there's no way I can avoid telling him the truth.

"Any chance we can talk about this another time?" I say under my breath, hoping he takes the hint.

"Oh." Realization lights on his face. "Got it. Yes. For sure."

Relief hits me, instantly easing the tension in my shoulders. Thank god.

He turns his back to the crowd, bowing his head, and mutters, "It'll be nice to have someone local to talk with."

"Absolutely." Now go away.

"Hey, Rach," Crystal calls from across the room. "Can I catch a ride home with you? Tony dropped me off, but now he's been sucked into something at the office."

"Of course." I glance back to Reese and give him a weak smile. "Duty calls."

He grins. "Have a good night. And we'll chat more soon."

Right. Ugh.

"What the heck was that about?" Crystal asks as we hit the sidewalk outside Books & Beans.

Ah. She must not have overheard. Thank goodness. She's already going to be mad that I didn't tell her about grad school. I don't need her being upset that I told Reese first on top of that.

"He was just asking if Mason's excited for sixth grade."

"Oh." She sighs, her shoulders sagging as we approach my SUV. "That's disappointing. Even if he isn't your type, anyway."

I hit the fob on my key ring, and we both climb into my SUV.

"How do you know what my type is?" I ask as I start the car. "I don't think I even know what it is anymore."

With a soft snort, she buckles her seat belt. "You like 'em with a little more swagger and a lot more muscle."

An image of Jinx immediately surfaces, and a smile spreads across my face unbidden. Yeah, he has both of those in spades. "You're right," I say as I pull out of the lot and start toward her house on the other side of town.

"See?" She swats at my arm.

"What about Jamie Stroud?" she asks out of nowhere, and I burst out laughing.

"Yeah, right." While Jamie is very attractive in a big, bearded, badass sort of way, he's a bit of a mess when it comes to women. He's divorced, with a seventeen-year-old son—Jack, who works with Jinx—and he has a five-year-old son with a woman who's closer to Jinx's age. That kiddo will be in my class this fall, and I'm already nervous about dealing with his mom. She's a lot, and I can only imagine how difficult she would be if I were dating her ex.

"Don't let Miranda scare you off," Crystal says, as if reading my mind. "Jamie's a great guy. He'd be worth it."

That may be true, but I have my sights set on someone else.

Someone who's already proved he's worth it.

Me: Hey you. You still awake?

Justin: Yep. Just crawled into bed to watch a movie.

Me: Anything good?

Justin: I don't know. Mission Impossible, I think.

Me: Ah. Brushing up on your spy skills?

Justin: Heck yeah. I've gotten real good at watching movies like this with my eyes closed. Don't tell anyone, but it's kind of a superpower.

Me: Haha. If it's any consolation, I'm in bed, too. Took the kids school shopping before they went to Craig's, and then we had a PTA meeting. I'm exhausted.

Justin: Want me to come over and give you a back rub?

Me: God, I wish.

Justin: I can be there in five minutes.

MY STOMACH FLIPS at just the thought, but is he being serious?

Me: Don't tease me like that.

Justin: Not teasing. Just be warned that when I do it, I'll be in my underwear.

With a giggle, I turn over onto my side and prop the phone up on the pillow beside me. I wish I could see his face.

Me: How about a video chat?

Justin: Say less, babe.

An instant later, the phone lights up with a request. I hit Accept and curl into my pillow with a smile. "Hi."

"Hey, gorgeous." He grins. There's a flash of skin, and when the image clears, he's got his phone on his lap, giving me an up close and personal view of his abs and the little trail of hair beneath his belly button.

"Damn. You just go right for it, huh?" I tease.

He laughs, making the phone shake. "Too much?"

"Not at all." I wet my lips and let the image burn into my mind. "I like it."

He quirks an eyebrow. "Tell me more."

"Your ego is big enough," I tease, filled with a lightness I only feel with him.

"It's not the only thing that's big."

"Oh my god!" I burst out laughing. "You did not just say that."

"What?" he asks with a smirk. "You've felt it. You know it's true."

Good lord, this man. Yes, I have felt it, but he was just pressed between my legs. It's not like I put my hands on it.

"Anyway..." I settle against my pillow, getting more comfortable. "What did you do today?"

"Thought about you."

Okay. This is going to be that kind of conversation, is it? Might as well play along.

"You did?" I tuck a hand under my cheek. "What about?"

"How sexy you are." Those blue eyes, so full of longing, sweep over every inch of my face.

"Are you trying to get me to show some skin, too?"

"No." He shifts onto his back and holds the phone above him. "I'm just telling you that I think you're beautiful. And smart. And strong."

Butterflies flutter low in my belly, but I keep up the teasing. "You said I was sexy."

"All of the above." He folds an arm behind his head against the pillows. "I also like your smart mouth and the way you give me shit all the time. You're not afraid to tell me how you feel."

Yeah, well, there are some things I haven't shared.

"What's that look for?" he asks, his expression sobering a little.

"Hmm? Oh. Nothing."

"I just said you don't hold back, and now you're gonna do it?" He chuckles softly. "Don't you go making a liar out of me, Sunny."

Well, I can't do that, now can I? "I was just thinking that there are some things you don't actually know."

"Like what?"

I wet my lips and swallow, pushing past my comfort zone. "Like how much I've thought about you, too."

His gaze dips to my mouth. "What kind of thoughts?"

"The kind that require access to the top drawer of my nightstand."

Holy shit. Did I just admit that?

The butterflies take flight, and tingles skitter down my arms and legs as he watches me, lips parted.

"Fuck, woman. Don't stop there. Keep talking."

I do one better. I roll over and grab my vibrator from the drawer.

"That's fucking hot," he growls, his irises igniting like blue flames. "What exactly do you do with your little friend? In detail, please."

I laugh softly, even as my heart rate picks up. "That's between me and Prince."

"Prince?"

"He's purple, so I named him Prince."

"Jesus Christ." He laughs, roughing a hand down his face. "That's hilarious."

I shrug lightly.

"If you don't want to tell me, how about you show me?"

Oh shit.

A wave of heat hits me, from the tips of my ears to my toes. Just the thought of getting off with him watching lights a fire low in my core, making me ache. I squirm against the sensation, and a little moan rolls up in my chest.

"That turns you on, doesn't it?" His voice is hungry again.

I bite my lip but nod.

"Don't get shy on me, babe. I think you want to show me as badly as I want to see it."

I do. God, I do, and this is a side of myself I haven't fully explored. Partly because I never had the opportunity, and partly because I've never been with a man I've wanted to share it with. There's only ever been Craig, but this...

"I want to watch you come, Sunny," he husks. "I'd rather be there doing it myself with my fingers and my tongue—"

My hips pulse forward in response to his admission and the desire in his tone, and I squeeze my legs together to savor the ache.

"—but we'll get there. For now, I want to see how you play when you think about me."

Sweet god, my panties are soaked, and I haven't even touched myself yet.

"Sit up against the headboard." The command is firm but gentle. "Prop the phone up on the blankets."

Hands trembling, I do as he says without hesitation.

"Take your tank top off."

I obey that command, too.

"Fuck, you're pretty." His lashes lower over darkened eyes as he drinks me in. "The number of times I've gotten off thinking about your tits since that night..." He breaks with a muttered "*fuck*."

Never taking my eyes off him, I skim my fingers over my breast until I find a nipple and toy gently as he watches. I want so badly to slide my hand into my shorts and panties, but that will come. He'll get me there.

"My mouth is watering, Sunny." He scrapes his teeth over his bottom lip. "I want to suck on you like I did that night, but I don't want to stop this time. Not until you're pulling my hair and screaming my name."

"Oh god." My hips flex off the mattress as a tug of pleasure zips through me, from my breast to my pussy, as if they're tethered and his words are pulling on that string.

"Two hands," he orders. "And don't you dare be gentle about it. I know you like it harder than that, baby."

My breath catches. How? How has he already figured me out?

"Pinch, Sunny. Tweak your tits until you can't take it anymore. Pretend it's my mouth and my teeth. Biting, teasing, tasting..."

"Oh shit..." I drop my head back against the headboard as I give into the pleasure. It feels good, but it's not enough. "I need more."

"Use your toy."

A shaky breath escapes me. Thank god.

I stick my thumbs into my waistband and push down my shorts and panties, only to have him shake his head on the screen.

"Uh-uh. Don't you even think about touching that sweet pussy yet."

My heart stops, and I stare at him blankly. Wait, what?

"Use the vibrator on your nipples."

Oh. *Oh*.

My face flushes, because again… how does he know?

A low, dark chuckle crackles in the air. "That's what I thought."

"How are you so good at this?" I kick my shorts aside and pick up the vibrator, not bothering to play coy. "Did you plant a camera in here?"

He flashes a crooked grin, and his phone shifts slightly. "No camera, babe. I just pay attention," he says, his tone strained and his abs flexing.

That fire in my belly flashes at the sight of him, at the desire in his expression. "Are you touching yourself?" I whisper as I turn on the vibe and tease it over one pebbled, aching nipple.

"Fuck yes, I am." He groans. "Do you have any idea how fucking hot you are?" His eyes flutter shut, and his phone slips until his fist appears. Just as quickly, it's gone as he works himself over.

I can't see more than the rhythmic pulse of his hand and the way his upper body tenses and twitches, but it's enough. It's enough to give me the courage to take the reins and return the torture.

"I've never watched before," I admit, my breath quickening. "Is that how you like it? A little rough, too?"

His eyes dart open, and his nostrils flare, but he doesn't stop. He squeezes and releases once, only to do it all over again. "No. What I'd like is to be buried between those tits right now. Fucking your mouth at the same time."

Holy. Shit.

"Play with your pussy, Rachel. I'm not gonna last much longer, and I wanna hear you come first."

Yes, please.

Emboldened by his genuine desire for me, I pull my knees up and then let them fall apart unabashedly. I've never done something so bold and brazen, but it feels so good. So right. Even in person, I've never felt empowered enough to let myself be seen like this. And I love it.

"Jesus Christ," he groans. Then, "Fuck, Sunny, that's pretty. Touch your clit for me. Show me how you like it."

Gliding two fingers between my swollen lips, I give him what we both want, teasing and stroking my aching bead until I'm panting and writhing. Only then do I add the vibrator, holding it just where I like it until the coil of orgasm begins to wind tight.

Then I move it away and focus on him.

His jaw is clenched tight, and there's a storm of arousal in his eyes. The muscles in his arms are bunched and tense, and a fine sheen of sweat glistens on his chest. He's beautiful, and to know that I'm the one who's turned him on like this...

"I'm going to come," I rasp. My natural instinct is to close my eyes, to block out every possible distraction, so I can greedily enjoy every last pulse that racks my body, but I can't look away from him.

"Oh fuck," he growls, pumping himself faster as he gasps for breath.

And I'm gone.

The wave of orgasm crashes through me, sending goose bumps racing across my skin as every nerve in my body sings. My pussy pulses, and my toes curl, and then the sexiest, most feral groan I've ever heard vibrates through my phone.

The tendons in his neck strain as we both watch the ribbons of white paint his golden skin, the evidence that I drove him just as wild as he drove me right there for me to see.

It is easily the most erotic moment of my life. As much

as I'd love to be there with him, touching him and tasting him, I wouldn't change it for the world.

As he lifts those sated eyes to mine, a slow smile teases one corner of his mouth. Then he lets his head fall back against the pillows. His chest rises and falls as I fight to catch my own breath.

And then I laugh. "We really just did that."

He swallows hard before clearing his throat. "Yeah. We did."

"You should probably get a towel."

He rubs a hand over his face, over that dark smirk. "I need a fucking shower."

And I need sleep. Because for the first time in months, I feel like it's possible.

"Thank you," I say softly, bringing the phone closer.

He picks his up, too, and the gentleness in his expression has butterflies whirling in my stomach. "Thank you, Sunny. That was amazing."

I blush, which is funny, all things considered. "You're welcome. Sorry about the mess."

His shoulders shake as he laughs again. "Never apologize for making me lose my shit, babe."

Lip caught between my teeth, I sigh. "Okay. But only if you promise we can do that again sometime."

His gaze flicks to mine, the fiery embers of desire still smoldering. "Oh, we will abso-fucking-lutely be doing that again."

Thank god.

TWENTY-TWO

JINX

Craig Perry is the last guy I want to see bright and early Saturday morning, especially after the night I had with Rachel, but sure enough, there he is. Almost like a reminder from the universe that I'm supposed to be taking things slow with her, not puddle jumping over every last barrier between us.

"Yo, Jinx." He raises a hand as he approaches from the gas pumps at the Cole Stop. Cady's in the passenger seat of his truck, and if the kids are in back, I can't tell.

"Hey, man." I lift my chin and toss the beef jerky and package of almonds I just bought onto my center console. "What's up?"

"Not much." He shoves his hands into the pockets of his jeans like he's going for casual, but the tense expression on his face gives him away. "I just wanted to thank you for working with Mason this summer. Cutting grass and coaching and shit."

I adjust my ball cap and nod. "Yep, no problem. He's a good kid. A hard worker, too."

"He loves being useful, and if he can do it outside, even better." He smiles, but it's fake as hell, confirming my suspicion that he's over here for another reason.

We've never been friends, even though he's close with Aiden and Jesse. He's always rubbed me the wrong way, and the way things have gone down with Rachel only proves that my instinct was right.

"He likes the cash in his pocket, too. You know how kids are."

I give a half-hearted laugh. "I thought he was saving for a car."

Craig snorts and gives his head a shake. "A car? He's not even twelve."

"He told me he was gonna start saving now so he can get something nice when he turns sixteen."

He specifically said he wanted a truck like mine, but I'll keep that part to myself. It's only a matter of time before Craig hates me for a slew of other reasons. There's no need to add my connection with Mason to that list.

"Anyway, no thanks necessary. It's been nice getting to know him."

Craig nods again, this time glancing past my shoulder like he's debating whether to bring up what's really on his mind.

"Saw the flowers you planted at the house, too," he finally says. "Rachel seemed to like them."

Bingo.

"Yeah?" I arch a brow. "Good to hear. That was my goal."

His gaze snaps back to me and sharpens. "Your goal?"

I lift a shoulder. "She said she wanted to do something

with the flower beds again but didn't have the time, so I thought I'd make it happen for her."

His face reddens a little further in response. It's hot out today; I suppose that could be the cause, but the way his eyes are narrowed on me says otherwise.

I just smirk. Am I playing with fire? Hell, yes, I am. This asshole fucked up the best thing that ever happened to him by being a selfish prick. Someone needs to make sure he realizes that. Might as well be me.

"So you two do talk," he says tightly, his tone edging on accusatory.

"Of course we do. It'd be rude to pick up and drop off Mason without talking to his mother, wouldn't it?"

"I'm not sure I like your attitude, man."

I chuckle. "You asked a question, and I answered it."

"With a fucking attitude." He works his jaw from side to side, still considering me through narrowed eyes. "Look, I appreciate what you've done for my boy, but if you're planning on doing more than that, you might want to think twice about it."

Oh really? This motherfucker has some balls, doesn't he?

I stick my tongue in my cheek and tilt my head. "Are we talking about Rachel now? Because if you've got something to say, you might as well just say it."

"I'm talking about my wife," he snaps.

It takes everything in me not to drive my fist through his goddamn nose, but I keep my composure.

"She'll be your ex-wife soon enough," I remind him. "Does Cady know you're over here whipping out your dick for a woman you're not supposed to care about anymore?"

He lowers his chin and balls his hands into fists. "I'm always gonna care about her, you little fuck."

Irritation rolls up my spine, but I'm not going to show him my hand just yet. I've already said enough where Rachel is concerned.

"That's good to hear," I say instead. "I'm sure the kids will appreciate that."

"You don't know the first fucking thing about my kids."

I knuckle my nose and stifle a laugh. "Actually, I do. And I notice they're not with you right now. Why is that?"

He doesn't respond. He's too busy huffing out breaths like a bull ready to charge, his nostrils flaring and his eyes flashing with anger.

Lowering my chin, I shake my head. "Seems to me like maybe you need to worry less about my relationship with Mason and Emma and more about yours."

With that, I shoot him a grin and climb into my truck.

He doesn't so much as move as I back out and wave to Cady as I pass.

Am I an asshole for poking the bear? Probably.

Do I care? Not even a little.

RACHEL

LAST NIGHT WAS INSANE.

I was insane.

In a completely uninhibited way that came out of nowhere.

Except... did it really?

Or have I denied that part of myself for so long that I forgot it existed? To be fair, I've never had the opportunity to take risks like that. And it's only been a few years since I got in touch with myself sexually.

So maybe I just needed the right moment and the right man to open that door.

And god, do I hope Justin meant what he said about doing it again.

My phone pings with a text notification, and I stretch across the mattress to reach it. I've been sorting laundry and am currently stuck in the middle of an archipelago of colors, whites, and bedding.

A giddy flutter of butterflies lets loose in my stomach when Justin's name appears on the screen. It's funny how one man can stir up such a mixture of feelings inside me in such a short span of time. It's exciting and nerve-racking all at once.

I really don't want to mess this up.

Justin: Hey gorgeous.

Me: Hey yourself. *kiss emoji*

Justin: Things got a little intense last night. Just wanted to make sure you're okay.

Be still my heart.

Me: I slept better than I have in months. I'm more than okay. How about you?

Justin: Fucking phenomenal now. *sunglasses face emoji*

I laugh.

Me: Glad to hear it.

Justin: What are the chances you're free later today?

I take in the half dozen piles of laundry and recall the mess of papers, sticky notes, and notepads in the living room.

Me: How much later?

Justin: I was thinking I'd bring dinner over.

Orgasms and food? What on earth did I do to deserve him?

Me: Consider me intrigued.

Justin: *laughing emoji* Dinner it is. See you around five.

Me: Looking forward to it.

"WHAT'S ALL THIS?"

Just after three o'clock—two hours earlier than expected—Justin shows up at my door with a load of grocery bags hanging off one arm and, of course, that adorable shit-eating grin of his.

"Don't worry your pretty little head about it." He bends to press a kiss to my forehead. "I know I'm early, so I'll do my thing, and you get back to what you've been working on. You won't even know I'm here."

His thing, huh? I cross my arms over my chest and purse my lips, pretending to consider his suggestion. There's no way whatever he has up his sleeve is anything I can ignore, so it's a good thing I got most of my reading done this morning. Also, he's dressed in a pair of gray jogger shorts and a sleeveless athletic top with his ball cap on backward. He has distraction written all over him.

He tilts his head and cocks a brow. "You gonna make this difficult, Sunny? If so, you should know I'm very persistent."

"Oh, I am well aware." I stick my head out the door and pointedly scan the freshly cut lawn and the flowers on either side of the porch.

He laughs. "Let me in, babe. I promise I'll behave."

I doubt that, but I step aside anyway.

"Go back to what you were doing," he says with a lift of his chin. "I'll make myself at home."

I give a half laugh and gesture to the groceries. "When you said dinner, I didn't expect you'd be making it."

"Listen, woman. If I'm going to wine and dine you, I'm sure as hell not going to do it with frozen pizza or takeout." He bumps me with his elbow and nods toward the living room. "Now, I mean it. Go. I got this."

He kicks off his sneakers and makes his way to the kitchen like he's been in my home a hundred times. I'm tempted to follow. The curiosity is killing me. But I'll play his game. For a little while, anyhow.

With a sigh, I pad back to the living room where my laptop, my books, and my notes are waiting. Classes don't start for another week, but we've been given early access since so many of us in this program are currently teachers who will be headed back to our own classrooms soon.

I've spent the last three hours looking over the intro material, scheduling due dates in my phone, and reading the first week's assignments. I've spent the last five or so years dreaming about the day I'd finally take this plunge, and now that it's here and literally right in front of me, it's surreal. And I'm really freaking proud of myself.

The sound of the fridge opening and closing, followed by the cupboard doors, makes me smile. I should probably be nervous, considering he's more of a frozen meal guy than a chef, but he could make macaroni and cheese, and I'd be over the moon. The effort is what gets me.

Also? I really like having him here. And I like that he's comfortable in my space.

So I pop my earbuds back in and let him do his thing while I work. Just like he asked.

JINX

THE LAST TIME my palms sweat like this, I was sixteen and trying to impress Gracie Janikowski with my new used truck. Now I'm twenty-six and trying to impress Rachel Perry with a home-cooked meal. Oh, how the times have changed.

I don't know whether she could tell how nervous I was or whether she's busier than she's let on, because it's taken me forty-five minutes to get this meal prepped and in the oven, and she hasn't popped in to check on me once.

Quietly, hoping I don't disturb her if she's engrossed in something, I creep into the living room, where I find her curled up on the couch and fast asleep. Her red-brown hair is twisted up in a bun, and her face is free of any makeup. Those pretty freckles add to her peaceful innocence in a way I wish I could see more often.

She's always moving, this woman. She's always got a million things on her mind. So seeing her at rest soothes something inside me, too. It eases my own mind to know that, at least for a little while, she can have these moments of quiet. Assuming, of course, that her dreams are as calm and serene as she is right now.

I take the blanket from the corner of the couch behind her and drape it over her carefully. Instead of waking, she snuggles deeper into the pillow with the softest, sweetest sigh.

I'm basking in the ripple of warmth that sound sends through me as I turn to close her laptop. With my hand on the top of it, I press gently, only to pause when I notice the window open on the screen.

She was working in an online classroom. I recognize the format from the handful I took when I was in college.

When she said she was working, I assumed she meant that she was prepping for the upcoming school year with kindergarteners, not college students.

Hmm.

I take in the notebooks and papers spread out on the coffee table, and my breath sticks in my chest.

Master of Educational Administration.

Administrative Leadership.

Principalship.

Holy shit. My sunny girl is going after her master's degree.

A sense of pride I probably have no right to feel wells up inside me. Damn, this woman impresses me at every turn.

The night we sat on her porch and ate cheeseburgers, she confessed that she'd felt held back in her marriage. That she'd wanted to do something more with her career, but she'd never felt supported in that desire. So she put that dream on a shelf. She didn't elaborate on what it entailed, but now I know. Now I see it, and I'll be damned if she ever feels held back or unsupported again.

Moving quietly, I make my way to the laundry room. There are two full laundry baskets in front of the wash machine, one that's clearly Emma's, with her assortment of brightly colored T-shirts and leggings, and one full of Mason's dirty practice clothes.

I only hesitate for a second before I remove the towels from the dryer and pile them on the laundry table. Then I transfer the wet clothes from the washer into the dryer and toss Mason's stuff in to be washed. I may not be confident in the kitchen, but I know my way around laundry. Despite how much I dislike the task, Ma made damn sure we all knew how to take care of our own shit by the time we hit middle school.

I fold the towels next and put them away in the main bathroom. She probably has a master bath that could use replenishing, too, but entering her private space is a step too far, even though it's damn tempting to go in search of the bathtub that's haunted my dreams for weeks.

With any luck, I'll be seeing that space soon, but for now, I'll wait for the invitation.

For now, I head outside and grab a few tools from the back of my truck. I noticed the railing on one side of the porch was loose a few weeks ago, and now is as good a time as any to tighten it back up.

The Pruitts are outside with their chocolate Lab, so, keenly aware of the curious expressions on their faces, I lift a hand in greeting. I don't have my trailer or lawn equipment today, and Mason isn't here to help me out. Hell, I'm not even dressed for work. I'm just a man doing domestic shit like I live here, like I'm trying to be a good man for the woman inside.

I may not live here, but that last part is accurate. I want

to be the kind of man Rachel wants and needs. And I don't care who sees me doing everything I can to fit that mold.

Rachel has been dealt a shit hand these past few years—probably longer—and it's about time someone steps in and gives her the support she deserves.

Things between us may have started out innocently enough. I was just a nice guy lending a helping hand.

But I'm no longer interested in being a temporary solution to her problems.

I want to be a long-term part of her life.

TWENTY-THREE

RACHEL

The sound of the dryer buzzer stirs me from my sleep, and I stretch lazily on the couch. I shouldn't be so tired, considering how well I slept last night, but then again… I smile to myself. Maybe the excursions before the sleep have a little something to do with my lethargy.

The dryer opens and closes down the hall, and I bolt upright in response, my heart stopping.

Fortunately, the discarded Nikes in the foyer catch my eye before panic gets the best of me. With my hand on my chest, I blow out breath and will my muscles to relax.

Just Justin, my knight in a shiny white pickup truck.

But why on earth is he in my laundry room?

And where did this blanket come from?

Oh, this man. He's going to ruin me if I'm not careful.

"Um, hello?" I call, padding down the hall and rubbing the sleep from my eyes. "What are you doing?"

"Hey, sleeping beauty," he says when I hit the laundry

room doorway. He tosses a grin over his shoulder while he shakes out one of my shirts. Then he folds it on the laundry table. "Did you have a good nap?"

"Yes..." I take note of Mason's empty laundry basket and the washing machine hitting the spin cycle. "Are you doing my laundry?"

"Yep." He shrugs and presses his lips together in a modest smile. "I also put the clean towels in the front bathroom. Not sure if they belong there, but there was room."

I blink a few times, wrap an arm around my torso, and pinch myself.

Nope. Not a dream.

"Did you just pinch yourself?" He flashes a crooked smile.

"Are you for real right now? And what is that smell?" I pull in a deep breath, my chest expanding, trying to discern the aroma.

"Beef tips. I hope you like mushrooms."

Maybe I died in my sleep, and this is what heaven is like.

I close the distance between us, loop my arms around his waist, and bury my face in his chest.

Hmm. Smells like the real thing. Feels warm and solid like the real thing, too.

"You okay?" He holds me tight and strokes my back.

"What did I do to deserve you?" I ask into his shirt.

With a chuckle, he presses a kiss to the top of my head. "Um, you were born?"

"I'm serious. It's like you swept into my life one night and have done all the right things since. Like an angel or something."

A robust laugh shakes his chest. "I am no angel, Sunny."

He wasn't last night, that's for sure. "You could be a pervy angel. With devil horns."

"Now that's more like it." He leans back against the table, spreads his legs, and pulls me into the V. "Probably a tail, too."

"Mm-hmm." Sliding my hands around his hips, I squeeze what I can of his butt. "You've definitely got tail."

He arches back and lifts a brow. "I like fresh from a nap Rachel."

"Yeah? Well, I like you all the time." My chest goes tight as I make the admission. It's terrifying to bring my feelings out in the open like this, but it's the truth. He and I have evolved into this... *thing*. We haven't talked about it. We haven't named it. We're just... here. It's a little unnerving, but it feels so completely right.

With his pale blue eyes dancing back and forth between mine, he trails his knuckles along my cheek. "Seems we've found ourselves in a little situation, haven't we?"

With a nod, I bring my hands up to his chest, soaking in his warmth. "Is it weird for you?"

"Why would it be weird?"

"Because I'm older. And a mom. Who's technically still married."

"Nah, babe." He shakes his head, then, in a low, tender voice, says, "I don't give a shit about our ages. And your kids are amazing. The married part..." He hesitates. "It does trip me up a little. I want you to be ready."

I want to be sure I'm ready, too. But more than that, I don't want to lose this opportunity with him.

"I've tried not to rush this," he adds. "But you're so fucking hard to stay away from."

"I've noticed." I glide my fingertips across his chest and

then down to his abs, relishing how they twitch and tense under my touch.

One corner of his mouth ticks up in a grin. "Yeah?"

"You can't seem to help yourself when it comes to doing things for me." Over the fabric of his T-shirt, I tease a fingertip along the waistband of his shorts. "I'm not sure I've ever properly thanked you for all you've done."

He tips his head, his smile softening. "You've thanked me plenty, Sunny. And I'm happy to do it."

"That may be, but..." Lip caught between my teeth and nerves skittering through me, I regard him. I may be older, but there is no doubt he's more experienced. What we did last night was a first for me. "I enjoyed our video chat. A lot."

He zeroes in on my lips, and his lashes fall heavy over hazy eyes. "Me, too."

"There was one part that didn't work for me, though." I casually slip a hand beneath the hem of his shirt.

He shivers at my touch, but a moment later, when my words register, he frowns. "Did I do something wrong? Tell me."

I ease his concern with a stroke of my thumb over the V of muscle just above his hip. "I wanted to see you." Feeling bold, like I did last night, I hook my fingers in the waistband of his shorts.

"You..." He clears his throat. "You couldn't see me?"

I scrape my teeth along my bottom lip and shake my head. "I only saw your hand. And the mess you made."

A ghost of a smile flickers across his lips, and his eyes light with desire. "You should've told me."

"You were busy." I shift closer, my mouth a hairsbreadth from his. "Besides, I think I have a solution."

His breathing picks up, his chest rising and falling

against mine. "Sunny, I think I know where this is going and—"

I press a finger to his lips. "Don't argue with me."

His cock twitches in his shorts and hardens against my stomach. Even if his head tells him he should deny me, his body clearly disagrees.

"I want to see you," I murmur, gently tugging at the cotton of his shorts and then his boxer briefs beneath. "I want to touch you, too."

"Sunny..." My name is a raw warning. Or maybe it's a plea.

"You've done so much for me..." I slip a hand inside the fabric. He's thick and hot to the touch. The heavy fullness of him is in complete juxtaposition to the smooth satin of his skin. And the way his lips part and his eyes darken as he watches me empowers me to tug his shorts down just a bit farther and drop to my knees.

"Ah, fuck, Sunny." He gently tangles his fingers in my hair.

Focus locked on his face, I lick along the underside of his cock. He's perfect and beautiful, and the heady look of arousal in his eyes fuels my desire to do this for him even more.

He's already done so much for me.

He's been so good to me when he didn't have to be.

And there's nothing sexier than a man who knows how to be exactly that... *a man*.

I pull back just enough to wet my lips and tease my tongue around his crown before taking him into my mouth. He's big, and I'm out of practice, so I take my time, learning his body and letting myself acclimate. In return, he's patient and his hands in my hair are gentle.

"That's so fucking sexy," he murmurs as he watches my

every move. The way I take a little more of him with every bob. The way I fist the base of his shaft and work my hand in tandem with my mouth. "I didn't think you could get any prettier, but you're absolutely stunning with my dick in your mouth."

Excitement flutters in my stomach and warm arousal spreads through my body like a slow burning wildfire. Encouraged by his praise, I open wide and take him as deep as I can until he hits the back of my throat and I gag.

Instinct tells me I should be embarrassed, but I'm not. Not with this man. He's already figured out so many of my weaknesses and he's never once made me feel ashamed. This is no different.

So I do it again and again, until I can take all of him, and until his hips begin to pulse in time with my mouth.

"Ah, shit, that's good." His hands fist in my hair as he bares his teeth in a hiss. "You like sucking my cock, Sunny?"

I nod eagerly around him despite my watering eyes. I don't just like it; I *love* it. And my drenched panties are proof.

I've never enjoyed giving head before. In fact, I despised it because it was always obligatory and never reciprocated. But this is different. This *man* is different, and right now, I want to give him just a little bit of the relief he's given me.

He runs his knuckles along my cheekbone. "Relax for me, baby. Let me fuck that pretty mouth of yours."

Jesus. If he keeps talking like that, I might come without laying a single hand on myself.

"That's it." He curls a hand around my throat as he strokes in gently but intently, giving me a little more of himself with every thrust. "Look how good you swallow me."

Oh my god. *Oh. My. God.*

"I'm not gonna last long," he warns. "Not when you look like this. If you don't want to taste me, Sunny, you better let me—"

I curl a hand around his balls the second he hits the back of my throat and I swallow. I have no idea what I'm doing, but it must be right, because his legs begin to shake and the sexiest, most guttural groan rolls up from his chest.

"*Fuccck.*" He pulls back and pushes in again, and I swallow him down a second time, tears streaming down my cheeks.

Once, twice, three times more, he thrusts, and when he thickens on my tongue and tries to push me away, I hold on tight.

"Ah, shit. *Ahhh.*" He comes hard with his head thrown back, the tendons in his neck and the muscles in his arms and torso twitching.

I barely taste his release before swallowing it down and then quickly pulling back for breath. My chest heaves and my pussy aches, but I have no intention of doing anything about that. This was about him.

"Holy shit," he pants, his hazy gaze falling on mine as I wipe my tears and smile up at him.

"You good?"

He laughs devilishly, tugs up his shorts, and hauls me up to my feet, his big arms wrapping me up tight. "I'm so fucking good. Thank you for that."

What am I supposed to say to that? You're welcome? Ha. No way. So, I say nothing at all, and just enjoy being close to him like this. His proximity calms something in me and makes me feel safe. His presence in my life has filled a loneliness I hadn't fully acknowledged, either. It's not just him and me.

It's *us*.

Us.

It's a simple word. Just a single syllable. But it holds so much potential and so much promise. A promise I didn't realize I even wanted or needed anymore. A side effect, I suppose, of living in an essentially loveless marriage for as long as I did.

He pulls back and regards me for a beat, his eyes darting back and forth between mine. "What's wrong?"

"Nothing." I smile up at him. "I just... I think part of me gave up on ever feeling like this again. So, moments like this? They're so surreal sometimes."

His jaw tightens and understanding sets into his gaze. "I hate that you felt that way."

So do I. But it's how things were, and a small voice in the back of my head warns me to be careful now. I've enjoyed having Justin in my corner, but there's no guarantee it will last.

As much as I want this, I have to be real with myself, too.

TWENTY-FOUR

JINX

"So you can cook." Rachel smiles as she sets her napkin beside her empty plate and sits back in the chair, looking satisfied. "And well, too."

I fork up the last bite of beef tips on my own plate and laugh off the compliment. "I wouldn't say that, but I do know how to follow directions."

She tilts her head. "Directions?"

I set my fork down and wipe my mouth. "I found a recipe online."

Her brows rise. "Oh my god. Could you be any cuter?"

The laugh that rolls in my chest this time is far less humble. "I'm going to pretend you didn't just stereotype me."

"I'm sorry." Her cheeks go a little pink. "I didn't mean to offend you."

"I'm not offended, babe. I'm just sorry that your experience with men has shown us to be incapable of doing something as simple as looking up a recipe, following instructions, and preparing a meal for the woman we care about. It's not rocket science."

She clears her throat and reaches for her glass of water. "Wow."

I study her for a beat, hit with a flurry of nerves. What's going on in that head of hers? It didn't take me long to figure out that her marriage wasn't much of a marriage at all. Instead of a partnership, she was mothering three people rather than two. But until this moment, I didn't realize just how deprived of the simple things she's truly been.

She swallows audibly and bows her head just a little, tentative. "Is that how you feel?"

I dip my chin. "I do."

"You care about me?"

Ah. That's the part she's hung up on, huh?

"If you haven't figured that out yet, then I'm not doing a very good job of showing it."

A flush creeps up her neck and into her cheeks. "It's not that."

I reach across the table and take her hand. "What is it, then?"

She watches me for a moment, her eyes full of fear and hope, before she pulls in a breath and lets it out carefully. "I just didn't expect any of this."

"If it's too much..."

"It isn't. I'm just... a little afraid. You know?"

I nod, my damn heart aching for her. "I understand. And I'm going to do everything in my power to ease that fear. Because I do care about you. And I don't want you to ever doubt my intentions."

"And those are what, exactly?"

"To show you that I see you. And I get you. And that I

think you're an amazing, selfless woman who deserves to have someone in her corner."

She tilts her head, sweet emotion in her eyes. "Where did you come from? Because I swear you swept into my life one night and never left."

I chuckle. "Is that your way of telling me I'm being a pain in your ass?"

"No." She lets out a teasing scoff. "I'm trying to tell you that I see you, too."

For a silent moment, we regard each other, so much passing between us without words. It's unlike anything I've ever experienced, this deeper level of comfort and connection that feels so damn right.

"Speaking of seeing things..." I tip my head toward the living room and the homework on the coffee table. "You want to tell me what that's all about?"

Her eyes widen briefly. Then she sighs, her shoulders sinking just a little. "You saw all that, huh?"

I nod.

"It was a spur-of-the-moment decision. To apply, I mean. I didn't expect to hear back until the fall, but the acceptance came in just a couple of weeks. I took that as a sign."

I can't keep from grinning. "Hell yeah, babe. I didn't mean to snoop, but I saw something about principalship. Is that what you want? To be a principal?"

"Mm-hmm. Or maybe even a school administrator. I'd probably have to get my MBA, too, but—"

"Do it." I squeeze her hand. "If that's what you want, do it."

She gives a nervous laugh. "Not sure my bank account could handle it. In fact, this degree may very well do me in."

"Okay, so what do we need to do to get ready for that?

To make it happen?"

She blinks once, then again, like the question caught her off guard, then she opens her mouth to answer, only to shut it again.

"What's that look for?"

She tips her head and wets her lips. "What do you mean *we*?"

God, she's cute.

"Maybe I haven't made it clear..." I smooth my thumb over her skin. "But I'm not going anywhere. You can take whatever time and space you need to get through the divorce and what comes next, but I'm here. In whatever capacity you need me to be."

With a sharp breath in, she stands, then she rounds the table and throws her arms around me, pressing the longest kiss into my hair.

"How am I so lucky?" she asks, her voice filled with emotion. "How did the universe know that you're exactly what I need in my life?"

I shift in the chair, wrap my arms around her, and pull her close. She cups my stubbled jaw, and as I look up at her, I wonder the same damn thing.

"The feeling is mutual, babe. So let's just go with it and see where it leads."

"HOW ARE you feeling about the meeting with Jesse next week?" Rachel asks a couple of hours later, as we're snuggled up on the couch, watching a home renovation show and sharing our disgust at how overpriced everything is.

"Pretty good, thanks to your suggestions for the business plan. Just have to print everything out for Monday."

"What do you think he's going to say?" She turns her face so her forehead is pressed into my neck and draws lazy patterns on my chest with her fingers.

"Honestly, I can't decide whether he'll love it or hate it. Right now, I'd say we're leaning a little more toward him hating it."

She hums. "Because you stood up for yourself and told him how you felt about him making that call for you?"

"That and because there's a good chance he'll want to keep the company to himself." I don't want to believe that's true, but it's a possibility I have to be prepared for.

"Hmm." She continues drawing circles on my chest, soothing me with her touch. "I don't think that's the case. He's too family-oriented for that."

"That's just it. He could want EE for his family only."

She shakes her head. "No. Your dad wouldn't approve of that."

I chuckle. "Do you even know my dad?"

"Sure, I do. He plays cribbage with my dad."

"Okay, so..."

"I get the impression that he's a traditional kind of guy. Just like you and Jesse. I don't think he'll shut you out."

With a sigh, I settle deeper against the cushions. "I guess we'll see."

She presses a kiss to my jaw but pulls back quickly when her phone pings with a notification on the coffee table. She leans forward to pick it up and frowns.

"Everything okay?"

She studies the device for another moment before clicking it off and setting it aside. "Uh, yeah. It's just..." She shoves a hand through her hair. "The coworker that's figured out I'm in school... he asked if I wanted to get together this week to talk about our classes."

"Ah." My gut tightens possessively and, more than likely, unnecessarily. "For coffee or something?"

She shakes her head and scrapes her teeth over her bottom lip. "He asked me to have dinner with him."

What the fuck? She's not even divorced yet.

Says the guy she blew tonight and got off with last night.

Shit.

"That's..." I rub a hand around the back of my neck and fight the tension coiling my muscles. "That's great."

"What?" She laughs. "Another guy asking me out is great?"

"For you, yes." Me, not so much.

Her mouth drops open. "I'm sorry, but I thought—"

"That we're a thing?" I nod, keeping my breathing steady. "But you just told me that you haven't dated much."

"I haven't dated at all."

"Exactly. And that's why you should have dinner with this guy."

She stares at me like I've lost my mind, and maybe I have. But it's the right thing to do.

I clear my throat and lock eyes with her. "You should see what else is out there. Live a little."

At the end of the day, I want her to know for sure that it's me she really wants. Everything I've done for her and with her... it's been for *her*. I can't hold her back now.

"I doubt he's anywhere near as funny as I am. Or as good of a kisser." It's a pathetic attempt to lighten the mood, but I'm out of my element here.

She squeezes my hand and gives me a look that almost resembles a smile. "I don't like him. I already know that much."

I shrug. "So you'd say no even if I weren't in your life?"

She pauses long enough to give away her answer. He may not be Mr. Right, but she'd say yes, even if out of curiosity.

"Go on the date, Sunny. If it doesn't work out, I'll be here." I'll hate every second of watching and waiting, but I set myself up for this.

"But what if—" She ducks her head, hiding behind the curtain of her hair.

"What if what, Sunny?"

I know what she's thinking, and I know she doesn't want to say it out loud. She doesn't want to hurt me.

Tangling my fingers with hers, I give her hand a squeeze. "Sometimes we don't know what we really want until we try a few things out. It's okay. I'm a big boy. I understand that."

"What if I have fun?"

I laugh, even as my chest constricts. "That's the point, isn't it?"

"But—"

"But nothing." I smile, even though it fucking hurts. "You haven't done this kind of thing before. Not as an adult, anyway. And the chances..." I break off and swallow hard. Fuck, I don't want to say it, even though it's the truth. "The chances of you finding the right guy straight out of the gate aren't likely, though I know I'm one hell of a catch."

She laughs softly, sadly.

"If it turns out you want to be with someone else more, then so be it. I'll be your friend. That's not going to change."

As much as I want to be her endgame, she was right earlier. I dropped into her life and made myself at home. Maybe it's time I take a step back and let my sunflower bloom.

TWENTY-FIVE

RACHEL

It's been years since I've put my sneakers on for a run, but after last night's rain, the temperature is cool. I crave the fresh air in my lungs just as badly as my muscles crave the burn.

It's all Justin's fault. Things between us have heated up so fast and yet not fast enough at the same time. We need to go slow and not get ahead of ourselves, but he is a hard man to resist. My body hated me for letting him leave last night, but it was for the best, no matter how hard my reawakened libido tried to convince me otherwise.

So a run will have to do. For now.

Earbuds in place, I stretch in the driveway, then take off at a light jog. By the time I turn onto the last street on the north side of town, I've hit my stride, and it feels damn good.

As I approach the trailhead near one of the smaller lakes in town, I make a last-minute decision to run the three-mile loop. I may very well regret it, but pushing myself is empowering, too.

I've learned a lot about myself since Craig and I separated, and it took far too long to realize that I was mistaking unhappiness for weakness. All that time, I remained silent when I should have been speaking up for myself. Especially when Craig walked away, and I was left feeling stupid for pretending for so long. In reality, it took a lot of strength to stick it out, too. My kids have always been my number one priority, and so much of what I did—so much of what I set aside—was for them. There's nothing wrong with that. It's what mothers do.

The weakness came in when I set myself aside for Craig, too. Not only did he know I was doing it, but he took advantage of it. The more I gave, the more he took. And when I was maxed out and had nothing left to give, he made me feel like a failure. Like nothing I did was enough. And if I fell short—figuratively and literally, like I did the day I brought donuts to his work—he took it personally, as if I was an embarrassment to him.

From where I am today, I can see that he was actually so unhappy with himself that he projected that disappointment onto me. And I took it. I carried it around because I thought it was my responsibility as his wife and his partner. Only, he had stopped being my partner years ago. He was merely a bystander in our life, letting me shoulder the burden of damn near everything while believing himself above me because he was bringing home a paycheck.

While I run, I replay argument after argument we had over the years. So many of the times I'd tell him that I needed more, only for him to make me second-guess myself. He knew what to say or how to look at me to make me wonder if I was truly the problem.

When I finally shut down and put up my walls instead of letting him get to me, he moved on to someone new. I have to wonder if he chose Cady because he already knew he could manipulate her.

With my chest aching and my thighs burning, I round the last corner on the trail and head back into town. Aiden, Justin's brother, and Olivia Bishop pass by in Aiden's truck, and I lift a hand in greeting.

I've never understood how an honorable, respectful man like Aiden could be so close to someone like Craig. They went to high school together, sure, and Craig works for Aiden's brother. But in every way, they're vastly different. Aiden is the quieter, more reserved of the Enders brothers, so maybe his hardened exterior allows him to put up with more crap, too. Jesse is probably somewhere in the middle, and then there's Justin, who has no tolerance for Craig's crap at all.

Maybe that's part of the reason we get along so well.

As I round the corner onto my street, Craig's truck comes into view. It's parked in the driveway, but it's empty.

What the heck? He isn't supposed to bring the kids home until dinnertime.

Unless he saw Jinx's truck here last night...

My stomach sinks as I continue toward the house.

I knew it would happen sooner or later, but why today? I was having such a good morning.

My feet pound against the porch steps at a quick pace, and as I pull open the screen door, I take my phone from the pocket in my leggings to turn off my music.

That's when I see the missed calls and texts. Craig's dad woke up with a stomach bug, and he thought he'd bring the kids back before they got sick, too.

"Good to know you're all right," Craig grumbles from

the kitchen, where he's made himself at home with a cup of coffee. "I was about to call Aiden and report you missing."

I roll my eyes and kick off my sneakers. "Oh, please. It's been a half hour since you called."

With a smirk, he gives me a once-over. I'm going to assume the creepy grin is because he's surprised that I've gotten back into exercising and taking care of myself and *not* because he likes what he sees.

"You've lost weight," he says, his eyes lingering a bit too long on my stomach, which he knows I've been self-conscious about since having kids.

"Is that supposed to be a compliment?" I pick up my water bottle with a huff.

He dips his chin. "You're looking good, Ray."

"Shut up, Craig." I intentionally bump his arm on my way to the sink to refill the bottle. "Where are the kids?"

"Their rooms. Emma has a headache, and Mason's pissed at me."

Color me surprised. Mason hasn't been happy with his dad in months.

Shutting off the tap, I turn and lean against the counter. "What happened?"

He runs a hand around the back of his neck and casually strides to the other side of the kitchen island. "We had a talk this weekend," he says, his attention fixed on his coffee. "Disagreed on pretty much everything."

"Like?"

He lifts a shoulder. "Nothing important."

"It's clearly important to Mason if he's upset with you."

With an irritated glare, he claims a stool.

Go ahead. Make yourself at home.

"We discussed spending more time together, and he more or less told me he's not interested."

Ouch. That hits me right in the heart. But did he honestly expect a different reaction? He's made it clear since he left that the kids aren't his number one priority. Sure, he shows up for his visitations like he's supposed to, and he makes it to most of their games. But he's still living with his parents, so they're rarely alone. And the time they could spend together, just the three of them, is usually shared with Cady.

"No comment?" he snipes.

"You need to find your own place to live." It's not what he wants to hear, I'm sure, but I'm done holding back with him. He held *me* back for long enough.

"For fuck's sake." He folds his arms on top of the island and glances away. "Everyone is so damn concerned about where I'm living."

I lift a hand. "The judge is going to ask you next month, too." He more or less told Craig it was a must. It isn't the Perrys' job to help their adult son raise his kids.

"I fucking know that, okay?"

Then do something about it.

"Anyway, about Mason..." I steer us back on course. "He's been practically begging for time since you moved out, and you've ignored him over and over again. Of course he's upset."

"Why do you think I wanted to have that conversation?" His tone starts out defensive, but he tamps it down. "I just want to make this right."

"I understand that, but you're six months too late." I tilt my head. "The world isn't going to wait while you figure things out. Especially not a hormonal kid who's dealing with his own issues."

He nods and laces his fingers on the countertop. "I

know. Doesn't help that Jinx has been spending so much fucking time with him, either."

Really? And to think I almost believed he was remorseful.

I successfully bite back a scoff and cross my arms over my chest, ready to level with him. "You may not like it, but it probably does help."

He recoils immediately. "Fuck that. And what the hell is going on between you and Enders, anyway?"

Flashbacks from yesterday and the night before race through my mind, and I do my best not to react. I don't want to lie about seeing Justin, but I would like to wrap my head around what's happening between us before I share it with anyone. Especially my soon-to-be ex-husband.

"Can we please not do this?"

"We've danced around this for long enough, don't you think? If there's something going on, just tell me."

"I think it's time for you to go." I hold my chin high. "I need to check on the kids anyway."

His brow furrows, but not in anger. No, the look on his face is one of surprise. Maybe a little fear, too. The man didn't think I'd move on, did he? He really thought I'd sulk and pine for him forever.

God, I was an idiot.

I close my eyes to shut it all out. I don't want to see his disappointment, and I refuse to feel bad for him. I put him first for far too long already. It's time I protect myself.

"Fine. I'll go." He gets to his feet and picks up the folded Enders Excavating hoodie I set on the island after Justin left it here the day he fixed the washer. "I'm taking this with me."

Heart lurching, I clear my throat. "That's not yours."

He frowns and looks down at the sweatshirt. "Uh, yeah, it is."

"No." I hurry across the room and snatch it away. "It isn't."

His eyes dart back and forth between mine for another moment before it clicks, and his expression hardens. "He's been here."

Swallowing hard, I step back.

"He's been in my fucking house," he grits out, face turning red.

"This isn't your house anymore." Or at least, it won't be in a few weeks.

He scrubs his hands over his face, laughing bitterly. "I can't fucking believe this. He not only moves in on my kid, but now he's moving in on you."

"Please keep your voice down."

The glower he hits me with in response sends chills down my spine. "You're not even going to deny it."

I ball my hands in the sweatshirt. "I don't owe you anything, Craig. You were the one who chose to leave. To end our marriage. And then you moved on."

His nostrils flare and his lip curls, and my heart begins to race.

What is he really upset about? That another man is possibly interested in me? That I'm actually moving on? Or is it that I'm finally being treated the way I deserve?

"He's using you, Ray." He shakes his head. "It's what he does. Look how many years he's been riding Jesse's coattails."

"That isn't true—"

"The hell it isn't!" he roars. "He sees you as a fucking opportunity." He looks me up and down with a sickening smile. "An easy, desperate piece of ass."

I almost laugh. And maybe I would if I weren't also on the verge of tears.

"Get out." I stab a finger toward the door. "Now."

"Mom?" Mason calls from down the hall. A heartbeat later, he appears, looking from me to his father, his expression full of concern and confusion. "What's going on?"

"It's okay, honey." My voice cracks. I hate—hate—that he's witnessing this. I swore I would never put him through this again. "Your dad was just leaving."

Craig makes a disgusted sound and sneers at the hoodie still gripped in my hand. "Keep that shit away from my kids."

I bite my tongue as he storms out, letting the screen door slam behind him.

TWENTY-SIX

JINX

Either Craig thinks I'm pretty, or he's really not happy about me seeing Rachel.

The steam coming out of his ears during our staff meeting hints at the latter, but the last time someone stared at me as intently as he has this morning, she ended up asking for my number.

"All right." Jesse slaps his denim-clad thighs and gets to his feet. "Have a good week, boys. Be safe and get your vacation requests in ASAP if you plan on taking any extra time off around Labor Day."

"You already got my request, right, Hayden?" Craig asks as the other guys shuffle out.

"Yep," she confirms as she pulls up the calendar on her laptop. "The whole week, right?"

He nods, then glances my way like he wants to come over and say something. Maybe even kick my ass. But Jesse steps in front of him and dives into a conversation about their new excavating job and all the shit they have to get done this week.

"So," Hayden says in a hushed voice, sidling up beside me, "you ready to do this?"

My chest may be a little tight, but I give her an easy nod and hold up the folders I prepared last night. "Ready as I'm ever gonna be."

"I'm excited for you." She grins, her eyes dancing. "And just so you know, I haven't told Jesse anything. This is all yours."

I give a short laugh. "Thanks, Hay. I appreciate that."

She gives my arm a reassuring squeeze just as Jesse clears his throat.

"You still need to talk to me, Jinx?"

Hayden and I share one last private glance before I set my shoulders and turn my attention to my brother.

"Yep. You ready now or…?"

He holds up his coffee mug. "Just let me grab a refill."

Two minutes later, we're seated in the office he shares with Hayden. Thunder rolls in the distance, and the breeze coming in through the open window smells like rain. The storm isn't supposed to start until this afternoon, so its early arrival feels ominous. I'm about to start shit in here, and Mother Nature is about to do so outside.

"So, what are we doing here?" With a deep exhale, Jesse leans back in his chair. "Hayden won't tell me a damn thing, and given the last conversation you and I had, I'm a little nervous."

Jesse nervous? He's usually the calm and collected one, but today, I'm wearing that hat. Maybe it's because I did my fair share of stewing and stressing yesterday. Though most of mine was about Rachel and her date.

Nope, dude. Don't go there right now.

I tilt my head to one side, then the other, shoving the thought away, and pull in a breath. "First things first," I start. "I'd appreciate if you'd hear me out before you get pissed off."

He lifts a brow. "I'm gonna be pissed? Thanks for the warning."

Fucking guy. "Second thing. This is gonna seem like it's coming out of left field, but I've been thinking about it for a while."

He folds his hands over his stomach and listens.

"In fact, I probably should have brought this up a long time ago. The truth is, I was stubborn. And a little scared."

He frowns, his brow pulled low. "Scared?"

I nod. Might as well get this part out of the way. "Yeah, man. I look up to you, and I sure as hell don't want to let you down."

He sits forward quickly and rests his elbows on the desk. "What? Why would you let me down?"

I lift a hand. "Because that's what I've always done?"

"What are you talking about?" His frown has deepened into a full-on scowl now.

"It's what I've done since I was a kid. Some of it comes with the territory. Me being a younger brother, especially behind guys like you and Aiden. Regardless, you've made it plenty clear over the years that you think I'm a fuck-up."

He laughs defensively and roughs a hand down his face. "Okay. It's a good thing you warned me about getting pissed. Let's move on before I do just that."

We need to dive deeper into that topic sooner or later, but for now, he's right.

I take another deep breath and tamp down on the nerves skittering through me. "You know I've been working a lot of hours. In the beginning, I did it because we were getting our feet wet here, and the profit margin on the landscaping side of things was slim. We were trying to bump up the residential piece since Dad hadn't done much with it. So I did what I had to do to build our client list and save money."

With a roll of my shoulders, I assess my brother. The frown is gone now, but his expression is still serious.

"When things started to pick up and I couldn't keep up on my own, we brought on Connor. And for a couple years after that, he and I handled things just fine. Again, I was putting in more time than I clocked because this is our family business. It's never been about a paycheck to me.

"These past two years have been fucking amazing." I pull my ball cap off and rake my fingers through my hair, then settle the hat on my head again. "I never imagined we'd find as much work as we have. I don't want to toot my own horn, but I think a lot of the business we have is because I've gone the extra mile where I didn't have to. Word of mouth travels fast, and I've busted my ass to live up to the standard I've established for us."

He narrows his eyes, still listening, and laces his fingers on top of his desk.

"Hayden put together a spreadsheet with the official numbers, but I've been working on something for a couple of months now, too." I slide the folder I put together for him across the desk. "I've kept records for the past several years. Everything I turned into you, I kept a copy for myself as well. It's not that I didn't think you were doing the right thing with the information, but because I wanted to keep track of things, too."

Silently, he opens the folder and flips through the pages.

"At first, I did it to get a feel for things without the pressure of actually having to do them."

He straightens the papers and glances up.

"And then I realized that I actually enjoy that side of the things."

"The numbers?"

"The management. The organization. And yes, I suppose the analysis." I swallow past the lump in my throat, because this is the part where he might really get angry. "At some point, I started to resent you for not offering me another partner opportunity," I admit.

He opens his mouth, but I hold up a hand.

"I know that's not fair. I told you I wasn't interested, and it's only been six years. I really have worked as hard as I have because I love it. But part of me hoped you'd see it, too."

He closes the folder and tips his head, and even though I don't want his sympathy or to be seen as weak, I look him in the eye, unwavering.

"I've always wanted your respect. And I hoped you'd eventually look at me and not see me as the kid who used to screw up all the time, but as a man. As an equal."

"Jinx..." He blows out a breath and looks up at the ceiling, his throat working as he swallows. "I do respect you, man."

"To a certain extent, maybe. You've given me a lot of space to do my own thing with the landscaping part of EE. But I've outgrown the leash. And frankly, I don't want to do things the way we've been doing them anymore."

Expression unreadable, he regards me for a beat. "You want to be partner now."

I dip my chin and clasp my hands to keep them steady. "Yeah. I do. It doesn't have to be fifty-fifty. I know your work is the primary focus of the business. But mine isn't anything to sneeze at anymore, and if we expand like I want to, it's only going to keep growing."

He drums his fingers on the desk and hums, thoughtful. "What are you thinking?"

"I don't know. I couldn't even begin to compare and do the math because I haven't seen the numbers for your side of things, but honestly, it doesn't matter. I just want a bigger stake in this. It's our fucking legacy, man, and it's just as important to me as it is to you."

"Can you give me some time to look at things? If you've already talked to Hayden, then I'm sure she's got something started."

I nod. "Take some time. Talk it over with her. I just want to open the door and see what's feasible."

He rocks back in the chair and scrubs his hands over his face. "To tell you the truth, I was thinking about broaching the subject again before she came on board, because this shit is too much for one person to handle."

"I wish you would have come to me. Not just because of my personal interest in things, but because, at the end of the day, I'm your brother."

He nods slowly, his eyes fixed on me intently. "I know, man. And someday, we should have a heart-to-heart about this fuck-up thing you mentioned."

I chuckle, even as my stomach twists. "Yeah, probably. But I'm gonna need a few beers for that conversation."

He grins. "I have a feeling I will, too. Do we need to invite Aiden?"

"Probably. Might as well drag Amelia into it, too."

He groans and tosses his head back, his chair squeaking beneath him. "Come on, man. She really is a pain in my ass."

"Yep, but we're stuck with her."

"She's a good babysitter, at least." Jesse sighs.

"And she can cook."

"Yeah, but she has horrible taste in men."

I laugh. "You're right about that."

Scowling, he shakes his head. "The next one has to be better than that mustache guy."

"We can only hope."

Rachel: Dinner with Reese is Friday night.

HER TEXT CAME over an hour ago, and I've spent every minute since wondering if I fucked up by telling her to go.

In my head, I know I didn't. But in my heart? Fucking hell. I don't want another man to even look at her, let alone get close enough to breathe the same air.

But it's the right thing to do. And all I can do in the meantime is keep showing her who I am. And maybe go to church and pray for once.

"Hey, Jinx." Connor waves to get my attention. We've been installing paving stones for the Carlisles' backyard project all day, and it's well past time for lunch.

"Break time?"

"Yeah. I'm meeting my brother in town for a burger. Might be a little longer than usual."

"No problem. Take your time." I plant my hands on my hips and survey what we've done so far. "I'm gonna take a break myself, but I'll be here."

"Thanks, man." Jug of water in hand, he heads for his truck.

I wipe the sweat from my forehead and get back to work

while I contemplate how to respond to Rachel and consider what comes next.

Should I stay away this week? It'd be hard to see her anyway, with the kids at home. That's another thing that's been bugging me. I don't like feeling like we're sneaking, especially when it comes to Mason. He and I have built up a rapport, and I'd hate to screw that up. But telling them now seems pointless if she's going to date other people.

Other people.

Fucking hell, I should have thought this through before I suggested it. How am I going to keep my shit together while she does this? And what if it blows up in my face?

When I've finished the section of pavers, I stand and stretch. Then I head to my truck, unstrapping my knee pads as I go, and climb behind the wheel. I leave the door open to keep the air moving, even if it's thick. The rain has held off, but the gray clouds overhead promise a storm is brewing.

After several gulps of water, I snag a granola bar from my lunchbox and pull out my phone.

Me: You gonna wear that blue dress?

Her reply is almost instant.

Rachel: No way. That's a special dress.

Me: This isn't a special date? It's your first one in how many years?

Rachel: Let's not count. But yes. It's my first date. Officially anyway. You did take me to the sunflower farm, and you fed me a couple of times, too.

Hell yes, I did. And thank god she vetoed the dress,

because I'd go out of my damn mind knowing how good she looks in it.

Me: Don't worry, babe. I'll take you on a real date one of these days, too.

Rachel: I'm already looking forward to it.

Damn. That admission is like a shot to the heart. Let's hope this Reese guy doesn't put a damper on that happening.

Rachel: I'm at my dad's right now. He and Mason are trying to install new boards on the porch. If you hear sirens, it's probably the ambulance because Dad's either cut off a limb or he's given me a heart attack.

I laugh.

Me: Don't die on me before our date, Sunny. And tell your dad I'm happy to help if he needs it. Just holler.

Rachel: I'll let him know. Talk to you later?

Me: *heart eyes emoji*

TWENTY-SEVEN

RACHEL

"Can we please get ice cream?" Emma pleads from the back seat as we pull out of my dad's driveway.

Fortunately, no one hurt themselves during the porch repairs, and Dad had a package of hot dogs in the fridge, so we were all fed.

"I've got some money." Mason digs into his pocket and pulls out a small wad of cash.

Laughing, I shove his hand away. "Put that away. You worked hard for that, and you worked hard with Grandpa today, too. I'll cover the ice cream."

He and Emma give simultaneous whoops, and I hit my blinker as we approach the ice cream shop.

Ten minutes later, we've claimed a table outside and are digging into our sundaes.

"So..." I start, spooning up a bite of hot fudge and vanilla ice cream. "Are you excited for school to start?"

Emma practically bounces in her seat. "So excited.

Tessa says we have a new kid. It's a boy."

Mason rolls his eyes. "What happened to Drake?"

Her cheeks go pink, and she kicks him under the table. "Mind your business, *Mason*."

I hold a hand to my mouth to keep from laughing. "What about you, honey?" I ask Mason.

He shrugs. "I can't wait to get sixth grade over with."

"Why is that?"

"In seventh grade, I can play middle school football." He shoves a spoonful of his treat into his mouth and gives me a *duh* look.

Okay, then.

"Hey, I think that's Jinx." Mason hops to his feet and waves a little wildly.

Sure enough, a familiar white truck pulls up to the stop sign across the road and honks. Then, instead of turning left to head home, he turns right and cranks the truck into the ice cream shop parking lot.

Emma wiggles her way to one side of her bench to make room. "He can sit by me."

Mason scoffs and gives his sister a stereotypical condescending big-brother look. "You don't even know him."

"Yes, I do," she argues and then snaps a bracelet on her wrist. "We're friends."

They are? That's news to me.

Justin hops out from behind the wheel and tucks his hands into the pockets of his jeans, inadvertently showing off a friendship bracelet, as he strolls over.

"Hey, y'all." He flashes a megawatt grin, all white teeth amidst that brown-sugar stubble. His hair is curling around the bottom of his baseball cap, and damn, it affects me far more than it should. "You save me any ice cream?"

"I saved you a seat." Emma pats the space next to her.

He tips his head toward the counter. "Let me go grab something. I'll be right back."

In no time at all, he's back, already licking a chocolate ice cream cone. With a wink at me, he sits sideways beside my little girl, who beams up at him. For a second, I worry that she might be crushing on my man, especially when she leans over and whispers in his ear.

My concerns are assuaged when she straightens, and Justin responds.

"Oh man," he drawls, his brows jumping to his hairline. "What about Blake?"

"It's *Drake*," she corrects him with a dramatic eye roll. "And he didn't even say hi to me when I saw him at the lake the other day."

When the heck have these two been talking? Or did all of this transpire during their run-in at the Kaminskis'?

Justin presses his lips together and gives her a sympathetic look. "Dudes are weird like that, Em. Was he with his friends?"

She nods.

"See, that's how we are. We don't like to let on that we're into a girl until we're sure she's into us. Wait until school starts and see how it goes."

I clear my throat and glare at him. "She's eight."

"I'm almost nine, Mom."

Justin chuckles and gives his cone a long, slow lick, effectively turning my brain to mush.

When he winks over the top of the melting chocolate, my insides liquify, too.

Why must he be so sweet *and* so sexy? And the friendship bracelet... I could kiss him for humoring her like that.

"You got any work for me this weekend?" Mason pipes

up. "I can help in the evenings now, too, since football is done."

Justin nods and wipes his mouth with a napkin. "Yep. Gotta cut the cemetery this weekend. But I'll be working late all week at the Carlisles', so evenings probably won't work."

Mason sighs, his shoulders sagging a fraction. "All right."

"Hey..." I bump my shoulder into his. "Grandpa has plenty for you to do, remember?"

"I know," he says, his eyes downcast. "But I like hanging out with Jinx."

Me, too, kiddo. Me, too.

Justin and I share a secret smile, and then I force myself to look away. They know about my date on Friday night, and I don't want to confuse them by getting caught making heart eyes at Justin, too.

"Could we go to some high school football games this year, Mom?" Mason asks around a bite of his sundae.

"Oh. Um, maybe. I guess we'll have to see what the schedule looks like." And how deep I've buried myself in homework and life.

"Jack is playing this year," he adds.

"Jack?"

"Jack Stroud." Justin wipes a bit of chocolate from his lip. "He works with me. Or he did until practice started."

"Ah. That Jack."

"I can take you, Mase. I plan on going to at least a couple of the games." He flicks his gaze to me. "Assuming it's okay with your mom."

"And your dad. You'll be with him every other Friday."

"What about me?" Emma pouts, dropping her elbows to the table. "I want to go."

Justin chuckles and bumps her gently with his elbow. "I've got plenty of room in my truck. Your mom could even come if she wanted to."

The image of the four of us pulling up to a Friday night football game with nearly all of Cole Creek in attendance comes to mind, and my stomach whirls in immediate anticipation. Anticipation that I promptly tamp down.

Yes, I would love to someday do those kinds of things with him and the kids, but we're not there yet. And he's encouraging me to date other people first. I'd do well to not get ahead of myself.

"We'll see." I smile and take a bite of my ice cream.

Another big truck rumbles past, then makes a quick turn into the parking lot. This one is also familiar, with an Enders Excavating logo in the back window.

Justin lifts a brow as Jesse gets out of the truck and starts our way. The man looks downright pissed off.

"Ah, crap." He takes another lick of his cone and rises from the table with a sigh. "I better deal with this."

"Okay." I give him a small smile as trepidation runs through me. From the look on Jesse's face, whatever's on his mind isn't good. "Thanks for hanging out with us."

He gives me a lopsided grin, and his gaze drops to my lips just long enough to make me squirm.

He may be in trouble, but *phew*.

He's not the only one.

JINX

"ARE you out of your fucking mind?" Jesse stabs a finger toward the table where Rachel and the kids still sit, finishing their ice cream. We're wedged between his truck and mine, thankfully out of view.

"This is what you've been doing?"

I turn away and trek to a trash can to toss my cone. "You talked to Craig, huh?"

"Answer the fucking question, Jinx. Is this what you've been doing?"

I pull in a breath and harness all the patience I possess. "Have I been hanging out with Rachel and the kids? No."

He drops his chin to his chest, seething. "Don't play games with me. You know what I goddamn mean."

I do, but what I don't understand is why it's any of his business.

"I'd rather not do this here."

Him pulling in and storming over like he did is too reminiscent of my old man coming to chew me a new one when I was a kid. I don't need him making a bigger scene when he learns the truth.

"Too fucking bad," he growls. "Craig already told me all I need to know, so I don't need to hear you say it."

"Say what?" I retort, my own temper piquing. I knew he wouldn't be thrilled about me seeing Rachel because it would make things awkward for him at work with Craig. I get that. But he has no right to give me shit about something that's otherwise none of his concern. "That I've been spending time with Rachel? Maybe you do need to hear it from me, because I can guaran-damn-tee that my version is different from Craig's."

Jesse's hands tighten into fists. "She's not even divorced yet. And those kids... fucking hell, Jinx. Those kids have been through enough."

"I know that." Annoyance courses through me, mixing

with hurt. How the hell can he think I haven't thought about that? That I don't care? "We're just friends."

"Right." He laughs bitterly. "Friends with fucking benefits." He shakes his head. "I thought you were smarter than this shit. I thought you'd grown up."

Teeth gritted, I blow out a long breath, working to keep my fury in check. "You couldn't be more off base right now if you tried, man. I think you should take a step back and—"

"No." He closes the distance between us and stabs a finger into my chest. "You sat in my office today and tried to sell yourself as responsible and ready to become a partner. And I believed you, Jinx. I fucking believed you. Then I not only hear about how untrue that is, but I see it with my own eyes."

I turn my head for breathing room and tamp down every instinct to react. But I swear to god, if we weren't in public and Rachel and the kids weren't only a few yards away...

This is the shit he's done all my life. Jumping to conclusions without giving me a chance to explain. Blaming me for shit without knowing the full story. Throwing his fucking weight around because he can.

"I think it's time you stop listening to selfish motherfuckers like Craig Perry." I shove him away. Not hard but enough to tell him I'm not letting him win this one. "And maybe you should get your eyes checked too while you're at it, because what you saw over there?" I point toward the table. "You don't know the first thing about it."

"Then tell me," he snaps.

"Too fucking late." He doesn't get to come screaming in and throwing accusations around, then expect me to explain myself. "You want to talk man to man? Fine. But we're not doing it like this."

For a second, I consider getting in my truck and leaving. But I won't let him get to me.

I walk back to Rachel and the kids and hope he takes it for what it is.

Fuck you, Jesse.

TWENTY-EIGHT

RACHEL

To find a prince, you've gotta kiss some toads.

In my case, to be sure the prince I've found is the real deal, I've gotta humor a few imposters.

Ugh.

I tug at the too-high collar of my sleeveless top and do a couple of squats to stretch out my jeans. My feet despise the heels I'm wearing, and my bra is digging into my left boob.

I haven't even left my bedroom, and I'm already uncomfortable. Put a margarita and some nachos in me, and I'll be fantasizing about my pj's before the date is halfway over.

This does not bode well for poor Reese. Though, let's be honest, he never stood a chance.

"You can do this," I tell my reflection. "All you have to do is chat about your classes and make small talk about teaching." With a long breath out, I fuss with my hair in the mirror. At least that looks good, thanks to Crystal insisting she curl it before she took the kids for a few hours.

A notification pops up on my phone, and in response,

my stomach twists into a knot.

Reese: On my way. See you in a few.

Too late to back out now.

Me: I'll be here!

No *can't wait!* or *I'm so excited!*

In reality, I'm kind of excited, but not for any of the reasons Reese would probably like me to be. I'm looking forward to getting out of the house on a Friday night, and I've been dreaming about raspberry margaritas since he asked if I liked Mexican food. And maybe a small part of me is eager to go on a date. To see if it's anything like I remember. To simply experience it again.

If only Justin were the one about to knock at my door. I love spending time with him, and I love the way he makes me smile so much that my cheeks hurt. That he gets me without me having to explain myself. And that, with just a simple touch, he can set my body on fire.

That's not going to happen with Reese. I've worked with him for years, and not once has he made me laugh like Justin does. He's never made me blush, either.

Okay, Rachel. Get it together. The last thing you need is to call your date the wrong name tonight.

At the sound of the doorbell, I grab my purse from the dresser and take one last look in the mirror.

Date-night me looks pretty good, I'll give myself that.

Now to make the most of tonight... and get it over with at the same time. The sooner I humor these imposters, the sooner I can claim my real prince. Or as I like to think of him...

My knight in that shiny white truck.

JINX

THE GUY who thought Rachel going on a date with another man was a good idea is the dumbest son of a bitch on the planet. Masochistic, even. It's only been two hours, and I'm already three beers in and pacing a damn groove in my living room floor.

Is she having fun? Is she laughing? Blushing? Did he bring her flowers?

I swear to god if he kisses her, I'll lose my shit.

She'd have to disclose the details for that to happen, and I hope like hell she doesn't. I really don't want to know. Reese whatever-the-fuck-his-last-name-is doesn't want me to know either, I guarantee that.

A series of hard knocks sounds on the front door, and before I can take a single step that way, Aiden lets himself in.

"Break and enter often?" I snarl.

"Shut the hell up," he mutters as he closes the door behind him. When he looks my way, he recoils. "What the fuck is wrong with you? You look like shit." His gaze sweeps to the empty beer bottles on the table and the one in my hand. "Are you drunk?"

"I've had three beers, asshole."

He continues to scrutinize me, brow furrowed. "Is this about Jesse?"

Great. He's already heard, which means Jesse's been running his damn mouth.

"Or is it about Rachel?"

The mere mention of her name makes my already pounding heart quicken and the knot in my stomach tighten. "Why the hell are you here?"

"Holy shit." My brother lets out a deep exhale and rakes a hand through his hair. "I was hoping Jesse had it all wrong, but he doesn't, does he?"

And there's my answer.

"He doesn't know the first fucking thing," I growl. "And let me guess, you're here to make assumptions, too."

He holds up his hands in defense. "Actually, I'm not." He takes a tentative seat in one of the living room chairs, hands still held out in front of him like he expects me to pounce.

Smart, since I could really use a good knock-down drag-out right now, and he's as good a target as any.

In a tone so calm it only makes me want to take my anger out on him more, he says, "Why don't you take a seat and tell me what's going on?"

Focus locked on him, I shift my jaw from side to side. I have no interest in discussing this with anyone. Especially right now, while the woman I care about is out with someone else. Then again, maybe talking it out will keep me from doing something stupid.

Dropping onto the couch, I set the beer aside and scrub my hands over my face. "What did Jesse tell you?"

"That you're sleeping with Rachel."

"That motherfucker." I shake my head and let out a begrudged laugh. "Of course he'd jump to that conclusion."

"So you're not?"

"No, I'm not," I snap. "But am I seeing her? Yes. Sort of. It's fucking complicated."

He lifts a brow. "And here I've been worried about her getting hurt. Maybe it's you I should be concerned about."

I huff out a breath, willing the tension in every one of my muscles to ease. "What?"

"I'm a detective, Jinx. Did you really think I wouldn't figure out that you're seeing her? I knew a month ago."

What the hell?

He shrugs. "I kept my mouth shut because it wasn't my business. That, and I didn't want to get in the middle of you and Craig."

"Fuck him," I spit out. "How the hell are you even friends with that prick?"

"Same way you're still friends with Ty." He shrugs and leans back. "We go back a long way. Doesn't mean I support everything he does. Hell, doesn't even mean I like him most of the time."

"Sure doesn't look that way. He's been sleeping on your couch on and off for the past six months."

He lifts a hand. "I wasn't there most of the time. And I kicked him out the second Olivia started staying with me."

He should've let the asshole sleep in his truck for pulling the shit he did with Rachel.

But then again, if he hadn't left her, she wouldn't be in my life like she is.

She wouldn't be mine.

"What's got you so worked up tonight? Did Jesse say something else?"

"Jesse's avoided me for four damn days. If he's talking shit, it ain't to me."

Aiden leans forward, elbows on his knees. "Then tell me what's going on, man. I'm too fucking tired to try my hand at reading your mind."

I roll my shoulders, still fighting the tension, but the movement only makes it worse. "You don't need to mediate, man. You've got your own shit to deal with." Not all that long ago, he was fighting demons from Olivia's past. His blood pressure probably still hasn't recovered.

"My family *is* my shit," he retorts. "And this may come as a surprise to you, but I'm actually on your side here."

That grabs my attention and does something funny to my chest.

"Jesse's out of line."

Well, cover me in sprinkles and call me a fucking donut.

"Rachel may have put up with Craig for too damn long, but she's not stupid. She's sure as hell not going to let another man use her."

My blood boils at just the thought of her being used. And it pisses me off that my own brother thinks I'd be capable of doing that kind of shit. I'd go toe to toe with any motherfucker who tried to take advantage of her. Hell, I did that night in the pub.

"I've never seen you this wrapped up in a woman before." Aiden gives a small smile. "And the way you're invested in her kids?" He whistles and leaves it at that.

No shit. Because I've never felt this way.

Rachel is nothing like any woman I've ever been interested in. She knows what she wants in life. She's settled and stable—even in the midst of a divorce—and her quiet strength blows my damn mind.

As grateful as she's been for my help, she doesn't need me. She never has. That woman is a badass. Damn, I hope she realizes it someday.

"Man, if you don't talk to me, then I can't defend you," Aiden prods.

"Look," I say, scratching at an invisible spot on my jeans. "I appreciate the thought, but I don't need you to defend me. And Jesse can kiss my ass if he truly believes I'd ever do Rachel dirty like that."

Lips pressed together, he considers me for a beat. "This is serious, then."

I swallow hard and glance away, chest aching at the thought. "I don't know. I really friggin' like her, but I don't want to be her rebound."

"Ah. Now we're getting somewhere."

"Yeah." I grab my beer and take a swig. "I tried not to let this happen, but here we fucking are."

He nods, thoughtful. "These things tend to take on a life of their own. They don't care about our plans."

I snort. "You would not have said that a few months ago." Before Olivia came back into his life, he was so cynical it was sickening.

He smirks. "Happens to the best of us, man."

I tap the beer bottle against my knee. "I'm still trying my damnedest to do this right. It might kill me, but I'm trying."

"Is that what this is?" He nods at the empty beer bottles.

Jaw clenched, I crane my head from side to side until my neck cracks. "She's on a date right now."

"Are you serious?" He stiffens and blinks at me, his mouth slack. "With who?"

"Some guy she works with. She didn't want to go, but I told her she should."

He barks out a disbelieving laugh. Clearly, he thinks I'm an idiot. And I'm not sure he's wrong.

"She hasn't dated much, and I don't want her to make the same mistakes she made with Craig all over again."

He rubs a hand around his neck, still chuckling. "Wow."

"Yeah, I know."

"So, what? You're just gonna drink yourself to death while she spreads her wings?"

I huff and take another pull of my beer. "What else am I going to do?"

"How long do you expect this to take? A few months? A year?"

My gut churns at the thought of standing on the sidelines for even a few weeks. "I don't know. However long it takes, I guess."

"You know it doesn't matter, right?"

I flick my focus back to him, waiting for him to elaborate.

"If it's right, it's right. If it's not, it's not. The only way you're gonna know that for sure is by giving it a shot. Not by watching her try on other dudes."

Try on? Like she *tried me on* in her laundry room? The thought of her getting anywhere near another guy's dick makes me want to smash something. *Several* fucking things, in fact.

I know she wouldn't. It's not the kind of woman she is. But I know too much about her past—or lack of one—to deny that she needs to explore a little. To see what else is out there. Who else is out there. Even if that means more than just dating.

Yeah, I want her for myself, but more than anything, I want her to be happy. After giving up so much of herself to be a mom and a wife, she deserves it and so much more.

"She needs to do this." I tip back the last of my beer, then run my wrist across my mouth. "I don't like it, but it's the way it's gotta be."

Aiden sighs and rubs at his forehead. "I get that. You've got balls for encouraging her to do it, knowing it might blow up in your face, but I get it."

"I can't promise I won't go apeshit at some point." This is only night one—and with a guy she claims is harmless—and I'm close to going out of my damn mind.

He gives a half laugh. "Yeah, well, you haven't yet. I'd

call that a success." He waves a hand at the empty beer bottles. "You're playing with fire by getting drunk and loosening up your resolve, but lucky for you, I came over."

"I wouldn't call you nosing into my business *lucky*."

He grins. "Don't get pissy. I'm on your side here, remember?"

I grunt.

"I'm glad to hear you're not just fucking around with Rachel. I don't mean in the literal sense because that's not my business." His face twists like the idea of me having sex makes him want to puke.

Serves the asshole right.

"As long as you're treating her right, and you're doing this because you genuinely care about her, then you've got my support."

Well, shit. That simple comment makes the backs of my eyes sting. I sniff the sensation away and give him a nod. I don't need anyone's approval, but I'll take it, nonetheless.

"I appreciate that."

"I'll talk to Jesse—"

"No." I cut him off with a stern shake of my head. "This is my shit. I'll deal with it."

He regards me for a beat, lips turned down, then nods. "All right, then." Exhaling heavily, he gets to his feet. "I'll leave you to your pity party."

I stand as well, and before I know it, he's got me in a headlock and he's giving me a noogie.

"I love you, you little fuckhead," he grumbles as he rubs his knuckles against my skull. "Believe it or not, you turned out all right, considering you had me and Jesse as role models."

With a laugh, I shove him away. "Get the hell off me."

He smirks as he heads to the door. "Don't do anything

stupid once I leave, or I'll take back everything I said here tonight."

"I'm not making any promises," I mutter, knowing damn well I'm not going anywhere. I can't stand in her way, even if it hurts like hell to watch it happen.

"Uh-huh." Aiden grins over his shoulder. "Ty's on duty tonight. I'll have him park down the street and keep an eye on you."

"Ty would one hundred percent have my back on this. Hell, he'd probably drive."

He scoffs. "Yeah, you're probably right."

I hold the door open for him as he steps out into the night. "Thanks, man. I appreciate this."

He dips his chin. "No problem."

As he heads to his truck parked behind mine in the driveway, my phone sounds from the living room.

Closing the door, I pull in a deep breath and muster the fraction of additional control Aiden's visit has given me.

I know it's her without having to look. Though I don't have the first clue what she has to say. Maybe we should have talked about it beforehand. Set some rules or some boundaries, because as badly as I want to know how things went, it's probably for the best that I don't.

Inhaling again, I pick up my cell.

Rachel: I'm home.

Nothing more, nothing less. It's all I need.

Me: Thanks for letting me know.

Rachel: Good night.

Me: G'night, Sunny.

TWENTY-NINE

JINX

The grass at the cemetery didn't need to be cut today, but when Mason texted this morning to ask if I had any work for him to do, I didn't want to let the kid down.

I didn't want to miss an opportunity to see his mother, either.

When I rolled up, though, Mason was outside waiting for me. According to him, Rachel was in the shower and aware he was leaving. It's hard not to wonder if her timing was intentional, or maybe I'm just paranoid.

It's killing me not knowing how her date went.

It's also killing me that she left me hanging with those two simple texts.

I tossed and turned all night, imagining every scenario, from awful and awkward to the teacher trying to put his hands on her.

Worse? What if it went better than expected and she wants to see him again?

"Hello." Mason waves a hand in front of my face. "Earth to Jinx."

"Huh?" I snap out of the trance. Shit. I've been standing at the trailer with a ratchet strap in my hand for god only knows how long. "Oh. Sorry."

He gives a grin and shakes his head. He's fair skinned like his mother, so the sun has already turned his cheeks pink.

"You forget your sunscreen?" I ask with an arched brow. "Your mom is gonna kick my butt if I send you home sunburned, boy."

He snorts. "Sorry."

"Mm-hmm." I give him the side-eye as I tighten down the equipment. "You're lucky it's a short day."

"You mean *you're* lucky," he snarks back.

With a guffaw, I reach for him so I can give him the same knuckles Aiden gave me last night, but he jumps out of the way just in time.

"You better run," I joke as I wrap the excess strap around the clip and knot it.

His face is still lit up as he grabs a bottle of Gatorade from the cooler in the back of the truck and twists it open.

"So, two more weekends until school starts, huh?"

He sighs, and his shoulders sag a little. "Yeah."

"What's the sigh for? Aren't you excited to see your friends?"

"Saw most of them during football."

"Yeah, but that's over now."

He shrugs. "I know. I wish there were more games."

"Me, too." Can't say I don't like having my evenings and Saturday afternoons back, but the kids were fun. "You can play next summer, right? You won't be too old?"

"Nope. If I have a ride again, I'll play. I can play middle school football, too."

"Yeah?" I lean up against the truck beside him. "You gonna keep at it? Be an all-star someday?"

He laughs. "Maybe."

"Good. But you better remember me when you turn pro." I nudge him with a playful elbow.

"You want tickets, huh?"

I give his hair a good tousle, catching him before he can duck. "Dang right, I do."

He takes a couple of gulps of his drink and then wipes the back of his hand across his mouth. "This is kinda awkward, but I wanted to ask you something."

My stomach instantly ties itself into a knot, but I keep my expression neutral. If it's awkward, the question might be one best kept for his parents, but I want to be an outlet for him, support when he needs it. "Sure. What's on your mind?"

"You like my mom, don't you?"

Ah, shit. I had a feeling we'd be having this conversation sooner or later, but that doesn't stop heat from burning up my neck. "What makes you think that?"

He cocks his head to the side and gives me a disappointed look, his lips turned down. "I might be a kid, but I'm not stupid."

I chuckle, doing my best to ignore the discomfort creeping through me. "All right, then."

"You talked to her a lot this summer. And you made her smile."

His words hit me in the gut. "Yeah, we have talked. And I'm glad. To have made her smile, I mean."

"She likes you, too, you know."

Yeah, I think she does, too. "What do you think about that?"

"I want you to answer my question first. Do you like my mom?"

Kid holds back no punches, does he? "Yeah, Mase, I do. I like her a lot."

He nods and ducks his head, kicking at the grass beneath him. "She cried a lot when my dad left. I don't want that to happen again."

Fuck. "I don't want that to happen again, either. That's why..." How the hell do I explain this to him? "That's why I've been giving her space and time. I haven't been through a divorce, but I imagine it's hard on a person. Especially someone with a big heart like your mom has."

"She does a lot for me and Emma. And she did a lot for my dad, too. And Grandpa Kaczmarek when he needs help."

I dip my chin. "She's a giver for sure."

His expression tightens. He keeps his head down, and for a moment, he holds his breath like he's trying not to cry. "She needs someone to do nice things for her, too. Not because she can't do them herself, because she can. But I think she wants someone to help, you know?"

I chuckle. "I sure do. And I've been working on that."

"That's how I knew you liked her."

With a long breath out, I rub my neck. "I was kinda obvious, huh?"

He gives a half laugh, finally looking at me full-on. "A little. I saw you staring at her a few times, too."

Oh. "Uh... sorry about that."

He rolls his eyes. "No, you're not. I'm a guy. I know how it is."

He does, huh? I bite back a laugh. "How do you feel about me maybe dating your mom?"

"Maybe? I thought you already were."

This kid does not miss anything. Damn. "Not officially." And that's all I'm going to say about that.

"I think I know what that means." He makes a disgusted face, his lips pursing and his eyes pinching. "You should take her on a date at least."

Shit, if I thought this conversation was awkward before... "You'd be okay with that?"

The disapproving frown he gives me is reminiscent of many I've received from my old man over the years. Damn. "You should buy her dinner if you're gonna be kissing on her."

Okay, this kid is way too fucking smart. "I... don't know what to say to that."

He smirks, perking up a little, but just as quickly, he deflates. "Wait. If you marry my mom, can I still work with you?"

"Whoa, dude. Slow down." I hold up a hand, laughing again. "We're talking about a date, not a marriage proposal." But I'd marry her in a fucking heartbeat if that's what she wanted.

"Yeah, but my mom is pretty awesome. If you go on a date with her, you're gonna fall in love."

I don't need to take her to dinner for that, buddy.

I lift my ball cap and scratch a hand through my hair. "One thing at a time, kid."

He grins again, standing a little taller, chest puffed out, all confidence.

Dammit. I'm fucked. The kid sees right through me.

"I don't see any reason why you couldn't keep working with me," I say. "It'll be stuff like we've done this summer for a while. When you're old enough, you can move on to some of the bigger jobs."

"Good," he says, wiping at the sweat on his forehead. "Because I don't have enough money saved up for a truck yet."

I chuckle. "Nah, that's gonna take a while."

"Maybe I could help you shovel snow this winter, too."

Damn. I don't think I've ever met a kid this motivated. "That's a great idea. I always need help with that."

With another kick to the grass, he nods. "If you fall in love with my mom..."

Ah, Christ. Here we go again. What's it gonna be now? *Are you going to start sleeping over? Will you be my stepdad?*

"Yeah?" I prompt, bracing for the worst.

"Will you sell me your truck for cheap?"

RACHEL

"MOM!" Emma calls from the front of the house. "Mason is home! I'm gonna ask Jinx to look at my bike tire before he leaves!" she hollers. An instant later, the screen door slams, and then the house is silent.

I pull in a few deep breaths, then I set my cleaning cloth aside and follow after her.

Now that football is over and Justin isn't picking up Mason for practice, he and I have hardly seen each other. In fact, I haven't seen him since the night we had ice cream together. The night he and Jesse got into an argument about him being there with us. Thankfully, the kids didn't overhear any of the exchange. Becca and her kids showed up as the guys were storming off, and they ran off to play. But I heard enough, and guilt has been gnawing at me ever since.

Add in my date last night, and I've been on pins and needles, waiting to see him. When he picked up Mason this morning, I was in the shower. Needless to say, my house is cleaner than it's been in weeks. I've spent the day nervously scrubbing and dusting every surface. I've been too preoccupied with this inevitable conversation to do anything else.

"Hey, Mom." Mason approaches the front porch, carrying his water jug. His forehead is smudged with sweat and dirt, and his dark hair is damp and sticky.

"Hi, baby. Looks like you worked hard today." I resist reaching out to ruffle his hair and settle for a smile instead.

He nods. "Yup. I'm gonna take a shower. Can I make pizza rolls when I'm done? I'm hungry."

"Of course. But don't you dare leave your dirty clothes in the bathroom. I just cleaned in there."

"I won't." He skirts around me to head inside, and I traipse casually down the steps to join Justin and Emma by his truck.

"Mason says I need a new tire, but when it did this last year, Dad fixed it, and it was fine," she explains. "Will you look at it for me? Mariah and I want to go for a bike ride later."

Dressed in his usual jeans, a snug T-shirt, and a ball cap, Justin nods. "Sure, I can take a peek. Did Mason try to put air in the tire already?"

Our eyes meet over the top of her head, and he gives me a soft smile. Then those light blue eyes sweep all the way down to my freshly polished toes and back up again.

"Hey, Sunny. I like your hair like that."

I reach up and touch it, mostly because I've forgotten what I did with it after my shower. Just a messy knot with lots of stray strands from my vigorous and cathartic cleaning binge.

"Thank you. This is called the shabby chic cleaning lady style. Saw it on Instagram and just had to try it out."

He half snorts, half laughs and follows Emma to the garage. The door is already open, and her bike is parked out front. Clearly, she's been waiting for him to bring Mason home. That makes my mom heart happy.

Knowing that the kids like him as well as they do makes the decision to spend time with him so much easier. The way he is with them in return, how well he treats them, though, is the part that really eases my mind.

With one quick lift and twist, Justin flips the bike upside down, resting it on its handlebars and seat. The move makes it impossible not to home in on his biceps as they flex. And when he squats to inspect the tires? Not checking out his ass is impossible.

The man really does have a nice butt... among other things.

"Do you have a pump for the tires?" he asks, giving them both a squeeze.

"Yep. Hold on." Emma hurries into the garage and grabs the pump. "It's not a great one, but it works."

"Doesn't need to be fancy." He takes it with a grin and pumps up the front tire first. For a moment, he inspects it, turning it slowly. "Hmm. I think you have a leak, Em."

"We have a patch for it." She rushes away again and digs around in an old toolbox that I forgot we even had. A moment later, she holds her arm up, producing a little orange square with a black patch on it. "Ah-ha!"

With a chuckle, Justin scratches at his jaw. "Are you sure you need me to help? You already know what's what."

She beams as she hands over the patch, and her expression turns serious as she watches him work.

"Yep, here's the spot." He holds a finger over a spot on the exposed tube beneath the tire. "Give me your hand."

She does.

"Feel that air?" He holds her finger over the leak and squeezes the tube.

"Yep. That little bugger." She shakes her head.

I bite back a laugh at how adorable the scene is.

A few minutes later, with the front tire repaired, the back tire pumped up, and her chain greased, Justin flips the bike back onto its wheels.

"There you go. She's good as new."

Emma jumps up and down, her ponytail bouncing. "Yay! Can I try it out?"

"Of course," I tell her. I'd love a minute alone with her bike mechanic anyhow.

"You got a helmet?" Justin cocks a brow at her.

She huffs and fists her hands at her sides, frowning. "Yes."

"Better put it on. That patch should hold, but you never know. Don't need you wiping out and cracking that smart noggin of yours." He tugs on a lock of her hair.

Her cheeks go pink as she turns toward the shelf where her helmet sits. "Fine," she says. She straps it on and hops on the bike. "I'm just going to the end of the street," she tells me.

"You can go a little farther if you want. Just watch for cars and stop at the stop sign."

With a thumbs-up, she takes off.

Justin and I watch her go, and when she's far enough down the street that we have some privacy, he grabs my hand and pulls me hard against his chest.

"I've fucking missed you," he growls. He slides his hands to my butt and presses his lips to mine.

He tastes like coconut lip balm and an addiction I don't ever want to kick.

Last night, when I was supposed to be enjoying the company of another man, he was all I could think about. These kisses, the way I feel simultaneously protected and free when I'm with him.

I thought about his body, too. About the way he holds me and touches me and makes me want him like I want my next breath.

He breaks away with a knowing smile and grasps my arms, easing me to the balls of my feet. Because somehow, I've managed to crawl halfway up said body, desperate to get as much of him as I can.

"Oh..." I take a step back and lower my head. "I'm sorry. I..." Got a little carried away.

That ridiculously sexy dimple in his cheek pops. "You didn't kiss the teacher like that last night, did you?"

I give a small scoff, even as my heart twists. "As if."

He chuckles, but a hint of trepidation shines in his eyes. "Why not?"

"You know why."

He sticks his hands into his pockets and rocks back on his heels, instantly smug. "You're supposed to be giving these guys a real chance, babe."

"You make it a little difficult. And *guys*? Plural?" Exactly how long does he expect this dating experiment to last? I already know what I want, and that's him. Preferably naked, really freaking soon.

"There will be more."

Ugh. My heart sinks.

"Don't look at me like that, Sunny." He shakes his head

and glances away, a sudden tension in his neck. "When you do, all I wanna do is toss you into my truck, drive us someplace private, and fuck every other man out of you."

My core clenches in response to that declaration. I would absolutely let him. God help me, but I would.

"There's only been one." The confession rolls off my tongue easily, but the second it's out, I hold my breath, waiting for his reaction. I suspect he's probably figured it out, but I need him to know.

Jaw tight, he grits out a feral "one too fucking many."

Oh, sweet Jesus. The possessive side of this man is quickly becoming my favorite.

"We need alone time soon," he murmurs, closing the distance between us again. He tucks a strand of hair behind my ear with one hand and uses the other to pull my hips against his so I can feel his erection.

Blood rushes to my lower belly, my body aching for him.

"I want that, too," I rasp. "But I don't know when I can."

A low growl vibrates in his chest, and his lips find mine again. I part for him, welcoming him, savoring the way his tongue teases against mine in a slow, sensual dance. It's impossible not to wonder if that's how we'll make love. Or will our first time be more like that first kiss? Rushed and frenzied and—

A car horn sounds in the distance, and I jerk away, fingertips pressed to my guilty lips. The garage door is wide open. Anyone driving by could have seen us making out like a couple of horny teenagers.

Justin gives a sly grin. "Afraid of getting caught, Sunny?"

"By my children, yes."

His tone is low and full of mischief when he says, "We may have to get creative."

I'm all about creativity. I don't know how much longer I can pretend that he hasn't woken a need in me that I wasn't sure I'd ever feel again.

Last night's date with Reese proved what I was already pretty sure about. We talked entirely about school and our classes, and it was no different from chatting over lunch in the breakroom. There was absolutely no spark between us.

But Justin...

Good god. The buzz in my veins and along every one of my nerves is entirely his fault.

"Hey, Mom..." Mason's voice cuts into my greedy thoughts.

I spin toward the door between the garage and the kitchen, where he's standing, freshly showered. "Where are the pizza rolls?"

Thank goodness for that horn.

"Check the top left of the freezer, baby." I force a smile, then I flick a sidelong glance at Justin, who's stuck his tongue in his cheek, probably to keep from laughing.

"'Kay, thanks." Mason pulls the door shut, and a heartbeat later, Emma rolls back into the driveway.

"Still holding air!" she calls out with a huge grin.

"I better get going before I do something stupid," Justin mutters. "Text you later?"

Anticipatory butterflies take flight in my stomach. "You better."

"And about that alone time..." He lowers his gaze to my lips. "I'll find a way to make it happen."

"Promise?"

He flashes a wicked grin. "Oh, I promise."

THIRTY

JINX

I hate Mondays.

Especially when they begin with my brother blatantly ignoring me in front of not only his crew members, but mine.

Connor is somewhat aware of the situation between Jesse and me, but by the end of our staff meeting, Matt, my new hire, whose first day is today, looked like he already regretted his decision to take the job.

Jesse wouldn't so much as look at me, let alone ask what the landscaping crew had on the agenda this week. He was nice enough to Matt when he introduced him to the rest of the crew, but the tension between Jesse and me was thicker than his damn ego.

I kept my cool, but only because Hayden pulled me aside before the meeting and told me that his pissy mood was mostly due to the call she'd gotten from her ex over the weekend. Lane apparently reached out, wanting a visit with Jett. My nephew is biologically Jesse's, but Lane, the ex, helped raise him for a few years before Hayden and Jesse got back together. They extended the visitation offer when Hayden and Jett moved to Cole Creek, but I don't think they expected him to take them up on it.

Jesse's gotta be stressed the fuck out over it. And because I understand that, I didn't call him out when he adjourned the meeting without asking about the landscaping plans for the week.

"Well, that was awkward," Connor mutters as we head outside to the storage yard to get our equipment ready for the day. We're installing the water fountain at the Carlisles' today, so we won't need much more than our tools and maybe some mortar, but nonetheless, it's all out back. "He's still not talking to you, huh?"

"Guess not." I drop the tailgate on my truck so we can load up, then turn to Matt. "My brother and I are in the middle of a little lovers' quarrel."

He snorts. "What the hell kind of family business is this?"

With a laugh, Connor slaps him on the back. "I see you're gonna fit in just fine."

The new guy grins, probably in relief.

"Why don't you two head over to the Carlisles' and start uncovering everything? Make sure there aren't any issues with the brickwork, too, now that it's settled. I'll grab the tools we need for the day." I glance over my shoulder at where Jesse and his guys are figuring out who's driving which truck and trailer. "I want to try and grab Jesse before he leaves."

"Gotcha." Connor tips his head toward his truck, where it's parked a few spots down from mine. "You can ride with me," he tells Matt.

Once the two of them head out, I load up the supplies

we'll need for the day. As the overhead door of the storage garage descends, Craig heads over, presumably to grab something from the bay next to mine.

Perfect. While he's getting his shit set up for the day, I can talk to Jesse without being overheard. I haven't taken more than a handful of steps that way, though, when Craig steps into my path.

"Heard that Rachel was out with someone else on Friday," he says with a sardonic sneer. "You two didn't last very long, did you?"

This fucking guy, I swear.

"Look, man, I'm not interested in talking to you about my relationship with Rachel." I try to side-step him, but he follows, blocking me again.

"Your relationship?" He gives a wry laugh, his lip curled in a way that makes me want to knock him to the ground. "Is that what you think it is?"

What the hell is his issue? Is he all of a sudden second-guessing his feelings about her because she's ready to move on? Or is he really so petty that he can't stand the thought of her being happy? Or does he feel threatened by me?

My gut tells me it's a little bit of everything. He's petty and threatened and finally realizing that he's actually losing her.

I can't find an ounce of sympathy for the guy. Maybe if he hadn't run to Cady so quickly after he left Rachel, I'd feel differently. But from where I'm standing, the only person he has the right to be pissed at is himself.

"What goes on between Rachel and me is none of your business." I grin over gritted teeth. "But I'll tell you this: I won't be intimidated into backing off just because her moving on hurts your ego."

He rubs his palm against his jaw, chuckling. "You think this is intimidation?"

I lift my hands. "If it's not, then what is it?"

"This is me trying to protect my fucking kids," he snarls, puffing up. "They don't need to witness their mother being used and tossed around by some—"

"By some guy who actually gives a shit about her? A man who wants her to be happy?" I take a step closer. He needs to hear me loud and clear. "I'm not going anywhere, Perry. I already care too damn much about her and those kids. All I want is to be there for them. I don't give a fuck what you think about that. *They* are my priority, not you, your ego, or your friendship with my brothers."

He glares at me, ready to spit venom. Instead, as if suddenly remembering he's at work, he takes a few steps back and glances to the street, his hands balled into fists at his sides.

"This is bullshit," he grumbles. "I don't like it one fucking bit."

I can't imagine he does. "I'm sorry you feel that way."

He scoffs. "Yeah, I bet you are."

He's right. I'm not. He did this to himself, and I have no sympathy for the guy.

Without another word, he turns, boots grinding in the dirt, and stalks off. When he gets to his work truck, he slams the tailgate and climbs behind the wheel. A second later, he cranks the engine and peels out, kicking up gravel and dust without a single fuck given to the people standing nearby.

I scrub a hand over my face and let out a long exhale. I'd love to think that's the last I'll hear from him on the matter, but I'm sure as hell not going to hold my breath. It's pretty clear he's only now understanding how badly he's fucked up. Unless he finds another outlet, I'm the most convenient target for his frustration. Better me than Rachel, though.

As I turn back to my truck, I catch a glimpse of Jesse in my periphery. He's standing with his hands on his hips, focus locked on me, no doubt having witnessed the entire encounter.

Good.

I hope he heard every word of it.

With any luck, he'll realize how wrong he's been about me, too.

But if not, so be it.

I know who I am, and I know what I'm capable of. I'm done letting Jesse determine my self-worth.

I've got my own ruler now, motherfucker.

RACHEL

JUST A FEW HOURS into hauling out all my classroom supplies and getting most of the wall art and educational materials tacked up, I feel pretty good.

With the tortoise and hare themed items I bought last spring set up and the new white boards that were installed over the summer, the place looks fresh and cheery, just like a kindergarten classroom should.

"Phew." I blow my hair out of my face and take a second to catch my breath. Then I push to my feet and inspect the racetrack taped across the bottom of the wall. The animals in the race are seriously adorable. It would be super cute in a nursery, too. If only that train hadn't left the station years ago.

"Knock, knock." Reese pokes his head in from the

hallway and does a quick scan of the room. "Dang, Ms. Perry. You work fast."

I wipe my hands on my jeans and adjust my ponytail. "I'm a woman on a mission. How's it going in your room?"

He stuffs his hands into the pockets of his cargo shorts and shrugs. "Eh. I'm debating if fifty bucks is enough to bribe Kenzie to come and do it for me."

"Fifty bucks is a lot of cash to a thirteen-year-old. I say go for it." Come to think of it, Emma would have loved to help me, too. Darn it. Why didn't I think of that?

Because you've spent all your free time thinking about your new man.

Which reminds me...

"I'm glad you stopped in," I begin, wandering over to my phone to turn down the volume on my music. "I had a good time on Friday night."

Reese nods, but the smile on his face is reluctant. "Yeah, me, too. Did you, uh, get any work done in our classes over the weekend?"

"No. I've probably done as much as I can until classes actually start."

"Same here. It's great that they give us early access, but now I just want to get the show on the road."

"Exactly." I laugh softly again. "Anyway, about the date... I really did have a good time. I'm glad to have a friend in these classes. I have a feeling I'm going to need someone to freak out to every now and then."

He grins. "You've got my number."

"I do." I pull in a breath, bite my lip, and come out with it. "But I don't think I'll be using it for any other reasons."

Reese's shoulders relax immediately. "Thank god. I mean..." He gives an awkward laugh, and his cheeks turn a little pink. "I had a good time, too, but I'm not sure I'm ready for anything more. It probably sounds ridiculous since it's been a couple of years since my divorce. It's just... singlehood and I get along really well. I think I'm gonna keep schmoozing her instead."

The sound that escapes me in response is half snort, half laugh. "Totally understandable." I thought I wanted to enjoy being by myself for a while, too, but it turns out that when the right person comes along, nothing compares to being by their side.

"I'm so glad we're on the same page."

"Me, too." I sigh, relieved as the tension I've been carrying since our date ebbs out of me. "And if Kenzie doesn't want to help you with your room, I'm happy to help once I'm finished in here." I hold an arm out and pan the space. "But you better claim my time before Crystal does or—"

"Who's talking about me? Better be something juicy." The devil herself appears in the doorway. Her hair is twisted on top of her head, and she's dressed in a 3rd *Grade Rocks* T-shirt and leopard-print leggings. "Oh, hey, Reese." She gives him a wave, then drops into a tiny kids' chair with an exhausted huff. "I'm too out of shape for this."

"I was thinking the same," Reese says. "That or I need more coffee."

Crystal points a finger at him. "Now, that's a great idea. If you make a run to Bobbie Jean's, I'll buy."

He raises a hand. "Say less. Text me your orders, ladies."

"Sweet." Crys pulls her phone from a pocket on the side of her leggings. "I'll Venmo you the money."

"Perfect. Be back in a few." With that, he's gone.

"I like that man." Crystal gives another heavy exhale. "I

texted both our orders. I told him to get you an iced chai, since it's hotter than balls in here."

"That's for sure. I regret not bringing my fan in with me." I take a seat in my more size-appropriate chair and survey my progress. The walls are decorated, and the centers have all been reorganized. Not bad for day one.

"Did you break the news to him yet?" She tips her head toward the door.

I nod. "Yep. He wasn't feeling it, either."

"That's a relief. It would have been crazy awkward around here otherwise."

"Probably."

"And..." she says, drawing out the word, "I also kinda sorta gave someone else your phone number, so..." She winces, but the devilish glint in her eyes belies the repentant gesture. The woman has no shame.

"Oh really." I tilt my head. "Who?"

"Jamie."

"Oh my god." I drop my head back and huff. "You were serious about that?"

"Heck yes, I was. He's a great guy. And he's asked about you, too."

A little ball of dread forms in my stomach at the idea. I should probably be flattered. Jamie really is a good guy. Attractive, too. But he's missing that dimple in his cheek. And the blue eyes that see through to the heart of me, as well as the arms and hugs that feel like home.

"Go out with him, Rach. Just see how it goes. I'm not saying you have to marry him or anything. And for the love of god, if you sleep with him, make sure he double wraps. The last thing that man needs is another baby mama."

Just the thought makes me recoil. "I'm not going to sleep

with him, so you don't have to worry about his child support."

She quirks an eyebrow. "You didn't say you wouldn't go out with him, though."

No, I didn't. Because the more toads I toss, the sooner I can have my prince.

"Tell him to call me. The sooner, the better, too."

Squealing, she does a ridiculous happy dance in her ridiculously small chair.

I simply smile.

And pray she's as excited when she finds out that I already have a man in my life. A man I fully intend to keep.

THIRTY-ONE

RACHEL

"Bye, baby." I kiss the top of Emma's head and soak in the feel of her arms around my middle. "I'll see you later tonight."

"'Kay." She jogs down the front steps to join her brother and Craig at the truck. "Love you!"

"Love you, too." I blow her a kiss and then do the same for Mason. Naturally, he rolls his eyes in response, then turns and climbs into the passenger seat.

One side of Craig's mouth tips up in amusement as he watches Mason slam the truck door. Then to me, he says, "See you in a few hours. Enjoy your alone time."

Yeah, right. On instinct, I huff a laugh, only to stop myself at the genuinely friendly expression on his face.

Wait. Is he being sincere?

Holy crap. I think he might be.

I give a little finger wave to the kids as they back out and then retreat into the house. My phone dings with a notification almost immediately.

Justin: The kids leave yet?

Oh, he's good.

Me: Just left.

Justin: Perfect. Now go for a walk.

Go for a walk? I rode my bike for forty-five minutes this morning. I don't need another workout. Unless...

Alone time.

I grin like a fool and type out my response.

Me: Okay. Anywhere in particular I should walk?

Justin: Surprise me.

Ah. Excitement stirs low in my belly. We're going to play, are we? I can get behind that.

Me: Give me five.

He doesn't respond, but the *read* notification appears on my screen.

Giddy with anticipation, I change quickly. Rather than pulling on a sports bra, I go with a feminine but still practical white lace one with a matching thong. A woman wearing Lycra leggings can't have panty lines, after all. And the white tank top paired with the purple pants makes my curves look pretty damn good, if I do say so myself.

Hair in a messy bun and feet shoved into my sneakers, I grab my earbuds and my phone and head out. I'm tempted to keep the volume down so I can hear Justin approach, but that feels like cheating. And far less fun.

With my favorite rock playlist blasting in my ears, I make it past the edge of town and head for the trail that circles the lake. As I approach the entrance to the trail, the feeling of being watched sends a shiver down my spine.

Seconds later, strong hands grip my hips and haul me back against a hard, formidable body. I gasp as a rush of fear and excitement washes through me.

Warm breath teases against my temple as he plucks the earbuds from my ears. He hums as he tucks them into the pocket of my leggings. Then he murmurs, "Pretty girls like you shouldn't be out in the woods alone."

"Handsome boys like you shouldn't tell them to go there, then."

He nips playfully at my ear. "I told you to take a walk, not play hide and seek."

A zap of elation courses through me. "Oops."

Thick arms wrap around my waist as he curls down and buries his face in my neck. It feels like his big body is trying to swallow me and keep me safe. I close my eyes, wishing he could.

"I think you like playing games," he says, his lips grazing along my skin. He gently bites the flesh of my neck, then soothes it with his tongue. "Don't you, Sunny?"

"I-I think I do."

"You're not sure?"

I shake my head, the move jerky. "I've never... before."

"Ah."

He smiles against me. It's no doubt one of those wickedly delicious ones that turns me into a puddle of want.

"Should we experiment then?"

"Yes, please." My voice is a pleading whisper, so raw and needy that I almost don't recognize it.

"You trust me?"

So much so that it should probably frighten me. I never thought I'd want to give this much of myself to another man, but with Justin, I can't imagine not. Being with him, trusting him, completes me in a way I never thought possible.

"I do."

"Good."

With his arms still wrapped around me, he lifts me off the gravel and spins around. Silently, he carries me to his truck a few yards away. When we approach the passenger side, I expect him to open the rear door and toss me inside. Instead, he opens the front passenger door and pins me between the truck and his body as his rough, eager hands tug up on my tank top.

"Anyone could drive by right now," he husks as he cups and then kneads my breasts. "Anyone could see me touching you like this."

I sink my teeth into my lip to keep from moaning. What does he have planned for me? Will he strip me bare right here on the side of the road? Have his way with me in his truck?

With a yank of my bra, he frees my breasts so he can stroke his thumbs over my nipples.

I hiss and arch back against him, not surprised but spurred on when I find that he's already hard. We've had so few intimate moments like this. How is it possible that he's already figured out just how to touch me and how to make me so freaking wet?

"More," I beg. "Please."

A satisfied laugh rumbles out of him, then he's pinching my peaks between his thumbs and forefingers. My butt slams back into his lap again, and this time, there's no stopping the low, greedy groan that rises from my belly to my throat.

"So needy." He tsks, sliding one of those big, calloused palms down my stomach and to the waistband of my leggings. "Maybe I should check and see just how badly you want me."

My eyes roll and my lashes flutter when he slips his hand into my pants *and* my panties. He parts my flesh with his middle finger. It glides easily over my clit because I've been dripping for him since the moment he snuck up on me.

"*Fuck*. Is this all for me?"

I nod, my body trembling with every stroke of that single finger. He delves deeper and deeper into my panties until he finds my opening and dips inside.

"Oh god." My knees nearly buckle, and I have to grip the seat for leverage.

"Lean forward." He presses between my shoulder blades with his free hand, gently urging me down onto my chest. Then he tugs my leggings and panties over my ass, baring me to him and the warm summer air. "So fucking perfect," he murmurs, smoothing a hand from my hip to the curve of my ass and then squeezing. It's not hard enough to bruise, but it is enough for me to wish he'd do it again.

"More," I beg. "Please."

"What do you need, baby? This?" He slaps my ass and then soothes it with another tender squeeze. "Or this?" His finger retreats, then quickly returns, joined by another.

I bite my arm to muffle my cry of pleasure.

"Both?" He chuckles darkly. "I think you like both." Gripping my hip again, he grinds his hard cock against me while he continues to fuck me with his hand. It's slow and tender at first, and then harder and deeper until my head spins and arousal dampens my thighs.

I want to come so badly.

I *need* to come.

But I've never orgasmed like this. Never without a toy.

Emotion burns in my chest and in my throat, and my traitorous body gives me away by shaking when I try not to cry.

He gentles his movements, his thumb rubbing lazy circles over my clit as he leans down and places a reassuring kiss between my shoulder and my neck. "It's okay, baby. Don't overthink it."

How does he know? How does he *always* know?

"Focus on how good it feels." He slips those fingers inside me again, crooking just right and with so much tenderness and determination that I do cry. Not out loud, but I surrender to the emotion and let my tears fall.

Letting go makes it easier to concentrate on his touch. On the way he fills me and loves me and makes me feel so many things at once.

The fire builds again, slowly but fiercely, the low flame turning into a fiery blaze. I want this. I want this so badly with him.

He kisses his way down the middle of my back, his lips so warm and so hungry against my skin until he's *right there.*

The caress of his breath against my slickened skin is my only warning before his tongue flicks across my pussy from behind. With hand and fingers still pumping in the front, he laps at the arousal that weeps from me, drinking me down like a starved man. And the sounds he makes... the moans... *my god.*

I should be embarrassed.

I should be ashamed of how much it turns me on.

But I'm not.

Not with him.

JINX

I DIDN'T PLAN for this to happen.

I didn't plan to accost Rachel on the side of the fucking road, let alone give in and finally taste her.

But the second I discovered how badly she needed me, how badly she'd been deprived, I had no choice.

There isn't a thing I wouldn't do for this woman, not that burying my face in her pussy and devouring her is any hardship. She tastes like fucking heaven, and the way she pulses back against me, trying to capture more of my mouth, is the sexiest thing I've ever experienced.

"That's it, baby. Fuck my face," I growl into her as she reaches back and fists my hair to keep me where she wants me.

"Oh god," she pants. "Oh god. That feels so good."

"Mm-hmm." I try to catch her clit with every backward shift of her hips, but the position isn't right. And her pants... the fucking pants have to go.

Without a word, I grip her hips, spin her around, yank her leggings down to her ankles, and discard a shoe. Once that one leg is free, I spread her wide before me, and I damn near come from the sight alone.

Just the faintest strip of auburn hair, puffy lips, and a swollen pink clit that practically begs to be sucked.

"Fucking hell, Sunny. You're so much prettier in person."

A ghost of a smile dances across her lips as I lift her leg to my shoulder and dive in.

Tongue, teeth, lips, fingers... I give her everything. Sucking and teasing, humming and lapping. I explore until there isn't a single bit of her perfect pussy that I haven't tasted and claimed.

She is mine.

There's no question in my mind.

And I take care of what's mine.

"Oh god." Her hands wind in my hair as she gives herself over to me. With every flick of my tongue and every pull of my lips, her hips rise to meet me, fucking my face while fire blazes in her eyes.

I love that she watches. That she can't take her eyes off me while I devour her.

I'll eat her every day just for her to look at me the way she is now. Like I'm her sin and her salvation.

"J-Justin..." Her breath quickens and her tits, still spilling from her bunched up bra, rise and fall with every frenzied inhale and exhale. "Oh god, oh god, oh god..."

Lost in euphoria, I stay the course, using my fingers and my mouth, sucking her clit and fucking her with my hand like my life depends on it. My beard is soaked, and gravel digs into my knees through my jeans. It's the greatest fucking sensation.

I need to give her this. I *want* to give her this.

I break away long enough to encourage her, to coax her. "Come for me, baby. I wanna taste it. Wanna feel it on my tongue."

Her dilated gaze locks on mine for a heartbeat, then her lashes flutter shut, her nostrils flare, and her cheeks stain the sexiest pink. She's right there. I can feel it in the way her body tenses and in the way her walls tighten around my fingers, the promise of her release *right fucking there.*

In the next second, the orgasm crashes over her. Waves pulse through her from head to toe, puckering her nipples and sending goose bumps across her bare skin. When she comes back down, she's wearing the prettiest, most sated smile.

For several moments, she keeps her eyes closed and just breathes, almost like she's savoring every last bit of pleasure still humming in her body.

One thing I know for sure: I'm going to do this for her every damn chance I get. No matter what it takes. This woman is a goddess, and she deserves to be treated like one, well and often.

With a deep breath, she finally opens her eyes and strokes her fingers against my cheek. "That was amazing."

I kiss one thigh, then the other, then haul myself up from the gravel, gathering her close, and kissing the top of her head. "You're fucking gorgeous when you come."

She gives a light, somewhat embarrassed laugh. "I'll take your word for it."

"I'm going to get you a mirror."

"Oh my god."

She shoves me away and reaches down for her leggings and panties, but I gently bat her hand out of the way.

"Uh-uh. I undressed you, so I get to redress you," I say as I guide her leg into her panties and then her pants.

She steadies herself with her hands on my shoulder. "You're too much."

I'm not. She's just been with the wrong guy.

"Hop up on the seat. I'll put your shoe back on, too."

She rolls her eyes but climbs into the truck. "I can't believe you just did that."

"I can't believe it took me this long," I counter. "You can bet your sweet ass I'm gonna be doing it all the damn time now."

She gives a soft sigh, even as the pink stain in her cheeks darkens. "I wouldn't complain."

"Good." I move in for a kiss, but she pulls back suddenly.

"Wait..." She presses a finger to my lips.

Ah. She's not into kissing after eating. All right. Not a big deal.

"I have to tell you something."

My heart stumbles in my chest. That doesn't sound like it's a flavor issue.

"Okay. Let's hear it."

"I have another date."

What the fuck? That simple sentence sends the damn organ in my chest plummeting.

"Tomorrow night." She ducks her head and presses her teeth into her lip.

Is she seriously going to see the teacher again? She said she didn't like him. And what about what we're doing now? Am I mistaken to think we just upped the ante in our relationship?

Like me, she didn't know this was going to happen, so I can't fault her there, I guess.

I clear my throat and go for neutral. "With that Reese guy?"

She shakes her head, her eyes averted.

Another dude? I force myself to take a breath and not get pissed. I'm the one who told her she needed to date, after all.

"All right." I force a smile I'm sure she can see right through. "Who's the lucky guy?" *Just don't tell me it's Craig.*

"Jamie Stroud."

Fuck me with a chainsaw. His name hits me like a punch to the solar plexus. It's enough to steal my breath.

"You know him, right?"

Do I know him? I almost laugh. "He's Jack's dad."

"Exactly." She wets her lips. "That's why I figured you'd be okay with it. Crystal says he's a nice guy."

Right. Nice. Nice and jacked, too. The guy is massive. Has a good job, and he's apparently a ladies' man.

He's the only guy in town that I'd want to see her with less than Craig.

"You don't look happy." She reaches for my arm, warm fingers wrapping around my wrist. "Should I cancel?"

Laughing, I rough a hand over the back of my head. "No, you shouldn't cancel. And you shouldn't ask me if it's something you should do, either. You're supposed to be doing this for yourself, Sunny, not me."

Her concerned eyes dart back and forth between mine. "I don't want to see anyone but you."

I don't want her to, either, but she's only been on a single date so far. I can't suggest she call it quits already.

But Jamie Stroud? Fucking hell.

I suppose I should have seen that coming, considering we live in a small town and he's supposedly a hot commodity. The worst part of it all is that I can actually see Rachel with him. In a hazy shade of red, naturally, but she could do a lot worse, that's for damn sure.

"Look, babe, we knew this wouldn't be easy. But we've gotta stay the course." I grip her upper arms and stroke my thumbs over her skin.

She fists my T-shirt and pulls me close. "Even after what just happened?"

Closing my eyes, I swallow hard. I can still taste her, and I'm already looking forward to doing it again. But maybe we need to slow things down. "Yes, Sunny. In fact, maybe this—"

She presses her fingers to my lips, silencing me. "Don't say it."

Whether I say it or not doesn't make it any less true.

She needs time to do this the right way, and if we keep hooking up like this, there's no way she can do that.

Fighting back the emotion welling up inside me, I tuck a strand of auburn hair behind her ear. "Go on your date, Sunny girl. We'll figure things out from there."

She leans into my hand, her eyes swimming with sadness. "Are you sure?"

No, but I'm a man of my word. I told her I'd be okay with this, and I will be.

Somehow.

THIRTY-TWO

RACHEL

Eleven.

That's how many times I picked up my phone to text Jamie to cancel our date. I was sick, I'd decided. Something contagious, I was sure.

Each time, I'd remind myself that I didn't want to lie. More to the point, I would *not* lie. Because if I learned anything during the last few years of my marriage, it was that lying to placate a man never solved the issue. Not really.

No, I never technically lied to Craig. But a lie of omission can be just as harmful, and in the end, not being honest about how unhappy I was hurt me more than it hurt him.

I also really want to get through this little game Justin and I are playing, and there's only one way to accomplish that.

That's why I kept the date, and that's why I'm currently sitting in the passenger seat of Jamie's truck as he drives toward Copper Crossing.

"I hope you're okay with steak and seafood." From the driver's seat, he hits me with a kind smile. His nicely groomed beard pairs well with his neatly cropped hair. His jeans are definitely not of the work variety, and the sleeves of his pressed black button-down are rolled up, revealing ink on both arms.

My memory of him from the time I bumped into him at the grocery store not all that long ago was spot on—he is one very attractive man.

"I love both, but seafood sounds especially good tonight. Where are we going?" I ask, folding my hands in my lap.

"The Crossing Steakhouse. It's been forever since I've been there. I thought tonight was a good night to fix that." He gives an almost timid shrug. It's adorable on such a foreboding man, but it does nothing for me. Not like a certain someone's charming and ridiculously sexy dimple.

"I haven't been there in a long time either, so you chose well."

He gives me a sidelong glance, one brow lifted. "You can probably tell from my dad bod that I like to eat. But just in case, consider this your warning."

I laugh. "Noted."

As we approach the road for the farm with the sunflower field, I smile to myself. My sunflowers have wilted, but I saved the seeds in hopes of planting them in my flower garden next year. They may not match the overall vibe, but I don't mind. My vision is less about aesthetic and more about savoring the memory of that trip.

"I heard your son is playing football this year," I say. It'd probably do me good to at least try not to think about Justin for the entirety of this date, so Jack seems like a safe topic. Though Justin *is* the one who told me about him.

"Yep. I'm sure you know about his friend Noah's accident."

I nod. "I did. His mom was on the PTA for a while, and believe it or not, I remember both of the boys when they were in elementary school. They were inseparable even back then."

Jamie's throat works as he swallows hard. "Yeah. Jack's had a hard time with it. Playing football is his way of supporting Noah."

My heart aches at the thought of his son hurting like that. "It's really sweet. You've obviously raised him right."

"I can't take all the credit, but yeah... he turned out all right." He dips his chin proudly.

For a little while in high school, I worked at Tulah's diner with Jamie's ex-wife. From that experience alone, I'm sure Jack gets plenty of his heart from her, too.

"Tell me about your kids," Jamie says.

Sticking with the easy topic, I spend a solid ten minutes telling him about Mason and Emma, and he shares more about Jack and his youngest son, Parker. By the time we pull into The Crossing Steakhouse parking lot, we've commiserated about how tough parenting is these days and we're in agreement that single parenting is not for the faint of heart.

"How's the coparenting going?" he asks as we walk side by side toward the restaurant's entrance. "If you feel like sharing, of course. I won't be offended if you tell me it's none of my business."

I smile, genuinely appreciative of Jamie's candor but also his easygoing attitude. "No, it's okay. I don't mind. It's going okay, I think. No major issues, but it's only been seven months."

He holds open the door, and the aroma of delicious food makes my mouth water.

"That's good. Hopefully it stays that way," he says as he follows me inside. "I've been lucky, too. With Jack and Cece, anyway." Jamie scratches at the back of his neck and gives me a rueful smile. "It's a little touchy with Miranda and Parker from time to time, but nothing's ever perfect."

Lips pressed together, I peer at him over my shoulder as we approach the hostess stand. "That's true. Initially, Mason struggled, but the last few months have been a lot easier." Thanks in part to Justin.

"Jack said Mason worked with Jinx this summer, too."

I shoot him a pointed look, hold a finger to my lips, and whisper. "We're not supposed to talk about that. Child labor laws and all that."

He tips his head back and lets out a rich laugh. "Ah. Forget I mentioned it, then."

With a shrug, I step to one side and focus on the hostess as she asks whether we'd like a table overlooking the river or something closer to the bar.

"Do you have a preference?" Jamie asks me.

"The river sounds nice."

Jamie hits me with a kind smile, then turns to the teenage girl behind the podium. "The river it is."

The hostess leads us to a corner table at the back of the restaurant with a great view of the water. In no time, the sun will set and the view will be even better. Maybe we'll get to watch the storm that's predicted to roll in tonight.

Once the waitress takes our drink orders, we peruse the menu and make small talk. He launches into a story about working with Crystal's husband, Tony, and some of the shenanigans they get into, and I fill him in on how my dad is doing and show him pictures of my older brother and his family.

"I bet it's been twenty years since the last time I saw

FJ." Jamie grins as he swipes through the images on my phone. "Probably for the best, too. We got into so much shit when we were younger."

"I bet you did." My brother was a hell-raiser before he joined the military. Jamie is a couple of years older than him, but FJ was always a little ahead of his time like that.

"How long have he and his wife been together?"

"I think it'll be fifteen years next month."

"Damn. That's a long time." He hands back my phone. "How long was it for you and Craig?"

That ache that flares every time I'm reminded of the day Craig left me does its thing in response to Jamie's question, but the pain is duller than it's ever been. "Twelve years and three days when he told me he wanted a divorce."

With his brows furrowed, Jamie scoffs. "You're kidding me. Three days after your anniversary?"

"Yep." I pop my lips. It's just one item on a long, long list of shitty things Craig has done over the years. Anymore, though, I realize I shouldn't have been surprised.

"Cece and I were married for seven." He shakes his head and fixes his attention on something over my shoulder, a little lost in the thought. Then, "Shit, I'm sorry. I'm sure you don't want to talk about any of that."

"It's okay. It's natural conversation." I give him a knowing smile. "We've both been through it, so it's common ground."

He lets out a long sigh, his shoulders relaxing. "Exactly. Then again, I don't know what it says about me that I've been divorced for ten years, and it still feels like yesterday."

Hmm. Maybe it's less about finding common ground between us and more about him needing someone to talk to.

"I don't mind talking about it," I admit. "To be honest, the only part about my divorce that came as a surprise was that Craig asked for it. I knew it was coming. I just thought I'd be the one to make the move."

His brow creases, and there's a tension in his eyes that looks an awful lot like pain. "Cece was the one who wanted our divorce."

I remember hearing that. They got pregnant and then married young, and Camille—as far as I know, Jamie is the only one who calls her Cece—ultimately decided she wanted more out of life. It's a sentiment I know all too well, only I didn't have the courage to leave.

"Do you mind..." He clears his throat. "Do you mind telling me what went wrong?"

"I think my story is similar to yours. Actually, Camille's."

He clasps his hands on top of the table and nods. "I figured. Honestly, that's why I'd like to hear it. After all these years, I think I finally understand, but I'm sure there are plenty of things I haven't considered."

Ten years or not, it's pretty clear this man isn't nearly as over the demise of his marriage as he wishes he were. Knowing that adds to the comfort I already feel tonight. This date isn't leading to anything more. I knew it from the start, but now it's obvious he knows it, too.

"The short version is that I gave up a lot of myself when I became a wife and a mom. That's bound to happen to a certain degree, sure. No one ever stays completely the same. But, as cliché as it sounds, it's like I woke up one day and didn't recognize the woman looking back at me in the mirror. I saw Mason and Emma's mom, and Craig's wife. Rachel had all but disappeared. I had stopped doing nearly every single thing that made me who I was before I got married and had kids."

Jamie tips his head, his jaw working. "Please don't take

this the wrong way. It's just a question, I swear." He lets out a long breath. "You couldn't get back to being that person once you realized what had happened?"

My heart gives a little pang in my chest. "No." I shake my head and wring my hands in my lap. "I tried, but it seemed like every attempt to do something for myself was met with confusion or contempt. Why did I suddenly want to go to grad school? Why did I want to travel? Why did it bother me that he didn't help with things around the house when I never had an issue with it before?" I give a heavy exhale, willing myself to tamp down on my frustration before it boils over. Just the thought of all the arguments Craig and I had over the years is enough to raise my blood pressure. "Some of that was my fault, of course. I lost sight of myself, and it took me a long time to realize it. I allowed and, in some cases, created situations in my marriage that led to resentment and anger."

Jamie's cheeks puff out as he blows out a breath. "That sounds a lot like what Cece said when she left."

My heart goes out to both of them for that. Her then and him now.

"Can I ask how you handled that?" Now it's my turn to turn the conversation into one that might feel a bit uncomfortable.

He sits back in his chair and shrugs, though his expression is one of pain and remorse. "Not well. I was angry, and I felt betrayed. Like she'd lied to me early on. Even when she tried to explain over and over again that she'd changed—that she'd grown up, actually—it just didn't make sense to me."

"But now you see it differently."

He nods slowly, his attention fixed on me. "So differently. And I feel like an ass for not understanding before. I think she and I could have worked things out if I had been more mature and open-minded myself, but I wasn't." He gives a self-deprecating laugh. "I don't think I've ever admitted that to anyone before."

I smile. "Your secret is safe with me."

He ducks his head and gives a chuckle. "Yours, too."

The server appears at our side with a basket of bread, and Jamie digs in.

"Can I butter your biscuit, ma'am?" he teases with a southern accent that makes me giggle.

I pick up my glass of wine and hold it up. "With a twang like that, how can I say no?"

"THE SHRIMP SCAMPI was so good. Probably the best I've ever had." Pushing away my plate, I let out a contented sigh. "How was your steak?"

"Amazing." Jamie dabs his mouth with a linen napkin. He's reaching for his water when our server materializes out of nowhere to clear our empty plates.

"Room for dessert?" she asks cheerily.

"Ha. As if I have room."

Jamie nods in agreement. "Same here. But thank you."

"Another drink, then?"

When we both decline at the same time, I can't help but laugh.

Once the server has excused herself, I angle forward and rest my forearms on the table. "We almost get along too well."

Jamie leans back in his seat and chuckles. "We do, don't we?"

Yes, but this is where I have to tell him the truth.

Before I can, though, he clears his throat. "As nice as this has been, I have to be honest." His brow furrows slightly as he meets my gaze. "I'm not sure I'm in the best headspace right now. And I don't want to mislead you."

Reaching across the table, I squeeze his hand. "You have no idea how glad I am to hear that."

His eyes widen, but there's more amusement in his expression than surprise. "Damn, girl, just stomp on my ego, why don't you?"

"Um," I say, tilting my head and giving him a pointed look, "you're the one who started the honesty train, sir."

He chuckles and gives my hand a quick reciprocating squeeze, then fidgets with his napkin on the tabletop. "I know where my hesitation comes from, but what about you? Is it because your divorce isn't finalized yet?"

"No." I cross my legs beneath the table and smooth my hands along the tablecloth. "Our final court date is the week after next. It's just..." How much do I want to tell him? Being honest about my failed marriage is one thing, but discussing my relationship with another man doesn't feel right. Still, I don't want to lie. "I think my heart may already belong to someone else."

Jamie rears back in surprise, his brows jumping into his hairline. "No kidding."

Nope. And there's no *thinking* about it. Justin is my future. The only reason I'm here tonight is to give him some peace of mind, as ridiculous as that seems. This way, he can be certain that he's the man I want. After this, I have to hope he'll see that he isn't a rebound. Rebounds are like bandages for broken hearts. They're temporary, and they only help us hide our wounds.

Justin, on the other hand, has woven himself inextricably into my life and into my heart. Our bond is permanent, and his presence in my life has done so much more than cover up my emotional wounds. He's helped me heal. There's no ripping what he's done for me away. Not without tearing me apart in the process.

"So, who is this lucky guy?"

I tsk as I pick up my wineglass. "A woman doesn't share her secrets, Jamie. You know that."

He continues to grin as he regards me. "Why on earth did you agree to go out with me tonight, then?"

I tilt my head and grin right back. "Why did *you* ask *me*?"

His eyes crinkle at the corners. "If I say peer pressure, will you think I'm a pussy?"

"Nope, because then I'd be one, too." I wink.

The laugh that escapes him echoes around the dining room. "We're a hot mess, aren't we?"

"Oh, yeah." Setting down my empty glass, I sigh. "As enlightening as this evening has been, maybe we should call it a night before this wine catches up to me and I say more than I already have."

He holds up a hand. "Hey. I already said I wasn't gonna spill your secrets."

"Good." I angle in and whisper. "And I won't tell anyone you're still hung up on your ex-wife."

He gives a light chuckle, and his face heats a little. "I appreciate that."

After Jamie insists on paying the bill and signs the credit card receipt, we step out into the late August night. It's warm, and the air is thick with the impending rain. I can't wait to get home, open my windows, and listen to the storm.

Hand on the small of my back, Jamie leads me toward his truck near the back of the lot.

The breeze kicks up, and I turn my head toward the sky and breathe deep. Justin comes to mind immediately. Will I always think of him like this? I hope so.

Suddenly, Jamie's steps falter, snapping me out of the moment.

"Hey, man. How's it going?" he asks, his tone friendly.

I glance at him, then look ahead to see who he's talking to.

Justin stands before us, arms crossed and feet planted wide on the asphalt. Behind him, his white pickup is parked beside Jamie's.

Despite Jamie's question, he doesn't say a word. He doesn't shake his hand. He doesn't even look at him.

No, his fiery blue gaze is locked on me. His nostrils flare and his throat strains as he swallows, but the thick emotion radiating off him isn't anger. At least, I don't think it is. He has nothing to be angry about. He told me to do this. He encouraged me.

No, this is fear.

And if I have it right...

There's a heavy dose of possession there, too.

"You all right, Enders?" Jamie steps forward, genuine concern etching his features. But just as quickly as that expression lands, it disappears. He glances from Justin to me and back again. "Ah. I see." He barks out a laugh. "You're the one, huh?"

With his jaw clenched tight, Justin flicks his gaze in Jamie's direction. "Thanks for taking care of my girl, but I'll be the one taking her home."

Oh, he will, will he?

It's about damn time.

THIRTY-THREE

EARLIER IN THE EVENING

JINX

There's nothing like physical labor to keep a man distracted.

At least that's what I'm telling myself as I unload retaining wall block from my trailer into the Pruitts' backyard.

It's more torture than distraction, if I'm being honest. Across the street, Rachel's house is quiet and dark, and to make things worse, I passed her and Jamie on my way over. She was laughing in the passenger seat, so caught up in their conversation, I don't think she even noticed me or my truck.

In that instant, I was hit with the urge to throw up, and it hasn't left me yet.

I thought I was okay with the dating thing. I was sure it was what she needed. But what about me? Is it wrong to want to say fuck it all and make her mine regardless of the circumstances? Because right now, tonight, I don't give a damn about the risks. If I get hurt, I get hurt. It's a possibility no matter what I do. So why put myself through hell now? She's already told me she wants me. Maybe I should believe her.

"You need help out there?" Mr. Pruitt calls from the patio door.

I situate another block on the pile and wipe the back of my hand across my brow. "Nah, I'm good, but thank you."

The older man dips his chin. "All right. We're headed into town. We'll be back in a half hour."

"Sounds good. I'm almost done here anyway." Then I'll have to find something else to do to keep from going crazy. Maybe I'll go for a run.

A few minutes later, I hear their car back out of the garage out front, and I stand back and survey my progress. I only planned to unload the blocks tonight, but taking my frustration out on my body has made the process go faster than expected. Maybe I should start digging out the embankment, too.

The sound of a truck approaching on the street grabs my attention, and I straighten, listening carefully. It's only been an hour since I passed Rachel and Jamie on the road, so I doubt it's them already, even if a selfish part of me hopes it is.

It takes everything in me not to stalk around the house to investigate. That would be some creeper level shit, and I'm already straddling the line by working across the street tonight.

A minute later, I wish I had gone to scope things out. Then I could have stopped Jesse in his tracks. But he's already halfway across the backyard by the time I notice him.

"Kinda late to be working, isn't it?" he asks as he strolls over a little too casually, his hands tucked in his pockets.

"Since when do you check up on me?" I turn my back on him and grab a couple blocks from the trailer, then add them to the stack on the ground. "Or are you here to bitch me out some more?"

"I'm here to apologize, asshole," he grunts out. "So maybe dial back the attitude."

Apologize? Jesse? I'll believe it when I hear it. With a huff, I turn for another couple of blocks.

"Can you stop for a minute and at least look at me?" The hint of regret in his tone takes me aback.

"I want to get this done," I grumble, sloughing off the curiosity building in me. "Could get it done faster if you helped."

He makes a throaty sound but steps up to the trailer and grabs a couple of blocks. "I heard you talking to Craig the other day in the storage yard."

My chest pinches, but I don't stop my movements. "Yeah?"

"You really do care about her."

I turn to him with a scowl. "Of fucking course I do. I told you that."

"I know." He nods, keeping his focus set on me. "And I should have listened to you."

With a huff, I shake my head. "Why is it always like that with us, man?"

"What do you mean?"

"You question everything I do, and instead of giving me the benefit of the doubt, I have to prove myself to you." Blood heating, I tear off my gloves and toss them onto the trailer. "It's bullshit, and I'm sick of it."

A crease forms on his brow. "I didn't realize—"

"Because you never listened when I tried to tell you."

"It wasn't intentional, Jinx. I honestly didn't know."

Seriously? He's a smart guy. How could he have not known?

"To be fair," he says, "I don't think I'm that hard on you about everything." He tips his head. "In fact, sometimes you're the one who gives me hell. So this isn't completely one-sided."

I scoff. "The difference is that when I give you shit, it's for good reason. You, on the other hand, shoot first and ask questions later." I run a hand around the back of my neck. "I'm not a kid anymore, man. You can stop assuming everything I do is based on hormones and stupidity. I outgrew that shit a long time ago."

His jaw tightens. "I know. Now, I mean."

I regard him for a beat, frustration coursing through my veins. "And overhearing my conversation with Craig did that? I don't buy it."

He lifts a shoulder and gives me a contrite smile. "Hayden helped."

I give a laugh. "You'd be so fucking screwed without her, man."

"You think I don't know that?" He shakes his head, then gives a heavy exhale. "But the truth is, I'd be screwed without you, too."

Damn right he would. As far as the landscaping side of the business goes, anyway.

"Look, man, I'm not really good at this apology shit, but I owe you a big one." He cups the brim of his cap and rounds it, ducking his head. "I'm sorry that I failed to realize you'd grown up and that you actually turned out to be a pretty decent guy."

"Is that supposed to be a compliment? Because you say it like you're surprised."

"Yes, it's a compliment." He sighs. "But no, I'm not surprised. We were raised by the same people, and I think they did a pretty damn good job with all of us."

I can't argue with that. Ma and Dad long ago mastered the skill of giving us the right mix of unconditional and tough love. I might've thought differently as a kid, but these days, I wouldn't change a thing.

"I've been tougher on you than I should have been, probably because you've always looked up to me. In a way, I've always believed that how you turned out is a reflection of me and the example I set." He lifts his ball cap and shuffles a hand over his hair. "And I'm only now realizing that I don't need to do that anymore. You grew up. A long time ago. You're not looking at everything I do anymore. You've become your own person."

I get it. I figured out his reasoning a long time ago. Even so, it pisses me off that, no matter how many times I tried to call attention to it, he refused to hear me out. If he hadn't been so damn stubborn, we could have addressed this years ago.

I stuff my hands into the front pockets of my jeans. "I'm always going to look up to you, man. No matter how old I get."

He gives his head a brief shake. "See, that makes me nervous."

I chuckle. "Why?"

"Because I've fucked up plenty. Especially these past few years."

"If you're talking about the situation with Hayden and Jett, you didn't fuck up. You did what you needed to do. I know you wish you two could've worked your shit out sooner, but things happen for a reason. It wasn't your time before."

Thinking about it like that hits home. It's like a punch to the gut.

Maybe the timing for Rachel and me is right. Because the only thing that's been holding me back is fear.

Jesse glances off toward the tree line. "Why is Rachel with Jamie Stroud right now?"

My stomach sinks at the reminder. "How do you know that?"

"I saw them in Copper Crossing before I came here."

So that's where they were going.

I scrub a hand over my jaw. "I thought her seeing other people would be good for her, but I'm starting to wonder if it was a bad idea."

He snorts. "You think? If you want to be with her and she feels the same, then why are you playing around?"

I clench my hands at my sides, then stretch my fingers out again. "Like I said, I thought it was the right thing to do."

He shakes his head. "Sounds familiar. And it sounds like something you're gonna regret."

"I already do."

"So fix it."

How do I do that without going back on my word? "I told her I'd be okay with this."

He nods. "I get it. But do you have any idea how much I regret not trying just one more time with Hayden? If I had, everything would have been different. We wouldn't have lost four goddamn years, Jinx."

The pain in his expression and in his voice is palpable. As stubborn as he can be sometimes, he's always worn his feelings about Hayden on his sleeve.

"Is this pep talk part of your apology?"

He shoots me a sidelong glance. "This is me telling you not to follow my example. If you're serious about Rachel, stake your claim. Don't let someone else move in and keep her from you."

That's the last thing I want, but what if the way she feels about me now doesn't last? Will she give months or even years to our relationship, only to realize she was wrong?

"How does she feel about you?" he asks.

Yanking off my hat, I rake a hand through my hair. Then I blow out a breath. "She thinks seeing other people is ridiculous."

He laughs. "She told you that?"

My chest tightens at the incredulity in his tone. "More or less."

"So she's doing this to appease you?"

Jesus. When he says it like that, it makes me sound like an asshole. Makes me feel like one, too.

"You're not a kid anymore, Jinx. I'm sorry that it took me so long to acknowledge that. But if there's any part of you that's holding back with her because of the way I've made you feel..." He breaks off, shaking his head. "Stop, man. Stop second-guessing that you're enough for her. If she says she wants you, believe her. And believe me when I say that I am really fucking proud to call you my brother."

Holy shit.

Emotion builds in my chest like a damn bomb, threatening to explode right here in the Pruitts' backyard.

He slings an arm around my shoulder and gives me a side hug. "Go get your girl, man. And once you get that shit figured out, we'll talk about the partnership. I promise you,

I'm not going anywhere. But she may be if you don't set things straight."

Maybe.

Probably, if she spends any more time with Jamie fucking Stroud.

Fuck. The idea makes my gut twist painfully.

"All right?" He gives me a shake.

"Yeah," I say hoarsely and then clear my throat. "Thanks for this."

He grins. "I can be something other than a pain in the ass sometimes."

I snort. "You're still a pain in the ass. But a little more tolerable. Like a cramp instead of a hemorrhoid."

With a laugh, he shoves me away. "Get the hell out of here, man. I'll finish unloading the block."

I scan the dozen or so remaining and then the dirt that needs to be dug out.

"I planned to dig out the wall tonight."

He follows my gaze and sighs. "I guess I'll do that, too, then."

I bite back a smirk.

After that ice cream shop incident, damn right he will.

THIRTY-FOUR

JINX

Surprise, surprise. He took her to the most expensive restaurant in Copper Crossing.

He probably thinks he can throw around a little cash and win her over. Maybe convince her that he's a catch over a bottle of fancy wine. Prove he's virile and shit by devouring a big-ass steak the size of his fat, too good-looking head.

Fucking guy.

I'd hate him if he wasn't so goddamn likable.

I sit in my truck, parked right next to his, ruminating over how much of a scene I want to create. More to the point, I have to consider what's least likely to piss Rachel off. Or worse, embarrass her.

If I go inside, that'll happen. She's been through too much to have any interest in drama. And if I wait, it'll give him more time to talk her into seeing him again.

I guess that's the chance I have to take.

Fortunately, I don't have to wait long.

Ten minutes after I've parked so I'm facing the entrance, the front door of the Crossing Steakhouse opens, and Rachel steps out ahead of Jamie. She's wearing dark wide-leg pants that flow around her and a cropped white top that not only shows a sliver of her stomach, but her bare shoulders, too.

Teeth gritted, I tug the keys from the ignition.

With the contrast between that white top and her skin and the way her hair is piled up at the back of her head, there's no way that asshole didn't notice all her freckles. My fucking freckles.

Possession roars through my veins as I hop out of the truck and step into their path.

Jamie grins when he spots me, totally at ease. "Hey, man. How's it going?"

I don't respond. I don't even look at him. It's impossible to when I can't take my eyes off her.

My woman.

Her steps falter and her breath hitches when she finally looks up. With parted lips, she regards me, her wide eyes dancing back and forth between mine. I don't need to hear the questions going through her mind to recognize them.

"You all right, Enders?" Jamie frowns at me, then glances back at Rachel. Then his shoulders drop. "Ah, I see." He gives a light laugh, then nods almost to himself, before returning his focus to me. "So you're the one, huh?"

The one? Did she tell him about me?

She tilts her head almost imperceptibly. Guiltily, too.

Yeah, she told him. Just like she told me. Like Jesse said, I should have believed her.

I should have believed my own mind, too, because this woman is it for me. I knew it the moment she stood on her back porch and yelled at me for cutting her grass.

She's feisty, my Sunny. Beneath the sweet and pretty exterior is a strong, determined woman who knows what she wants.

How could I have ever doubted her?

I clear my throat and give Jamie a quick nod. "Thanks for taking care of my girl, but I'll be the one taking her home."

He holds up both hands and steps back. "If that's what Rachel wants, she's all yours."

She wets her lips and nods, her attention fixed solely on me. "I do."

Thank god.

RACHEL

JUSTIN IS quiet behind the wheel. Too quiet. I don't know what to make of it.

He knows he's the one I want. At the restaurant, I got the impression that he'd finally figured that out. That he'd finally had enough of the silly game he wanted me to play to prove that to him.

Maybe I should have pushed back. Maybe I should have fought harder. Told him that, no, I would not date anyone else. I didn't need to because he already has my heart.

Oh my god.

Why the hell didn't I do that?

Fuck, Rachel. Fuck, fuck, fuck.

What is wrong with you?

I ball my hands into tight fists in my lap and stare at the road ahead of us, praying the emotion burning in my throat doesn't make its way to my eyes.

I did it again.

I let another man convince me that I should do something other than what I really want, and I did it to make him happy. I set aside my wants, what I knew to be true. Now, wallowing in silence, I see it all so clearly.

I don't know why he showed up tonight. All that matters is that he did. And that I've been given the opportunity to fix this.

"We need to talk," I say and then clear my throat. "About a few things."

His hands tighten on the wheel, and the little muscle at the juncture of his jaw pulses. "Not really in the mood to talk," he mutters, not bothering to look my way.

"Are you mad?" I swear to god, if he's going to be audacious enough to try and flip this around—

"Not mad."

"Good." I shake my head, biting back a harsh laugh. "If you were, I'd make you stop this truck right freaking now."

The faintest flicker of a smile softens his cheek for a moment, but just as quickly, his expression goes tense again.

We come to the first stop sign in Cole Creek, but instead of turning right to go to my street, he goes straight through town. "Where are we going?"

He doesn't answer. Just keeps his gaze trained on the road ahead like he didn't hear me.

"Okay..." Now I do laugh, but I'm not amused. "I think we're about to have our first fight."

In response, he grunts. Freaking *grunts*.

"You don't get to show up like a damn Neanderthal at a date *you* told me to go to and then give me the silent treatment for twenty damn minutes, Justin Enders." My voice is unnecessarily loud, but I'm done playing games. "What the hell was that back there?"

He tips his head from one side to the other, straining the thick tendons in his neck and making my mouth water, dammit.

"Hello?" I shift in the seat so I'm facing him full-on. "You've never held back before, so why are you doing it now?"

It isn't until he hits the blinker that I realize he's turning onto his street instead of mine.

"I'm thinking," he finally mutters, his voice as rough as the gravel beneath his tires.

"About?"

"I'd rather show you." He cranks the wheel into his driveway, slams the truck into park, and jumps out.

"Are you freaking kidding me?" I hop out and stomp to the front of the truck. When we meet, I shove at his chest. "You don't get to do this. You don't get to go all broody on me when this whole thing is your fault."

He grasps my wrist, blue flames blazing in his stupidly sexy, hooded eyes. "It is my fault," he admits, his voice low and husky. "It's my fault that I thought I could just be a nice guy and not fall for you. It's my fault that I didn't try harder to stay away when I knew you needed time. It's my fault that I thought I could step back and let you take that time after the fact, too."

My breath hitches in my chest, and my heart beats so hard that I can feel it in my ears.

"I was wrong, Sunny," he says, hanging his head. "I'm not that fucking strong. Is that what you want me to say?"

"I-I don't know. I..." I step in close, push up on my toes, and kiss him. Hard. *That's* what I want. Turns out I don't actually want him to talk. I want him to kiss me and touch me and make me forget we ever thought we could control this thing between us.

A low, feral growl rises in his throat as he lets go of my wrists in favor of palming my ass and lifting me off the ground.

Hands in his hair, I tug and claw, trying to get closer to him while our lips and tongues battle over who's more desperate for the other.

I don't even realize he's carried me into the house until he slams my back against the wall just inside the entry.

He tears his mouth from mine and trails wet kisses along my jaw. "I'm done playing. You hear me, Sunny?" He bites at my neck, making me arch into him with a hiss. "You're mine now. No more dates. No more bullshit."

Yes. *Yes, yes, yes.*

"Just you and me as soon as I can get you out of these fucking clothes."

With a breathless laugh, I try to rotate my hips to show him just how much I agree. His hold on me is too fierce, though, and his body is too wrought with hard, unyielding tension.

"Be careful," he warns, fingers digging deeper into my ass as he grinds back. "I'm already a man on the edge."

Gripping his head, I pull him back from my neck and grin. "Then quit talking and get me out of these damn clothes."

Those wicked flames flash in his eyes again, and then it's on.

He sets me back on my feet and gets to work on tearing off my shoes and my pants. While he's busy with that, I strip my top over my head.

He fists the back of his shirt and tugs that off, too. My greedy hands are everywhere at once. His wide, muscled shoulders. His thick, flexing biceps. And the hard, sculpted planes of his chest.

I angle in, placing frantic kisses on every inch of bare skin I can reach. I want to experience every bit of this man. To touch him and taste him everywhere. He's already under my skin, but I want to feel him in my veins.

I flick my tongue over one of his nipples, eliciting a groan from him, and while he unclasps my bra, I undo his belt and his fly with eager hands. I need to touch him. To feel him skin on skin.

"Ah, fuck," he rasps when my fingers wrap around his hard, thick cock. "You better be sure about this if you're gonna touch me like that."

A wanton laugh escapes my chest. "I'm sure that if you don't get inside me soon, I'm going to go out of my damn mind." I shove down his jeans, fist his dick again, and give him a pointed glare. "Tell me you have a condom."

He hits me with a wicked grin. "I have a whole damn box."

"Then fix this problem, Justin."

In one quick swoop, he swings me up into his arms and deposits me on the kitchen table a couple of feet away. The last time I sat at this table, he ate my cookies. Maybe tonight he'll eat me.

"Don't you dare move." He points a finger at me while he kicks off his boots and jeans. Then he sprints his bare, sculpted ass down the hall, presumably to the bedroom. He's back in less than a minute, already rolling on the latex.

"Panties," he demands, lifting his chin to the lace still keeping me hidden. "Take 'em off."

I don't know what comes over me then. Maybe I'm emboldened by the need coursing through me, but I lean back on one palm and spread my legs just enough to slide my hand into the damp fabric. "Don't you want to do it? I mean, you should probably check to make sure I'm ready."

Nostrils flaring, he adjusts the condom and stalks forward. Then, with his hands planted on either side of my hips, he dips in close. "I don't need to check, baby. I can already see how wet you are for me. Can smell how ready, too." He pulls in a deep breath and lowers his focus to my core, watching me play.

Heat blooms in my cheeks and spreads down my neck, pebbling my nipples.

"Ah, that's pretty." He hovers closer, capturing one peak between his lips.

My hips lift from the table the second he sucks.

"Such a greedy girl," he murmurs. "You think you can handle my cock, Sunny? Or are you gonna come undone the second I touch you?"

I rub circles around my clit, the ache already building. "That's the point, isn't it?"

His eyes flick to mine, full of mischief, and he shakes his head. "There's no race to the finish with me, baby. Be damn sure about that." He wraps his fingers around my wrist, halting my play. "When I touch you, whether I'm buried inside your sweet pussy or eating it, you *will* come. I don't care if it takes a minute or an hour."

I swallow hard. "So no faking?"

His eyes flash with a dark intensity. "If you have to fake it, then I'm not doing my job. We clear?"

I nod and wet my lips. From what I've experienced thus far, I can't imagine it'll be a problem with him, anyway.

"Now lift your ass so I can get those fucking panties off."

The heat building low in my core ignites at the command. God, I love this demanding side of him.

Leaning back on both hands, I do as I'm told, letting

him peeling the damp lace from my body. When he fists the fabric and brings it to his nose, I almost die.

"You told him about me." One side of his mouth ticks up in a smug grin. "Were you thinking about me, too? When you let him buy you dinner?"

Every cell in my body trembles with anticipation. "Y-yes."

He gives a feral laugh and tosses the panties onto the table.

The table.

Holy crap, he's going to fuck me right here on the table.

Nudging his way between my thighs, he strokes his cock, eyes never leaving mine. "I'm sorry I put you through that, but I'm not the least bit apologetic for being the one who made you wet."

Dick in hand, he rubs the tip through my slickness, sending a full-body shudder through me. There's no doubt in my mind that I'll come tonight. Just that light tease against my clit already has my blood roaring.

"Don't tease me," I beg. "I need to feel you inside."

Hooking an arm around my back, he hauls me to the edge of the table and notches the head of his cock at my opening. "You're gonna be the end of me," he warns. He's looming over me, cast in shadow, looking as though he's ready to eat me whole. "There isn't a damn thing I wouldn't do for you. You know that, right?"

He doesn't wait for my response before he pushes inside. The move is so slow and torturous that I almost weep with the frustration *and* the pleasure of it.

He's big and it's been a while, so I appreciate the gesture, but my god, I need him. I need to feel him stretch me and fill me and own me.

"So good," he murmurs as we both watch him sink

inside. "Ah, baby, you feel so fucking good." His arms *shake* on either side of me and his jaw clenches, and I suddenly can't breathe.

"More," I plead, my chest rising and falling as I watch him watch us finally crossing this line. As we finally give into this.

Somehow, it's simultaneously too much and not enough.

Yet it's *everything*.

My hips pulse, pulling him into me. Begging for him. "*Please*."

"So desperate for me," he praises, inching in further. "So fucking greedy. Look at us, Sunny. Look how good we fit together."

I see it. I feel it. He's not even fully seated, and it's already the best sex I've ever had. Because it's him. *It's us*.

Finally—finally—he thrusts forward, burying himself to the hilt, and every fiber of my being comes alive.

It's like nothing I've ever felt before, being connected to him like this. Being as close as physically possible while knowing that it's so much more than sex.

Maybe that's why I'm already on the edge, the coil of arousal wound so tight. Because this man takes away every one of my worries and fears. He doesn't ask questions or permission, either. He does it because he understands that I need it.

"You're not going to hurt me," I pant as he pulls out and slides back in like I'm a fragile, priceless work of art. "We've got all the time in the world for slow and easy, but right now..." I cup his face and lock eyes with him. "I need you to fuck me."

Shadows of desire darken his expression, and finally, he pumps in hard.

I gasp as pleasure ricochets through me. "Harder."

A feral grin ticks up one corner of his mouth. "You sure about that?"

Licking my lips, I lean back and spread my knees to give him better access. "Do I look unsure to you?"

He chuckles and pounds in again. And again. And again. All the while teasing my clit lightly with his fingertips.

The contrast is maddening, and my head buzzes with frustration and anticipation. I want to come so badly. Not only for the release, but to show him how crazy he makes me.

Suddenly, he scoops me up again and carries me to the living room. I cling to him as he tosses a pillow and lays me on the couch. He never leaves my body, and the second my ass hits the pillow, he cages me in, his hands pressed to the cushion on either side of my shoulders, and drives into me again.

"Oh god!" I grasp his forearms and meet his thrusts. "Why does that feel different? Oh, shit. *Oh, fuck.*" My nails dig into his skin and my back arches. And holy freaking hell, this angle... the way he hits every nerve—

"That's it, baby," he growls, his arms and neck straining. "Take me deeper. Take me all the fucking way home."

"*Ahh.*" My head spins and my nipples tighten in response to the sensation. The way his thighs press against the back of mine while he strokes that spot deep inside is so perfect.

The heat in my lower belly spills over like molten lava, and my orgasm hits so hard that all I can do is cling to him as I'm washed away in the most exquisite rush and then pulled back in again as pulse after pulse of pleasure rocks my body.

I'm still breathless and reeling when he lifts my ass even higher, his hips like pistons as he fucks me with an animalistic ferocity. A man of power and possession on a mission to please.

"Yes, baby." I scrape my nails down his chest, loving every move he makes. "Come for me. Fill me up. Make me yours."

Two more hard, punishing pumps, and he throws his head back with a roar. His cock thickens inside me, and every muscle in his body strains as he comes.

It's beautiful and breathtaking, witnessing this big, protective man lose control. It's empowering, knowing that I was the one who made him so wild.

When the last spasms subside, he drops to his elbows above me, his face buried in my neck as he catches his breath.

I kiss his shoulder as I cradle him close. "You okay?"

His body, covered in a fine sheen of sweat, shakes with silent laughter. "I'm supposed to ask you that."

"Oh, I'm more than fine." I bite my lip as heat creeps up my chest and into my cheeks.

"Please tell me that wasn't fake."

"Definitely not fake." The giggle that escapes me is one of pure joy. "And definitely the first time that's ever happened."

He lifts his head, surprised eyes darting back and forth between mine. "Are you serious?"

With a nod, I swallow down the embarrassment that tries to rise up. "I've only ever come with Prince. But you, sir, are two for two."

A crooked and all too satisfied smile spreads across his face. "Well, shit. Feels like I just won a damn award."

"Oh my god." I shove at his stomach, but there's no

budging him. "We really need to do something about that ego."

"And this." He pulls the throw pillow from beneath me and tosses it to the floor. "She's gonna need a good washing, for sure."

There's no stopping the wave of embarrassment that hits me. I scrunch up my face and peer up at him with one eye. "I'm sorry?"

He chuckles. "No, you're not. And neither am I. In fact, I might start carrying her around with me, just in case."

I burst out laughing, a lightness flooding me. Never have I had this kind of silly interaction while naked with a man still firmly inside me. "Oh really? You plan on going around town, seducing random women with your pillow magic?"

With a cheeky grin, he pushes himself up and grabs a couple of tissues from a box on the coffee table to take care of the condom. "Just you, Sunny girl. Anywhere and everywhere you'll have me."

Good lord, he's cute. And sexy. And so damn lovable.

"You sure about that? Because now that I know you have the golden touch..."

He cocks a brow. "Don't challenge me, babe. Because I'll take it every fucking time."

I hope he does.

THIRTY-FIVE

JINX

Angry thunder rolls outside, but beside me, the most peaceful angel sleeps.

She took her hair down before we showered and crawled into bed, and though she cut it a while back, it's still long enough to drape over my shoulder like a soft silk blanket. Her breath against my chest is warm and sweet. A complete paradox to all the dirty things she said on the couch. And her body, so warm and content as she curls into me, makes it difficult not to wonder how the hell I've managed to survive this long without her.

Call me a romantic like my mother, but I've always dreamed of finding a woman to share moments like this with. I've never been cynical or bitter about love, but holding Rachel like this... it's more than I ever expected and certainly more than I've experienced.

Sure, I've had other women in my bed. Not as many as people assume, but I can confidently say I've never held a single one of them and imagined our future together while they slept.

With Rachel, I can't think of anything else. If I'm honest, this sensation isn't new. It's not like I'm suddenly pussy whipped now that we've had sex. No, I've caught myself making plans for us in my head far too many times to count over the past month. Not just plans for Rachel and me either, but for the four of us. Emma and Mason, too. What we'll do for Thanksgiving and Christmas. Where we might go on vacation for spring break next year. If I'll eventually move in with them or if we'll find a place of our own.

"Whatever you're thinking about must be serious." Rachel's sleepy voice cuts into my thoughts. Then she presses a kiss to my chest. "You okay?"

I clear my throat and stroke gentle fingers up and down her arm. She's wearing one of my T-shirts, and the sleeve hangs almost to her elbow. "I'm perfect. You comfortable?"

"Mm-hmm." She snuggles in closer, lifting her leg a little higher on mine. "So comfy. This is a great bed."

I give a soft laugh, even as warmth blooms in my chest. "Just the bed?"

"The pillow is nice, too, albeit a little distracting." She pokes my abs playfully. "And very sexy."

"A sexy pillow. Huh." I grin into the darkness and shake my head. "I guess I've been called worse."

With a giggle, she trails her fingertips over my bare skin, making my muscles jump. "What time is it?"

"Ah..." I crane my neck so I can see the clock on the nightstand. "Almost two."

"You haven't slept, have you?"

Swallowing, I hum. "Nah. Not yet."

"Not used to sharing your bed?" She pushes up on her

elbow. Wearing a concerned expression I can just make out in the glow from the clock, she studies me. "I could go crash on the couch."

"Fuck that." I loop my arms around her and drag her on top of me.

She laughs and squirms but not hard enough to actually get away. Instead, she adjusts her position so she fits perfectly against me. Like she belongs like this. Like we belong.

"I was thinking about where we go from here," I admit. We have to talk about it eventually, and now is as good a time as any.

"And what did you come up with?" she asks with her face pressed to my neck.

Hand running up and down her back, I brace myself to be completely open about my thoughts. "I don't care where we go as long as we do it together."

She lifts her head and searches my face. For a long moment, she's silent, just taking me in as lightning flashes outside, followed by distant thunder. Finally, she speaks. "I like that plan. Are you thinking something like... an overnight trip here and there? Maybe a weekend away? Or something more complex, like a road trip?"

My heart pounds out a rhythm it's created only for her. "I was thinking more like a trip around the world."

A slow grin spreads across her face. "On a plane?"

"A boat. Without a motor."

Her eyes widen. "Oh, wow. That could take a long time."

With one hand still holding her to me, I smooth the hair back from her face. "It'd be a commitment, that's for sure."

She nods slowly and pushes upright so she's straddling

my hips. Without panties, because hers are still somewhere in the kitchen.

"Is that too much?" I grip her waist, either to keep her from getting too close to my dick or to help guide her there. I'm not sure.

"Does that thought scare you?" she counters, shifting back a bit so the heat from between her legs is centered over my hardening cock.

Instinctively, I press up into her, though my boxer briefs keep things from getting too out of hand. "Doesn't scare me at all." I grind again, and she sucks in a breath as she splays her palms over my chest for leverage. "You?"

She shakes her head, pulsing her hips ever so slightly like she's begging my dick to hurry the fuck up and find its way home. "It doesn't scare me anymore. I know what I want. What I've wanted from the beginning. Now that I know we're on the same page..."

I bite back a groan as she grinds against me. The friction of her pussy and my underwear sends a bolt of desire through me. "I need to feel you again."

"See? Something else we're in agreement on."

She lifts just enough to push down my briefs while I grab a condom from the box on the nightstand. Together, we roll it on, and in less than a minute, I'm balls deep inside her.

"We have a lot to figure out," she says as she rides me slowly. "But we'll get there."

I thumb a nipple through the cotton covering her. "You say the sexiest things."

She grins and pauses just long enough to whip my shirt over her head. "Who knew I had it in me?"

"I did," I grit out, holding her hips tightly to keep her

from making me blow my load two seconds in. "I knew it the second you told me off for cutting your grass."

A soft, sexy laugh spills from her throat as she arches back, her hair falling over her shoulders, and braces her hands on my thighs. She's a fucking goddess, riding me with the confidence of a warrior and paying no mind to the storm raging outside. This is her show. Her stage.

"You bring out the best in me," she pants. "What can I say?"

I jackknife up and gather her to me, desperate to be as deep and as close to her as I can get. When she slides down, I push up, filling her over and over again until our ragged, desperate breaths drown out the storm.

"Ah, fuck." I've never had a problem with stamina, but then again, I've never been with her until tonight. I swear she could make me come in seconds like a teenager if I wasn't so determined to make it good for her first. "You're killing me, Sunny," I rasp. "Every fucking thing about you drives me insane. Your strength. Your fire. This fucking body."

She rolls her hips, then rises up, arching so her tits are in my face, and I swear to god my vision blacks out for a second.

Grasping for control, I roll us over and pin her hands above her head on the mattress. "My turn, Sunny girl. I love the way you fuck me, but right now, it's my turn."

Her lashes lower over hazy eyes as she bites her lip in silent assent. Her submission is like fuel to the fire already burning in my veins. She's been strong and independent for so long, and I fucking love that she trusts me enough to hand over the reins. That she knows I'm not the kind of man who'll let her down in any regard. I can't imagine it's been easy for her. Hell, I know it wasn't. I was there to witness every second of it, from her snark in the bar that first night to her staring me down from her back porch when I cut her lawn. Even tonight when she chewed me out.

I'll do what I can to ensure she never loses that fire again.

But goddamn, it's like a sucker punch when she lets down her guard just for me. I want to be that person for her. Nothing in my life has mattered more than our connection.

That realization has me slowing my pace, easing in and out of her with lazy, drawn-out strokes as our breaths mingle and our eyes remain locked.

"I love you." The confession leaves my mouth without a trace of hesitation. She's probably not ready to say it back, but I need her to know what she's done to me.

Her eyes widen as she pulls in a quiet gasp.

"It's okay." I let go of one of her hands and cup her face, brushing my thumb along her cheek. "You don't have to say anything. I just want you to know."

She swallows hard and closes her eyes. When she opens them again, she sucks in another shaky breath. "I-I love you, too."

Holy shit. Damn if my heart doesn't explode into a thousand pieces at the sound of those words. "Babe..."

Tears fill her eyes, but she smiles. "More than that, I am *in* love with you."

My chest fills with a mix of pride and devotion, and not just because she feels the same, but because I put myself out there and made myself vulnerable to her in a way I've never done with before. I took a risk, hoping she'd see me for the kind of man I believe I am. And she did.

She tugs her hand free, curls them both around my jaw, and pulls me down for a kiss. "Now that we're clear on that..." She sighs when we break apart. "You should probably make love to me."

Grinning like a damn fool, I shift so I'm on my knees, lift her ass with both hands, and drive in deep. "Sweetest words I've ever heard."

THIRTY-SIX

RACHEL

Twenty-four hours ago, I never would have guessed I'd be waking up in Justin's bed like this. No, with the date with Jamie looming, I imagined that I'd be relieved that it was finally behind me—one more down on my path to getting the man I really wanted—but that I'd spend Friday morning detoxing. Maybe go for a run and then stop in for a chai and chat with Bobbie Jean while I picked out a new romance novel as a treat to read between my grad school assignments.

Justin going caveman and showing up at the restaurant last night proved to be all the detox I needed. That possessive, growly side of his? Good lord, it *works* for me. The man made me come *twice,* no toys or batteries required. I gave up on the idea that my body would ever work like that long ago. But one thing is clear where Justin Enders is concerned: where there's a will, there's a way, and my man aims to please every damn day.

I stretch like a cat after a perfect nap and grin at the delicious ache in my muscles.

My reverie is interrupted, though, by the sound of footsteps in the hallway outside the bedroom.

"What's that smile for?" Justin pads into the bedroom in a pair of black boxer briefs, holding two steamy mugs of coffee.

"Mmm..." Tucking the sheet around my chest, I sit up, and after I give my shoulders a good roll, I accept the coffee. "Just thinking about how I should be way more tired than I am."

With a flash of a smug grin, he takes a seat on the edge of the bed beside me. "Did I keep you up too late?"

"Yes." I bring the mug to my lips and blow over the top of it. "But it was absolutely worth it."

He chuckles. "For the record, you were the one who initiated round two."

I did, didn't I? Hmm. I think I like this new, sexually empowered side of myself.

"Not that I'm complaining," he adds with a little bounce on the mattress. "I'm gonna need to tighten the screws on this bedframe, though."

"Whoops." I shrug. "Sorry about that."

"No, you're not." He cocks a brow and takes me in for a long beat. His bright eyes scan my face, my hair, and my body wrapped up in nothing but his bedsheet.

I can only imagine what he sees. I went to bed with wet hair, and I scrubbed my face free of makeup in the shower we took together. I'm probably a wreck.

"You know, I didn't think you could get any prettier." His voice drops to a low, husky pitch. "But this just-fucked glow you've got going on right now? It's breathtaking."

And that's how women accidentally get pregnant... over and over again.

"Thank you for that. The compliment *and* the glow." I give him a coy smile. "We should probably talk about birth control."

He swallows down a gulp of coffee and nods. "I was thinking about that, too."

"I had an IUD for years, and the experience was awful. I had it removed a few months ago." Once Craig left, there was no point in suffering through the cramps and irregularity. Our sex life didn't really warrant that kind of protection in the first place, but I wasn't taking any chances, so I dealt with it.

"That's an implant, right?"

"Yes. They can be a great long-term option for women who are done having children or don't want more for a while."

He smooths his thumb over the enamel on his mug, focus fixed on the movement. "Which of those categories do you fall into?"

My heart does a weird little flip, and to keep my cool, I shove a hand into my hair and blow out a breath. "Jeez, Justin. Jump right into the tough questions, why don't you?"

"You know I don't hold back." He winks, easing the conversation back into lighthearted territory.

Thank God for that. It makes it easier for me to be just as forward.

"I've always wanted more kids," I say, voicing that admission out loud for the first time. "At least one. Maybe two more. It was just FJ and me growing up, and while there was nothing wrong with that, I always wished I had more siblings."

"Being one of four could be a pain in the ass from time to time, but I love being part of a big family now."

"I bet. I would've loved that for Mason and Emma..." I trail off, searching for the words for what I want to say next, hoping I won't scare him off. We just crossed the line into this new phase of our relationship. How deep is too deep right off the bat?

Justin dips his chin and catches my eye. "But?"

"But I didn't want more with Craig." Guilt swamps me as I make the admission, but it's the truth. He gave me incredible children, and I would never change that. But he's a better coparent now than he ever was when he lived with us.

Justin knuckles his nose. "So, you'd be open to more kids someday?"

With him? In a heartbeat. "I would."

A pleased, almost goofy smile makes that dimple in his cheek pop. "Noted."

I laugh, and the tension from moments ago dissipates. "But not anytime soon. I have a master's degree to finish first."

"Dually noted." He lifts his cup for another drink, his grin promising that, if and when the time comes for us, I'm going to be in trouble.

"Anyway, I'll make an appointment. Go on the pill. I used it before without problems, and as long as I'm the only one you're sleeping with..."

He cocks an eyebrow. "You're not insinuating that I'm a manwhore, are you?"

I giggle. "No. I'm insinuating that maybe we can forego condoms at some point. If you're comfortable with that."

His eyes widen, and I swear the man gasps. "Fuck you bare?"

Good lord, the mouth on this man.

"Don't play with me like that, Sunny. I'll drive you to the damn doctor right now if it'll make that happen faster."

Yep, I'm definitely in trouble.

"While we're on the subject of us spending more time together, I might've done some finagling this morning."

Nerves skitter through me at the possibilities. "Oh, boy. What kind of finagling?"

"I made plans for us this weekend."

Be still my heart.

"Starting in about two hours."

Two hours? I splay a hand over my chest and blink, suddenly a little panicked. "I have to get the kids from Crystal's and—"

"Bobbie Jean said she could keep them today. She's taking her kids to the lake for a beach day, so the more the merrier."

"Oh." He made plans for Mason and Emma on his own? Can he see the hearts in my eyes right now?

"I probably overstepped, but I didn't want you to have to worry about anything."

I appreciate that, and I'm not upset that he took it upon himself to make plans for them, too. He's more than proved that he has their best interest at heart. So I trust him to do the right thing when it comes to all of us. It's just...

"Craig is supposed to pick them up later this afternoon." And I'm going to have to explain why I'm not there to see them off.

He sets his coffee mug aside and squeezes my thigh through the blankets. "Is that what's bothering you? Or is it making plans in general? It's okay if it is. We've gone from, like, thirty-five to eighty overnight, so I get if it's too much."

I shake my head and swallow down the lump of emotion in my throat. "I'm okay with the plans. And it's not that I care what Craig thinks..." Though, there is a teensy part of me that doesn't want to make waves with him right now. The divorce is so close, and I don't want to give him any reason to be an ass in court.

"I can talk to him if you want. I know he isn't thrilled about us seeing each other, but I think he understands that there's not much he can do about it."

I scrape my teeth over my lips. "No. That's not necessary. I'll tell him. And I think..." I pause to pull in a deep breath. "I think we need to tell the kids, too."

He swallows audibly. "Mason already knows."

"What?" My heart lurches so violently I almost spill my coffee. "How?"

He shrugs. "Just figured it out, I guess. He asked me about it the other day."

Oh my god. I wrap both hands around my mug to hold it steady. "What did he say?"

"He asked if I liked you. And then he wanted to know if I'd sell him my truck if we got married."

If my jaw could physically detach from my body, it'd be on the floor. "He did not."

Justin nods once. "He sure did."

Hand to my forehead, I try to imagine the conversation. "But he wasn't upset?"

"Nope. Actually seemed pretty cool about it." He smirks, clearly pleased with that fact.

I suppose I am, too. Mason was the one I was worried about, given how much time they've spent together. I was afraid he'd think I was stealing Justin from him.

"Okay, so it's just Emma, then." I have no idea how she'll react. She's only nine, but she's already bouncing between being a sweet little girl and a cranky-for-no-reason almost-teenager.

"I actually have an idea that might help." He takes my cup from me, sets it aside, and grips both of my hands in his. "I want us to do something with them, too. If you're okay with it."

"Of course I am. They already love you. They just have to get used to me loving you, too."

He closes his eyes and gives a small smile. "Damn, I like hearing you say that."

Good to know, because I'm pretty sure I've been in love with him since the day he ate my chocolate chip cookies and told me he was going to help coach Mason's football team.

"Anyway..." he continues. "I was thinking we'd take them to Wisconsin Dells one of these weekends. Do they still get a long weekend off school in October?"

October. Yes. The one that always falls somewhere in the second half of the month. He's talking about taking a trip with us two whole months from now.

We're really doing this, aren't we?

"Yes, Sunny girl." He leans in and pecks my lips. "I still plan on being around then, if that's what you're thinking." He smooths his thumb over my cheekbone. "You okay with that?"

"I'm more than okay with it," I squeak.

He chuckles. "Good. So we'll tell them this weekend is for us, and then the weekend in the Dells is for them. Whatever they want to do."

"But I'll probably have class. And homework."

"Which we'll work around. I can take them to the water park or the arcade if you need to study."

Mental note to give Janice Enders the biggest hug ever next time I see her, because she raised this man right.

"So..." He wraps his arms around me and playfully rocks us from side to side. "Are we telling the kids you love me today or what?"

Oh, but that ego. That ego could still use some work.

"I WANT MY BRACELET BACK." On the other side of the kitchen table, Emma screws up her face in disgust.

We did it. We told her and Mason that Justin and I are officially dating. Putting the status of our relationship into that category doesn't feel right when we're so much more, but I don't want to overwhelm them right now, either.

"Aw, man." Justin frowns at the bracelet on his wrist. "Really? And here I was thinking about making you one."

She rolls her eyes. "You were not. You were too busy kissing my mom."

"Whoa." I hold up a hand. "I know this is probably hard for you, but there's no need for an attitude, missy."

Emma scowls and crosses her arms. "But he was. I saw him."

Justin clears his throat and side-eyes me. "Uh, you did?"

"Uh, yeah," she mocks. "In the garage the day you fixed my bike."

"Oh." He shifts forward in his seat, elbows on the table, and clasps his hands, clearly uncomfortable. "I, uh, I'm sorry you saw that."

"Me, too," she snarks. "I rode all the way to the end of the street again and almost kept going."

I fail at holding back a laugh. I suppose I'll take her sass over tears and confusion any day. "I hate to tell you," I say, sitting straighter, "but you'll probably see more of that. Not that we're going to be kissing all the time, but we do like each other, so..."

Mason lifts his chin to Justin. "I still got first dibs on your truck, right?"

Justin snorts. "Dude. Let me finish paying it off first."

Mason gives a lopsided grin. "That wasn't a no."

Oh my god, these kids.

"Okay, you two. Clearly, Justin and I seeing each other isn't a surprise to anyone, so—"

"Why do you call him that?" Emma pipes up. "His name is Jinx."

Ah, yes. We should probably clarify that. But it doesn't feel like my story to tell. So I sit back, giving him the floor.

"Jinx is my nickname," he says. "But Justin is my real name. Your mom calling me that... it's kinda personal. Something special between us."

I lean my head on his shoulder and give his bicep a squeeze. "He calls me Sunny sometimes, too. It's what people who like each other do."

Mason wrinkles up his nose. "TMI, Mom."

Justin laughs, his whole body shaking. "All right. I think it's time we end this conversation and give you two some time to think about it."

I nod along. "Yes. When you get home from your dad's on Sunday, we can talk more if you'd like."

Emma slides off her chair in a rush. "Nope, I'm good. I'm going to get my backpack ready." With that, she skips off to her room.

Mason, however, glances back and forth between us with narrowed eyes. "Don't make this weird, okay? Like, I know what going away for the weekend means."

My cheeks flame instantly. Oh, the joys of having a too-smart tween.

Justin clears his throat. "I've always respected your mom, Mase. That isn't going to change."

He gives a skeptical side-eye as he gets to his feet. "I'll be the judge of that." Then, just like his sister, he heads off to his room to get ready for the weekend.

"Well." With a soft laugh, I cover my face with my hands. "That went better than expected."

Justin drapes an arm over my shoulders and pulls me close so he can kiss the top of my head. "Of course it did. I'm a hell of a guy."

I melt into him with a sigh. "What have I gotten myself into?"

THIRTY-SEVEN

JINX

I left Rachel and the kids to get ready for their respective weekends while I stopped home to get my own bag packed and run a few errands. Little does Rachel know that this weekend away has been on my mind for a while, and I've made some plans. Plans that I cannot wait to make happen.

I pull into a parking space in front of Books & Beans just as a text lights up my phone.

> Rachel: Dropped the kids off at Bobbie Jean's, but I can't get a hold of Craig. I don't feel comfortable leaving town until I do.

The thought makes my chest constrict, but it's understandable. Do I wish we could just say fuck him and leave? Absolutely. But that's just asking for trouble.

Me: Fair enough. You want me to find out where he is today?

I took the day off—to say Hayden was shocked when I texted to let her know this morning would be an understatement—but as of our staff meeting on Monday, his crew was set to work on the site for the new dollar store all week. I could do a quick drive-by and solve this problem in five minutes.

Rachel: Do you mind?

Me: Not at all. Give me a few.

Rachel: Thanks, babe.

Babe. Damn, I love that.

While I'm here, I run into the coffee shop for our travel drinks. Becca is behind the counter today, presumably because Bobbie Jean is spending the day with the kids.

"Hey, little cousin." Becca flashes a bright grin as she tightens her blond ponytail. "I heard a rumor about you."

I give a light laugh and dig out my wallet. "It's probably true."

"Oh, I have no doubt it is." She leans across the counter and whispers conspiratorially. "Heard you've been seen coming and going from a certain kindergarten teacher's house all summer long."

I lift a hand and smirk. "Like I said..."

With a laugh, she slugs my shoulder. "Jinx Enders, you sly dog."

"You don't have to whisper about it anymore, either. We're out now."

She shakes her head and grins, the expression a mix of

surprise and approval. "I'm glad to hear it. You shouldn't have to sneak around."

"Anyway, we're headed out of town for the weekend, so I'm here for some liquid sustenance."

"Ah, I got you. A large Americano for you and an iced chai for the lady coming up." Winking, she gets to work making the drinks.

While I wait, I head for the books. I'm only slightly embarrassed by the idea of checking out with this particular purchase. Asking Amelia for a recommendation has been the worst part of my scheming, by far. She knew damn well why I was asking, but she had to throw out a few guesses for fun, including my inability to get it up *and* my lack of skill when it comes to getting my girl off without a little smut to help. Putting the book on the counter for Becca is far less painful. In fact, rather than razz me as she rings me up for the paperback and the coffee, all she does is smile and zip her lips.

Book tucked under my arm and coffee in hand, I head back to my truck. I've got the drinks situated in the cupholders and I'm just about to climb inside when a familiar truck pulls up behind me, almost like I manifested the asshole.

I shut the driver's door and lift my chin to Craig as he hops out. "Hey, man. Rachel's been trying to get a hold of you."

He has sunglasses on, so I can't see his eyes, but I imagine my knowledge of that has got him spitting daggers.

He stuffs his hands into the pockets of his jeans and steps forward. "Yeah, I just got her texts."

I lean against the rear fender of my truck, considering whether I should say more. Rachel wanted to talk to him herself, but I can't help but feel like he and I still have a few things to clear up.

"You going out of town with her, too?" he asks, finally removing his sunglasses and hanging them from the collar of his T-shirt.

"I am. Figure she could use some time away before school starts up again."

"So, this is a real thing, then? The two of you?"

I nod. It's strange, the way elation courses through me, mixing with apprehension now that I'm face to face with Craig. "It is."

Grunting, he scans our surroundings for a long moment. "I'm gonna be honest, man. I know I'm not supposed to care, but I do. I care a fucking lot."

"I get that. I'd rather you care than not give a shit. It tells me you probably want what's best for her."

He swallows hard and meets my eye. "I do. I know that might be hard to believe after the last couple of months, but I don't wish her any ill will. I might want to jack you in the face right now, but Rachel... she's the mother of my children."

Damn if that single sentence doesn't ease my mind in a way I never would have expected. I give him a smile. "I've wanted to punch you plenty, too, so I guess we've got that in common."

He scoffs, then says, "Yeah, I probably deserve it."

Yep. Not going to argue with him about that.

"Just promise me you're not playing around, man. I don't think I can walk away right now if I'm not clear on that."

I lower my head and give it a shake. "No offense," I say, focusing on him again so he can see how serious I am, "but I'm not promising you anything." My relationship is with

Rachel, not him. "But I have promised her, and that's the best I can give you."

He holds my gaze for a moment, then dips his chin. "Fair enough."

"You should still call her, though. She wants to talk to you about this herself."

He runs a hand over his bristled jaw. "All right. I can do that."

I push off the truck and pull in a breath. "Are we good, then? Or am I going to have to watch my back?"

The faintest smirk flickers across his face. "We're as good as we can be. Unless you do something to hurt my kids."

I hold up my hands and wince at the verbal blow that hit me straight in the chest. "You've got nothing to worry about where that's concerned. I love those kids."

He flinches at that last statement, but I don't take it back. I won't apologize. I *do* love them, and if he has a problem with that, then maybe we need to have another conversation.

"I'm not trying to replace you. That I can promise you."

He surveys me, brows lifted, and his expression softens. Like maybe he's actually paying attention and can see my sincerity. "I appreciate that."

I resist the urge to clap him on the back like we're old friends. Instead, I take a step back. "I've gotta get going."

"Yeah, me, too. I'll call her, though."

"I think she'd appreciate that." I offer a smile, hopeful that he means what he says. It'll be a hell of a lot easier for everyone—especially the kids—if we keep this civil.

He starts for the coffee shop door but pauses before he goes inside. "By the way, Jesse told me that things are gonna be changing at EE. For your sake, I hope that means what I think it does."

Jesse's been talking, huh? Can't deny that a little flicker of satisfaction doesn't hit me. I guess he meant what he said last night, too.

I bite back a grin. "I do, too, man. I do, too."

RACHEL

AT THE SOUND of tires crunching on the gravel in the driveway, I hurry around the house one last time to make sure the windows are all closed and that I didn't leave anything unnecessary plugged in. Justin should let himself in, so I quickly double-check my small pull-along suitcase while I'm at it, too. I have no idea what he has planned, so I packed a swimsuit and that navy dress I've been dying to wear. I want that to be a surprise, so in the suitcase it went, rather than in a garment bag. I'll just have to iron it. I might've tucked Prince inside, too. Just in case. Though based on my experience with Justin, I probably won't need him.

A knock on the front door startles me—and makes my cheeks flush. I hurry to zip up the suitcase before calling out for Justin to come in.

But it isn't his voice that sounds down my hall. No. This one has my heart lurching rather than somersaulting. "Ray?"

Shit. Craig.

Why didn't he just call me back?

Probably because you tried to call five times like a crazy person.

"Uh, hi." I force a smile as I round the corner with my suitcase in hand. "I'm sorry. I know I called a few times, but this isn't an emergency."

He eyes the suitcase and shuffles inside, but he remains close to the door. "I know. I read your texts. I was nearby, so I figured I'd stop by before I head back to work."

"Ah." I park the suitcase next to the table, where my purse, toiletry bag, and phone charger are ready to go. "I already dropped the kids off at Bobbie's. I told her you'd be by around five-thirty."

He nods casually, his demeanor ten times more relaxed than the last time he was here. "Sounds good." Then, he adds, "I ran into Jinx in town just now."

"Oh." And he's not spitting venom? Huh.

"Wasn't hard to figure out that it's him you're going away with."

I wring my hands together, bracing myself for the other shoe to drop.

"He's not a bad guy, Ray. I just didn't expect to feel this way about you seeing someone else." His brow creases with a sincere, almost pained expression that shocks me after how angry and irrational he's been about Justin and me up until now. "Splitting up was the right thing. For both of us. And I obviously didn't wait long to move on, but it's gonna take some getting used to, knowing you've found someone new."

Now he knows how I felt all those months ago. "It isn't easy, is it?"

He hooks his thumbs in his pockets and shakes his head. "No, it isn't. And for what it's worth, I'm sorry for making you feel the same. Shit, I didn't even give you a month."

The laugh I let out is soft, but it's laced with plenty of bitterness. I'm as over it as I'll ever be, but the principle of it still irritates me. We were married for twelve years and together for fifteen.

"I've started therapy," he admits so quietly that I'm not sure I've heard him correctly until I see the tears in his eyes. Tears he quickly blinks back with a sniff. "Probably should have done it a long time ago. Turns out I have a lot of shit to work through."

I don't doubt that. He didn't have the easiest of childhoods either, and obviously, our marriage had its issues, too.

"I'm not sure why I'm telling you this." He shrugs and gives me a facsimile of a smile. "I guess maybe I just wanted you to know that I'm really not trying to be an asshole."

I gulp down the lump forming in my throat. "Thank you for telling me."

With his lips twisted to one side, he ducks his head, scuffs a shoe along the floor in the entryway. "I might want to bring the kids with me at some point, too. If that's okay with you."

"Of course."

"And," he says, his voice hoarse. He clears his throat and focuses on my face, his eyes earnest. "I hope he makes you happy."

That confession was definitely not on my bingo card. The little sob that escapes me in response is such a surprise, I don't have a chance to stop it.

"He does," I whisper. Sniffing, I chase away my tears with the back of my hand. "I hope you find what it is you're looking for, too."

He gives a sheepish shrug. "Still trying to figure that out, but I'll get there."

I hope he does. Mason and Emma deserve the best version of their father he can give them.

"I should get going." He tips his head toward the door.

"Jesse's probably blowing up my phone, wondering where the hell I am, and Jinx is probably parked around the corner, waiting for me to leave."

I expected Justin to be here by now, so it's possible.

"Thanks for coming by." I give him a gentle smile.

"Have a good time this weekend. I'll see you Sunday afternoon." He pushes the screen door open. "Let me know if you're gonna be late coming home. I can keep the kids longer."

The easy offer nearly bowls me over. He's just full of surprises today, isn't he? "Thanks," I say, keeping the surprise out of my tone. "I'll keep you posted."

He steps out onto the porch just as Justin pulls into the driveway. "Fucking guy," he mutters under his breath.

I laugh. "What was that?"

He shakes his head as he clambers down the steps. "I'm working on it, all right?"

"Uh-huh."

Justin strides are way, lifting a hand in greeting, and Craig lifts his chin in return. I never imagined the day when my ex-husband and my boyfriend would pass each other in the driveway, and so casually, at that.

"Everything okay?" Justin asks, brushing a kiss to the top of my head when he meets me at the door.

"Believe it or not, yes. What did you say to him when you saw him in town?"

"Honestly, not much. He seems good, though, huh?"

"He does." I watch as Craig rolls by, lifting a hand as he passes. "It's strange."

He frowns. "Strange like we should be worried?"

"No." I shake my head. "Strange like maybe everything is going to be okay after all."

A crooked smile lifts one corner of his mouth. "Of

course it's gonna be okay." He snags my hand and pulls me to him. "Because, when it's you and me, ain't nothing gonna stand in our way."

He's such a cheeseball, but I love him all the more for it.

Smoothing my hands up his chest, I bite my lip. "You ready to get this weekend started?"

He swings me up into his arms like I weigh nothing at all. "Oh, Sunny girl, I am more than ready. The question is, are *you*?"

THIRTY-EIGHT

JINX

"I never want to leave this place." Rachel holds her arms out at her sides, turns her face up to the sun, and smiles into the breeze coming off Lake Michigan.

I scored the vacation rental this morning because of a cancellation. I have to believe there was some kind of divine intervention involved. The cabin is perfect. Cute and quaint, with a sandy beach and this little dock that's perfect for a couple of chairs or beach towels. There's a hot tub on the back patio, and the master bathroom has a tub that I definitely plan on breaking in. I've been fantasizing about Sunny in nothing but bubbles since she answered my call from the bathtub all those weeks ago.

"It's quite a view," I say, wrapping my arms around her from behind. "Then again, you're in it, too."

I find that sweet spot behind her ear and press my lips to her warm skin.

With a giggle, she leans into the kiss. "You're just full of all the right words, aren't you?"

"They flow when I'm around you. What can I say?" And damn if that's not the truth. My heart is so full when I'm with her. The words can't be contained.

She turns and loops her arms around my neck. "Can we have a campfire tonight? Looks like there's plenty of wood."

I nod. "Absolutely. I even grabbed supplies for s'mores."

Her eyes widen eagerly. "Did you really? I haven't had one yet this summer."

"We'll remedy that in no time." I dip low and steal a quick kiss. "But first, I was thinking maybe we'd break out the suntan lotion and soak up some of these rays."

She wrinkles her nose, drawing attention to the freckles scattered across the bridge. "You mean the sunscreen."

I laugh. "I got you covered, babe. I hope you brought a swimsuit."

She waggles her brows. "I did. And not my mom-bod one, either."

My dick twitches at the image that flashes in my mind. "Please tell me it's a two-piece."

She purses her lips. "It is. As secluded as it is here, there's a chance, if you're extra sweet, that it'll become a one-piece."

Hell yes. Then again, if she goes topless, it'll only be a matter of time before we're both skinny dipping.

"Maybe you should show me."

She wriggles out of my grasp and slowly walks backward a couple of steps before she strides to the end of the dock and across the yard. "Maybe you should catch me."

I barely have time to register her words before she takes off at a sprint toward the cabin.

Five minutes later, our clothes are in a pile on the cabin floor, and she's bent over the back of the couch.

I didn't steal her away so I could fuck her every chance I get, but I won't lie...

This is a damn good way to kick off our weekend.

JINX

"THAT WAS the best grilled cheese sandwich I've ever had." Rachel leans back in the big Adirondack chair with a satisfied sigh. "I've never had one made on a campfire before."

"Me neither, but they *were* pretty good."

I'm not much of a cook, so our menu for the weekend is fairly basic. Knowing Rachel, she won't care what I make as long as she doesn't have to cook herself.

"We should get one of those contraptions." She points at the sandwich maker I found with the grill tools. "The kids would love it."

"I noticed you used to have a fire pit in the backyard. Would it be okay if I fixed it up?"

Her eyes light up even brighter against the orange glow of the fire. "Could you? It doesn't have to be anything fancy."

Oh, it'll be fancy, but I won't spoil the surprise and tell her that just yet.

I affect a bland expression and toss our paper plates into the fire. "I'll see what I can do next week."

She tips her head and squints. "Don't you dare. You already took off work today. I'm sure you have plenty of other things to do."

I lift a shoulder and poke at a log on the fire with a stick. "I'm not putting in as many hours these days, so I'll have time in the evening."

"Things still rocky with Jesse?"

"Actually, I think they're all right." And damn, does it feel good to have that weight lifted off my chest.

I tell her about how he showed up at the Pruitts' last night. Not the part about me pulling my head from my ass, but the part about the two of us planning to sit down and talk soon.

"Baby, that's amazing." She hops up from her chair and crawls into my lap so she can hug me. "I'm so happy for you."

"We haven't talked yet, so don't get too excited."

"It's going to work out." She pulls back and holds my face in her hands. "You and I are unstoppable together, remember?"

Grinning, I loop my arms around her waist. "I'd like to think so."

"So have faith." She plants a kiss on my lips. "But if that's not possible, I have enough for both of us."

Something inside me warms. It takes a second for the realization to hit. This is what it's like to be part of a couple. This connection and this belief in one another.

"I love you."

She smiles and taps the tip of my nose. "I love you, too."

I stretch up for another kiss just as fireworks light up over the water from somewhere down the beach. We're tucked into a little cove, but the trees closest to the water are low, giving us a clear view of the night sky.

"Oh, I love fireworks!" She shifts around so she's facing the water.

We sit like that, watching the colors burst in the sky for

several minutes before I pull her back against my chest. When she snuggles in close, I'm not sure there's ever been a more perfect moment.

"Tell me something about you no one else knows," I say, my lips against her temple.

"Hmm. I think Crystal knows it all, so that might be tough."

"You two have been friends for a long time, huh?"

"Since the year we were both hired at the elementary school. So, eleven years now."

"What's she going to think about us? She won't be too disappointed that her matchmaking wasn't successful, I hope."

She gives a light laugh. "She had her suspicions, so she won't be surprised."

"Ah. In that case, I might have to give her hell for trying to set you up with Jamie fucking Stroud."

"What?" She prods my stomach playfully. "Were you really that worried?"

"Uh, I showed up to intervene, did I not? Of course I was worried. The guy is built like a brick house."

"Trust me, you had nothing to worry about. He was just appeasing Crystal and Tony, too. He's still hung up on his ex-wife."

"No shit. Jack's mom?"

"Yep." She pops her lips. "And that reminds me of something I don't think I've ever told anyone."

"Yeah? What's that?"

She pulls in a deep breath as another round of fireworks goes off. When the sky has gone dark again, she lets it out and shifts so her eyes are on mine. "Jamie didn't come out and say it, but I suspect part of the reason Camille left is that after they got pregnant and married so young, she felt like she'd never had time to grow up herself. To figure out who she was as an individual. She never had the opportunity to do her own thing."

"Okay..."

"I can relate. Yes, I went to college and established my career before I had Mason, but I had been in a relationship with Craig since I was seventeen. At that age, I wanted to do everything I could *for him.* I was never a priority, not even to myself."

That's why I'm going to make damn sure she takes that opportunity for herself now. Why I've made her *my* priority.

"I've never told anyone this, but for a long time, I blamed my mom for making me think that giving up on myself was what I was supposed to do." Her voice cracks on the last few words, but she clears her throat and continues on. "When I was a little girl, I was in awe of her. She'd teach all day and come home every night to make dinner, take care of me and FJ, and tend to my dad's every need.

"My dad said something not long ago about my mom not being perfect. That comment opened up a ton of memories for me. Memories of finding my mom crying in her garden and memories of her sitting on the stool in the laundry room with her head hung in her hands. She even disappeared one weekend. She never came home after school that Friday. I was beside myself, but Dad didn't seem all that surprised. And when she showed up on Sunday, things went right back to normal. Like she'd never left at all." She gives a soft laugh through her tears. "Somehow, I forgot about all of that. Probably because I was so traumatized when she left."

I give her a gentle squeeze. "Childhood fucks us all up

in one way or another." I don't say that to diminish her experience, but rather to reassure her.

"It's ridiculous that it took me so long to remember that she wasn't perfect. And that she wasn't always happy. She struggled just like I did. And in the end..." She sucks in a tremulous breath. "In the end, she died without ever having the opportunity for more."

My heart aches for her. Fuck, I wish I could take away her pain. But it's obvious she needs to get this out, and my role right now is simply to listen.

"I was so bitter and so freaking mad at her," she cries. "I glorified her to the point of begrudging her because the shoes she left behind never fit me quite like they did her. They cramped my style and, ultimately, my heart." She chases away her tears with the heel of her hand. "But she never forced me to wear those shoes, you know? I did that all on my own."

I rest my chin on her shoulder, my heart pinching with sympathy for her. "But now you know the truth. Hers and yours."

"I do. But knowing it doesn't feel like enough. I have this..." She sits up and swallows hard, then presses a hand to her chest. "I have this ache... this feeling that I have to make it right with her somehow. But how can I do that when she isn't even here?"

I smooth her hair and tuck a strand behind her ear. "She wasn't here when you felt the way you did, babe. I don't think she needs to be here now for you to forgive yourself, either."

She holds my gaze for a long beat, letting quiet tears stream down her face. "You're right. Now that I'm being logical about all of this, I see it. But that doesn't ease the guilt."

"When's the last time you visited her?"

She frowns and tilts her head, and then her eyes clear when she realizes what I'm saying. "Oh. I went to the cemetery on Mother's Day. With my dad."

"How about by yourself? Just you and her?"

She chews on the corner of her lip and surveys the surface of the lake. "A long time."

"Maybe you should start there."

She nods slowly. "Yeah."

"I can almost guarantee your mom isn't looking down on you right now, shaking her head. I bet it's the opposite. She's gotta be damn proud of you for figuring this all out. And for finally doing a few things for yourself."

She pulls in another shaky breath. "I hope so."

"Hey..." I turn her face back to mine and smile gently. "I'm proud of you, too."

Her eyes glisten in the moonlight as she whispers, "Thank you. For that and for loving me despite my issues."

I give a light laugh. "Your issues make you human, Sunny. And a pretty amazing one at that."

THIRTY-NINE

RACHEL

In true Justin fashion, he woke me up with breakfast in bed. Naturally, he delivered it wearing nothing but boxers and a buffalo plaid apron with *Kiss the Cook* embroidered on the chest. For a man who claims he doesn't cook, he nailed the perfect Denver omelet, and his homemade hash browns were better than any I've ever made.

I expected to spend the day hanging out by the water like we did yesterday afternoon, but he'd barely cleared the tray from the bed before he told me to hop in the shower and put on the comfiest clothes I brought.

That was an hour ago, and now we're headed toward Green Bay. For what, he will not tell me.

"The suspense is killing me, you know."

He chuckles from behind the wheel. "I can tell. You can't sit still over there."

"Are we at least getting close?"

"Yep." On cue, he hits the blinker and merges right

toward an exit. But it's not for one of the bigger streets that I'm familiar with, so I'm not any closer to getting answers.

"How about a hint now?" I've asked three times already, but that was miles ago.

"Your students have more patience than you, don't they?" He shoots me a sidelong smirk.

I tip my head from side to side. "Hmm. Probably."

He lifts his chin toward the windshield. "Keep looking. We're almost there."

With a sigh, I concede. In a matter of moments, he pulls into the parking lot of a two-story white brick building lined with lush, lavender hydrangea bushes. My pulse picks up at the sight of the gorgeous place. But as breathtaking as it is, I have no clue *what* it is.

Until the sign near the door comes into view.

A spa? Am I reading that correctly?

I turn to Justin as he parks the truck, my mouth agape. "Are you serious?"

With an adorable smile, he unbuckles. "I didn't drive us all the way here just to park. Let's go."

I poke his arm from across the console, then break the news. "I hate to tell you, but places like this usually book out for weeks. There's no way we're getting service today." I appreciate the thought, though. Even if I am a little disappointed that this won't happen today like he probably hoped. I've been to a spa once in my life, and that was for my cousin Louella's bachelorette party. I was sixteen. It was literally half my life ago.

"I know people." He flashes another grin and hops out.

I stare in disbelief as he rounds the front of the truck and comes to open my door. "Like who? Actually, no. Don't tell me." He probably used to date someone who works here.

"Amelia works in Green Bay a lot. She has tons of friends down here. One of them happens to manage this spa."

"Oh." The giddy butterflies that were too hesitant to flutter moments ago let loose in my stomach. "So, you are serious."

He rolls his eyes and reaches around me to unbuckle my seat belt. Then he hooks an arm around my waist and tugs me out of the truck. "Let's get inside before we're late."

I manage to hold back my excitement for two point three seconds before I squeal and clap my hands like a little girl in front of a pony.

The place is fancy. Like fancy-fancy. The instant we step inside, a peaceful ambience settles over us. The air here feels lighter. Cleaner. The lobby smells amazing, too. Like citrus and something slightly masculine. Sexy. And maybe a little erotic.

Soft music plays from overhead, as well. I can't tell what it is because it's so quiet, but the culmination of it all immediately puts me at ease.

Though there's a quiet voice in my head stealing a little of my joy and warning me that this place must cost a fortune.

"Justin, this is too much," I whisper, looping my arm around his. I have no idea what comes next, but I can't imagine it's anything less than five-star luxury.

He kisses the top of my head. "Nothing is too much for you." He stops a few feet in front of the receptionist, who holds up a finger to indicate she's on the phone. Turning to me, he lifts my chin, ensuring that I can't miss the soft but resolute look in his eyes. "I take care of what's mine. And make no mistake about it—you are mine."

Those silly butterflies whirl in my stomach anew. I'll

never tire of him saying things like that, just like I'll never tire of being his.

"I love you." I press up on my toes and kiss him.

"I love you, too. But you're going to have to keep all that love in check for the next couple of hours."

"What do you mean?"

He waggles his brows. "Naked couple's massage."

"Ha-ha. Funny guy."

The receptionist clears her throat. "Undressing is optional, but many couples"—she angles herself over the counter and winks—"find that being naked just a couple of feet away from each other heightens the experience."

What the heck kind of spa is this?

Justin grins. "You feeling bold today, Sunny?"

I wasn't, but the challenge in his voice is loud and clear. "I think I might be."

His brows lift in surprise. "You know I was only kidding, right?"

With a one-shoulder shrug, I grin right back. "That was your first mistake."

The receptionist gives a soft laugh. "Let's get you checked in, Mr. and Mrs. Enders. Then I'll give you a few moments to make some decisions before I take you back to your room."

Mr. and Mrs. Enders? Oh, he's on fire today, isn't he?

He steps up to the counter, takes care of the payment, and joins me in the sitting area with clipboards and paperwork.

"Mister and missus?" I mutter.

He shrugs, and the expression on his face is the opposite of apologetic. "Has a ring to it, doesn't it?"

Heat ignites in my chest and radiates through me. Even so... "You should let me get divorced first."

"Eh, that's just a technicality."

I bite back a grin, but it slips just a little at the reality of this moment, though not for long.

I'm moments away from getting buck naked in a room with my new man and a couple of strangers, and thinking about my impending divorce doesn't make me want to run to the bathroom to lose my breakfast.

Who the heck am I?

And when did I become so damn happy?

JINX

I'VE BEEN semi-hard since Rachel accidentally-on-purpose dropped her towel before *and* after our couple's massage. And when she moaned every time the guy who gave her a pedicure rubbed the arches of her feet, it was all I could do not to crawl out of the pedicure chair and break the guy's hands.

Now she's leading me into the restaurant I've been looking forward to trying since I made the reservation yesterday, and I can't keep from staring at her ass in that goddamn navy dress she taunted me with two friggin' months ago.

I'm not even hungry anymore. Not for food, anyway. But her? I laugh to myself, but there's not a bit of humor in it. Her, I'm starving for. And I plan to abso-fucking-lutely devour her when we get back to the cabin tonight.

"You seem tense," she says once the hostess seats us at a table overlooking the lake. There are a couple of boats out on the water, their lights and the moon casting beams of silver on the surface.

"I am." I shake my napkin out onto my lap to cover my half erection. "I hope you enjoyed our spa day, because I certainly didn't."

She tucks a lock of hair behind her ear, her cheeks going pink. "I enjoyed it very much. My muscles haven't felt this relaxed in ages."

Uh-huh. She'll be changing her tune later. That accolade will be mine and mine alone.

"And I think you enjoyed yourself plenty. You just don't want to admit it."

I half snort, half scoff. "The towel drops? Yeah, I liked those. But witnessing the way that guy almost made you come by massaging your feet? I could've done without that."

Lips pursed and sultry lashes lowered, she reaches across the table and takes my hand. "You have nothing to worry about, handsome. You're the only man who's ever made me come without help."

"Damn right I am. And I'll be the only one to ever do it, too." I lock my gaze on hers to solidify my point. "Mark my words."

That light blush deepens, and she adjusts a bit in her seat so she can cross her legs.

"How does it feel?" I taunt. "To be turned on and unable to do a damn thing about it?"

"Hmm." She lets go of my hand and picks up her water glass. "The difference between you and me is that I like the build-up and the anticipation."

"Oh, so now you have patience?" I laugh.

She simply smiles as the waitress appears with our drinks, ready to take our order. Luckily, Rachel read the menu choices off to me on the way here, so we both knew what we wanted before we stepped inside.

Kinda like I knew I wanted her before she was even single.

That might make me an asshole, but I saw something in her that day she came to the office with Craig's coffee and lunch. I recognized the neglected, lonely woman beneath that fitted skirt and blouse, and I knew then and there that, if the opportunity ever presented itself, I'd do everything in my power to make her smile.

Now she's mine. And she's happy. It's a boost to the ego to know I had a hand in that.

"So, there's something I've been meaning to talk to you about," she says, her tone soft but serious, clearly shelving the flirtation for a bit.

"All right." I lift my bottle of beer. "Is it about the divorce?"

"No." She shakes her head. "That's the last thing I want to talk about. Court is in ten days, and I can't wait to put it behind me." She clears her throat. "I talked to Dalton the other day. We ran into each other at the Cole Stop. He's impressed with how much Mason improved from last summer to now."

"I am, too. You ever think about sending him to football camp? He could learn a lot and develop skills that could help him if he wants to play in high school and beyond."

She frowns. "No. I mean, yes, I have thought about that. But that's not where I'm going with this."

Despite my best effort to stop them, a rush of nerves skitters down my spine at her serious tone and expression. "Okay..."

"I know what you did."

Oh. My stomach twists itself into knots. She wasn't supposed to find that out.

"He told me that *you* asked *him* if you could help coach, not the other way around."

Heat burns up the back of my neck, but I shrug it off. I don't regret the decision one bit. Even if I wish she hadn't found out about it.

"Mason told you he wasn't going to play because of the transportation issue," she says, leaning forward, getting closer, "and you offered to coach so he'd always have a ride to practice and his games."

No point in denying it. "That's accurate."

"Justin..."

I lift a hand, swallow past the lump in my throat. "The kid wanted to play, Sunny. I had to do what I had to do."

"While you were also working eighty-million hours a week."

I give a crooked grin. "I survived."

"Barely."

Okay, now she's being dramatic. And it's cute as hell.

"You are too good to me. And to my kids. You know that, right?"

I shake my head. "Nah, Sunny. I'm really not. I'm just more than you're used to." I reclaim her hand. "But you better get used to it, because I plan to be around for a long time."

Her lashes flutter as she bites her lip. "You're going to ruin me, aren't you?"

"No." I bring her knuckles to my mouth. Press a kiss there. "But I am going to love the hell out of you."

"Well, you're off to a great start," she says, tears shimmering in her eyes. "Now I wish we were back at the cabin so I could love the hell out of you right back."

Chuckling, I thumb toward the door. "We could take our food to go."

She laughs. "You're not eating a forty-dollar steak out of a take-out box, Justin Enders."

"I would for you."

She rolls her eyes as the hostess approaches with another couple in tow. I do a double take when I catch a glimpse of the guy's face.

"Holy shit."

The familiar man wears a scowl as he turns our way. That's when I notice the toddler on the woman's hip.

Holy crap.

"Colton Wade." I get to my feet and extend a hand.

My old buddy blinks for a second, then breaks out into a grin. "Jinx Enders. Well, I'll be damned."

We do the part handshake, part hug thing and then stand back, both of us shaking our heads in disbelief.

"What's it been? Eight years?" I ask.

He used to come up north with his buddies to tear up the back roads on their dirt bikes. Then he took his skills to the big leagues and earned himself a couple of motocross titles. Not on the courses, though. The high-flying stuff. Tricks and shit.

"Something like that." He stands back and gestures to the woman and the little girl. "This is my wife, Taylor. You might've met her before. And our daughter, Freya. She's new."

I chuckle and offer my hand to Taylor. She looks vaguely familiar, but I can't say for sure. "Nice to meet you both." I gesture to Rachel, who also gets to her feet, her focus already on the cute curly-haired little girl.

"Aren't you a spitting image of your mama," she says, tickling the girl's cheek. "I'm Rachel." She smiles at Taylor. "Jinx's girlfriend."

The two make small talk, presumably about the toddler,

while I try to focus on Colton and not on the fact that Rachel just called herself my girlfriend. Obviously, she is, but hearing her say it...

That one word is nowhere near enough.

She's my all-in. My ride or die.

And as soon as she's ready, I'm going to make her my wife.

I don't care whether I have to wait a year or a decade.

She's already planted her seed in my heart, and I will nurture our love for as long as it takes.

FORTY

RACHEL

Could it really be this easy? To find love again and be so happy?

I'll be honest; rekindling my love life was the very last thing on my mind when Craig and I split up. But then Justin Enders saved me from myself that night in the pub and then came to my rescue time and time again in the three months after.

The part of me that's become so strong and independent over the past decade or so of my life has reared her determined little head a few times, questioning whether this is the softer, needier side of me giving in to what she's wanted for so long or whether this is the real deal. If what Justin gives me is truly the perfect balance of everything I've ever wanted, wrapped up in one handsome, selfless package.

I believe that he is.

I don't know what I did to deserve him, but I'll be

damned if I'm not going to jump head and heart first into this opportunity.

Losing my mom at twelve taught me so many things, many of which I'm still figuring out, but I do know this:

Life is too short to live in fear.

And when something—or someone—comes along that makes you feel safe in the storm of your own chaos, you hold on tight.

"I'm ready for you." Justin appears in the doorway that separates the main part of the cabin from the bedrooms. He's shirtless and wearing jogging pants, and when he leans into the wooden frame, all sexy in his tanned and muscled glory, with that mischievous glint in his eye, I swear I swoon.

"What are you up to?" Tipping my head, I get to my feet from the sofa where I've been listening to the crickets and the frogs and the subtle whoosh of waves in the distance.

When we returned from dinner, he gave me firm instructions to remain in the main part of the cabin while he went to the bedroom to apparently prepare. For what, I don't know.

"You'll see." He holds a hand out to me as I approach.

"I feel overdressed compared to you." I'm still in the navy dress I've been saving just for him.

"I'll take care of that," he says softly as he pulls me close, his free hand sliding back into my hair as he leans in for a kiss. "In fact, before we get started, you should know there are a couple of rules."

"Rules?" I shiver when his lips trail to my jaw and then down the column of my neck.

"Mm-hmm." He nips at my collarbone, and goose bumps lift on my skin. "The first rule is that tonight is about you. The second is that I'm in charge."

"I like the sound of that, but what if—"

He presses a finger to my lips, his eyes sparkling with sultry amusement. "Hush, Sunny. Just let me do my thing."

I smile against his finger. "Okay, then."

"Good girl." He winks and then, fingers tangled with mine, leads me toward the master bedroom.

The scent of sandalwood and something fruity hits my nose before we step into the room, which is aglow with candles. On the dressers and the nightstands, even a couple on the floor leading to the bathroom.

"Wow. You've been busy."

He turns and walks backward toward the bathroom, still tugging me along. "I have a confession to make," he says, eyes twinkling with a boyish gleam. "I've been fantasizing about you, naked and wet and in the bathtub, ever since I caught you taking a bath that one night."

"Oh, really?" I chuckle softly and then gasp when I see what else he's done.

The enormous tub is full of bubbles, and there are more candles on the vanity, the windowsills, and the ledge around the bath. Red rose petals are strewn across the floor, leading to a massive bouquet on a wooden chair in the corner, and the soft chords of sexy, indie rock play from his phone. There's even a tray of chocolate-covered strawberries by the tub. And Prince.

"Oh my god..." I press a hand to my chest, which suddenly aches with excitement and a little overwhelm. He did all of this. For me.

"I hope you don't mind that I went into your bag, but I had a feeling you might've brought your friend along. Just in case."

I open my mouth to respond, but nothing comes out. I'm just so... wow. No one's ever done anything like this for me before. And no one's ever gone out of their way to plan an entire weekend like this for me.

He shifts in close and cups my face. "I love you, Sunny, and I want to show you how much I mean that."

"You already have. You've..." I break off with a heavy sigh. I don't need to say the words. He knows what he's done, and maybe it makes me a little greedy, but I want what he's offering. I want all of it and all of him.

"Let's get you out of this dress." He shifts around me and gently lifts my hair, but before he goes for the zipper, he presses slow, wet kisses along the back of my neck and my shoulders.

Heat pools instantly in my lower belly, and I want so badly to squeeze my thighs together to quench the ache. But I also don't want him to know how easily he's turned me on. If I have to play by his rules tonight, making him work for it is the least I can do.

"Thank you for saving this dress for me," he murmurs. "You look fucking stunning, but I'd be lying if I said I haven't been thinking about getting you out of it all night."

I shiver at his words and the warm breath on my skin. "What if I told you I bought it with you in mind?"

He gives a low laugh as he smooths his free hand over my hip and to my belly, inching lower toward the hem of the dress in what feels like slow motion.

I bite my lip to keep from moaning in anticipation.

"I'd say you're a smart woman, but we already knew that, didn't we?" He sinks his teeth into the swell of muscle between my neck and shoulder as he slips his hand beneath my dress. He wastes no time in finding my panties and cupping me over the fabric. "Always so wet for me, aren't you, Sunny?"

"You're not the only one who's been waiting for this dress to hit the floor."

With another husky chuckle, he abandons my panties and quickly unzips the dress before sliding it off my shoulders and letting it fall from my body.

He groans instantly, his big, calloused hands coasting down my arms and to my hips so he can jerk me back against him, the hard length of his erection undeniable against my nearly bare ass.

"Sexy lingerie, too, huh? Seems I'm not the only one who had plans for tonight."

"You've brought out the bolder side of me. What can I say?"

"You can say you'll let me strip you out of it so we can get in that bathtub and live out all my fantasies."

I tip my head back and moan as one of his hands finds its way to my breast, his thumb stroking over my nipple. "Your rules tonight, handsome. You want me in that tub, you better get me there."

The growl that vibrates in his chest is damn near feral as he tugs down my thong, curses the fact that I can't wear the heels in the water, and then relieves me of my bra before he pushes down his joggers.

I turn to look, of course, and bite my lip at the sight of his thick, proud cock jutting from the dark, trimmed hair between his legs. His balls are full and heavy looking, and I squirm at the thought of how good he's going to feel when he buries himself inside me. And that close, delicious contact of his body and mine that makes me feel like we're truly one.

With a hand around the back of my neck, he lowers his mouth to mine. His tongue gently coaxes mine in a slow, sensual dance as he backs toward the tub and helps me in.

The water is the perfect temperature, and the tub is even bigger than mine at home. When Justin lowers into the water behind me and pulls me onto his lap, there's more than enough room for both of us.

"How's the temperature?" he murmurs against my shoulder. Beneath the water, he glides his hands from my hips to my stomach and then up to my breasts.

"Amazing. This bubble bath is amazing. Smells good and it's so silky."

"Imagine how soft our skin will be when we crawl into bed later."

Leaning my head back against his shoulder, I sigh. "Feels pretty good now." And how am I already so relaxed?

"Champagne?" He lifts a glass from the tray and offers it to me.

"Thank you. You really thought of everything, didn't you?"

He gives a soft chuckle, his chest vibrating against my back. "Like I said, I've been fantasizing for a while."

"Tell me about those fantasies." I take a small sip of sweet, bubbly liquid.

His lips are on my shoulder again, then my neck. Hot and wet, sending heat pooling in my core. "I could show you instead."

Goose bumps wash over my skin. "I like the sound of that."

Rather than caressing me again like I expect, he dries his hands using a towel on the ledge and picks up a paperback I hadn't even noticed. I recognize the cover immediately, and a thrum of excitement pulses through me. He brought along a steamy romance novel?

"Where on earth did you get that?"

"The bookstore." He holds the book in front of me like

it's no big deal and opens to a dog-eared page. "I imagined you relaxing in the bath, enjoying a little lady porn with your toy."

I bite my lip as my cheeks heat. "Are you sure you haven't been looking in my windows?"

He lets out a wry laugh. "So I was right."

"Sorta. On occasion, I've been known to listen to spicy scenes from audiobooks while I, uh, take care of business."

"Ah, perfect." He tips his head toward Prince. "I'll read and you play."

A zing of excitement rushes through me. Dirty words and his voice? Yes, please. Thank god for waterproof toys.

With shaky fingers, I grasp my vibrator. Then I shift on his lap, so I have room to let my legs fall apart. That movement alone has his cock twitching against my ass. Instantly, all I can think about is how easy it would be to lift, impale myself on him, and make love just like this. No condom, no cares.

Soon enough.

Gently clearing his throat, he begins to read, and I push my hesitation aside. With my toy set to the speed I like best, I get comfortable and close my eyes.

The first touch makes me jolt a little, and behind me, Justin grows harder.

"You're so fucking beautiful," he reads. "Do you have any idea how many times I've gone home and jerked off, thinking about you? I've come to images of you in every possible position. On your knees for me, your cheeks pink and your eyes watering from sucking me off. The sight of my cum on your tongue and dripping from your pussy after you let me fuck you and fill you up."

I bite back a moan as the pleasure builds and the picture he paints becomes clear in my mind. I know what happens next. I've read the book more than once. Even so, something about him reading it makes it feel new and even naughtier.

"Will you let me do that?" he continues on, the rasp in his voice giving him away. This is turning him on as much as it is me. "I want to make you mine in every way you'll let me, baby."

Yes. The word is on the tip of my tongue. I know it would be risky, but I want to feel him like that so damn bad.

"I'd let you." The concession is a greedy pant as blood pulses between my legs, my orgasm already so close. I've gotten good at making myself come, but the culmination of this romantic bath, Justin's husky voice, and his rock-hard erection have multiplied the pleasure.

With a low growl, he tosses the book onto the floor and gets to his feet, taking me with him. He turns and deposits me on the ledge next to the tub, his gaze darkening as he drops to his knees in front of me and lifts one leg, then the other, to his shoulders.

He doesn't dive in with just his mouth like I anticipate. Instead, he takes hold of the vibrator as well, using his tongue, his fingers, and the toy to bring me to the brink of release... only to pull back and deny me.

"Ahh!" I cry out in frustration, hands slipping on the wet tile.

His only response is to lock his eyes on mine and do it all over again, two fingers pumping in and out while he tongues my clit and keeps the vibe pressed just to the side.

It's maddening and amazing all at once. But in no time, I'm right there again. My ears ring and my vision tunnels. I'm helpless to do anything but fist his hair and ride his face, desperately trying to beat him at his own game.

"Justin, please." My moan is as much of a plea as it

praise. Nothing has felt this good before, but if he keeps teasing me...

"I want more, Sunny. I wanna fucking taste you."

Isn't that what he's doing? My god.

"Come on, baby. I know you can do it." He kneels upright suddenly, one forearm braced on my thigh as he works the vibrator with one hand and fucks me so hard with his other that I see stars.

It's the most erotic feeling, being so open to him and so completely at his mercy. My pleasure is literally in his hands.

And when he quickly pulls them from me, the toy now fully on my clit, I come so hard that my body does something it's never done before...

I squirt.

"That's my fucking girl," he murmurs with a wicked smile as he coaxes every last pulse of orgasm from my body. Only then does he dip his head and lave at the insides of my thighs and then straight up the center of my pussy like he starving for me.

It's easily the hottest thing I've ever experienced, and when his lips tug on my still tender clit, the tension of another orgasm sparks anew.

"Need you inside," I beg. "Please."

"Ask and you shall receive, babe." He pushes to his feet, water and suds sluicing down his body. His stomach is tense, and his erection looks almost painful as he procures a condom from the same mysterious place he found the book. "Stand for me," he demands as he tears the package open. "Turn around and hold on the ledge."

I do as I'm told without hesitation, bending down and presenting myself to him like the wanton woman I am, desperate to be completely owned by him. As much as I'd love to feel him raw, his restraint is damn sexy.

"You're swollen," he growls behind me. "All that hot water and finger fucking... your pussy is cherry red. Wish you could see yourself right now."

My hips twist of their own accord, trying to squelch the throb that his words elicit.

"You're dripping, too, and it's not the bath water." He gives a wicked chuckle and glides the tip of his cock through my folds. "Sexiest thing I've ever seen, watching you come like that. Think we can make you do it again?"

I don't know, and right now, I don't care. I just want him inside. "Quit talking and fuck me already."

"Uh-uh, Sunny..." He tsks. "My rules, remember?"

I groan, engulfed by a wave of sweet agony.

"It might feel like fucking, but know this..." He grasps my hair and wraps it around a fist, tugging gently as he lowers his mouth to my ear. "When I'm inside you from now on, we're making love. Every touch, every kiss, every moan... they make me love you a little more. Do you understand that, Sunny? Do you know what you've done to me?"

I barely have time to nod before he pushes inside, slowly filling me until I can't take any more. Like this, he feels even bigger. Hot, too. Or maybe that's me.

"Nothing feels as good as you wrapped around me," he husks, letting go of my hair to curl that arm around my waist. "Nothing feels as good as you taking my cock over and over again. You giving me your body and your heart, trusting me with every part of you." He thrusts in hard and groans. "It does something to me, baby." Retreating, he drives back in and snarls, "It's driving me fucking wild. I can't get enough."

Tears burn in my eyes, and as much as I want to

respond, I can't. I'm helpless to do anything but let him love me like he needs, because he isn't the only one who feels the spark of something deeper and more intense every time we're together.

I'm right there with him, feeling it in a way that should probably scare me, but there isn't an ounce of fear in my veins.

Not with this man.

With him, there is only love and hope and faith that this time...

I got it right.

And I'm never letting go.

FORTY-ONE

JINX

True to his word, Jesse asks me to stay after our Monday team meeting to revisit our partnership discussion. Of course, he first tried to get me to spill the beans about what happened with Rachel when I broke up her date, but I reminded him that I don't kiss and tell. It's a lesson he taught me years ago and one we've both abided by since. Mostly, anyway. I did confess that she'd only be dating me from here on out, and that seemed to curb his curiosity.

With that out of the way, I'm more than ready to get this ball rolling and get down to business.

"If I do come on board as a partner, how much will it cut into your income?" That's the question that's been weighing on my mind since I showed him my business plan. I want this for myself and my future, but the thought of taking away from Jesse and his family doesn't sit well.

He lifts a shoulder. "Honestly? Not at all. It will cut into the company's overall profit, but with the plan you've put together, that number should return to normal in no time. And in a couple of years, it'll grow even more."

I was hoping he'd say that, but I didn't want to make assumptions. Jesse doesn't live a glamorous life, aside from that monstrosity of a house he built, so I didn't get the impression he was pocketing all the profit.

"Hayden took a closer look at your projections and updated them based on the actual numbers from the past few years." He slides a folder across the desk. "Take a look and tell me what you think."

I crane my neck and clear my throat, then, with a shaky hand, I open the file. This kind of shit always makes me nervous. Makes me feel greedy, despite how hard I've worked to make this happen.

I scan the first few pages. They're updated versions of my own. Hayden even highlighted her changes and explained her rationale in a few places. There's nothing surprising or significantly different.

Until I turn to the fourth page.

"What's this?" I frown when the number in bold at the bottom of the page jumps out at me. Specifically, all the zeros.

"That's what EE owes you in overtime for the past few years. It's an estimate, of course, but Hayden's confident that it's close to what you're due."

Hard pressure builds in my chest, making it difficult to breathe.

My heart hurts, too.

And I think my arms are tingling.

"You all right?" Jesse leans forward, his brow pulled low with concern. "Or were you thinking it should be more?"

I cough. And then cough again. Then I toss the folder onto the desk and hang my head between my knees. That's what you're supposed to do when you hyperventilate, right?

"Jesus Christ." Jesse hurries to his feet and strides to the water cooler in the corner. He fills a paper cup and passes it to me.

Grateful, I sit up and take a drink, but when he claps me on the back, I choke and sputter.

"Shit. Sorry." He holds his hands up and backs away.

I laugh and cough at the same time, wiping tears and spit from my face. "Sit down," I croak when I can finally talk.

He does, but his expression is still pensive.

"I didn't ask for that." I stab a finger at the folder. "And I don't need it."

His shoulders relax as he pulls in a breath. "I know you didn't ask for it, but you earned it. And paying you is the right thing to do. Hayden's already cut the check." He angles forward and turns to the next page. There in front of me is an electronic copy of said check with today's date. "It's probably already in your bank account."

Holy shit. He's serious about this.

"Jesse..." I shake my head. "That's not why I want to be your partner. It isn't about the money."

He nods and clasps his hands on top of the desk. "I know that. If it were, you would've taken me up on the offer years ago."

I sit back in the chair and study him, absorbing all the information.

Not only is he offering me a partnership, but he's back paying me. Check that—he's already done it. There's a quarter million dollars in my bank account right now.

Mind. Blown.

He flips to the next page in the folder. "This is what

we're thinking for an annual salary, but it's negotiable." He taps another unimaginable figure before he turns to yet another page. "And here are the profit projections for the next five years. This is the perfect time for us to do this, Jinx." He looks up and regards me with a hopeful smile. "We could really take EE to the next level if we bust our asses."

My dad said something similar when Jesse took over. That EE was ready to grow, and sure as shit, we did it. Now, we can do it again.

"This is really happening." I say it more for myself than for him.

He nods. "Yeah, man. I've already made an appointment with the lawyer. I hope you're free on Friday."

Friday. Just four more days.

"I'll have to ask for time off work," I tease, the shock finally wearing off, "and since I took this past Friday off, too, I'm not sure it's possible. My boss can be a pain in the ass."

He snorts. "Shut the hell up. The appointment is at ten. I was thinking we should invite Dad to come along, too."

Now that thought has my chest hurting in another way altogether.

"Did you mention this to him?" I ask.

Jesse shakes his head. "Didn't want to do it without you."

With a nod, I swallow past the lump in my throat, working to keep my shit together. "Can we do it soon?"

"Is right now soon enough?"

MY PALMS HAVEN'T SWEATED this much since that night Dad caught Gracie Janikowski and me with our pants down and then made me sit next to her old man in church the next day.

I'm not worried about whether Dad will like the agreement Jesse and I have come to. If all four of us worked at EE, he'd be in heaven. The company is his pride and joy, just like it was my grandfather's.

But I should have done this sooner. I shouldn't have left him to worry that I might never get to this point. I have a lot of making up to do. And a lot left to prove.

"Hey, boys." Ma waves. She's standing at the stove, where—shocker—she's stirring something in a big pot. Smells tomato-based, and there's a huge head of cabbage on the counter behind her. If I had to guess, they're having *gołąbki* for dinner tonight. Tomorrow and Wednesday, too.

"Hey, Ma." I dip close and peck her cheek. "Smells good in here."

"Thank you. If you come back later, you can have supper with us." She flashes a cheeky grin, because it wouldn't be a visit to our childhood home if she didn't try to feed us or guilt us into coming by more often.

"I might just do that." Rachel's spending the evening with the kids, going through their things for school next week. And after spending the last few days with her, going home to an empty house doesn't appeal.

"Don't tease me, Justin Andrew," she warns with a stern finger.

I hold up my hands. "Not teasing. I'll be here."

With a chuckle, Jesse stuffs his hands into his pockets and glances out the patio door. "Dad outside somewhere?"

"Probably. He was grumbling about needing to cut the grass. Haven't heard the mower going, so he's probably messing with that. It was giving him grief the other day."

Humming, I scan what I can see of the yard. "Sounds like we came at the right time, then."

Ma makes a throaty sound. "He's never going to let you take over our lawn care, Jinx. At least not while he's still got two arms and two legs."

Maybe not, but it won't stop me from reminding him that I'm more than happy to do it.

"Ah, I see him." Jesse lifts his chin. "No mower, but he does have a shovel and his pellet gun."

"*Na miłość boską.*" Ma looks up at the ceiling and makes the sign of the cross. "Please go save him from himself."

"On it." Jesse slides the patio door open, and I follow him out back. "Squirrels or rabbits?" he calls out to our dad.

"Skunks," the old man snarls back. "Damn things keep getting into the trash in the garage."

"You try closing the door?" Jesse asks with a grin.

Dad just flips him off. "Aren't you two supposed to be at work?"

"We're on the clock." I shrug.

He leans the shovel and the gun against the patio skirting and wipes the sweat from his brow with a handkerchief. "Then why are you here?"

"Was hoping we could talk to you about something." Jesse tips his head toward the cluster of chairs on the patio.

"Something wrong?"

"No," my brother answers before I can.

I kind of want to be the one to tell Dad about our plan, and thankfully, I catch Jesse's eye as we follow Dad. He takes one look at me, gives a small smile, and nods.

Funny how in tune we can be when we want to be. Then again, we're rarely on the same page, but that's because it's fun to try and piss each other off.

"Any day now." Dad rolls his hand impatiently as he sits. "At this rate, I might keel over before either of you spit it out."

Chuckling, I fold my hands between my knees. "Jesse and I have been talking."

"To be fair, he brought it up," Jesse interjects.

I shoot him a glare, and he holds up a hand.

"He's right. I did bring it up. Now, we want to run it by you."

"I'm not interested in un-retiring, so if you're about to ask me to come back to work..."

"We're not." Jesse groans. "Jesus, Jinx, just tell him already."

Here goes. My stomach's twisted in knots, but the words come out easier than I expected. "I want to become a partner at Enders Excavating."

Dad's head snaps up in surprise. "What now?"

I nod. "You heard me. It's been a long time coming. I know you and Jesse thought it might never happen. But the truth is, I've always wanted in. It's our family business, so of course I do. I just wasn't ready when I was nineteen. But I'm ready now."

Dad regards me for a beat, like my confession is too good to be true and he's afraid to get excited. "You're serious."

"I am." I dip my chin. "We've already talked about what that means for the company and for each of us individually. I put together a plan to expand the landscaping portion of the business, and Hayden's taken a look at things from an objective standpoint. We're all in agreement that we can do this and do it well."

Dad eyes Jesse, one brow lifted. "That all true?"

"Yep. The only thing he didn't tell you is how hard he's worked behind the scenes these past few years."

"It wasn't really behind the scenes," our father mumbles. "But you're right. He did work damn hard."

I clear my throat. "I'm right here."

"Good thing we're not talking shit, then, huh?" Dad jokes. "Anyway, you know I'm happy to hear this. It's how I've always wanted things to be. Hell, I'd be thrilled if all of you kids were there, but two out of four is just fine."

"So, you approve?" I need to hear him say it, even if it's just for my pride.

"Hell yes, I approve. Your grandpa would, too. And someday, when you're my age, hopefully your kids will be having this same conversation with the two of you."

"Jinx would have to settle down for that to happen." Jesse shoots me a knowing smirk. "But maybe someday."

Maybe someday sooner than either of them realizes.

Behind us, the patio door slides open, and Ma pokes her head out. "Jesse, can you come and help me core this damn cabbage? It's stubborn as hell."

Sighing, he pushes to his feet. "You should be good at dealing with stubborn things, Ma. You're married to Dad, after all."

She snickers, and Dad rolls his eyes.

When the door closes behind them, Dad gives me a sidelong glance. "I figured this was coming."

"Yeah? Why's that?"

He sits back in the chair and studies me. "You've been carrying yourself differently lately. Like you're more confident, which, as far as I'm concerned, you never should have had an issue with. You're a good kid, Jinx. No, scratch that." He lifts a hand. "You're a good *man*."

That chest pain that hit me in Jesse's office flares back to life. I rub at the spot as emotion thickens in my throat. He's never made me feel like I didn't measure up next to my brothers, but his words are reassuring in a way I didn't realize I needed.

"Thanks, Dad."

We get to our feet and exchange a hug that drives home the point—he really is proud of me.

I hope he's just as proud when he finds out that I've met the woman I plan to spend the rest of my life with. And I've done my best to live by his words from all those years ago.

The true measure of a man can be seen in how he treats a woman.

Maybe it's time I told the rest of my family just how much those words have impacted me.

Scratch that.

Maybe it's time I *show* them.

FORTY-TWO

RACHEL

I'm not sure which I'm more anxious about: telling my dad about Justin and me or telling Justin's family.

Both are equally nerve-racking, mostly because my divorce has only been final for a few days, but also because of our age difference and because I'm a mom. Granted, the six-year gap has never been in issue, aside from my initial assumption that his age meant he was immature. But he wiped that concern off my list of worries the moment he started showing up for me. Literally and figuratively.

Being fresh out of a twelve-year marriage is a more reasonable concern, especially for those who don't know that my relationship with Craig was over a long time ago. Jesse and Aiden know the truth, but their parents and my dad... well, they come from an older, more traditional generation, and they may not be as open-minded about that.

For that reason, I'm not sure telling them together—and in front of the rest of the family—is the best idea. But nonetheless, that's how it's about to go down. As soon as Justin gives me the signal, anyway. For now, I'm biding my time in the kitchen with his mother, trying to focus on Polish cheesecake.

"And that's it." Janice turns off the mixer and clasps her hands triumphantly. "We pour the filling into the pan and bake it. Easy peasy."

It certainly seems easy enough, but it's also exactly how I've tried to make it myself in the past and failed. "There aren't any secret ingredients?"

"Nope." She unlatches the mixing bowl and pours the buttery yellow mixture over the crust in the springform pan. "You could always add caramel or fruit like you might a traditional cheesecake, but this is the base. No secrets."

"Other than lots of butter," Hayden chimes in as Janice scrapes the bowl to get every last bit of mixture out.

"True. And not margarine, either. Only real, honest-to-goodness butter will work."

"I can't wait to try it." Hayden grins. "Lord knows, I love butter."

I laugh. "It's delicious when made right. Then again, it's been almost twenty years since I had it."

Janice gasps. "You haven't had *sernik* in twenty years?"

"I've tried to make it on my own, but it was never good. It always tasted like scrambled eggs."

Janice grimaces. "You might've been using extra-large or jumbo eggs."

I tip my head. "Would that make a difference?"

"Absolutely." She gives the springform pan a little shake to even out the filling. "Always use regular eggs when baking unless the recipe calls for something bigger." Then, with a devious smile, she waggles her brows. "Bigger is only better in the bedroom. Not so much the kitchen."

"Mom!" Amelia gasps from the kitchen table, where she and Olivia are cutting up vegetables for our cookout. "Could you not?"

The older woman snickers. "What fun would that be?"

"Ugh." The youngest Enders sibling groans. Then to Olivia, she mutters, "See what I have to put up with?"

"Oh, don't act like little miss prim and proper, Amelia Jane. We know better."

Hayden gives a quiet laugh. "She has you there, Lee."

Amelia launches a stick of celery across the kitchen and hits Hayden in the chest. "Zip it, blondie. We all know what you and Jesse have been doing to *make up for lost time* these past few months."

Hayden scoffs, but there's no animosity behind it. In fact, the blush in her cheeks says she's guilty and she knows it.

Across from Amelia, Olivia presses her lips together, and if she could somehow blend into her seat and become invisible, I suspect she would.

"Same goes for Olivia," Hayden says, gesturing wildly to Aiden's rekindled flame. "Rachel and Jinx, too."

If Janice hadn't just placed the cheesecake in the oven, I'm certain she would've dropped it.

"What?" The Enders matriarch spins on the toes of her socks, gray-blond hair lifting around her shoulders. "Rachel and who?"

My face flames hot, and I feel like a deer caught in the headlights of a big ole Mack truck.

"Whoops." Hayden covers her mouth belatedly. "Is that cat not out of the bag or...?"

"It is now." Amelia grins from ear to ear. "Damn, that was a hard secret to keep."

Janice continues to stare at me, blue eyes round as she

digests this information. "You're the one Jinx was talking about."

I'm not sure which conversation she's referring to, but clearly, there's been one. About me.

"Um..." I have no idea how to respond. This is his mother, for Pete's sake. I want her to like me—or rather, continue to like me—rather than think I'm a new divorcee who's latched her needy claws into her baby boy.

"Ladies, if you'll excuse us." Grabbing my hand, Janice pulls me out of the kitchen and down the hall toward the back of the house to what I assume is a guest bedroom. Only when she's closed the door behind us does she look at me again. "Spill it, young lady. Tell me what's been going on between you and my son."

JINX

"KIDS THESE DAYS HAVE IT EASY," Dad says to Felix, Rachel's father, as they pick up the discarded bean bags near their cornhole board. "When we were young, we didn't have games like this. We had to make our own. Out of sticks and rocks."

Mason rolls his eyes dramatically while we stand away from our board, waiting for the old men to play. "Let me guess... you had to walk to school uphill both ways, too."

Felix points a bag at him. "You're darn right we did. And twice as far when it snowed."

"That doesn't even make sense, Grandpa."

"Doesn't have to make sense," he counters. "All that matters is it's true."

"No, it isn't." Emma giggles from the sandbox where

she's been humoring Jett for the past hour. He's taught her how to properly load the trucks with rocks and sticks, and they have a route all mapped out like it's a job site. "Maybe it just felt like it was farther because you're *old*."

"Ouch." Even I flinch at that one. "Take it easy, Spitfire. Those old folks have fragile egos, too."

Thwap!

One of my dad's bean bags smacks me upside the head.

"What the hell?" I rub at the spot while Mason mutters an impressed "nice."

"Who's fragile now?" my dad retorts before he and Felix fall into a fit of laughter.

"You did take that a little too far." Mason speaks up. "But I'm glad you did, because your dad laying the smack down on you was pretty funny."

Jesse raises his beer from the patio. "Dad should get at least two points for that hit. Just sayin'."

"I'd give 'em the game." Aiden flashes a grin from the preheating grill. "Then again, if they keep playing, maybe Jinx'll get pegged again."

"What kind of example are you all setting for these kids?" I throw my hands in the air. "I make one little comment, and you're out here promoting violence."

Aiden waves me off. "You ain't seen nothing."

I'd argue with him, but considering everything he's been through in recent weeks with his job and with Olivia, I don't have a leg to stand on. So I let it go, and we continue our game of cornhole.

Just before Mason and I are up again, Emma tugs on my shirt.

"I have to use the bathroom."

"Ah. You want me to show you where it is?"

She shakes her head. "No, that's okay. But I'm not sure which door to go in."

"You can go in through the patio. Your mom and the other ladies should be right there in the kitchen."

"'Kay." She jogs off but stops once she reaches the top of the patio steps. "Hey, Jinx?"

"Yeah?"

"If you and my mom get married, does that mean Jett will be our cousin?"

Oh, for fuck's sake. She did not just ask that in front of everyone.

Jesse, prick that he is, clears his throat. "Yeah, Jinx. Will he?"

He's dead. And I'll use his backhoe to dig the fucking hole.

"Just go to the bathroom, Em. We'll talk about that later, okay?" Way later. Because right now, I have more important things to explain.

The patio door shuts behind her, and my dad laughs.

"You should see your face right now, boy."

I bet.

Rubbing a hand around the back of my neck, which suddenly feels sunburned, I hedge. "We, uh... we were going to tell you about that. Today."

"You're getting married?" Aiden damn near flies off the patio.

"No. Jesus. Settle down." I hold up a hand. "We're just dating."

"And kissing. Probably other things," Mason mutters, and I shoot him a death glare.

Jesse chortles. "Wow. This is going so much better than I expected."

"You knew about this?" Dad asks. Then he looks to Felix. "How about you?"

Rachel's dad lifts a shoulder. "I suspected. I mean, it's not every day some young buck shows up at the door asking what kind of flowers your daughter likes. I figured he was sweet on her."

"Am I the last to know?" Dad holds up his hands.

"Probably." Ma's voice sounds through the patio door screen before she slides it open and steps out with Rachel in tow. "I've got you beat by ten minutes."

Great. Not only does everyone know, but Ma's going to make it into a competition. Her favorite pastime.

"I'm sorry." Rachel pads across the lawn in her sandals, her peach sundress fluttering in the breeze. "But it wasn't my fault. Hayden let it slip."

"It's all right." I sling an arm around her shoulder and press a kiss to her temple. "We planned on telling them today anyway, right?"

She nods and places a hand on my stomach as she glances at her dad. "Now you know why I wanted you to be here."

He frowns. "So there's no *sernik*?"

My father snorts. "Oh, I'm sure there's cheesecake, Felix. There's probably enough pie and pierogi, kluski and kielbasa to feed the whole damn town. It's how we do things around here."

The softest smile curls on Rachel's lips. "I wouldn't lie to you about *sernik*, Dad. I know it's your favorite. And maybe that's why I agreed to let Janice teach me."

His expression softens, and the love and adoration between them is palpable. With FJ living so far away, all they've had for a long time is each other. But now, they have us. And we're damn lucky to have them.

Still irritated, my dad lifts his hands and scans the small crowd that's gathered in the backyard now that the ladies and Emma have joined us, too.

"So, was I the last to know about Jinx becoming a partner at EE, too, or…?"

Jesse groans, my mother gasps, and Amelia and Aiden say a simultaneous "uh, what?"

Rachel curls into me, laughing quietly. "I already love this family."

I wrap my arms around her and laugh right back. "You sure you want in on this?"

"Absolutely." She presses a sweet kiss to my chest. "I want in on anything that involves you."

RACHEL

"TODAY DID NOT GO AS PLANNED, DID it?" Sitting beside me on my front porch steps later that evening, Justin bumps his shoulder into mine. "It's almost like they knew what they were doing, outing us the way they did."

"Right? I still can't believe Emma asked about us getting married in front of all the Enders men. She's supposed to be my girl! You know, have my back and whatnot."

He grins. "She's awesome. Gotta love a woman who gives no fucks about what she says."

"Ugh." I turn my face to the evening breeze and close my eyes. "That could bite her in the ass someday."

"Maybe, but for now, it's good she's so comfortable speaking her mind."

Ah. I can't argue with that. I'd rather she grow up with confidence and conviction than bite her tongue to protect other people's feelings. That's a lesson that took me far too long to learn.

"Your dad seemed to enjoy himself today, too."

"He did, didn't he? He gets out plenty for his coffee clutching and bunko with the guys, but that's not the same as spending time with family. I know he misses the way things used to be when FJ and I were kids and Mom was still alive. I try to visit him as often as I can with the kids, but it's just different." I bump him like he did me. "Thank you for inviting him."

"Of course. He's always welcome, and you heard my mom before we ate. We're all family now."

Silly emotion burns in my eyes now, just like it did when Janice wrapped her arms around me in their guest bedroom and told me that she'd prayed that Justin would find someone like me someday. That she was proud of the way I've always handled myself and of the way I've mothered my children, and that my mom would be proud of me, too.

"Hey..." He frowns at the tears in my eyes and pulls me close. "I didn't mean to make you cry."

I wave a hand in front of my face. "You didn't. It's just... your mom reminds me so much of mine."

"Ah." He kisses the top of my head. "Well, I'm happy to share. There's plenty of her Polish attitude to go around."

I choke on a laugh.

"How did your visit go earlier?"

Pulling in a shaky breath, I swipe at my cheeks. "It was good. I got a lot off my chest." My mom might not have been there physically, but I felt her presence when I sat in front of her grave and told her everything. "Funny thing, though. Someone brought a huge hanging basket of flowers for her.

Dad says it wasn't him. You wouldn't know anything about that, would you?"

Justin glances ahead toward the street, tongue stuck in his cheek. "Nope. Not a thing."

"You're such a cute liar."

He chuckles. "You said the same thing the night I brought you home from the bar. Sitting right here on this porch."

"Did I?" I still don't remember all the details of that conversation. "What did you lie about?"

"I didn't lie. You asked if a hot guy like me would ever be interested in a cougar like you. I said I absolutely would, but you didn't believe me."

Oh my god. My cheeks flame. "First of all, I'm not old enough to be a cougar, and second, there's only six years between us."

He nods in whole-hearted agreement. "That's what I said."

"Hmm." I sigh. "We've come a long way since then." I was worried he was too young, but that was before I found out that being older doesn't necessarily make a man a man. At twenty-six, Justin is the best one I've ever known.

"Nah, I knew then that I wanted you," he muses confidently. "You're the one who needed convincing."

Lips pressed together, I give him a sidelong glance. "Maybe I didn't want to get my hopes up."

"That's the thing, Sunny. When I tell you something, I mean it. I keep my word, every single time."

"I know that now." And it's part of the reason I love him so much. "When we were out of town, you said I was yours. You meant that, too, right?"

He dips his chin without hesitation. "Damn right, I did."

"Forever?" I know the truth in my heart, but I want to hear him say it, too.

"Yes, Sunny." He turns and takes my hand into his, squeezing gently. "You're it for me, if that's what you're asking."

My heart beats a little faster as I nod. "It is."

He brings my knuckles to his lips. "You are it for me, and I'm willing to go as fast or as slow as you need as long as we're together."

I don't need more time, but I also want to be sure we do this right.

"I don't see a future without you in it, either." I lean in for a kiss. "And not just because you're hot."

He smiles against my lips. "It's the lawn tractor, right? Gets you all hot and bothered."

"Mm-hmm." Sliding a hand up his thigh, I trail a fingertip over his zipper. "Makes me think about all that power between your legs."

He groans. "You think the kids are sleeping yet?"

"Not sure. How quiet do you think you can be?"

His eyes flash, intrigued by the challenge. "You serious?"

I lift a playful shoulder. "It's going to happen sooner or later, handsome."

Getting to his feet in a rush, he pulls me against him and kisses me hard. "God, I love you."

I wriggle away, reach for the screen door, and toss a saucy glance over my shoulder. "Maybe you should come inside and prove it."

He strips his T-shirt off right there on the porch. "Say less, babe."

EPILOGUE

RACHEL

The Board of Regents of the University of Wisconsin System, on the nomination of the faculty, have conferred upon

RACHEL EILEEN PERRY

The Degree of

Master of Education

I did it. Holding my diploma in my hands is nothing short of surreal.

Time has flown since I enrolled in the master's program a year and nine months ago. I was nervous about how I'd handle being a mom, a teacher, and a student at the same time, but somehow, some way, life fell into place exactly as I needed it to. There were only a handful of days that wreaked havoc on my nerves. And most of them were as the final semester of grad school wound down and the next phase of my life began. And even those days weren't really so bad with Justin by my side.

We've been together just as long as it took me to get my degree. And somehow that man finds ways to make me love him a little more every single day.

He moved in just over a year ago. When he was sleeping here far more than he was at his place, it seemed silly for him to pay rent on a house just to store his things. Especially when it was obvious that he belonged here with me and the kids. They've come to love him just as much as I do, and he settled into the role of a pseudo stepdad just as easily as he transitioned into being a full-fledged partner at Enders Excavating. He was born to do both, and he's thriving in ways I suspect exceed even his own expectations. He still takes care of the cemetery and the public gardens in town, but the rest of his time is spent designing custom backyards and gardenscapes. He's incredibly talented, my man, but then I already knew that.

I set the diploma aside and pick up the next package. This one sends a rush of excitement through me.

I know what it is without looking, just like I knew when the bouts of nausea started a couple of weeks ago. The repulsion to my beloved chai came next. At that point, taking a pregnancy test was really just a formality. Heck, I'd already ordered the item in this package. That's how confident I was.

The only question now is whether I wait until Justin comes home to give him his gift and break the news, or drive out to where he's working with Jesse and the excavation crew. Out to the site of our new house.

"Hey, Mom. Mariah and her mom are on their way." Emma emerges from the back hall in her swimsuit and a pair of shorts. At nearly eleven, she's almost as tall as me and her once-brown hair has taken on an auburn hue. Her freckles have come out in full force, as well. Even if I wanted to deny her, there's no way anyone would believe me. She's my mini me in every way possible.

"Okay, honey. Did you remember sunscreen?"

"Yep, got some on." She pats the side of her beach bag. "I have more for later, too."

"Good girl. Have fun. And behave!"

She laughs as she scoots in for a quick hug. "I always do. Jeez."

Uh-huh. Just like I did at her age.

A horn sounds outside, and she sprints for the door. The "I love you" she throws over her shoulder is punctuated by the slam of the screen door behind her.

Sighing, I pick up the package and bite my lip.

I really wanted to make a production of telling Justin about the baby, but it was hard enough holding out for this gift. I'm not sure I can wait any longer now that it's arrived.

Maybe if I hurry, I can catch him when the crew breaks for lunch. Knowing him, he'll keep working, especially because it's our house. This is the perfect reason to force him to take a break. And then hurry home tonight, too.

Once I've run a brush through my hair and put on a little lip gloss, I hurry out of the house with the package and my diploma in hand.

My palms sweat on the drive across town and then farther out toward my childhood home, but I can't keep the smile off my face.

So many amazing things have come my way in the past two years. I'll forever be grateful for every one of them, including the ten acres of land Dad gave me as—wait for it —*a divorce present.*

Funny guy, my father. He knew I'd always wanted a house out in the country, and he saw my fresh start as a good time to help me along. With the nice chunk of change Justin received for all those years of unpaid overtime, we broke ground on our future home, putting down some roots together.

And now that there's a little bean growing in my belly, those roots are only growing deeper.

Just as expected, the majority of the guys are hanging out in the shade by their trucks when I pull into the driveway down the road from my dad's. Jesse lifts a hand in greeting before starting my way.

"What's up, Rach?" he asks as I climb out.

I tuck the package and the diploma under my arm and smile. "Not much. Just have something I wanted to show Justin. Is he around?"

Jesse points to the shell of our future home. "He's inside with Mason. Head on over. Just watch your step. We've got things pretty torn up right now."

They do, but I don't mind one bit. The nicer weather has finally allowed them to get some of the more extensive landscaping done. In the fall, when we broke ground, they only did what they had to do so we could get the foundation poured. Now, with spring turning into summer, they can finally clean things up and make it look pretty.

Every weekend since March, Justin, his brothers, his dad, and Mason have been out here doing the actual house construction. And in a few weeks when the inside is ready, I'll be here, too, doing my part.

As I make my way to the rocky path that leads up to the house, I catch a glimpse of Craig in my periphery. He lifts a subtle hand in greeting, and I offer a small smile in return.

Is it awkward that he's been here, working on the site of

my future home? A little, yes. But he and Justin have found a way to remain civil and respectful with one another, and that's all that matters. They will never be friends, and I don't think I'd want them to be, just like I imagine Craig would prefer I steer clear of the women he dates now that he and Cady have broken up. It's easier this way, and it works for us, so who am I to complain?

"What the heck are you doing here?" Mason asks when I step through the space that will eventually be the foyer door. He's sweeping up sawdust in the living room area. Just a little farther in, Justin is on a ladder, using a nail gun to fasten some kind of bracket to a two-by-four.

"Got some mail I wanted to show you." I hold up the diploma and flash a cheesy smile. "Ta-da! It finally came!"

Mason grins and sets the broom aside to come over and take a closer look. I did walk for my graduation a few weeks ago, but per usual, the actual document wasn't ready.

"Good job, Mom." He wraps an arm around my shoulders and jostles me in his version of a side hug. It's more than I expected, to be honest. At thirteen, he typically dodges me at all costs. Some days, I'm lucky if I get more than a grunt from him. He's better with Justin when they're working together like this, and as long as he keeps communicating with him, I'll let him be. Justin assures me that Mason is perfectly fine. He swears he went through the same thing, and that in no time at all, my momma's boy will return bigger and even better than before.

"Got your diploma, huh?" Justin climbs down from the ladder, one boot-clad foot at a time, and then wipes his hands on his jeans. "Lemme see."

I hurry over like a giddy kid and hand it to him.

"Wow. Look at you, all official and shit." A dimpled grin

spreads across his face as he reads it. "Get your butt over here and give me a kiss."

Mason groans behind us. "And that's my cue to leave." A moment later, the thump of his feet sounds on the steps outside.

"Poor kid." I laugh softly and press up on my toes for that kiss. "He's got it rough, doesn't he?"

Justin chuckles, too. "Just wait until I get home later and we can really celebrate."

Oh, boy.

Which reminds me...

"I have something else, too. For you." Of course, now that I'm here, I'm second-guessing the decision to tell him in the middle of the workday, especially with everyone outside.

"Yeah?" He tips his head, a mischievous gleam in his eye. Paired with the light brown hair curling around the edges of his ball cap, he's as swoony as ever. There's no way I can go home without telling him. He's just too damn charming, and hello, I'm having this gorgeous man's baby.

"Here." I thrust the package at him and step back nervously.

He hands me the diploma, and takes the package, one brow cocked. "What's with the jitters? Should I be afraid to open this?"

"No." Maybe. I mean, our lives are about to change yet again, but in a good way, I think. "It's just... my timing may be a little questionable, that's all."

"Okay..." He continues to watch me as he tears the small box open. "Feels soft," he says when he gets to the plastic packaging inside.

I swallow. "Yep. Take it out."

With narrowed eyes, he tears the plastic and pulls out the white fabric.

My heart races and my stomach whirls with what I hope is anticipation and not the baby disliking my late breakfast.

"My hands are shaking," Justin admits as he unfolds the tiny T-shirt. Immediately, he goes stock still. For a split second, he's frozen like that, but then he breaks out into a megawatt smile. "Are you shitting me right now, Sunny? Daddy's little helper?"

I shake my head, the lump in my throat making it difficult to speak. "No to the shitting part. Yes to the helper."

Laughing, he drops the packaging to the floor so he can hold out the baby tee with both hands. "Daddy's little helper," he says again, his tone a mix of excitement and disbelief. "I dig the lawn tractor."

"I figured you would." The second I saw it, I knew it was the perfect way to tell him, even if the rush shipping fees were astronomical.

"We've having a baby." He points to himself and then to me. "Us."

I nod as tears begin to well in my eyes. "We are."

He pulls me to him in a rush and then lifts me off the floor as he spins around. "I'm going to be a dad!"

"Shh!" I laugh. "Everyone outside will hear."

"I don't care." He puts me down and cups my face in his hands. "I want to tell the whole damn world." Dipping close, he peppers dozens of kisses all over my face. Finally, he pulls back, a little breathless. "Okay, so I'm going to do something really crazy right now. I wanted to wait until the house was done, but nothing is going to top this day, so I'm just going to do it now. Hold this." He gives me the T-shirt, darts over to a toolbox on the far side of the room, and crouches. When he stands and whips around, he's holding a little black box.

And my already racing heart takes off like a derby horse.

"It's kinda ironic that the first time I considered what it'd be like to be with you was that day spilled coffee in front of all the guys." He takes one slow step at a time back to me. "And now you're here, with a bunch of them standing outside, not only as my girlfriend but as the mother of my child."

He stops just a couple of feet in front of me, his cheeks flushed and his eyes wide. "I love you so fucking much, Sunny. You already know that I plan to do it for the rest of my life." When he drops to a knee and opens the box, it's all I can do not to fall apart. "Will you marry me and make it official?"

My knees hit the floor as I throw myself at him and blubber through tears. "You already know I will."

"Thank fuck for that." Arms squeezing tight, he holds me for several beats before pulling back with the ring between his fingers. "Gimme your hand, woman. I wanna see how this looks on you."

I do my best to keep steady while he slips the ring on my finger, but it's a difficult task with the way I can't stop giggling. It's gorgeous and, if I'm not mistaken, sort of resembles a sunflower with its huge center diamond and smaller stones surrounding it. "Dang. You did good."

He shrugs modestly and then winks. "I did better with you."

"I think we both did pretty good." I wrap him up in another hug and let out a happy sigh.

The thing about Justin and me is that we both do better together. That's what makes us so strong. I can only imagine how much stronger we'll become as the years go by and the roots we've planted really start to take hold.

And to think none of this would've happened if I hadn't taken that first step out of my comfort zone. If I hadn't finally done something for me.

Now, I have him.

The love of my life.

The perpetual sun on my face.

And someday soon, my husband.

Life is so damn good.

~THE END~

Thank you so much for reading ***Measure of a Man***! If you enjoyed Jinx & Rachel's story and want to keep up to date on the next Cole Creek book, please join my mailing list: www.mollymclain.com/newsletter

Amelia's book, ***The Mistakes We've Made***, is the next in the series, and I do not think you're ready! Amelia's love interest is my first anti-hero! Does that give you any clue who the leading man might be??

Preorder your copy now!

AND… If you want to know more about the handsome Jamie Stroud... save your copy of ***When You're Ready***! This is a Cole Creek spin-off and a complete standalone! It's due to release later in 2024!

I'd love to stay connected on social media, too!
Join **Molly's Misfits (my reader group)** on Facebook!

MORE BOOKS BY MOLLY

<u>COLE CREEK SERIES</u>

We're Made of Moments (Jesse & Hayden)

More Than a Memory (Aiden & Olivia)

Pre-order now: The Mistakes We've Made (Amelia's book)

<u>THE MCMURRAYS OF MASON CREEK SERIES</u>

Perfect Secret

Perfect Chance

Perfect Scandal

<u>RIVER BEND SERIES</u>

Can't Shake You | Can't Hold Back

Can't Get Enough | Can't Walk Away

A River Bend Wedding | Can't Resist Him

Can't Let Go | Can't Forget Her

<u>VELOCITY SERIES</u>

Fly | Fight

<u>STANDALONES</u>

Bend | Rush

Kissing My Brother's Bride

(1st book in the multi-author Kissing Games series)

ACKNOWLEDGMENTS

Oh my gosh, I have so many people to thank for keeping me sane while I wrote this book!

To Sandra, Kaylee, and Rhonda for helping me come up with the book title and for always being there when I need to talk shop or vent about life!

To Julia and Amy for being my go-to girls for literally all the things, bookish and life-ish. I adore you both!

To Crystal, who game me a play by play as she was reading and then listening to the first two Cole Creek books. Your excitement made ME excited. I appreciate your friendship and can't wait to squeeze you someday! Also... this Crystal is all you, girl! Tony, too!

To Sommer for the gorgeous cover as always, AND for the Polish-inspired beauties, too! You are a rockstar!

To Mel for the book doula help! You are a true gem, and I am so glad we get to work together!

To my editor, Beth, whom none of this would be possible without. I probably just used whom wrong, but whatever. I love you and I am never letting you go. Ever!

THANK YOU ALL SO VERY VERY MUCH!

ABOUT THE AUTHOR

Molly McLain lives in a small Wisconsin town with her blue collar husband of more than 20 years. She's addicted to 80's ballads, 90's rock, cheesecake, and office supplies. She's been scribbling down love stories in spiral notebooks since she was old enough to daydream about hunky boys and happily-ever-afters. Now she turns those daydreams into steamy, small town novels.

Made in the USA
Coppell, TX
21 June 2026

82925196R00246